Levi's
Gift

Jennifer Burke

WARD
RIVER
PRESS

This novel is entirely a work of fiction. The names, characters and incidents portrayed in it are the work of the author's imagination. Any resemblance to actual persons, living or dead, events or localities is entirely coincidental.

Published 2015
by Poolbeg Press Ltd
123 Grange Hill, Baldoyle
Dublin 13, Ireland
www.wardriverpress.com

A catalogue record for this book is available from the British Library.

ISBN 978-1-78199-943-1

Printed by CPI Group (UK) Ltd, Croydon, CR0 4YY

www.poolbeg.com

For my grandmothers

Prologue

Lena

I brought you here to the south of Italy to tell you the story of a seminary, and the world I encountered within.

It was a plain school in many ways. Pupils lived, worked and prayed in a jumble of ancient structures lying in high rising fields too rocky to farm. Nestled in the Italian hills, it was charming and humble about all but its humility. The sunny yellow walls were scabbed where the heat had cracked the paint. Tiles of deep red rippled across the roofs like a holy sea cleansing those studying within. The vines cling to my mind as vividly as they did to the walls – green twists dotted with berries snaking their way up the sides.

Inside those walls was a man, as young as I was, learning how to become a man of God.

He owns my heart to this day.

PART ONE

ONE

Mattie

I like the dark. The semi-dark is best. Everything still has form but it's indistinct. I pretend you're still here, Ben, deep in slumber. All the books I read in preparation for motherhood said it's important to rest while your baby is sleeping. So I imagine you dozing in your crib while I grab a few precious minutes of peace and quiet.

Peace and Quiet.

Funny how concepts get coupled together. Love and Marriage. Father and Mother.

Those didn't work out for me, and neither has Peace and Quiet. I have quiet. It brings me no peace.

Maybe it would be different if your father had stuck around to fill the void you left with comfort and company. But he didn't. He walked out the second he heard about you. I was ready to raise you without him and I would have made sure I was more than enough for you. Besides, we wouldn't have been completely alone. We would have had Lena.

I should probably call her 'Granny' when I speak to you about her, since that is what you would have called her. I'm used to her being Lena; it's been years since I've called her 'Mom'.

My only blurry memories of my own dad are of him sneering her name. Screaming it back at her like an insult; a verbal fist.

When my childhood sadness and shame at her indifference towards me eventually turned to anger, I threw her name back at her as a test. She barely noticed.

I haven't seen your father since the day he disowned us but Lena said he called yesterday. It was my birthday, you see. I have finally reached my twenties – that decade of freedom and adventure I have coveted for years. Now all I see when I look to the future is a barren block of time sucking me further into its abyss, away, away from you.

When Lena arrived in the afternoon Tristan was standing outside, apparently steeling himself to knock on the door. Maybe to ask me to come back to him, now that he doesn't have you to worry about, or perhaps to chastise me for neglecting to invite him to your funeral. Why should he care? He never wanted you and, from the moment he admitted it, I stopped wanting him. I'm glad Lena kicked him to the kerb. My darling Ben, I don't want anyone or anything except you.

Tristan's hand was mid-motion towards knocking on the door, Lena told me, when she arrived at my apartment building, and he turned on hearing her growl from the street behind him. She all but beat him from the stoop. She looked comedic when she barged in after their confrontation. Her hair was ruffled and her cheeks flushed from the emotion. A laugh escaped me and my stomach tightened with the strange action. It hurt like sit-ups.

Lena was going out of her mind with worry about me at the start. Now she seems resigned. I'm glad. Losing you isn't something I will ever get over and she needs to accept that.

She forced me to go to a support group a few weeks after. Well, she didn't so much force me as lead me to the car and drive me there. I was so out of it I didn't object until I realised where she was taking me. I started to shout but Lena put her hand on my arm and, when I looked into her eyes, I saw hurt there.

"Please, Mattie," she said. "I know your attachment to Ben won't just go away but I'm trying to help you – you have to give me something. Just do this for me and then I'll take you straight home."

So I sat through it. I listened to an older woman named Lisa cry about how she still misses her little boy, but how she stays strong for her other kids. We heard from Ashley, a few years older than me, who has finally gone back to work after her daughter was killed by a drunk driver and is delighted to be back to some sort of normality. It went on and on. Jennifer – recovering. Mary – feeling like herself again. Jessica – happy for the first time in years, with the help of the group.

I could sense Lena's head jerk in my direction with each promise of better days and she smiled as she dropped me home, certain my contemplative mood was a sign I had been inspired and would soon turn a corner. That wasn't the reason for my reverie. Something about those women made me uneasy in a way I couldn't explain. I slept well that night, right through until midday.

I awoke refreshed. I remember frowning in the light of the room, puzzled. Then it hit me – the reason I was rested. It was the very thing doctors warned me should have happened within days but with my constant dreams of you, my body took longer to understand that you were gone. I looked down. My breasts had stopped swelling with milk. Without the uncomfortable pulsating, I had slept.

My howl echoed throughout the lonely apartment.

You were leaving me bit by bit. I was to consign you to a period of grief and continue life happy like Lisa, Ashley, Jennifer, Mary, Jessica and all the others.

I made my decision then. I would not be that poor a mother. I would never forget you or abandon you. I would never trade you off for a future of smiles.

Lena soon realised that the support group had been a waste of time. She has stopped trying to bring me there.

I wonder vaguely why I have not seen her today. It seems late, though time is a fluid concept these days. She usually comes before the brightness that slips through the cracks in the window blinds softens with the approaching dusk. Sometimes, if I'm weak, I let her feed me. Mostly, we exist in companionable silence.

She was acting strangely yesterday. At first I thought it was because of Tristan showing up. She kept fidgeting and her eyes darted constantly around the room. A few times she opened her mouth as if to say something profound. I watched her openly, waiting, until she shook her head and returned to fingering the buttons on her top. I didn't probe. For one thing, I didn't have the energy. Besides, I spent years trying to pry confidences from Lena only to be cast aside every time. I have learnt not to try to get to know her.

I craved her as a child. She worked, of course – she had to. It wasn't those absences that bothered me. It was her distance when she was there.

Like the day I first met Simon when I was eight years old. I came rushing home from school to tell her about my new friend and all she could say was a vague, "That's nice, dear." She was physically with me but never properly present.

I think about Simon, as I have a lot recently, and my mouth twitches into the shape that used to be a smile. It is impossible to think of Simon and not feel a warmth in the air, even since our teenage stupidities pulled us apart for good.

Simon has the biggest grin of anyone I've ever known. His laughter is a roar and his lips stretch across his face, drawing the same response from anyone near him. He chuckles like an old man.

And he was an old man from the time we were kids. His eldest brother Aaron was a saint. The middle boy, Joseph, rebelled. Simon was left trailing on the end. Laughing his way through life to get by. Terrified of enduring the wrath of his parents yet knowing he wasn't smart, daring or religious enough to please them.

Don't get me wrong, Ruth and Ed loved all their children. They lauded Aaron and worried about Joseph. Simon was just – Simon. The poor kid was nothing special. Except to me.

We bonded over our disappointing mothers, though they could not have been less alike. How they ended up best friends is beyond me. Ruth never stopped pressuring Simon for improvement, failing to see he was perfect already. He never resented her for it to the extent I blamed Lena for her shortcomings. I guess attention in any form, even smothering expectation, is better than none.

Simon and I were inseparable from the start. When, in later years, friendship bubbled over into love, he would positively beam, and I remember the day I threatened to start using Lena's name for him – 'Sunshine Simon' – in public. He pursed his lips in mock horror and his mouth quivered as he tried to keep his natural expression from returning.

"Oh don't," I laughed, pulling him close. "Don't stop smiling! I won't call you that, I swear."

He buried his face in my shoulder and I could feel the widening of his mouth against me. "It's okay. I have a name for you too," he whispered.

I waited, expecting a teasing taunt.

His voice was tender. "My Mattie."

Simon still lives here in Washington DC. He would never visit. I don't think I'll ever see him again. The only person left in my life is my mother.

I have never been able to forgive Lena her apathy during my youth but I have come to rely on her since you died. Her constant presence anchors me. There is no one else. I'm not in contact with my friends from high school. None of my college friends live here – not that I had many left by the end. Lena said Ruth is willing to come and see me but I don't want to put up with her gossiping queries about my mental state. Besides, she is Simon's mother, and I'm not strong enough to deal with that right now.

So it's just me and Lena. She has, quite literally, kept me alive since you died. Yet she must know that engaging with me now can't make up for an entire childhood of reserve. It is too late. My desperation for her attention morphed into accepted rejection during my teenage years. I couldn't wait to leave DC to escape her disinterest. Now, she's all I have.

But Ben, why am I thinking about Lena? Who cares if she's been acting oddly? She'll be here soon enough, to fuss and help and encourage like she should have done years ago.

I would have been a different kind of mother if you had stayed. I would have soaked up every second of you. Instead, I'll sit here and remember the only time I had with you – those few precious months when I could feel you moving and growing inside of me before they pulled you from me, floppy and quiet.

So quiet it would have been peaceful, had my heart not shattered loud and forever.

TWO

Mattie

"Mattie?"

I don't respond. She knows where to find me. Still, I am surprised at the relief that relaxes my shoulders when I hear the key turn in the lock and Lena call out to me. I have definitely started to become dependent on her.

"Sweetheart?" Lena's head appears around the bedroom door, her hair falling as it always does into her face. She shakes it away. "I'm starving, Mattie – I'll make some dinner for us."

I continue to look at her until she nods and disappears into the kitchen. I close my eyes, listening to the sounds of her humming in the next room and the clinking of cutlery. I am swaying in her papa's rocking chair, a family heirloom she gave to me when I became pregnant with you, Ben. Her papa used to rock her in it when she was a baby and years later she sat for hours in it with me, feeding me and singing to me. Perhaps that is why my favourite things about my mother are the tunes she lilts quietly onto the air when she thinks no one is listening.

I remember the day she gave me that chair. Until then, I hadn't known it used to be her papa's. It was the morning after I had spent my first night alone in the apartment. I was tired. I had barely slept. The nausea part was over but the fun was just starting. You were a sportsman from the beginning. Boisterous

11

and strong – I just knew you were a boy! You never stopped kicking and squirming inside me. For some reason you always gained momentum at night. It was as if you knew you wouldn't be around for long and you didn't want me to sleep through any of you.

I was meandering through my new home, dwarfed by my oversized maternity nightdress which I didn't need yet but liked wearing because it made me look the part, mentally furnishing the place for your arrival, when the buzzer went.

"Come on up, Lena," I said into the intercom, not needing to ask who it was.

She took ages. Eventually, I heard scraping noises out in the hallway. I opened the apartment door and stuck my head out to see Lena pushing a rocking chair forward, as a tall woman with perfectly blow-dried hair backed up to my door, pulling the front of it.

"Hello, Ruth." I'd know her anywhere.

She turned, her cheeks rosy from the effort of dragging the chair. On seeing me, her face lifted. "Mattie, my darling girl, how are you?"

I let her enfold me in her arms and press me tight against her ample chest. It was the first time I'd seen her since Simon and I stopped talking but I was too happily full of you to feel awkward. Her tact in not mentioning Simon as part of her greeting was enough to endear her to me. And I was delighted just to have another person to whom I could show off my pregnant belly.

I pulled my flowing nightdress tight against me so my neat stomach popped out. "Look!" I grinned widely.

Ruth tilted her head to take in my bump and made a noise of appreciation. "Congratulations, Mattie."

I thanked her. I knew she was judging me. Baby out of wedlock? No daddy in sight? Not the sort of behaviour a bible-abiding woman condoned. I was sure she was delighted that her son had escaped my clutches, me with my loose ways. But she didn't show it and I was grateful to her for that. I wanted only good wishes. After all, you were nothing to be ashamed about.

I leaned around her. "What's that doing here?"

Ruth butted in as Lena opened her mouth. "Your mother asked me to meet her on the pretence that we would have coffee. Turns out she was merely recruiting my muscle to get this piece of fine wood up to a third-storey apartment!" Humour softened her apparent reproach and my mother caught my eye, flicking her eyebrows up in amusement.

It was the first friendly gesture Lena had made to me in weeks and my heart lifted from a place I thought was the highest it could be.

"Out of the way, Mattie, dear," Ruth ordered, bending her shapely behind in the door, pulling the chair as it flailed back and forth on its rocker.

I offered help but Ruth hushed me.

"Don't be stupid, girl! You're not to move furniture in your condition."

Condition. What a clinical word for such a miracle. I sat on one of the high stools at the kitchen counter and watched them haul the rocking chair over to the corner. I rubbed my stomach, as though my fingers were tracing a brail-like language for you to read on the inside.

"Done!" Ruth's exclamation shook me from my silent conversation with you. "Well, Lena, I can see why you wanted to start furnishing," she said, gazing around at the nearly empty apartment.

"Would you like a drink, Ruth?" I started to stand, ignoring her comment, but she waved me away with a flap of her arm. She had to leave but promised to call again if I would be happy to see her. Although I agreed out of politeness, I shook my head patronisingly at Lena when Ruth turned her back. My mother did not respond.

As soon as Ruth left, I turned to Lena. "I was joking," I said. "Of course she's welcome back but she won't come. Not after what happened between me and Simon."

"You'll understand when that little one grows up." Lena nodded at my belly and beckoned me over to the rocking chair. "Their friends become your second children. Now, what do you think of this? I was going to bring your piano instead – I know

13

you miss playing it. But Ruth was cheaper than a moving truck! This is something for you and the baby."

I put my hand out to rock my mother's chair. The polished wood felt smooth to touch and the light brown was easy on the eyes. It rounded into a curve everywhere there could have been an edge. It felt sturdy when I lowered myself into it.

I looked up at Lena. "It's great!"

I started to grin but it slipped from my face immediately. She was crying.

"What's wrong, Lena?" I wriggled without finesse from the chair.

She shook her head and smiled through the tears. "No, I'm not upset, Mattie. These are happy tears. I don't think I ever told you that this chair was my papa's."

I stared down at it again, with a deeper sensation running through me than approval. I loved it. Suddenly, Lena was hugging me. Astounded, I returned the embrace.

We held each other close as Lena cried over the rocking chair and I tried to remember the last time we had made such a meaningful physical connection. She pulled back after a while – she was always the first to do so – and sat on the windowsill, beckoning for me to sit back in the rocking chair. I complied.

"I had you when I was very young too," she sniffed, wiping away the last of her tears. I nodded. She and my dad were barely out of college when I was born. "I was so scared when I first found out I was pregnant."

I gazed at her. Lena had never talked to me about this before. "As I grew big with you, I wondered how I was going to cope, even with Damien there to help me. It was only when you came out of me, when I looked down into your scrunched-up little face . . ." she laughed, her eyes warm and I melted at her affection, "that I fell in love with you."

She stood and walked over to the countertop.

"But you know that feeling already." She turned and pointed at my hand unconsciously caressing my stomach. "I can see it in you. The way you move, the way you talk about the baby."

"I love him, Lena," I gushed.

14

"You think it's a boy? I thought the scan was inconclusive?"

I laughed. "It was but I can tell he's a boy – my little man! I don't know how but I'm sure of it."

She came to kneel by me. "Well, you are going to be sitting in this very chair in a few months rocking him to sleep and, I guarantee you, you will know no greater joy."

Only with her acceptance could I bring myself to admit my fear. "Even without Tristan?"

She scowled at the mention of the man who wanted nothing to do with the wonder growing inside me. "Yes, Mattie. You will be fine without Tristan. After all, this chair," she stroked the armrest, "was built for one parent and their child. My papa and me. Me and you. And now you and your baby."

Presenting me with her papa's rocking chair had been Lena's way of forgiving me for getting knocked up at the age of nineteen and dropping out of college. It was a forgiveness I knew I did not deserve.

An unplanned pregnancy is the ultimate college failure and is warned against more than sexually transmitted infections or drugs. I never intended to get pregnant; it was the last thing I wanted. I had bigger and more exciting plans. I had pushed Simon away for suggesting we might start a family within a few years of my leaving college. Finding out I was not alone in my body should have been an unwanted, terrible shock.

But when the stick changed colour to confirm you were inside me – though deep down I had already known it was true – I felt a burst of joy like I had never experienced. I was overcome with an urge, as unexpected as you were, to scream with delight – to run into the street and hug complete strangers. Then I wanted to hole up alone and cradle my stomach, to warm you like a hen would her already laid eggs.

Delirious with happiness, I was unprepared for Tristan's reaction. After he made it plain that he wanted nothing to do with us, I took an overnight train from my college in Chicago home to DC. Aside from Tristan and my roommate Angela I had told no one. I just left. Home, whatever its shortcomings, pulls like a magnet in times of distress.

I made my way nervously to our house where Lena had continued to live after I left for college. She opened the door and literally jumped.

"Mattie!" She stared at my tear-stained face. "What's the matter?" Her face hardened with emotion and I knew a litany of wrongs that could have been done to me was racing through her mind.

I blurted it out. "I'm pregnant and Tristan doesn't want the baby."

Lena's reaction was indicative of the way she had always been: her lips tightened and her face closed against me. For an awful moment, I thought she would slam the door in my face. But she stood back to let me in without a word.

For the next few days, we lived as we always had, quietly and with minimal interaction. She asked me about my health and I reassured her. She made me appointments with doctors and spoke to the college about deferring my place for a couple of years. "You will go back though," she said, with conviction. Nothing was asked about how I came to be like this, what Tristan had said, how I was coping with the change in my life.

About a week after my arrival, she asked me what I wanted to do. "You can stay here of course," she added, "but it was small enough with the two of us when you were growing up."

So we went house-hunting. The money Lena had put aside for my college expenses now had a new claim. It took a few months to find somewhere Lena deemed suitable. We settled on this apartment eight blocks from her house. Far enough away that you and I would have our own space, yet close enough that she could visit and help.

I moved in straight away. At nearly five months, it was time to get ready for you. The apartment came unfurnished, of course, except for the few high stools, and we convinced the previous tenant to leave his bed.

Until the morning Lena arrived with her papa's rocking chair, my relationship with her had been almost business-like. Her gift didn't change everything – after so many years of emotional separation, how could it? But the presence of the chair in our little home, Ben, was a comfort and I couldn't wait to share it with you.

I had it moved to the bedroom when I came home from birthing you, empty-handed. It was too much effort to crawl from the bed to the chair when it was all the way out in the main room of the apartment. I spend a lot of time in it now. I listen to music and stare into space, seeing not the space itself but the very person who is not in it – you.

Lena is calling me out for dinner. I don't go. I never do. She always asks in case today is the day I get over you and begin to act normally again.

After a while, she brings my food in on a tray and I eat silently, tasting nothing, rocking in the chair. Lena sits on the bed, cradling a warm drink. Wordlessly, she takes the tray when I am finished and, by the time she returns to my room after tidying up, I am in bed.

"I have news," she says, her words wobbly. I look at her until she drops her gaze. "Perhaps you're too tired tonight." She strokes my hair.

I feel no sense of curiosity about her proposed announcement. I glance back at the rocking chair. It is my favourite thing in the apartment. Not only because it was going to be our special place, Ben, but because it was my grandfather's and it reminds me of the day Lena gave it to me, when she opened up to me just a bit and I felt like the three of us could start being a family. I feel a lump sprout from my tonsils, constricting my throat. My eyes water.

Lena had reverted back to her closed self as soon as she left me after dropping off the rocking chair. She was always around; she helped me furnish and prepare for your arrival. But there were no more meaningful conversations. No hugs or handholding. I didn't care. I had you.

Now, as I look at the rocking chair and remember that day, a weakness deflates me and the tears spill over.

"Oh Mattie," Lena sighs, drying my cheeks with her palm. Then she says the strangest thing. "I can help you. We're going to Italy."

THREE

Lena

Papa was all I had, after my mother died bringing me into the world. He could have blamed me for causing him more loss, when he had already borne so much. Born in Poland, he survived the war and was brought to America where he met and married my mother. Like so many ingrates of my generation, I never asked him for details of his surely fascinating past and, too traumatised, he offered few stories.

He gave me the name Magdalena – a Polish, religious name. When I came home from school crying that one of the girls teased me for having the whore's name, he told me firmly that I had a name of which I could be proud. Not only was Mary Magdalene Jesus's particular friend, the name had also been my mother's. I asked him once why he did not call me Magda, as she had been known. He said that seeing her in my face was painful enough, without having to call me by her name. So I became Lena.

Too many refugees of the war slipped through the cracks in America. Swallowed up by the sheer size of the continent, they were too scared to learn the language proficiently and too weakened by torture, death and displacement to compete with the entitled bully-boys of the new world. Business was the new war and they had no appetite for it. Unable to support themselves, they transformed into the vagrants, the homeless – the plague of the city of Chicago.

My papa was not one of those sorry men. He was fortunate, perhaps, to have had an unusual physical appearance that, combined with his fierce determination to succeed, paved the way for a thriving career. He looked the part of an academic – tall, with white tufts of flyaway hair springing from his otherwise balding head. His glasses and long, thin face gave an almost Jewish impression, though the man seemed to me more staunchly Catholic than the Pope. When the Polish John Paul II acceded to the Vatican top spot, Papa wept as if a brother rather than a mere countryman had been granted papal infallibility.

Most of our immigrant neighbours from Europe were Jewish, hence my learning to call my father 'Papa'. He didn't mind, so long as I practised Catholicism. Outwardly I did so, sitting through Mass and inventing confessions. But this life was so much more stimulating than preparing my soul for the next and I lost interest. This did not please Papa. Religion had helped him survive the camp in which he spent nights starving, without the energy to cover his ears against the cries of his friends as they welcomed death. Religion sustained him as he dug their graves. It gave him a purpose, a means to continue.

It could always be worse, he told me when I moaned about my homework, my curfew, my hundred teenage angst-filled tribulations.

He grouped my troubles with his own. Being scolded by a teacher in front of the whole class or watching elderly neighbours being marched away for a shower from which he knew they would not return. Forced to write a hundred lines for handing in homework late – or made to collect hastily discarded clothes from the changing room for the new arrivals, while the guards collected the bodies for the furnace: our grievances were equal to my papa. He listened with real compassion to my problems. He didn't flaunt his memories in my face. He didn't want to accept that he had suffered more than me. Maybe he just didn't want to let the hurt in.

I was never let wallow for too long. My problems and his, he insisted, could have been worse. No guard in the camps made him wear a crown of thorns. No bully in school flogged me until my bones glistened in the sun. No tyrant ever nailed us to a cross.

So he sympathised with the Lord's sufferings, and thanked Him over and over for sparing him death in that place, for giving him another life, for allowing him to procreate again even if it meant losing the co-creator along the way. It could be worse, he would always say, drawing me close.

"I cannot claim too much pity," he whispered once, holding me so tight it hurt. "I've lost parents, friends, my wives. I've had to endure the loss of the two people no man should have to outlive – my son and daughter. But I was given a second chance: a third child. I was given you."

Mattie has no idea of the physical pain it causes me to see her so bereft of life. It makes me regret every tear I shed in front of my father. I had not realised a child's hurt can so pierce a parent's heart.

Since she lost Ben, Mattie has not been my little girl any more. Her eye colour is hazel, I know that, and her hair dark as the night. But now when I look at her, I only see an aura of grey. Her tall and full figure, which she did not inherit from me, faded away after Ben. Even her naturally wavy hair seems to hang lank now, more like my mousy, straight hair. I don't want that for her. She looks through everything in front of her, even me. Sometimes though, at no prompt, she will twitch out of her coma-like existence with a shudder. I catch her eye, hoping for a revival, but she breaks down as it all comes flooding back, and clings to me like a thirsty babe in arms.

I was like her once. Alone. Grieving. Not for a child but for the one person who had anchored me, the one person around whom my life had been centred – my papa. Knowing he was dying, he gave me one final parental instruction, phrased like a request. After his death, I departed this great nation for Italy as a shy, unworldly twenty-two-year-old. I went there not on a pilgrimage, not in search of saving, but because he had asked me to go.

It is not hard to imagine why Papa wanted me to visit Italy. He had no desire for either of us to revisit Poland. Too many horrific memories. Italy, where he had studied as a youth before the war, contained the perfect combination of ancient architecture and religious focus.

When he saw me drawing pictures from a young age, he was determined I would follow in his footsteps and become an architect. I can see now, with the gift of age and hindsight, that he was desperate to leave a legacy. A basic need drove him to make sure that his life, during which he had witnessed so much waste, was not wasted itself.

I could find no beauty as my papa did in concrete, stone and brick. Chicago was the perfect city for him. From the dominant Hancock Centre to the understated grandeur of the museums, the individual structures of downtown were so sturdy that the river wound its course around them. The Windy City was a focal point for architects country-wide.

For me, truth lay in paintings, sculptures, mosaics. The functionality of buildings – which for Papa gave them purpose – diluted for me the meaning they could have exuded had they been created as pure works of art. We had flaming rows when I switched from an architecture to a history-of-art major without informing him. I shed tears every vacation when he belittled my view of passion over profession, becoming ever more cranky and unyielding with age. But when he lay dying all was forgiven, by both of us. I would have agreed to anything he asked. That is how I ended up in Italy and the small hilltop seminary outside of Rome that changed my life.

I have never told Mattie about the *seminario* before. It is a part of my life that I have kept for myself. The man I met there saved me and shaped me. It could never have lasted. I suppose we knew that from the beginning. Damien and Mattie were meant to be a new start for me, a chance to move on. That turned out to be impossible and the memories have stayed with me, and me alone.

I have tried everything I can think of to help my daughter – except the one thing that saved me from my misery.

It is a miracle that, a few days ago, my friend Ruth unwittingly offered me a chance to return to that very place. I rejected the idea at first. I had left with no intention of ever seeing it again. But chasing that good-for-nothing Tristan from Mattie's door forced me to accept that my daughter is alone in this world. I am the one who has to help her – and the *seminario* is the only way I know how. That is why I will insist we go to Italy. Perhaps Mattie can find something of beauty there too. Something to make her life worth living again; a version of herself that can live without Ben.

There is another reason too. While the *seminario* helped me through the grief of losing Papa, I left there with a different type of bereavement pulling on me. I left behind my love – my Levi.

I have carried that with me all my life. I know what it is like to spend years missing and regretting. I don't want Mattie's life to be lost to a loss like mine has been. I have to show her. The sin I committed. The love I cherished. The truth about who I am and who I became – the same half-person I'm afraid she might become if she lets her grief for Ben shape her identity.

I never intended telling a single soul the story of my time in the *seminario*, not even her. But my girl is falling and I cannot catch her. So I will cast beneath her the net that scooped me up when I was drowning. I hope that it will save her too.

FOUR

Lena

The miraculous invitation came last weekend when I met Ruth for a picnic in the park and she spoke of the seminary. She had not mentioned it in weeks. Hearing the name – *Seminario dei Discepoli di Pietro* – again was music to my ears. Like a lullaby from a father's lips or the calming pulse of Gregorian chant, it brought me instantly home.

Ruth can often go weeks, or sometimes months, without mentioning the *seminario*, ignorant that I spend every second with her in a state of anticipation. The sound of the name coming from another person reminds me it was not all a dream.

She doesn't know, of course. I was always determined that no one, especially Ruth, would ever know of my connection to that place.

I am used to hearing her speak the name without warning. I know how to internalise my response and arrange my expression into one of mild interest when inside my stomach is leaping and my heart pounding. But last week, my worry for Mattie was heightened by her upcoming birthday and so I was more vulnerable than usual. When Ruth said the name, I reacted. Luckily, my whimper was drowned by a gurgle from Ruth's grandson. His plump arm waved like a ship's mast from his pram and she got up and lifted him out.

"I'm sorry," she offered as she sat down again, mistaking the tears watering my eyes. "I shouldn't have brought him here."

"No. Don't ever feel you can't be happy with him when you're around me," I said as convincingly as my tired voice could manage. I reached out and took the baby from her lap to prove myself.

I meant what I said to her. I do grieve for Ben, of course. Sometimes I have to actively stop thinking about him because the pain tightens my muscles to snapping point. But seeing Ruth's little grandson doesn't make me envious or sad for Ben's absence. It makes me happy that the world continues to move; that babies are living even if he isn't. I don't feel disconnected from the world because of the loss of my grandmother status, or left behind as Mattie does.

The chubby bundle lolling on my lap reminded me that there are still some blessed wonders to behold in the world.

When I welled up at Ruth's mention of the *seminario*, I am ashamed to say I was glad to have Ben to use as an excuse. I could never tell Ruth the truth: that my history with it dates back decades.

When I first learned of Ruth's association with the *seminario*, I pretended I had never heard of it. Now I wait, quiet as a spy, for her to talk about it and when she does a shiver like an electric current runs through my body. A few years ago, she and Ed travelled there. When they returned, it was weeks before she could make it through a conversation, no matter how unrelated, without bringing it up. She described its unassuming beauty in depth and with pity for my ignorance. "I wish you could see it, Lena." I don't know how I managed to remain composed, merely murmuring polite agreement, when inside I was screaming, 'I know! I've been there. I know more about the *seminario* than you ever will!'

It has been more than twenty years since I strolled through its gravel pathways towards the vineyards with their view of the mountains, but the emotions are as raw as if it had been yesterday. I worry that this will happen to Mattie – that years from now she still won't have moved on.

Ruth patted my hand. I opened my eyes to return from my memories of a remote religious school in Italy to the crowded park in DC.

The sun had been blasting from the sky all day, causing a sudden heat wave. Mattie wouldn't know, having spent most of her days inside with the curtains drawn, that the city had experienced a curiously chilly and rainy start to the summer. The sun appeared that morning without warning, throwing the weather experts into disarray.

Ruth and I had spread out her old picnic rug on the grass alongside many others, watching the passers-by struggle with the change in weather. Men carrying suit jackets over their arms sloped along panting, their shirts patchy with perspiration. The few midday joggers had given up and slouched against each other as they queued at the drinking fountains dotted around the park.

"Isn't He putting on quite a show today?" Ruth sighed happily.

I felt my lips pinch together. I knew who she was talking about. She was only trying to divert me from what she thought was my upset about Ben, but her linking a positive empirical observation to the work of her divine creator grated on me. I have been unable to engage with the Church since leaving the *seminario* and Ruth's ever-religious conversation is a constant frustration. I said nothing.

"Remember when we used to bring the kids to this park to play?" Ruth tried again, this time with a rather shaky voice. She has grown steadily and more tearfully reminiscent as Aaron's ordination approaches.

"Yes, I remember," I answered, thinking of how her middle son Joseph, just before entering his rebellious teenage phase, would play cops and robbers with Simon and Mattie. Joseph was always the robber. Ruth said it suited him. But I knew he was doing it for the younger ones because even pretend-bold was too much for Simon, and Mattie was scared of being chased.

"You should get Mattie out here." Ruth slid her gaze up from her grandson's face. "The sun would do her good."

I smiled weakly, bouncing the baby, gazing around at the myriad of people milling, resting, chatting, laughing and drinking animatedly.

I didn't want to talk about Mattie. I didn't have the energy. The combined heat from the sun and the pudgy baby made me sleepy. My lethargy was not helped by the humid air, tainted with lunchtime smells from pop-up vendors to whom the sun meant business.

The truth was I hadn't been to visit my daughter yet on that magnificent day. I didn't know how long the bout of glorious weather would last and the thought of wasting the day – God-given, as Ruth would say, or just plain wonderful, as I would – inside that darkened apartment made me cringe into myself. The pull of the outdoors, real conversation and happy, noisy scenes being played out all around was too much of a draw. The joy of cuddling a grandson, even if not my own, captivated me for longer than it should have.

I did visit her later, of course. I had not abandoned her. Not one full day had passed since she'd given birth to Ben that I had not been with her, taking care of her. I simply waited until later in the evening to call by, when the sun dimmed low, like her.

"She wouldn't come here if I asked her," I said, in response to Ruth's suggestion. "She's still . . ." I cast around for the right word, ". . . falling." Conscious of Ruth watching me intently, I tried to lighten my tone. "Now, Ruth, you haven't finished telling me how your boys are doing."

It was true. Her mention of the *seminario* had prompted my tears and shifted the conversation.

She hesitated, clearly wondering whether she should push me about Mattie.

"Come on," I forced a smile, "tell me something good."

Happy to oblige, she shifted on the rug to face me properly. Joseph – the new father – was the one she wanted to talk about, I suspected. But, not believing my repeated promises that I did not need to be shielded from the joys of grandparenthood, she chose not to dwell on him and the conversation came back to Aaron. Her eldest. The one who, with no siblings to distract him for many years, was moulded easily with her bible and her search for the truth. The one who, against all the odds, was studying in the same *seminario* that changed my life.

Ruth's face lit up, as it always did when she talked about her oldest boy. "Well, as I was saying, Aaron should receive the date of his ordination any day now. We're so excited! As soon as we hear, we'll be booking our flights to Italy. It's going to be a fantastic celebration. *Seminario dei Discepoli di Pietro* has invited us all."

Again, the sound of the name caressed my ears like a lover's whispered declaration. In some ways, hearing it was as painful as admitting Mattie's disintegration.

Ruth was still chattering. "We're out of our minds with excitement. The whole family will travel to Italy for the ceremony. It will be marvellous to have all my boys together again."

When I picture her three sons in my mind, I see the young, eager-faced boys who took care of Mattie. Time has transformed them into singular beings with distinctive life markers. Aaron is almost a deacon, less than a year from becoming a priest. Joseph has a child. Simon – my favourite – can now be nothing more to me than the estranged love of Mattie's life.

I tried not to feel jealous of Ruth's full, growing family. "That sounds great."

If my mundane offering fell short, she did not complain. In fact, she extended to me a lifeline. "Yes, it will be incredible. It's such a special occasion and there could be no better backdrop. The seminary is so beautiful."

"I'm sure," I whispered.

"Lena . . ." Ruth leaned in and changed everything with a word. "Come."

FIVE

Mattie

"We're going to Italy," Lena blurts out as though she has finally figured out the way she can help me.

I had been curled up under the covers when she sat on the bed beside me to make her declaration. I wipe my eyes, feeling my face contort into the scowl of a stroppy teenager. What is this latest nonsense?

She speaks quickly, her tongue tripping over the words in her rush to get them out. "Aaron's ordination. It's next month. Ruth has invited us."

I almost laugh. Travelling to Europe, so far from your grave, Ben, is unthinkable in itself. To expect me to show up at Aaron's ordination where Simon, as his brother, is bound to be, is lunacy. "Lena," I turn back into my pillow, not attempting to hide my exasperation, "I'm not going to Italy."

She stands and moves around the room, kicking the clothes I recently shed in favour of my old maternity nightdress out of the way. I can sense her crinkle her nose up at the mess. Lena cleans every time she comes but, by the next day, I have upset the room again. I don't do it on purpose. I just can't bring myself to tidy and, as I've told her a hundred times, she doesn't have to.

"It's not up for discussion. We're going. I know you don't want to go anywhere but –"

"Lena, please!"

I push myself into a sitting position. I have to stop this now. It's just like the support group drama all over again except this time she wants me to travel to another continent. How far does she think she'll have to take me before I forget about you, Ben?

"You have to cut it out. You can't save me from my own son. And Italy? Really?" I sit up straighter, charged with a sudden energy. "Remember when I was in college in Chicago? Do you realise how difficult it was to convince you to visit me just a few hours away? And after everything that's happened you think you can drag me to the other side of the world . . ."

I stop, worn out. I haven't made such a lengthy speech in weeks. Lena is looking at me with worry lining her face. I know she remembers it too – her one and only trip to see me in college near the end of my first year. Everyone else's parents had been to visit numerous times but Lena had always made excuses. Though I had wanted nothing more than to leave Lena for college to escape the emptiness of our home, I soon found that my desire for her approval could not be quashed with physical separation. Loath as I was to admit it, I wanted her to visit. Eventually, she did.

It was a disaster. Lena had grown up in Chicago, not far from where I was studying at DePaul University, and the memories were too much for her. On the first day of her visit she arrived on campus as we'd arranged and embraced me fiercely at the gates. Delighted at how much she'd obviously missed me, I launched into my itinerary for her short two-day stay but she cut me off.

"I haven't been back to Chicago since my papa died," she whispered and then said she wanted to spend the day visiting her old haunts – where she lived with her papa, her school and neighbourhood. "You understand, don't you, Mattie?" she asked in a way that was more statement than question, looking around like she might spot her papa walking amongst the groups of students.

I said nothing as I watched her go, my fists clenched by my sides. I might have gone with her, had she asked me.

On the second day, she was less distant. I think she realised how disappointed I was at her preference for her past over my present. So she accompanied me through the college and, in spite of my residual annoyance from the day before, I couldn't help but point out where I spent my days – the canteen, my dorm, the library – with a childish eagerness.

I was nervous about introducing her to Tristan and my roommate Angela. Turns out I was right to be: she didn't take to either of them. It wasn't hard to predict her reaction to the girl who shared my dorm room. I had rebelled as a teenager but, aside from a few wild nights in town, I had done nothing worse than acquire a nose-stud and later a lip-ring. It had been Simon, rather than Lena, who talked me into losing them.

Angela had short, spiky hair dyed the darkest black she could find. She had a row of twelve piercings in each ear, a Celtic tattoo on each arm, and she was unafraid to show her skin. When Lena and I entered the dorm room, she was sprawled lazily across her bed in a black wife-beater and a mini-skirt that barely covered her behind. Thankfully she was smoking nothing stronger than a cigarette.

Angela and I had fun together, downing shots from her portable minibar and playing cards on the rare nights we were both in, but we didn't hang out otherwise. She was a different kind of partier to me, preferring weed and body art to the jock-filled, frat parties I liked to crash.

She coughed and stubbed out her cigarette when Lena came into our room.

"Lena, this is Angela." I stifled a snort as my roommate fanned the air in a doomed attempt to dissipate the smoke that was hovering like an atmosphere around her.

"Hello, Angela." Lena stepped forward to shake her hand, coughing pointedly.

Angela, who couldn't care less what her own parents thought about her behaviour, nonetheless made an effort to be civilised. "Nice to meet you," she said loudly. "Sorry about the smell. I don't usually smoke but, you know, exam stress."

I could barely contain my laughter. I couldn't tell if Lena

bought it because Angela kept talking, trying to redeem herself for my sake, which I did appreciate.

"So what do you think of the college? Great sporting facilities, right? Sorry about the mess. Well, Mattie's side of the room is okay! Have you eaten? Steer clear of the campus cafeteria whatever you do – am I right, Mattie?" She thumped me on the arm and where I would usually have cursed at her I gave a twisted smile that promised retribution later.

We only stayed in the dorm room a few minutes. Lena was perfectly amenable to my suggestion that we leave Angela to her 'study'. As I ushered my mother out the door, Angela stuck out her tongue and gave me the middle finger with an insolent grin. I wasn't oblivious to the fact that she waited until my mother's back was turned to make the gesture. Whatever Lena thought, I knew I had a decent roommate in that girl.

I had hoped that, regardless of how she rated Angela, Lena would approve of Tristan. She seemed wary. I put it down to his weak jokes and banal conversation rather than a genuine dislike. Since he left me, I have wondered if she saw something in him that intimacy masked for me.

Lena left Chicago unhappy. The memories unearthed on that first day had obviously distressed her, not that she discussed them with me. My life there had not been enough to distract her and I waved her off with that familiar sense of failure, followed by anger. I had tried so many times to make her happy but nothing I did could ever achieve it.

So why does she think, now, that she can do it for me?

She looks scared at the fury in my face or maybe she is simply not used to seeing me animated about anything. Recognising that she cannot make me accept her ridiculous travel plan, she tries a different tact. "Do you want me to tell you a story?" she asks, breathlessly. "How about the story of my papa?"

"I already know it, Lena." I feel a stab of guilt at dismissing her papa but there is only so much of her thinly veiled attempts at distracting me I can take.

"Not all of it." She pauses. "Did I ever tell you that, on his

31

death bed, he asked me to go to Italy?"

I open my eyes. My mother is smiling calmly and looking deeply into me, in the way I always wanted her to as a child when that look was far away and vacant. I sigh and consent with a nod. She can tell me all the stories she likes but she's not getting me out of this bed, never mind to Italy.

SIX

Lena

Yesterday, on Mattie's birthday, I went to Mass in secret as I do every year. I sat near the back, dressed smartly and plainly. Head down not in prayer, but in hiding. I always go to this church, where I sit through the long, sung Latin High Mass with a masochistic pleasure. Sometimes I laugh at my attempt to conceal my identity. I am unknown in this part of the capital city. No one is watching. There is nobody to care.

A collective shuffling jolted me back to reality and reminded me to kneel with the others. When I was a girl, Papa used to take me to Mass every Sunday without fail, and often one or two evenings during the week as well. I would watch him lost in prayer and sometimes I would try to copy him by pressing my eyes shut, peeping out every few minutes. When I got bored, I would count how many times the pious old ladies blessed themselves or try to decipher the prayer from the soundless movement of their lips. I never paid much attention to how music shaped the service. Until the *seminario*.

Yesterday, as a deep baritone rumbled lower than his natural range, I tried not to be drawn back there by the sound of a male vocalist. Usually, on my annual pilgrimage to this church I allow myself to be brought back without hesitation. This year, I had another focus.

This year, I was shielding myself not to escape the other congregants but to give myself time with Ben. "Hello, little one," I whispered into the sound when the responses were murmured. "It's me, your grandmother. Can you hear me?"

A few months ago, I broke my pledge of not entering a church between my annual visits. I had to. Someone had to be there for Mattie. To keep her upright when they carried Ben's tiny white coffin down the aisle. The surroundings meant nothing to me. The haunting requiem was just a distant detail. I couldn't concentrate on saying goodbye; all my attention was on Mattie as she wailed. The acoustic amplified her pain, catching her cries and filling the high, domed ceilings, booming them for the rest of us to hear. As Catholics, we don't tend to do that. We express our pain in a muted, respectful way. Since Ben was born, silent and still, my daughter has let go of all her schooled etiquette. She broke.

I know she was astonished that I was willing to attend the funeral. She had seen me show up to the afters of weddings, having avoided the church service. I went to her high school graduation – I was the proudest mother there – but I didn't go to the Parents' Mass. I even missed church funerals over the years: Ruth's mother, our neighbour who was my most reliable baby-sitter, even a girl in Mattie's class who died after years of battling an incurable disease. It didn't matter what had happened – nothing could make me step foot inside a church. Until Ben.

I held it together at the funeral; I didn't let the sadness in. I don't know if I was merely being strong for Mattie or if she was so full of grief there was none of it left for the rest of us. I was practical and strong, the way a mother should be when her child is falling apart.

Not entering a church was a rule I had kept since the day I left the *seminario*. We had a civil marriage, much to the disgust of Damien's family. I might have been the one who organised Mattie's birth certificate but it was Damien who took her to the church to be christened. Her pleas were not enough to persuade me to be a part of her First Communion. "Why, Mommy? Why won't you come?" she said, her eyes pooling with tears. I could give her no answer. It was impossible to explain. By her Confirmation, she didn't bother to cry. But she had looked so sad.

In spite of all that, I was almost offended that she assumed I wouldn't change for Ben's funeral.

"Of course I'm coming. He was my grandson." I had reflected my daughter's incredulous look back at her. I wanted to add, 'and you need me,' but years of holding back stopped me. She held my gaze for a moment before her eyes emptied once again of all emotion. She shrugged and turned away, almost bored.

Mattie lost interest in my hypocrisy years ago. When she was young, she could never understand why I sent her to a Catholic school and insisted she go to Mass every Sunday, when I rejected every invitation.

"If you don't care about it all, why do you want me to believe?"

I would always shake my head and walk away. There was no way to explain. It got easier when she befriended Simon; she gladly went to Mass with Ruth's family on Sundays and stopped questioning my aversion to churches.

Mattie is the sole light in my life.

When I returned to DC from Italy, I was lost. But my college boyfriend Damien forgave me and welcomed me back. Soon, we were husband and wife and parents to a baby daughter. It didn't last with Damien. Since before Mattie started school, it has been just the two of us. Me and my daughter. I didn't mind. It felt right in a way; it was what I knew. Growing up, I only had my papa.

I never regretted raising Mattie alone after Damien left. We were better off without him and she did not seem upset by his absence growing up. She asked me questions about him over the years, more out of curiosity than a feeling of loss. I don't think she remembers him, or the yelling and cursing and drink-induced rages. All she wanted was me. But I couldn't let go of the *seminario*. I carried it with me all those years and it drew me into myself more often than it should have. I can see that now. I assumed Mattie would lean on me, fall into my arms for consolation at the death of her son. But she didn't and that forced me to recognise that a distance has existed between us for a long time.

Although I can hardly bear to sit through a religious service that reminds me so much of the *seminario*, I do make myself go every year on Mattie's birthday to thank God for her. Even now, when I have too late realised that we have long since drifted apart and she has slipped far from herself into this shell of a woman, I have to be thankful for her. Only one person ever meant as much to me as my daughter and I left him, long ago, to his vocation.

Before I knew it, Mass was over for another week. Or, in my case, for another year. I waited until the church was almost empty before removing my mantilla and staring up at the altar. It is a majestic place of worship with high ceilings and thick columns. Statues of the Virgin and rich paintings of the Stations of the Cross adorn the side aisles. The ceiling above the tabernacle drew my attention as it does every year. The four apostles – Matthew, Mark, Luke and John – sit around Jesus, whose halo is the brightest of them all, in a cloudy heaven.

I thought of Ben up there with the other baby angels. Mattie thinks he'll be all alone in heaven without a mother. But as I've told her over and over, my papa will look after him.

I was reluctant to step out of the church into the sweltering heat. Inside was cool, so I stayed a while longer. Glancing at my watch, I saw that it was not yet noon. I had told Mattie it would be later that afternoon before I made it to her. I didn't know if I should bring a birthday cake. Celebration might be an insult.

I knew I would not be arriving empty-handed – I had news. When Ruth had proposed the trip to me just days before, I shook my head. But the more I thought about it, the more it started to make sense. Mattie is not simply sad. She is depressed. This is normal, I know, on losing a child. But she's spiralling. Every day she is worse. Ben has been dead six months. She needs at least to begin to come back to me.

Still, as I made my way to her apartment yesterday afternoon with a small, nondescript cake, I was not entirely convinced Italy was a good idea, until I saw him.

Tristan.

The boy who abandoned my daughter when she told him she was pregnant. He looked well – clean shaven and smartly dressed. The bunch of bright flowers clutched in his hand sparked my response. He had no idea how my daughter had crumbled and how all the vibrancy and colour had drained from her life. She had faded while he lived in a world of bright colours and hope.

I have never hit Mattie. Nor have I ever let her be hit. That was one of the reasons I left Damien. He never beat her, or me, but it was heading in that direction and I wasn't taking the risk. I am only partly ashamed to say I took my handbag and whacked that boy across his body.

"What the . . ." He cowered away from the blow which just made me angrier.

He should have taken it like a man. He should have been there for Mattie instead of shrinking from his responsibilities – offered to marry her, regardless of whether they were too young. The choice ought to have been hers. He should be there now, to lift her out of her heartache and show her a future. It was Tristan's job to revive Mattie and he had failed.

I didn't say a word to him. I didn't hit him again. I just stood, eyeballing him, my chest rising and falling with adrenaline. He looked directly at my hard expression and understood. It was too late; Mattie didn't want anything to do with him.

Taking an uncertain step towards me, he handed me the flowers. "Will you tell her I stopped by?"

I took the summery bouquet, stared at it for a second, then turned and threw it into the street. A car drove over it. Defeated, he left and I ran up the stairs to my daughter.

I thought about Simon as I made my way up to her. He had been such a sweet kid and, if the baby had been his, he would have stepped up without a thought. They were buddies for years before they ever became a couple but I knew they were made for each other. They would have been about thirteen when Simon broke his wrist. Mattie insisted on wearing her arm in a sling too until Simon's cast came off. Even at home, when Simon wasn't there, she refused to remove it. When the school rang wanting to know why she was handing in homework half-done on 'medical grounds', I could do nothing to dissuade her. Honestly, I admired her for it and delighted in watching the connection between them grow stronger. Her judgement clearly failed in later years, as it was Tristan she chose in the end.

I watched her eat the cake I had brought, slowly, seemingly unaware it was for the occasion. Seeing Tristan solidified my decision to take her to Italy but I was too agitated after my altercation with him and I couldn't collect the words to tell her.

It was not until today, after we had eaten in silence and the tears had slid down her cheeks seemingly without a prompt, that I finally broke the news. As I expected, she brushed the idea aside but she did listen with interest to how Papa convinced me to go to Italy.

It won't be easy but it is time, I know, to make her move on. I will start where it hurts most, by removing Ben.

SEVEN

Mattie

I sit in the rocking chair in my quiet and empty apartment, slightly dazed, clutching the delicate photographs. I can't believe I have agreed to go to Italy. I tighten my grip.

At first, I told Lena I had no interest in her travel plan. I had no desire to go anywhere. She knew that. This was just another one of her desperate schemes to help me.

She is obsessed with the idea of depression.

"You mustn't let the depression take you over, Mattie," she would say as I tried to close my ears to her. "Feel sad, of course you'll be sad, but don't lose yourself."

She just didn't get it. I already lost myself the day you left me, Ben.

The support group was the first of her many attempts to cure me. After that came individual counselling and forced exercise, talk of vacations and rekindling old joys, like playing the piano.

Since none of those had worked, I couldn't figure out what she thought attending an ordination in Rome would do for me. I never had the slightest intention of going. Forget about not having the energy to get out of bed, never mind travelling to another continent – there were other turn-offs. For one thing, Simon was bound to be there. Then there would be Ruth, flapping her mouth about the wonders of Aaron which would make me feel bad for the shunned Simon, regardless of our rift. Ruth would be sure to have her bible ready for me, highlighted and tabbed with sympathetic passages. And of course, Joseph would be there too with his baby boy. Even now, a sickly taste coats my throat at the thought.

Lena's pleas were pointless. Nothing would change my mind – until today, when I found the photos.

Lena and I had fought fiercely when she proposed the Italy trip like it was already a done deal. Eventually, I reached the end of my reason.

"*I said no!*" I shouted. We had been talking against each other for an hour and I was exhausted.

"But, Mattie –"

"No! I'm not going to Italy, now or ever. I don't care what you say and I don't care what your papa said years ago either. I'm staying here with Ben, so you can fuck off, Lena!"

Even while adrenalin coursed through my body with the satisfaction of finally saying that to her, tears sprang to my eyes. I ran to my bedroom and locked the door. I sat into my rocking chair with my hands over my ears to block out her weeping.

Whether it was the physical exertion of arguing or guilt at making my own mother cry or just another particularly strong bout of missing you, I don't know, but I slept for almost two full days. Every now and again I would hear Lena shuffling around the apartment.

It was not until I finally stumbled from my room, weak with hunger, that I realised what she had been doing.

Lena was standing in the middle of the room sweeping, a light-coloured bandana holding her hair back. Boxes surrounded her. All your baby paraphernalia was gone.

When I went into hospital to give birth, I had left the apartment ready for our return: a sturdy wooden crib stuffed with soft toys, bottles lined up like soldiers on the kitchen counter and stacks of diapers. Of course, I didn't touch any of it when I came back alone. Now Lena had tainted it, hidden it all away in brown, durable packaging.

My mother, the culprit, stared at me with chin-jutting defiance.

I screamed and ran at the boxes. She didn't try to stop me. I caught a few feeble explanations – she had wanted it all gone before I woke up, a clean start – but I ignored them all, diving into the boxes head first. The door clicked and she was gone, leaving me with arms full of teddy bears pressed to my face so hard it hurt. How could she ever understand that the new-toy smell was all I had left of you?

It was while carefully returning your things to their proper places that I spotted the photos in a drawer. I had forgotten that Lena gave them to me before you were born.

"They're from my papa," she had said, handing them over in a way that indicated they would crumble at a mere touch. "The only man this baby has to look up to." She hadn't meant it as a slight on Tristan's desertion. After all, she had raised me without a husband too.

Gingerly, I sat on the floor beside the last remaining full box and ran a fingertip over the happy faces. Papa was long gone. I had never met him but I grew up with hero-like stories of him. He was a brave man who suffered through the worst humanity had to offer and still thought it worth procreating. He was the type of man I had wanted you to have as a role model.

I stared at the memories. I had been too busy and excited to do more than glance at them in the run-up to your birth.

The first photograph was square – a Polaroid. It was dog-eared and black-and-white. The second was a rectangular photograph, less faded but blurred.

The second picture I had seen as a girl. It was of my mother as a newborn, in the arms of a pale woman, with her papa leaning over them both, beaming with joy. It was the only photograph taken of the three of them before my mother's mother died of blood poisoning brought on by a birthing infection. I turned the picture over.

Long, slender handwriting was etched into the back. *Family Number 2.*

I turned my attention to the older photograph. Except that I

41

knew the man to be Papa, I would never have recognised him. Tall, yes, but plump with a thick mop of hair and a young, unlined face. He was standing proudly beside a pretty young woman, his hand on the shoulder of a boy who could have been no more than five years old. A smaller girl leaned shyly back into the legs of her mother, a finger twirling her hair into a curl. Afraid that I already knew what it would say, I slowly turned it around. *Family Number 1.*

I cried for Papa and his lost families. I wished he was alive. He would have been able to identify with what I was going through.

When Lena arrived back later, she found me still sitting beside that one unpacked box, her father's photographs in my hands.

"He loved me so much," she sighed, taking the second picture in her fingers. "He was all I had. After he died, my school and college friends scattered. Neighbours helped out for a few days after the funeral but I had no other family. I was all alone."

We both looked at the photographs rather than each other, as though conversing through him. "With his last words, he told me he wanted me to go to Italy. That's the reason I went. He thought it might save me. And it did."

I looked at her finally. "How?"

She sighed again, walked to the counter and stood, her back to me. I waited. Finally she faced me. Again, she asked me to come, but this time in a way that assured me she would accept it if I said no.

She said she could help me by showing me the truth about her past. We would become close like a family should be and I would come out of my depression. I nearly screamed when she said that. She will never comprehend, Ben, that you are not depression. You are my life and I have no desire to live a life that doesn't include remembering you every second of every day. But I thought of Papa and his courage to make himself happy a second time.

So I finally agreed to go.

Lena all but skipped from the apartment. Ruth was calling

over to her house for a late evening drink and she couldn't wait to tell her.

I stare at the photos again as I rock slowly back and forth. Lena has people – real people – with whom she can share her good news. I only have you, Ben, but that's okay. I am driven by the past, now that you are in it. It took a photograph of a dead man to prompt my movement and when I leave for Italy you will be my constant travel companion, if only in my heart.

EIGHT

Lena

Ruth is thrilled when I tell her we are making the trip. It will be a chance for her to show off Aaron, her favourite son. Joseph gave her a grandson and Simon is the baby but Aaron is her first, her darling, and he's becoming a priest. I think I can appreciate the special place he occupies in her heart. I never had any other children after Mattie but I can't imagine it's possible to love another child more than – or even as much as – I do her.

I suspect that Ruth has two reasons for inviting me and Mattie to Italy: first, she wants to display Aaron in all his glory and, second, she believes that when Mattie feels the sun on her skin and sees the wonders of another culture, she might start to recover. Mattie, I know, finds Ruth overbearing and has a notion that Simon deserved a better mother. I have been friends with Ruth long enough to know her intentions are good, just like her. Beneath her outward persona of self-importance and her need to control, she has a heart.

"Oh Lena, that's marvellous," she says when I accept her invitation, hugging me hard. "And it will be as good for you as it will be for Mattie." She looks me up and down like I am a calf that needs fattening. Ruth, so curvaceous and womanly, often comments on my small, skinny physique with motherly concern.

I agree with a nod and thank her again for inviting us.

Happy with my reaction, she is all business. "Why don't you call over for dinner tomorrow evening? Ed will be away so we can have a good chat."

I happily agree.

The next day, on my way to Ruth's, I make a quick stop in to Mattie. It has been a difficult few days. In my attempts to compel her to come to Italy, I pushed Mattie too far and she snapped. Thankfully, Papa intervened from above and she finally agreed. She hasn't been lifted out of herself but, when I arrive, her suitcase is standing open in her bedroom. Every now and again she bends to pack something. It is a start.

"We won't be staying with Ruth over there, will we?" she asks.

Amazed and thrilled to be getting any conversation from her that isn't accompanied by sorrowful tears, I assure her it will be just us.

When Mattie first became friends with Simon, she was scared at the prospect of introducing me to his mother – the bible-bashing, ten-commandment-reciting Jesus-freak. What could I, the church-shunning single mother, possibly have in common with her? Turns out, there was one thing.

Mattie and Simon were nine before Ruth and I met. Aaron was almost eighteen and he was there with his mother, collecting Simon from school, when my daughter ran up to me and tried to pull me away. I recognised the younger boy from those mornings when I would double back to watch her playing in the school yard before the bell rang for class. So I approached him.

"Hi, Simon." I smiled down at the wide, pale eyes of Mattie's friend. They had probably traded stories about their mothers and must have been worried Ruth would deem Mattie a bad influence if she met me. I continued, unyielding, directing the conversation now at the boy's mother. "I'm Lena, Mattie's mom."

"Oh yes – Mattie." She nodded in recognition as my daughter continued to pull my hand in the opposite direction.

I cocked my head as I surveyed the mother of the boy Mattie would never shut up about. She was tall and shapely with immaculate nails and shiny hair – and shiny nails and immaculate hair.

Her attention locked in on Mattie. "Nice to meet you, young lady. Simon talks about you all the time."

The boy reddened and slunk behind his brother in protest.

"A pleasure to meet you too, Lena. I'm Ruth." She held out her hand. Her words and mannerisms were friendly but she remained reserved, as though waiting to see more before casting judgement. "This is Aaron, my oldest."

Mattie would probably be surprised that I remember every detail of that first meeting with Ruth. But I do and it wasn't because of Ruth herself or even little Simon. It was because of Aaron.

He was a tall young man, with broad shoulders and a handsome, symmetrical face. Very different from the freckly visage of his younger brother. To avoid Ruth's continuing stare, I asked Aaron whether he had finished high school and how he was planning on spending his summer.

Here Ruth jumped in, and with her answer the kids must have felt all was lost. Religion was the one topic that would surely divide us.

"Aaron is finishing high school this year and is spending the summer with his uncle in Italy!"

"My uncle is a priest," Aaron elaborated. "I'm thinking of entering the priesthood myself so he offered to let me spend some time with him in his order, to see how I would take to the life."

Ruth beamed with pride in the background. Mattie was still pulling at me, scared I would purse my lips against the religious Aaron as a sign that she could no longer play with Simon.

My head started to spin but I controlled myself. After all, Italy was home to so many orders, so what were the chances that he was going to *that* place? I didn't have the breath in my lungs to ask but he offered it up anyway, like a gift.

"It's near Rome. *Seminario dei Discepoli di Pietro*."

A sickening weakness flushed through my body. I gaped at this would-be priest and his mother – living connections to a past I could never forget. Fantastical plots of escape flashed through my mind. I wanted to grab Mattie and run away as fast as I could. We could move school, move state. At the very least I could forbid her from being friends with the freckle-faced boy. She would accept my reasoning; she knew how I felt about the ones who pushed religion like a drug.

But instead my past in the *seminario* crashed down upon me and my head swam at the mere possibility of retaining a link. In an instant, it became clear to me that I had been running from such an opportunity for years and could do it no longer.

So I smiled at Ruth. "That sounds absolutely wonderful."

I watched the scepticism lined into her face melt away at my words. We have been friends ever since.

Years of arriving at Ruth's large house has not diminished my awe of the place. Mattie calls it a mansion. They are well-off rather than rich but Ruth's family home, and her family, dwarfs mine. Their house is a large, detached suburban – a stand-alone with not only a sloping front entrance but a large back garden as well. When Mattie was younger, she used to love visiting their house just for that. She and Simon could run and dash and hide without me shouting at her to stay close like in the park.

The house is always pristine, despite Ruth being the only female in the family. The downstairs is open-plan and connected circularly around a grand, centred stairs leading to the bedrooms. Simon is the only one who still lives at home but the three boys always had their own rooms growing up and there was still one left over for guests. I might have been jealous had Papa's attitude to money not stayed with me.

Papa earned a lot of money as he moved up the ranks in his architecture firm, but we never moved out of the modest house we lived in. Once, he brought me to a 'family lunch' one of his colleagues had put on for the employees in his Beverley Hills-style home. I naively asked Papa whether we could ever afford to move somewhere like that. His answer surprised me.

"Lena, we have enough money to buy somewhere like this now. But what do you and I need with a huge house? Aren't we happy where we are?"

I think Papa was more content living in our neighbourhood. He volunteered at the refugee centre and liked to be close to the people on the ground. Besides, it was the house he had lived in with my mother before I was born and it would have been hard for him to move from there.

I ring the doorbell, as I have many times over the years, still gaping at the grandeur.

Ruth doesn't waste any time. As soon as she has me sitting on her sofa in the living room, glass of wine in hand, she produces the plane tickets.

"Now, I don't want to be presumptuous," she says with all the confidence of a woman about to contradict herself unconsciously, "but I've organised everything."

I take the papers she hands me in disbelief. Ruth has booked our flights. She has organised accommodation. She has even arranged for us to be collected from the airport and dropped to the self-catering apartment she has rented for us. When she finally stops talking, I look up from the information and confirmations she has thrust into my hand. Someone else might find it meddling to the point of inappropriate. But at this moment, it is exactly what I need and she knows it. So many times since he died, I wanted my papa to take care of things for me and I had to do it alone.

I try to express to Ruth how grateful I am but she holds up her hand and won't accept any thanks. Or money. We row. I tell her firmly that I cannot allow her to pay for transatlantic flights and over a week's worth of accommodation. She will brook no refusal.

"You are doing this for me. Flying across the world to see my son be ordained. Of course I will cover the cost. Now come on, let's go in for dinner."

She stands and I make to follow her to protest some more when the front door slams and a deep call reverberates through the house.

"Mom, it's just me! I forgot my laptop!"

He freezes when he sees me.

"Hello, Simon!"

My heart warms at the very sight of him. He feels like a son to me in many ways. Mattie had girl friends over the years but Simon was the one who stuck. He was the boy she ran to when she was upset and the one she called when she got good news. I was not surprised when they started dating and I guess I wasn't hugely surprised when they broke up, if only because young people often do before coming back to each other. What has astonished me is the total halt of communication between them. I know they kept in touch after the initial break-up, when Mattie went off to college. Simon took a trip to see her and, according to Ruth, they haven't spoken since. I'm sure it bothered Mattie in the beginning. But it was not long after their major falling out that she became pregnant and stopped caring about anything or anyone except the angel growing inside her. I used to joke that she would be more of a helicopter parent than Ruth if she didn't watch out but, even with her aversion to Ruth, she took that as a compliment.

After she lost Ben, I thought Simon might come to see her. Whether he tried to or not, I don't know.

But when I saw him stepping through the door into Ruth's house, a feeling of love bubbled up inside me. He is a good kid, the best of all Ruth's children. I miss him just like I miss the old Mattie.

"Hi, Lena." He comes over and bends down to give me a loose, unsure hug. He was always tall, and at almost six foot has a natural stoop from years of trying to blend in.

I return the embrace with a tight hold. "You look great, Simon. How's the business?"

"Oh, busy as ever." He reverts to his standard expression, a genuine grin. "Dad is away visiting clients so I'm keeping it going as best I can." His face tenses. "How's M-mattie?"

He stumbles on her name as though not used to pronouncing it. I pause, unsure how to answer. Thankfully Ruth cuts in.

"Lena and Mattie are coming to Rome for the ordination, Simon. Isn't that great?"

I can tell from Simon's dropped jaw that he had no part in planning our journey. It was all Ruth. To save him having to respond I pipe up, conscious that we are all standing in the hallway like strangers.

"Your mother very kindly arranged all the details for us, Simon. We're delighted to be going." I know I sound stilted and I hear the sincerity of my declaration waver. It all seems suddenly too much. Returning to the *seminario* is a massive decision on my part. I honestly don't know if I will be able to handle it. But throw in an unwanted reunion between Mattie and Simon, and I begin to doubt whether I can go through with the trip.

Simon excuses himself, retrieves his laptop and is gone with a rosy smile for me but a glare for his mother. I let Ruth do most of the talking during dinner. I am busy concocting plausible reasons for cancelling the trip but cannot bring myself to spoil Ruth's excitement with any of them.

In the end, I repeat over and over in my mind that this is about Mattie, not me. I need to help her. I have to show her. So I swallow my excuses with Ruth's fabulous spread. We are going to Italy.

NINE

Mattie

Lena has gone out to buy some groceries, which gives me a few minutes to talk to you, Ben. I'm not crazy. I know you're not here in this room. But Lena, whatever her personal aversion to organised religion, chose to send me to St Nicholas's school and their teachings were not completely lost on me. I believe in the afterlife. In heaven. In you, listening to me like my ramblings are a bedtime story.

Rather than a hotel, we are staying in a self-catering apartment. It is small and narrow, with high ceilings and spindly furnishings. Ruth chose it mainly for its central location and the cold-air unit in the wall – apparently not everywhere in Italy has one. The shutters are wooden and not a crack of light gets in. There is no semi-dark here. I pretend you are beside me in the blackness while I talk out loud to you.

We have been in Rome for barely two days and my mother is a different person. And not just one different person – she has become a jumble of contradictions that is making me nervous.

Aaron's ordination is not for another four days but Ruth insisted on Lena and me coming early so we can do some sightseeing. I know Ruth's game; she doesn't want any excuses for escape come the ordination. Let us get the formality of actually seeing the country out of the way so we can concentrate on the important business of her son. Thankfully she has not joined us. She has been at the seminary every day.

I sound bitter or resentful which I am not. Ruth has certainly been a good friend to Lena. Still, her holier-than-thou act irritates even a Catholic-school girl like me. And I have never forgiven her failure to appreciate her best son over the solemn Aaron and carefree Joseph.

Lena has not commented on Ruth's busy schedule. She hasn't said much about anything over the past couple of days. At first, that was fine by me. It left me free to converse with you, Ben, though her presence meant I had to internalise the conversation.

We didn't take a tour guide and chose instead to wander the streets together. I will admit, son, that this city has been the first thing to inspire me since you were born. The beeping of mopeds and cobbled pathways – I have to keep watching the ground to avoid stumbling – have entranced me. The crumbly buildings and twisting streets stimulate my mind, and I love the graffiti. It's part of the culture, an art form in itself. I wish for a three-way conversation between me, Lena and her papa. He would argue for the architectural wonders of the churches, Lena would be drawn to the sculptures and paintings while I would point to the skilled work of the democratic artists.

I keep expecting to bump into Simon. Ruth never mentioned when he arrived or where he is staying but he is sure to be here. An ordination is the priestly equivalent of marriage. He would never miss Aaron's big day. Worry distracts me even from you, Ben. If it was anyone else, I would resent the intrusion into my thoughts of you. But not Simon.

We were tree-climbing, tomboyish friends. The ones who didn't notice the changes in each other. He started to stare at the cheerleaders and I giggled at MTV poster-boys with the rest of the girls. But he was as oblivious to my rapidly swelling chest as I was to his broadening shoulders. At first, we drifted from each other, uncomfortable discussing what had begun to consume our hormone-riddled minds. Until the day I saved him from Ruth.

We were both fifteen and hanging out in his house – his mansion, really. We were heading for the attic – a converted loft with video games and a TV and a pool table – when Ruth interrupted us.

"Mattie! How lovely to see you, dear," she exclaimed with an enthusiasm that emphasised my recent absences.

Simon looked at the floor while I stuttered a reply.

"Come on, Mattie, let's go." He made for the stairs but Ruth put a hand on my arm.

"Wait, Simon, I haven't seen Mattie in ages." Her statement was cutting and I sensed danger. She turned her sweet smile on me. "How are you, dear? How is your mother?"

"Fine, thanks," I answered apathetically, itching to get upstairs with Simon. He had started dating a blonde called Bonnie from the year ahead of us and she was part of the reason I hadn't seen much of him recently. I wasn't jealous; it was Justin Timberlake I wanted. I just missed being around him.

When we had bumped into each other in the school yard and he invited me over for pool – Bonnie had cheerleading practice that afternoon – I accepted at once. I knew he wanted an excuse to avoid his guy friends. I saw how they wouldn't leave him alone after he spent the night in Bonnie's last Saturday. Unused to such blatant attention, Simon squirmed at the raucous high fives and lewd questions shouted at him in the school corridors. I was impressed that his elevated status hadn't diminished him to their level.

Our talk on the way home had been somewhat staid. I didn't want to ask about Bonnie in case I embarrassed him but his stay-over was the sole topic of conversation amongst our class, and avoiding it only inflated its presence. But I knew once we got up to the attic we'd settle back into our old, effortless ways, and the last thing I wanted to do was make inane chit-chat with Ruth in the hallway.

"Tell me, Mattie," Ruth's hand was still on my arm, "how did you enjoy the play on Saturday night?"

"Play?" I glanced at Simon.

His face froze. He looked like he desperately wanted to say something but his mouth dropped slack and useless.

"Yes, dear," Ruth's eyes bored into mine. "Simon was telling me all about it. How you ordered pizza in your house afterwards and he didn't come home because he 'crashed'?"

Her pitch rose sharply on the last word. As I tried to decide whether I could sneak another look at Simon, Ruth delivered the final blow.

"Funny though, I ran into your mother at the school gates this morning and she knew nothing about it."

Ruth's scheming made my chest puff out and I straightened my stance. Lena was far from the perfect mother but she never went behind my back to poke into my life. She certainly never put my friends on the spot in a thinly veiled attempt to catch me out. Sympathy for Simon's constant struggle for acceptance in his family spurred me on. I could practically hear my brain whirr into action.

"It makes sense that Lena would say that," I answered confidently. "She didn't see Simon. She was at the refugee centre on Saturday night."

It was the perfect alibi. Firstly, Ruth was disinclined to question anything of a charitable nature lest she appeared less Christian. Secondly, it was true. Well, partly true. Lena and her papa used to volunteer at a refugee centre and she continues the tradition every Saturday. She was gone for no more than a couple of hours in the early evening. When she came home at seven o'clock she cooked me dinner and we watched *The Bourne Identity*.

"We got home before Lena. Simon had already crashed on the floor of my room and he left early the next morning for Mass. My mother didn't see him at all." I gave Simon a hard look and pre-empted his mother's next question by adding, "And I really enjoyed the play."

My quick thinking thawed Simon's terror and his voice returned, albeit slightly higher than usual. "Yeah, *King Lear* was pretty boring but our teacher wouldn't shut up about how we should see it for class. So we went . . ." He tapered off without conviction.

I nodded eagerly and Ruth finally removed her grip from my arm, defeated.

As I set off up the stairs, with Simon behind me, I threw him a condescending look over my shoulder. I couldn't believe he hadn't thought to warn me that he'd used me as an excuse for spending the night at Bonnie's. But he was so grateful when we reached the attic that sympathy overtook my frustration.

"It's okay, Si." I examined the pool cue intently. "I get why you didn't want to tell her where you really were."

There was a pause, and when I looked up he was standing awkwardly in the centre of the room. He was all arms and legs, his gangly uncoordination that of an overgrown kid.

"Nothing happened," he blurted out. "With Bonnie, I mean. On Saturday. I did stay over, but nothing happened. Everyone keeps saying stuff, but it didn't . . ."

He trailed off and a bubble of joy expanded in my chest. He was still like me. He hadn't taken that huge, terrifying leap into adulthood. I smiled and he grinned back, scratching his head to give his hands something to do. I threw the cue at him and challenged him to a play-off.

I think that confidential admission to me was the beginning of our adult relationship, although romance didn't flourish until nearly a year after. He broke up with Bonnie soon afterwards and had a string of other girlfriends. I filled out in a womanly way, acquired a nose stud and then a lip ring, and gladly received the attention, comments and kisses of some of the excitable teenage boys from our class. All the while, Simon and I stayed buds, providing cover stories when needed and enjoying the stress-free hours away from societal pressure in his attic.

When we finally kissed, on my sixteenth birthday, we laughed. Not because it was funny, but because it was so wonderful that simply smiling wasn't enough.

I imagine what life would be like if just a couple of things were different. If you had lived and if Simon had been your dad instead of Tristan. We could have come here, to this inspiring city, on vacation. I would have taken in recitals while Simon looked after you and we would have met up afterwards and strolled late into the night. Instead, I am trailing behind my mother, feeling more alone than I ever have around her and that's saying something.

Surprisingly, Lena has not tried to impose art museums on me and she sticks with her usual refusal to enter a church, even for sightseeing purposes. So we stroll around the city. Lena walks silently beside me, occasionally muttering to herself. Sometimes she puts her hand on mine to point out a sight but it would be nothing famous. Earlier today, ignoring a most magnificent cathedral, she pointed to the coffee shop around the corner from it. A while later, on an unremarkable road she squealed at a grotty hotel. She shook her head when I pressed her for the significance and eventually revealed that she had once stayed there. Often, she massaged the scar hidden at the back of her ear like a control.

I call her on her odd behaviour at dinner. I am tired – a combination of the travel and sight-seeing exercise after months of lying in bed – and I can't keep my patience any more.

"What's up with you, Lena?" I let my fork fall with a clatter. The couple at the next table glance over then hastily back down again. I drop my speech to a whisper. "You've been acting weird since we arrived."

"You're right," she whispers back, looking at me strangely. It is almost scary.

"Lena, will you stop acting like a psycho? What's going on?"

There is a pause. "Eat up," she says. "We'll go for a walk after dinner. I want to show you something."

We finish our meal in silence. I could spontaneously combust across the table and she probably wouldn't notice. After we pay the bill, I follow her outside and we walk for about ten minutes through the lively streets. We reach the same cathedral we saw earlier today.

"Do you know where we are?" Lena asks.

"Well," I say lightly, "I know there's a coffee shop around the corner that you were more excited about than the Colosseum."

Lena gives a small laugh. "I know. Come here." She leads me past the cathedral, down the street with the coffee shop and turns onto a wide side street that is strangely deserted. Halfway down, we stop at the entrance to a church. It is unusual, with thick black marble dominating the façade. A sign by the door promises world-renowned paintings inside.

"They really do have a church on every corner, don't they?" I say.

Lena is not listening. Her neck is tilted back like on a hinge. She stares up at the church in contemplative silence, then puts a hand on my arm.

"I had a very good friend once," she says so quietly I can barely hear her over the honking cars and mopeds on the adjoining street. "Her name was Agata. I met her in this church and she took me to that coffee shop around the corner."

I wait, my senses alive.

"She lived in a seminary, high up in the hills. She took me there, where I met someone. A man named Levi. And my life changed forever."

I gape at her. She is on the verge of revealing something to me, something huge. At that second, her mobile phone rings.

TEN

Lena

It is Ruth.

As though sensing that I am about to expose the *seminario*, she rings to offer to take me to that very place. Aaron is not due to be ordained until later in the week but Ruth is conscious that she hasn't seen us since we arrived.

"We're getting on fine, Ruth." I try not to let my irritation seep through the phone. After all, she cannot realise the courage it took for me to tell my daughter even that small amount of my history.

I link Mattie's arm as I speak into the phone and start to steer her home. I am suddenly exhausted and need to curl up in bed and sleep for days.

"I'd like you to see the seminary before the ordination. I want to give you the proper tour!"

I manage to stifle a humourless laugh and Mattie eyes me suspiciously.

"Ruth, that's very kind but I'm sure you want to spend some quality time with Aaron while he's preparing . . ."

"Well, that's just it, Lena. All of the seminarians who will be ordained this week are having their families up tomorrow. The rest of our family can't be there and I don't want Aaron to have no one except me. Please, Lena?"

I know I can't refuse Ruth, not when she so generously brought me here. I promise her that Mattie and I will be ready in the morning and snap the phone shut with force. Mattie knows better than to press for information and we walk back to our apartment without speaking. When the door is closed behind us and the shutters pulled, she braves it.

"What did Ruth want?"

I start to undress for bed. "She is taking us to the *seminario* tomorrow morning to show us around." I walk into the bathroom and shut the door. Leaning my head against the cool wall tiles, I take deep, steadying breaths.

When I have changed into my nightdress and returned to the bedroom Mattie asks her next question.

"Lena," her voice is soaked in curiosity, "were you trying to tell me that you have already visited the seminary where Aaron is being ordained?"

Slowly, I nod.

She shifts her position on the bed, trying to process this. "Your friend Agata who you met in that church took you there. And you met a man? Was he a priest?"

"No," I whisper. "He was a seminarian. Like Aaron. Mattie, I'm tired. Can we talk about it in the morning?"

"I thought we were meeting Ruth in the morning?"

I say nothing but crawl under the covers, my heart pressing in on me. Mattie, so used to me jumping for her every need since Ben died, is clearly confused by my sudden withdrawal.

"At least tell me why this is so important. Just tell me that. What was so life-changing about the man you met in Aaron's seminary?"

I roll over in bed and stare at her open face.

I sigh. I had promised Mattie that I would heal her by bringing her here, that I would share with her the truth about my past to help her understand me and, ultimately, herself. So I start to talk.

I had hinted to her earlier in the evening that *Seminario dei Discepoli di Pietro* means something to me. Now I tell her the truth: that it means *everything* to me. It was there that I met the love of my life, my one true soul mate. His name was Levi and he was on the cusp of ordination, like Aaron.

It's funny how a look of horror from one person can extract laughter from another. "If you are so appalled," I grin at how shock distorts her expression, "imagine how I felt at the time."

I was young, grieving for my papa, alone in a foreign land. The last place I expected to develop such a deep connection with a man was in a school for priests. And if I was astounded by such a development, I cannot begin to comprehend how troubling it must have been for Levi.

"Meeting Levi was so different to any experience I had before. Damien, for example."

Mattie's expression tightens at the mention of her father, but she says nothing and motions for me to continue.

I begin to tell her my story.

Damien and I knew each other for years before Papa died. He was a loud-mouthed, popular guy on whose arm I was proud to be seen around college, but who I never really loved. He had his finger in every pie, and there were plenty of pies in Georgetown University. Damien wasn't athletic enough to play sport so he ran the bets. He wasn't funny enough to perform at open mike night, so he became chief heckler. Untamed hair and ripped jeans with an ability to scrape through every exam without turning up for lectures imbued him with a roguish charm. Vanity buoyed me when he picked me. My own status in college was low-key. I was shy. I missed my papa and I was inexperienced with men.

Before we started dating, I had made only a few close girlfriends and Damien's crazy party antics came to our attention as an object of snobbish derision. What a jackass! What a waster! I never gave Damien a proper thought, until Papa took a shine to him.

Papa came to visit me in college and insisted I take him to Mass in the campus chapel. I avoided telling him I had not once been to Mass since moving from our home in Chicago to college in DC. It would have broken his heart. I walked into the small chapel with what I hoped was an air of confidence and Papa was soon too lost in the service to scrutinise my religious habits.

An hour later, we were walking out of the chapel when someone bumped into me, hard. I turned to glare at the perpetrator and, when I saw who it was, my eyes narrowed further.

"Sorry about that, Lena." Damien's expression was sickly sweet and he grabbed my arm in an attempt to steady me, not that I had been near falling.

My glare turned to an inquisitive frown. I knew who he was because everyone knew who Damien was, but we had never spoken before. How did he know my name? Taking advantage of my pause, he leaned across my body and thrust out his hand to my father.

"You must be Lena's dad." He carried it off like a self-assured gentleman rather than the cocky brat he was.

Papa smiled down at me, delighted to meet a friend of mine, particularly such a shiny-looking chap as the blazered nephew of the Head of Religious Studies. Oh, he managed to slip that into the conversation and could not have failed to notice Papa's face stretch with approval. Eventually, I insisted that we leave as I had booked us lunch in a restaurant off-campus. I couldn't believe it when Papa invited Damien along. Politely and with a slow tone of regret, he declined due to previous commitments, but Papa didn't shut up about him for the rest of the day. I don't know why I didn't tell Papa that I knew Damien by reputation alone. I longed to silence his probing questions about the clean-shaven boy we met at Mass by telling him the truth.

Not wanting to let down a parent is a powerful motivator. I couldn't explain why but I knew Papa would be disappointed if I confessed that we, Damien's campus contemporaries, knew him better as the gin-soaked gambler who escaped suspension because of his connections rather than his insincere apologies to the college authorities for everything from loitering to bar-side brawls.

That night I saw Papa to the train station and ran along the platform, waving furiously as the train carried him to the airport. I walked back to my dorm with my head down, the tears flowing. It was my second year but I still missed Papa so much.

"Lena!" I heard my name shouted brashly across the square when I was just feet from the front door. I turned to see Damien running towards me. I wiped my wet cheeks hastily. Mortification at being caught crying was mixed with uneasiness about his interest in me.

He skidded to a halt beside me, his enthusiasm dampened when he saw my red eyes. "Are you all right?"

For some reason, anger flared inside me. "I'm fine," I answered curtly.

He ran a hand through his scraggly hair. "I was coming over to see if you wanted to go for a nightcap. But if you're not feeling up to it –"

"I'm fine," I said, less harshly, wishing I could think of something more articulate to say. "Okay, let's go."

He eyed me uncertainly as he fell into step beside me. I didn't think I'd ever seen Damien look uncertain around anyone. We strolled to a bar a few blocks away. Two older men nursing pints tipsily tipped their glasses in Damien's direction. I felt uneasy but he just laughed. We slid into a booth that looked cosy but had loose springs under the seats and a table with a surface so sticky the drink seemed to penetrate the wood.

Realising that I was on a date, I tensed. Damien was relaxed and I couldn't help but be flattered at his singling me out. Suddenly, the party-hard stories he relayed were funny instead of pathetic. His attention made me find charm and humour in the behaviour I used to deride.

I began spending all my time with him. My friends were delighted with the gossip in the beginning but Damien showed no interest in them and they became frustrated when I stopped being available to hang out with them.

"Why is he after you, Lena?" one of the girls asked, her voice dripping with scepticism.

I chose to be offended, instead of confronting the validity of her question. I didn't know the answer. I wasn't exactly an easy target for Damien. I wasn't desperate for a lover and I made the poor guy work for my attentions.

He stuck with me. Never cheated, that I know of.

When he kissed me, it was all tongue and no finesse. I was surprised. I would have expected a guy like Damien to have all the moves. Somehow, his lack of grace made me more confident by comparison.

After a few more dates, I built up the courage to ask him why he'd picked me.

"You were on my radar from day one, baby." He sidled up to me and I wondered if it was a ploy, bringing girls to these dingy bars so that he could make them feel protected just by sitting close. He became serious then. "You're not like the rest of them."

"That's it?" I tilted my head at him patronisingly but I wasn't annoyed. I found his inability to say the right thing strangely appealing.

He dropped his gaze, his apparent shyness increasing my attraction to him. "You're not fake. You're your own person. I can tell." It was probably the most honest thing he ever said to me.

I ended it with him when Papa got sick. The problem with Damien was, although he loved me in his own way, he was his own main priority. He comforted me while I cried about my dying father but he was more concerned with how my desire to nurse Papa would affect our grand post-college plans.

I was sad when we broke up. He had been my first proper boyfriend. But in the two years as his squeeze, I never felt one ounce of the passion or the personal connection I did the very first time I saw Levi.

"The way you react when you first meet someone speaks volumes about your future with them," I tell Mattie, who is still sitting on the edge of my bed, apparently enthralled. "With Damien, I was wary and, as it turned out, rightly so. My first meeting with Levi was a divine moment."

I try to explain it to her. I ask her to remember the first time she laid eyes on her son. I know a mention of Ben will grab her attention and it is a good analogy. After all, I will never forget the first time I saw her. It was as if every smile I had ever smiled and every laugh I had ever laughed were diminished to nothing compared to the joy that filled me up when I looked at her tiny face. I thought I might burst with love. There are only two types of people who can enlarge your heart in an instant that way – your children and your soul mate.

Children are the poets, the sculptors, the artists of the world. Their teetering frames are too unbalanced for hours at an easel and their stick-like fingers are unable to record stories in written form. Yet they are experiencing for the first time what we adults consider normal and mundane. Their perspective is unrivalled, and all the more mysterious because of the certainty that it will have evaporated by the time their brains grow enough to enable them to communicate it to the rest of us.

So we can only watch as their eyes pop with possibilities looking at an ordinary cardboard box, or as they run in circles for hours, apparently transported to an arena of cheering crowds and triumphant victories.

The one aspect of their wild imagination that remains into adulthood is a dangerous one because it is distorted through the media's exploitation of our dream life. Hollywood. Her stories captivate us. We suckle at her as though her milk will nurture us.

Childish dreams of heroics morph into teenage fantasies of meeting his gaze across a crowded room. Hollywood ensures these illusions live on into adulthood: the rest of the world fading to a blur as the sparks of electricity shoot between us, unnoticed by even the nearest bystander. No one else mattering, as we know this is our soul mate.

It's the ideal we all grew up with. In a time when the American Dream was pushed on us like a drug, we had no reason to suspect we could not achieve such perfection. Of course, Hollywood's stories are not realistic depictions of how most couples meet. Ninety-nine per cent of the time, it's a mundane opportunistic encounter, not an orchestral decree. It's the boy next door, or the woman in the office beside yours. It's the man who has similar interests or the girl who is sensible with her money. And it's important to play the odds. People buy into the dream and wait around for something spectacular, wasting their whole lives on the hopes of being that special one per cent, when in fact they are just commoners, part of the majority. It doesn't mean they won't be happy. Plenty of the ninety-nine per cent are. They adapt to life with one another and honestly learn to love each other and their co-dependence.

Some say there's no such thing as the other one per cent who experience a transcendental combustion of lust and almost unbearable love. But I know they exist. I've known it since I first saw Levi across that crowded room.

His eyes should have been dark brown, almost black, to portray the smouldering passion I discovered when gazing within. Or they could have been a piercing baby blue, reflecting a goodness and purity that no man I have met before or after could mirror. Instead they were a diluted tan that reminded me of the hot chocolate I used to drink while sitting on Papa's lap.

A childlike sense of novelty overpowered me. Desire dizzied me and I felt like gasping. But I kept my lips shut, not wanting a fresh intake of air to cleanse the feeling. I stood immobile, watching, drinking him in as he stared back with equal intensity and disbelief. It was in that instant I knew Hollywood was no lie. I was the one per cent. I waited for a swell of self-importance at that realisation but it didn't come. It didn't come because I didn't care about it.

"From that moment on, Mattie," I say, and I know she believes me, "I didn't care about anything or anyone but him."

ELEVEN

Mattie

Lena is a twister this morning. When she rose at six I moaned pointedly but she ignored me. Like when I was a kid, she swept about pulling at loose objects, re-arranging, organising – all noisily. I used to think she did it on purpose to wake me. I soon figured out that she was just oblivious to me.

Desperate to escape the apartment, I announce that I am going out and will pick up some breakfast. No response.

"Lena?" I try again. "I said I'm going to pick us up some breakfast. What do you want?"

She ignores me, holding outfits up to her body in front of the mirror, muttering angrily as she flings each aside in turn. I shake my head as I grab the spare key from a hook on the wall and slam the door behind me. She is losing it.

Ruth is going to collect us in a cab at eleven o'clock to take us to Aaron's seminary. Lena hasn't given me any details except that Ruth wants to show us around. I don't know whether it is a tour for the two of us or the whole family. For all I know, Joseph might be there with his baby. I feel my shoulders hunch against the thought. And Simon could be there too.

It is all too much and if Lena wasn't acting like such a basket case, I'd be inclined to send her alone. I wish she'd pull herself together. I'm the one who should be freaking out. She made me swear not to say anything about her connection with the seminary to Ruth. "Or Simon," she had added as an afterthought, as if Simon and I have anything to say to each other.

The early morning air is not as stifling as it will be come noon. It is calming to stroll around the relatively quiet streets. My swirling thoughts slow as I absorb the sort of shabbiness of the city. In a strange way it only adds to its beauty.

I sense something is going on with my mother. This trip is supposed to be about healing me. She keeps insisting that Italy saved her when her papa died but so far I've heard no stories to which I can relate. Nothing that defines her or explains her. Last night she gave some detail for the first time, admitting she has a sordid past as a seducer of the clergy. Then she clammed up and refused to say anything further.

In losing you, Ben, I can see how like Lena I am. Both single women, our lives caught up in our children. Both abandoned. For most of my life, Simon was the only steady male around. At home it was just me and Lena and she would never elaborate on why my dad left us. I know only the bare bones of the story. After an extended trip to Italy following her papa's death, Lena returned home to America and immediately reunited with Damien, her college sweetheart. They started a family early and broke up within two years.

I have little substantive memories of my dad; I had been so young when he left us. But, as a girl, I did have an unnatural tic. Simon observed it in that straightforward way children do. "Why are you always looking behind you, Mattie?" he had wanted to know and I could give him no clear answer. Random bursts of terror that I was being pursued would often come upon me at no obvious trigger. Lena rarely spoke about my dad, not that I asked much. But she did say something interesting once that stuck with me. "I ran from him so you wouldn't have to any more."

It partially explained my impulse. Did I run from my father? Had he chased me? I had created a romantic notion of him over the years. I dreamed that he left us for a noble reason – to work undercover for the police or to protect us from bad men targeting families like ours. When I was old enough Lena admitted the real story about his drinking, gambling and verbal abuse. I suspected but didn't want to know for certain whether it had been him who instilled in me a fear of being hunted.

After that conversation with Lena, I began to remember things, though how much of it my mind created to fill unwanted gaps I don't know. Lena has always insisted my name be shortened to Mattie but he used to call me his 'Tilda' – in a whisper so she couldn't hear. That was the only time his voice was gentle like a father's should be. The other memories are of rough cusses and threatening orders. Mostly directed at my mother but not always.

She might have been the one who left but he didn't fight for me. He deserted us. Likewise went Simon – the love of my life, my best friend. Tristan had seemed solid. He idolised me but he had no wish to be a father to you and so he left me too. Finally there was you. My little man. I never imagined you cutting me out of your life like all the rest. But your own life was cut before you drew your first breath.

Without realising it, I have looped back around to our self-catering apartment. From the street I can hear through an open window my mother clattering around. The sound of her continuing her crisis without me produces that familiar feeling of uselessness, and tears spring to my eyes. She's supposed to be the one taking care of me, not the other way around. Why did she bring me here? What does she think she can possibly teach me? I have suffered enough.

Every heavy footstep drains me as I power upstairs, ready to confront her. I barge into the bedroom we share, mouth already open in defiance, but I stop at the sight that greets me.

Lena is standing in the room, clothes and make-up strewn all around, gripping her head in her hands and sobbing violently.

She looks like I feel on the inside when I think about how you left me. You died. Sometimes I simply cannot believe it. You died. You died.

"What did you say, Mattie?" Lena sounds stuffy, like she has a cold.

I draw in a breath, realising I have started talking aloud. Am I going mad? I look at my mother, all sadness and self-pity, and I can't stop myself. The harsh words spill out before I can stop them.

"Ben's dead, Lena. He's dead. I don't care about anything else, least of all the drama playing out in your head twenty years too late."

She stares at me, her mouth agape. I grip my stomach and bend over. Massaging myself, I feel the skin loose and untoned but still flat against my stomach. I am hollow inside without you. It hits me anew, just like the first time I gazed on your pale, white face. I remember everything about you. From the way you squirmed inside me, always kicking in the lower left of my womb, to the day we buried you. I start to cry.

Lena doesn't come to me like I expect. She doesn't soothe me as she has been doing for months. Instead she sits on the bed, buries her head in her hands once more and weeps anew. I walk into the bathroom and slam the door. I turn on the shower so she cannot hear me crying even louder than she is. I feel bad for shouting at her. Whatever her faults, I cannot deny that she has at least tried to help me since you died.

You died. Fresh tears fall from my eyes.

When I emerge from the bathroom an hour later, a migraine has taken over Lena. Wincing at a rush of guilt that I might have contributed to it, I tuck her into bed in the darkness of the shutter-locked room to recover. I offer to stay with her, but she murmurs that she wants to be alone.

So I leave her and sit on the kerb outside to wait for Ruth. Passers-by step around me without comment. The apartments block the sunlight. It is pleasant in the shade. I try not to think about anything, even you, Ben, and let the warm breeze be my body's only sensation. After a while, I hear a voice.

"Mattie?"

I look up at Ruth, squinting although the sun is not in my eyes.

"What are you doing sitting on the sidewalk like this?"

When I tell her Lena is sick, she insists on coming up. Lena has not moved since I left her. Ruth wets a towel and places it on her forehead.

"The best thing for her, Mattie," she says conspiratorially as if my mother cannot hear her, "is rest. You and I should let her be and go to the seminary."

Lena tries to sit up. "Will you be up to it, Mattie?" she croaks. "You don't have to go if you don't want to."

"Of course she does," snaps Ruth. "No point both of you missing out. We'll have a lovely day. Besides, the other seminarians will have their whole families there. I don't want Aaron to feel unwanted."

I make my decision to go when Ruth explains that Simon and Ed are not flying into Italy until this afternoon as they can't leave the business for too long. Joseph is already in Rome but his wife is ill from jetlag so they are staying in their hotel for the day.

"They want to be well for our dinner later," Ruth excuses their absence.

I had almost forgotten. So far, Lena and I have been given time to ourselves. But tonight the celebrations for Aaron are to begin, starting with a dinner for the family, of which we are considered a part. I am not sure if I will be able for both Joseph's baby and Simon. I might as well go with Ruth now, so that if I can't bring myself to attend this evening, or the ordination when the rest of Aaron's family are there, I will have at least been to the seminary once and that should keep Ruth from shunning me completely. Not that I care what she thinks, but she did pay for our trip over and she is important to Lena.

I think about Simon running the business with his dad. It was what he always wanted. But I had assumed it was a long-term plan, that Simon and I would live a grand life before ever settling down.

I should have known better. Even our first kiss was against the backdrop of Ed's business.

It was my sixteenth birthday and it fell on a Friday. Lena had taken me out for dinner. Afterwards, Simon invited a group of friends back to his house to continue my birthday celebrations.

Lena had been unsure but Ruth insisted Ed would be there to supervise. So he was, until he kicked everybody out before midnight because of a fire at his printing warehouse.

Joseph tried to convince us to sneak into town with him but Simon wanted to go with his dad to check out the warehouse. I was tempted to follow Joseph – my attempts at rebellion had been increasing in intensity. But ultimately I wanted to be wherever Simon was. So, as the others dispersed, I followed my best friend out to his dad's car and we drove to the warehouse. Leaving us strict instructions to stay in the car, Ed raced inside. A few employees were already there, as were two fire trucks with their flashing blue lights. We watched with bulging eyes for the first few minutes but it soon transpired that there had been no fire. False alarm. Ed began to rush around appeasing and explaining.

"Screw this," Simon said after about half an hour and motioned for me to follow him.

We crept around the side of the main warehouse to a row of smaller buildings. I craned my neck to spy in the windows as we passed them – some were offices, others were filled floor to ceiling with the leaflets and booklets Ed's company printed.

"Where are we going?" I hissed.

Simon put a finger to his lips and beckoned me on. There was no one around the back – it appeared the fire had only been suspected in the main building. After a few minutes we reached the end of the row of offices and storage rooms. I stopped short. A square plot of land was broken off and surrounded by a low wall that we could easily see over. Inside the space was a miniature grey fountain. Water trickled feebly from the top of the fountain and spilled down into the circular basin below. Wooden benches ran along its length and width. Yet there was no entrance to the tiny area.

"Hop over." Simon swung his legs over the low wall without effort and I followed him.

I sat down on one of the benches. It was cracked and loose under me but I didn't move. The enclosure was so small my feet could touch the fountain. "What is this?" I asked.

"We don't know," Simon answered, walking along the seats and finally sitting beside me. "It was here when Dad bought the land and he refused to knock it down, although they could have fitted an extra out-office in the space. The staff sit out here in the summer sometimes."

I turned to ask him something – I forget what. I was very aware of how close our faces were to touching. His fingers moved to my lips and I held my breath. He took my newly acquired lip-ring between his thumb and index finger.

"Can I take it out?" he whispered.

I nodded, staying perfectly still. He moved slowly and gently. I didn't wince as he slid the point from my lip. All I wanted to do was look away but his stare locked me in place. His breath was warm on my nose. I closed my eyes.

After we kissed, we looked at each other and laughed. Then we kissed again.

That night, when we were both so happy to have finally connected in that way, I never imagined there could come a time when, more than not wanting him around, I would feel active relief at his absence. It saddens me that I have been feeling it strongly since Ruth informed me Aaron is the only son we will meet at the seminary today.

The journey to the seminary is not as painful as I expected. Ruth won't shut up about Aaron's plans for the future, which range from a Vatican position to taking a parish back home, but I am not required to participate in the conversation aside from the odd murmur of agreement. So I have the chance to stare out of the window and take in the landscape. Once again, I appreciate Lena's fascination with Italy. The busy, honking streets soon give way to rougher side-roads. Rows of vines stand brightly against the blue sky. Trees and laneways weave around hills strewn with dusty red rocks. I am sucked into the scenery and can understand why Lena wanted to show me Italy so badly. It is certainly high on the list of countries I wish I could have brought you to, Ben.

The cab driver pays no attention to the speed signs or the pot-marked roads as he carries us through a remote village. I am looking down, thinking how high up this village is located, when our driver swings a left turn and revs up a winding road, taking us further towards the mountaintops. My head spins from the steep ascent.

"Don't worry, Mattie. They all drive like maniacs in this country – it's tradition." Ruth's knuckles turn white as they grip the seat in front of her.

After ten minutes of twisting turns, we swing ninety degrees onto a dirt track. It is barely visible from the road but the driver is obviously familiar with the terrain. It leads to a circular courtyard already bustling with cars and cabs. The first thing that hits me is the black. Against a setting of lush green fields and a bright sun glistening from the sky, the masses of priests and nuns wearing darkness seem out of place. It is only then that I realise Ruth is dressed sombrely as well. A few flecks of white soften her black dress which I hadn't noticed under her pale cream jacket. I look down at my own pink dress. Another time I might have panicked. I seem incapable of such emotions since I have been left childless.

"Aaron!"

Ruth's shriek stings my ears as she shoves me aside to get to her son. As she hugs him, I look beyond them to a light yellow building standing tall against the mountainous backdrop. I crane my head to take in fields of vines in the near distance and rows of colourful flowers by a little river flowing alongside the building. Other buildings are dotted around the main one. I get the impression it would take hours of wandering to properly figure out the layout of this seminary. I turn to smile politely at Aaron but when I see him the familiarity of an old acquaintance melts my heart and I don't have to fake it.

"Mattie!" His greeting radiates happiness and I walk quickly to him, almost with a skip.

He is even taller than Simon and he has to stoop low to catch me in his embrace. It is the first time I have seen him in a cassock yet it does not seem strange. Actually, he looks perfectly normal in it, like that is how he has always dressed. I murmur congratulations in his ear and pat his back. As I make to pull away, he holds me tight against him.

"I'm so sorry about your baby," he whispers.

I feel my body tense to a degree that I know can bring on spasms. I force him back from me and this time he releases me. I look at the ground, willing myself not to cry.

"Aaron," Ruth squeezes between us, not having heard her son express his sympathy, "show us where we can get a good seat for the Mass."

I let them walk ahead, ignoring Aaron's backward glances, and follow them through a courtyard into a small chapel.

I hadn't realised there would be a Mass but I suppose that should have been obvious. I sit where instructed by Ruth, not taking in any of the surroundings although I know Lena will grill me for details later. I close my eyes as hushed a cappella notes wash over me like waves, settling my nerves.

People filter in and sit beside us. I hear Ruth talking eagerly to someone. She nudges me when Mass begins and I sit up, focusing my attention. Aaron and a row of others dressed in black under their light purple robes file in from the side, Aaron at the head. I feel Ruth squirm in her seat beside me, glowing with pleasure at her son's leadership role.

We are in a section at the back, separated by a black velvet rope from the main body of the chapel into which the seminarians are filing. Aaron got us a space in the front row of the back section so we have a perfect view of them settling into their stalls. Beyond the rope, pews run along the sides of the chapel, so the men are looking at each other, rather than at the altar. That strikes me as odd but I don't dwell on it. My attention is consumed with Aaron.

He is the same as I remember him, if not improved. Tall, handsome. With the physique for sport but not the inclination. He was a musician – I remember Joseph seething with envy when his earnest brother was given an electric guitar. "He's not even in a band!"

Though religious from his schooldays, I never imagined Aaron ending up a priest. I don't know why I didn't see it coming

– with a mother like Ruth and a temperament for reflection. I suppose I didn't expect any of our friends to enter the priesthood; it's not really done these days. Even from St Nicholas's, which is by all standards an extremely religious school, only a handful of men were called to the vocation during my time there, and no women. No one from my own class had shown any inclination.

I move my eyes from Aaron to the other seminarians around him. Their heads are either buried in the books they hold in their hands, turned respectfully towards the altar or staring ahead in contemplation. I blush as I think of what they are giving up to spend their lives praying. In college, the lads had only one thing on their minds. Including Tristan. While he would happily spend time with me doing other things – drinking in a bar, going to the cinema, even studying with me – he always wanted the same thing at the end of the day. Everything else was a means to that end. Their conversation was full of it, especially if they thought no women were around to hear them.

I fell asleep at a party once – one of the few parties to which I had managed to drag Tristan – and woke up hearing his mates spout the things they wanted to do to me. They were laughing like hyenas. I think it was their laughter that roused me from my drunken stupor. Tristan was sitting beside me, head down in pretend contrition, but he was guffawing along with the rest. He actually defended himself later.

"For God's sake, Mattie, it was all talk!" He waved away my sense of violation and powerlessness. "I'd never have let them actually *do* anything to you."

I didn't drink for a month after that.

The men here aren't working towards the usual end goal. In fact, they are making a promise never to get there. I can't wrap my head around their motivation. Despite the teachings rammed down my throat at St Nicholas's, I'm not overly religious and the recent scandals have done nothing to endear the Church to me. Since leaving home, I haven't attended Mass every Sunday and I can't remember the last time I went to confession. I do believe in God; I have certainly prayed to Him enough for you, Ben. But I imagine giving up everything – travel, adventures, motherhood – to stay here and pray. It's beautiful, but small. Confining. Just like the effect it had on Lena.

TWELVE

Lena

My headache has subsided. It started to ease once Ruth and Mattie walked out the door. I lie back on the bed and allowed my body to relax. I hadn't realised it had been clenched so tight.

I thought I was prepared. After all, I made it this far. But in these past few days, in the last stretch of the journey back to the *seminario*, my breathing has become erratic and my brain pulses like someone is punching me from the inside of my skull. Revealing something of the truth to Mattie last night should have been cathartic but it seems to have made my head ache worse. I know admitting to her that Damien was not the love of my life must have hurt her. While she knows he was a bully and that we were better off without him, it must affect her to know that there was another man who captured my thoughts, and that our quick-fix family was not enough.

Still, I'm glad I told her. She is consumed with Ben and can't see it right now but I am starting to tell her my story and it will help her. This trip can only bond us and I fixate on that to see me through.

After an hour or more in bed, I peel myself from the covers, shower and change. It takes a long time. My movements are sluggish and my stomach swirls. I try not to picture Mattie in the *seminario* without me. My mind keeps throwing up images of her in the courtyard, in the chapel, perhaps even strolling past the main building towards the vineyards, if they are still there. She will be meeting different people than I did. No Levi, that's for sure. No Agata, Marthe, Christoforo. For her it will be the same faces as home – Ruth, Aaron.

"Agata." I say her name out loud. She was one of the best friends I ever had. "Marthe." My chest hurts. "Christoforo." I smile before I can help it.

Their faces appear clearly to me and I take a step back, having swayed on the spot. I feel so near to them here, so close. How cruel is the disconnect between space and time. I might be near the place I knew them but time has surely made it another world. I wish I had not let Mattie go to the *seminario* without me. I have to make her see it as I did, not merely as an extension of Ruth's family.

As I leave the apartment to buy food for dinner, a burst of early afternoon sun cuts into my pupils. I stop and punch a fist to my head, letting out a groan. An old man with a bushy moustache and kind eyes stops and enquires in Italian. I wave him along, indicating that I am well. I walk on, sensing his concerned gaze follow me around a corner. I have met nothing but kindness in Rome. Agata enters my mind again – how she plucked me from the streets and saved me.

Thinking about that now, another memory flashes before me – a memory of the day Papa saved someone from the street – and I sense karma passed on from his good deed. I was walking with Papa down Michigan Avenue, the main street in Chicago, when he dropped my hand. I had been at a young enough age for Papa to insist on hand-holding as a strict condition of afternoon strolls so I was stunned when he let go of me to run towards a complete stranger. I watched, scared, while the two men collided into a violent embrace and collapsed to the ground together, sobbing wretchedly. People stared, and hurried to pass the scene.

I regret my reaction now. I erupted into tears at the sight of Papa in such distress, and refused to be introduced to the cause of it all – the stranger with his sunken eyes and smelly clothes. I buried my head in my hands and bawled until Papa agreed to leave his friend and take me home.

It was the next week – with buried memories of the concentration camp revived by the chance encounter with a fellow survivor – that Papa insisted we volunteer at the refugee centre. His friend was there. Papa had returned to Michigan Avenue without me a few days after our encounter and, having found his friends on the same street corner, brought him to the shelter. I cringed when the man approached me. He had showered and was wearing clean clothes but all I could see was the man who had made my papa cry.

"Your father is a good man," he said in a thick accent. "You should be proud of him. He is my guardian angel."

Years later, when I was scared and alone on foreign streets, I was sent my own guardian angel in the form of Agata.

I arrive back to the apartment and spread out the food I bought. As I set about cooking for Mattie I remember that we are supposed to be meeting Ruth and the entire family for dinner this evening. Cursing aloud, I make my way to the bedroom and drop dejectedly onto the bed. Once again, I start to doubt my decision to come back to Italy. Mattie has visited the *seminario* without me. Ben is still occupying her mind to the point that she doesn't want to hear about my past with Levi. What if she can't cope this evening with Joseph's new baby? What if she and Simon rekindle their fight, whatever it was about? I was too fragile this morning to comfort her. I can't let that happen again. I have to pull myself together. My head resumes its throbbing and I lie back on the bed.

When Mattie agreed to partake in this journey, inspired by photographs of Papa's resilience, it was her first attempt at strength since losing Ben. It had not been an easy step to take.

The day before we were due to leave, I arrived at her apartment to find her missing. She didn't answer her cell when I called. I knew exactly where she was but I was worried because it was starting to get dark. If the caretaker tried to make her leave as he locked the gates for the night, I didn't know how she would react. So I went to the graveyard and, as I knew she would be, she was there, singing a lullaby as she rocked back and forth to keep warm. She didn't react as I approached her and draped my coat over her shoulders.

"I can't leave him, Lena," she said.

I bent down beside her and picked up one of the white pebbles covering his grave. I handed it to her. "You're not leaving him." I touched my heart. "You're taking him with you in here. We both are."

She shook her head. "He'll be lonely here, with no one to visit."

"He's at peace, my love. You know that. He'll be here waiting when you get back."

She turned to me finally. "Did your papa ever visit the graves of his first wife and children?"

I let my head hang in contrition. I didn't know the answer. From the few times he had spoken about it, I didn't think he ever found their bodies. But I couldn't be certain. I never asked. It haunts me that he was my whole life and yet I know so little about what he went through. My shame in that moment conjured a further motivation for bringing Mattie to the *seminario*. She might not be able to see past Ben now but there will come a time when, like me, she'll wish she knew about the parent who raised her.

She cried when our plane took off from the soil in which her child is buried. But she is here. She can do this. So I must too.

THIRTEEN

Mattie

Lena stares at me with wide eyes when I return. I don't have to lie to tell her what I know she wants to hear – the seminary is wonderful. Her taunt face brightens at my enthusiasm but when I start talking about the Mass we had in the chapel and the home-made wine they offered us in the main building afterwards, she starts to well up. I tell her that if she is not feeling up to it, we can skip the meal.

Her eyes dry and she surveys me astutely. "We came here to support Aaron," she says. "It might be hard for both of us but I will make it to his ordination and you will go to this dinner."

At Lena's return to motherly strength, my lip starts to tremble. She takes a step towards me with a compassionate tilt of the head. "Who is it you're worried about?"

"Joseph," I say without hesitation. "Not Joseph himself – his baby."

"And Simon?"

I turn away. "It doesn't matter about Simon," I say, my voice hard. "We haven't been together for years."

For the first time, Lena asks why. At first, I don't answer. I have never told her the reason and maybe she is only asking now to escape her own mind for a minute. But I need her to get me through tonight and so I decide to tell her. I move over to the window and look out at the dark yellow of the late afternoon sky.

The conversation took place during our final year of high school. We had applied for colleges the year before and were eagerly awaiting, and in my case receiving, offers. Simon had applied to the same out-of-state colleges I had, plus a few more at Ruth's behest. I had no idea he was mostly doing it for show.

We hadn't discussed our future much. Conscious that we could end up on opposite sides of the country, we stayed silent about it to avoid making it real. When I got the offer of DePaul, one of the colleges I knew he had applied to as well, I couldn't resist any longer. His response to my gentle probing about which university was his top choice astounded me.

"None of them. I don't think I'm going to college."

"What do you mean?" The question came out more harshly than I intended. I was blindsided.

Simon remained sitting cross-legged in the centre of the pool table in the attic while I scrambled up from my usual sprawl on the couch.

He stared back at me unashamedly. "Just what I said, Mattie. I probably won't be going to college next year."

"But your grades are good," I frowned. Simon wasn't top of the class but he never failed, not nearly. Always reliably in the middle. Maybe not good enough for Ruth but satisfactory for a college application.

"It's not that I can't get in, Mat." He circled one of the pool balls on the flat surface with his palm. "I don't like studying. I'd rather *do* something. Dad's getting on in years and is going to need someone to take over the business in the next few years. It makes sense to start training me up."

I shook my head in disbelief. Simon had worked odd-jobs for Ed's publishing company for years. They had a number of contracts with large organisations, including the Church, in DC and also in the surrounding states. They made their money from it and Simon often did local deliveries.

"Simon," I stood up, "if you're going to take over a business, shouldn't you have a college degree? In business or accounting or even religious studies, given your dad's clients?"

He laughed but I was serious.

"Will they not pay for you to study?" I asked in a whisper.

Simon sobered and clambered down from the pool table. "Mattie, I want you to really listen to me, okay? My parents would love to see me go to college. You know them – anything with a bit of prestige. But this is *my* life. I don't want to spend four years studying. I know you think I should want to escape Mom and Dad, but I like it here."

I bit my lip, not able to believe this was happening. I cast my mind back over the conversations we'd had about the future and suddenly recognised how one-sided they had been. How had I never noticed it before? I wanted to escape Lena's discouraging indifference and I assumed he needed to get away from his mother too. Ruth was stifling. I had talked about travelling and college life and he had laughed with my jokes but never committed.

"Why didn't you tell me this before?" I whispered.

"I tried," he said forcefully.

I took a step back. He sounded angry. I didn't think I'd ever heard him really angry before.

"You didn't want to hear it."

"Don't you want a life, Simon?"

"Of course!" He smiled again but it was different than usual. "We have to ask ourselves what we really want out of life, Mattie. Otherwise we'll just go through the motions, only realising what we've missed when we're on our deathbeds and it's too late."

He reached out and rubbed my arm. I thawed a little at his touch.

"So, what is it you want, Simon?"

"I want a family," he said simply.

I backed away as he moved towards me until I was right up against the wall. His expression held a trace of something I couldn't place.

"Not today, Mattie. In a few years."

Then I saw in his honest face what I should have known all

along. I couldn't understand how I'd overlooked it. Simon was never like Joseph. He was more like the serious Aaron. He knew it wasn't what people expected of a seventeen-year-old but Simon had never shied away from who he was. I couldn't help asking again, although I already knew the answer.

"What do you mean?"

"I want a wife and kids. A house and a car and a good job where I can dictate my own hours. And I want it all while I'm young and energetic enough to enjoy playing with the children. That's the adventure I want, and of course I want it with you."

"Simon," I breathed, winded, "we all want a family but now's not the time. Now is about living out our fantasies – going to college, travelling the world, meeting new people . . ."

"Why?" he interrupted. "You know me. You know I'm not a party animal like the rest of the guys. I know what I want from my life, so I'm going to set about getting it. Right now."

Church bells from down the block tolled. They sounded oddly distant.

"What are we going to do? When I go off to college and you stay here?"

"Well," he reached out a hand for me, "depending where you end up, I was hoping we would stay together. It's only for a few years. After that you can come back."

"Hang on." I let his arm linger in the air. "Come back?"

"Well, yeah. I'd never ask you to stay here now – I know how excited you are about experiencing college. Once you're done, I'll be well on my way in Dad's business. You can come back and we can settle down."

Stepping around him, I walked over to the skylight. I spoke while staring out at the vast blueness of the sky so I wouldn't have to look at him. There was no way I was returning here in four years. College was not a mere stopgap for me. It was a stepping-stone. A ticket. I didn't know what exactly I wanted to do or where I wanted to go. All I knew was that I wasn't about to settle back into my old life when the whole world was out there.

I could have survived four years of long distance if there had been the promise of exploration and travel and new beginnings at the end of it. But trying to clip my wings by tying me to domesticated life at the exciting age of seventeen was inexcusable.

I left the attic that day in a daze. After talking for hours, we hadn't resolved anything. The truth was too raw. Simon and I were on different paths. Not temporarily, but for the long term. Our lives were not destined for intersection.

It took another few months before I could verbalise that. Neither of us wanted to admit what our conflicting plans meant. We remained boyfriend and girlfriend until the day we finished high school. We let our mothers take photos of us in our graduation gowns like they would one day adorn a mantelpiece next to a wedding photograph. Our two families went for dinner that night. We smiled as they toasted us but every time I looked at Simon I saw his natural grin waver.

That night, we walked home early, leaving Lena, Ruth and Ed in the restaurant. I had taken up my college place in DePaul University in Chicago and everyone had accepted Simon's insistence on a 'year out' before making any plans. Even Ruth lauded his wisdom in taking his time, though I was sure weeks of Simon and Ed's controlled persuasion had been required to win her over.

"Ruth seems to think he needs another year to mature before college?" Lena had grilled me the week before when the news had leaked out.

I had murmured indistinctly, mildly amused at the role reversal – it was usually me trying to engage with her.

"Do you feel that way?" she asked, bluntly. "Are you happy to be going to college?"

I had stood and dropped my plate noisily in the sink. "Yes," was all I said before running to my room to cry, knowing my days with Simon were numbered. It was not that I hadn't considered his proposition. But I just couldn't do it. I couldn't commit to the type of life I was living with Lena, even if it was with Simon instead.

As we walked home from our graduation dinner, he finally

brought up the subject we had been avoiding since the conversation in his attic so many months before.

"Are you going to stay here until college or will you go to Chicago early to get set up?"

I paused. "Not much point staying."

"Why?" he asked.

I looked up at the injury evident in his voice. The last thing I ever wanted to do was hurt Simon. I adopted a conciliatory tone. "It will be harder to leave the longer I stay. Knowing that we have to break up."

Despite what we had admitted long ago in the attic, he seemed shocked when I said the truth out loud – that we would have to split up. I tried again to make him see that college was only the beginning of my journey and that I couldn't come back to DC, even for him. I started to feel stupid when he questioned me further and I could give him no answers. I responded with defensive defiance.

"I don't know what I'm going to do, Simon. That's the beauty of it. I can figure it out as I go along."

He scoffed. "Mattie, you have to plan. Otherwise you'll end up drifting. If there is some burning ambition you have to fulfil, I could understand you not wanting to come home. But you've nothing. Just a vague sense of wanderlust."

"So what?" I was aware of our raised voices ringing loud in the darkened suburbia but I didn't care. "This is my life, Simon. I'm not going to spend it in someone else's shadow. I want to do things, go places. I thought you'd want to come with me."

"I do want to be with you, Mattie. I want us to have a real life. Here. I thought you'd get it all out of your system in college so we could start for real. I'm willing to wait for you . . ." He let his offer hang like it was charity.

I stopped walking and turned to him to fight for us one last time. "There's plenty of time for settling down, Simon. Don't you want to live first?"

His face clouded and I could see him letting me go. "I am living. And if this life is so boring and repulsive to you, maybe you should just go."

There was nothing left to say. I looked around and saw that we had arrived at my street.

Sure of my future, I walked away from him and into my house without looking back. If Simon thought he could turn me into a bible-bashing soccer mom like Ruth, he was mistaken. I had plans. No fixed plans, but ideas and notions and choices that made me shiver in anticipation. I wasn't about to be chained to wifedom and motherhood.

The irony should be obvious, Ben. Two years later, I would have given anything for Simon to have been your father.

"Oh Mattie!" Lena shakes her head sadly when I finish my story. I can't tell if she is disappointed in me, Simon or the whole situation but it is clear she thinks we made a mistake. I don't argue with her. She is right.

I had not been fully truthful about my fears for the evening ahead of us – of course I am nervous about seeing Simon. Even before we became a couple, he was the person I went to for reassurance and now, in the depths of my despair, he is not mine any more. But more than Simon or Tristan or anyone, you occupy my soul space, Ben, and it is my reaction to a living breathing baby that terrifies me most. I don't think I will be able to control myself.

It's simple. I am scared.

It's very simple: I don't want to see Joseph's baby. I don't want to see his wife, smiling contentedly with her little boy. It's selfish, I know, but I can't help it. Fear is all there is inside me.

Lena makes me eat some bread – a snack to keep me going until dinner. The bread has a bulky, rubbery texture that makes it hard to swallow. I chew it slowly while I watch her dress for the evening. Then I change, apply some light make-up and walk ahead of Lena down the stairs to the outside.

Lena links my arm as we step out into the dark street. I am tempted to make a smart remark about her abrupt recovery but I know she is probably running on adrenalin for my sake so I hold my tongue. She, however, does not and keeps up a steady flow of encouragement.

"They are all going to be at the ordination. You might as well see them now and get it over with. Maybe it won't be as bad as you think."

I nod without listening as we walk along. Ruth had given me all the details of the family dinner on our way back to the city. Aaron is getting a cab from the seminary to the restaurant just north of the Vatican and we are to meet punctually at eight. That will give Simon and Ed enough time after landing to find their way to their hotel and change for dinner.

We pass by the front of the Vatican, turning our heads to marvel at the grandeur of the basilica. Statues look down on us from the roof and the Egyptian obelisk stands tall and proud in St Peter's Square. Though it is late, worshippers are there, staring upwards, some on their knees on the hard ground clutching rosary beads.

We loop around the side and down more streets. I don't know where we are going but Lena seems certain of the way. Eventually we find the restaurant up a narrow paved street. We almost walk by it but Lena spots the wooden sign hanging from the bricked wall of the alley above the door. An extensive and expensive menu is displayed in the window.

"Isn't Aaron supposed to be taking a vow of poverty?" Lena asks in the breathless way that means she's trying to distract me.

I pull my new evening shawl around my shoulders in an effort to stop shivering, though I know it is not the temperature that is causing me to shake. Lena has insisted on us being late so that we will meet them all together. It's her 'Band Aid' theory – get it over with quickly.

I swallow hard as we enter, the evening sun evaporating into the dullness of the restaurant, half-lit with what are clearly supposed to be atmospheric wall-lamps.

"Lena! Mattie!" Ruth calls us from a table at the far end of the long room.

My mother walks forward but, before I can follow, I hear a familiar greeting behind me.

"Sis?"

I turn, and my face breaks into a smile. It nearly cracks with the strange movement. I had been so focused on his baby, I hadn't given him a thought. Here he is – Joseph – standing in front of me with that familiar twinkle in his eye. His hair has started to recede but the rest of him hasn't changed at all. Unlike his two tall brothers, Joseph is a short, heavy-built man with dazzling features.

"Joseph!" For some reason, my reply registers relief. I sound like a lost child who has just spotted her guardian. Before I have time to be embarrassed, he pulls me into his arms.

"There's my little Sis!"

He grins against my neck and I melt further into his hold at the nickname. I haven't heard it in years, because I haven't seen Joseph in years. His younger brother and I were never apart as kids so he took to joking that I was part of the family – his baby sister. I used to love that. Joseph was the bold boy and the rebellious teenager. The fact that he deigned to pay me any attention always made me feel special.

A different voice, deeper and warmer, breaks through my reverie. "Another woman? Is this why you left your wife at home, Joseph?"

For an infinitesimal instant, I squeeze my lids shut.

"Simon." I say his name like an announcement. Extracting myself from Joseph's hug to face him, I try not to think about the last time I saw his eyes, so full of anger and disappointment. Now they are compassionate, measuring me anew.

He steps into his brother's place. Our embrace is charged with awkwardness yet it feels ordinary and right in another way. I pull away before my emotions muddle me more. I look at the two brothers and all of a sudden comprehend the meaning of what Simon had said to his brother.

"Your wife isn't here?" My whole body trembles, not daring to hope.

"No." Joseph's eyes bore into me, trying to explain with a look. "Serena's exhausted after the trip and the baby is whiny. They're back in the hotel."

My legs wobble but before I can collapse Ruth is upon me. Never so glad for her interference, I hug her and let her lead me to the table, only half listening as she berates her boys for keeping me to themselves. I sit beside my mother and grasp her hand. The baby isn't coming and Simon is being shunted to the other end of the table by Ruth. I can handle this.

Joseph shimmies in beside me as Ed reaches across the table to plant a kiss on my cheek. I always liked Ed – he is exactly how I imagine a father should be. His voice is gentle and there is a natural tenderness about his mannerisms that softens his imposing figure – he is even taller than his sons with a round bald head and wide eyes to match. I am still smiling at him as he introduces the two men beside him as Aaron's school friends who have travelled for the ordination.

"Where's the *vino*?"

"Joseph! Have some manners."

"Mother," Joseph holds up his hand in mock defiance, "I have been let off my chain for one night. I intend to enjoy myself. Particularly," he leans in to me, "when someone else is picking up the tab. Am I right, little Sis?"

Memories spin in my mind. Joseph winking at me as he sneaks a six-pack of beer into his room. Simon and I shielding a truant Joseph from Ruth behind the pool table in the attic. Standing on the front steps of their mansion as Joseph leaves for college, fighting back tears like he really is my brother.

Joseph was always portrayed as the bad apple. I hope Ruth can see how wrong she was about him. He was outgoing but never a bully. Unruly but not cruel. He was the first to marry, straight out of college – Lena told me the wife is a straight-shooter who tamed him – and the first to give Ruth a grandchild. I glance at him as he jokes about how he has been looking forward to Italian wine more than Aaron's ordination. He must know about you but he is not offering useless condolences. He is steering clear of any conversation about his new baby, although I'm sure it's all he wants to talk about. He is protecting me like a big brother should.

So I smile and nod and even laugh as he recalls some of the more sordid stories of his youth. I don't look at Simon. A few times I sense him staring at me but I don't give in to temptation.

The long-haired waiter is refilling our wineglasses for a second time when Aaron finally arrives. Ruth stands and shouts his name, stretching out her arms in welcome.

"You'd swear he was being made pope," Joseph mumbles through a mouthful of breadsticks. "What reaction do you think me or Simon would have got if we'd been this late?"

He cocks an eyebrow at me and I snort. Joseph would have been threatened with a hiding in spite of his age and Simon would have been waved to the side dismissively. Before I can stop myself, I flick my eyes to the end of the table where Simon is sitting, but Joseph leans forward at the same moment and all eyes, including mine, move to him.

"Oi, Aaron!" Bits of bread fly from his mouth. "What time do you call this? We're fucking starving."

"*Joseph*!"

Aaron laughs and makes a face at his brother. Joseph responds with a grin and a vulgar gesture. Ruth reaches along the table to slap his hand down as Lena and I exchange an amused look. Aaron greets us all briefly before taking his assigned seat at the head of the table with Simon on one side and of course Ruth on the other. He seems discomfited by his mother's attentions and keeps batting away her fussing hand. Joseph mimics his brother and Simon joins in. Eventually, at a particularly stern glare from his wife, Ed has to intervene.

It is at this point I recognise the odd feeling drifting through my body. I'm enjoying myself. You're still here, Ben, don't worry. But the others are actively creating a jovial atmosphere and I can't help getting sucked in, especially when Joseph keeps leaning in to share with me every joke that comes into his head.

I turn to see Lena deep in discussion with Aaron and Ruth. I suddenly find myself restless for more of her story about the seminary.

We take our time over the meal and it is nearly midnight by the time Aaron insists he must be getting back. The restaurant is full – Italians eat late – but Lena and I are yawning.

In the bustle of leaving, we get passed from person to person for our goodbyes. It is not on purpose that I bypass Simon. In the tussle, I end up skipping one of the school friends too. I do not rectify the omissions, and I walk outside as Lena is being crushed in a bear hug by a well-oiled Joseph. I breathe in the balmy night air.

Out of nowhere, Simon is there. His long body leans over me and he grips my arms with a startling strength.

"I didn't know the right time to bring it up. But I can't let you go without saying I'm sorry."

I wait, wondering what this apology is for: the way he acted at my college the last time I saw him; how he left things with us; not contacting me again? The list could go on. His next words wind me.

"About your baby. I'm so sorry about Ben, Mattie."

I'm not breathing. Just hearing your name spoken aloud freezes me. Before I can collect myself, his lips are on mine. A gentle, innocent kiss of solidarity.

Ruth calls his name. He goes.

Lena is beside me, pushing me along. I am inside a car. We are moving. I sit in a daze, letting my mother direct the cab driver.

It is strange missing something other than you. The dinner has reminded me of something else I have lost – my surrogate family. I stroke my lip where Simon touched it with his own. Suddenly, life doesn't seem so simple.

Lena is watching me. I know I must listen to her story. Simon and his family have shown me this evening that family is important. I only wish he was still a part of mine.

FOURTEEN

Mattie

Lena is different again today. She looks calmer than yesterday but is tense, and during the simple process of making tea she knocks over two mugs and a jug of milk. Her mouth is tight and I have a feeling she is preparing herself. The big talk is coming.

I'm not ready to listen yet. Our meeting with Simon and his family last night is consuming my thoughts and I need time to reflect. I tell her that I'm going for a walk for a few hours, that I need to be alone. She lets me go reluctantly, reminding me to be back for an early dinner, as we need to talk. She doesn't give up – and neither did Simon.

My head is full of him as I walk. His kiss last night was not a passionate attempt at a reunion. I have known him long enough to appreciate that it was merely his way of communicating care. But it re-awoke the memories of our love that I had stubbornly refused to dwell on since we stopped speaking. Now, after being thrown back into his physical presence, the last time we met rushes back to me in extraordinary detail.

When I chose adventures and excitement over a life with him, he did not let me go entirely. During my first year in college we kept in contact but only through infrequent and detached text messages or emails, and I didn't see him at all during my first summer vacation – my visit home clashed with his work travels.

At college, I was swept away by dancing, parties and ultimately Tristan. Looking back, it's a bit disconcerting the many ways in which my new boyfriend was similar to Simon. Content with the mundane, and he doted on me. I needed that. Even while relishing the fun and freedom of college life, my superficial socialising could not fill the hole Simon had left and I latched onto Tristan's affections gratefully.

I was in my second year when Simon came to see me in college. My stomach constricted at the unexpected and wonderful sight of him strolling along the shrub-lined pathway from the gates to the main door.

It could have been one of those defining Hollywood moments: I skip down the steps in a flowing summer dress, he drops his bag at his feet and opens his arms, as the music crescendos to its climax I land against him and the story for our grandchildren is complete.

Of course, it didn't happen like that. There was no orchestra. I was bundled up chastely against the winter snow in protective thermals and, perhaps predictably, my arm was wedged solidly through Tristan's. He caught my gasp of delight and linked me tighter as I pulled him along with me down the steps. We stopped in front of Simon, still joined like an absurd daisy chain.

"Simon!" I couldn't keep the joy from my exclamation although I didn't reach for him.

"Hi, Lena." He made the first move, leaning in to kiss my cheek. He smiled his wide grin, clearly relieved that I was happy to see him so long after our angry break-up.

I had to wrench my arm from Tristan's hold and for a second I hated my new boyfriend.

"Nice hair." Simon raised a single eyebrow.

I scratched at my new short cut, catching some of the pink and blue strands I'd recently dyed at my roommate's insistence. "Do you really like it?" I teased.

Simon smirked back. "It's not another lip ring at least."

We laughed together and I allowed myself an extra-long hug with the man who had not only been my first love and first lover, but my best friend since I was eight years old. He smelled of my childhood. A rush of memory and nostalgia flooded through me, making me feel as old as my mother's papa. I was taken aback at the depth of my emotions on seeing him. It was worth that year apart, just for the strange combination of intensity of feeling and lightness of heart at our reunion.

Perhaps, Ben, in the same way there is a direct correlation between the extent of the hurt I have suffered since losing you and the joy I will feel when I finally meet you in heaven. But I cannot let myself think that or I won't be able to wait.

Simon and Tristan eyed each other suspiciously. I tried not to stumble over the words as I introduced them as "my new college friend" and "my friend from home". Neither seemed happy with their description, though Tristan was visibly relieved that I had not deemed this tall stranger to have any more significance than an old buddy.

Simon was not so naive. "So," he grinned in his familiar easy way as the two of us tucked into chicken wings in a local fast-food joint an hour later, "who's the new guy?"

I coughed loudly and pulled a stray bone from my mouth to show it was the food, not his flippant remark, that had choked me. The restaurant was stiflingly hot. Beads of condensation ran down the windows from the body heat of customers escaping the cold. I could feel my cheeks redden at Simon's gaze and hoped I could blame it on the heat.

"He's just . . . Tristan," I finished lamely.

I had insisted on eating alone with Simon, reminding Tristan that he had a tutorial he shouldn't miss. He had reluctantly agreed but grabbed me for a passionate kiss before strutting off. Simon had raised his other eyebrow at that. I ignored his response, linking his arm as I had Tristan's and promising him the best chicken wings in all of Chicago. If he noticed that I lured him away from anyone I might know – off campus, through the local park and down a side road way off the main street – he did not comment.

We sat in silence as I contemplated Simon's motivation for his unannounced visit. Was it simply to see me? Or was he planning on asking me back? Nothing had changed. Or had it?

"How's the business?" I tried not to sound like I had an agenda.

"Good." Simon sat up straighter, more animated than I had seen him all day. "Really good actually. Dad sent me to visit a potential customer in Florida last week and I bagged them. Got a better deal than Dad expected."

I smiled. It was a rare thing to hear Simon talk of his achievements. He was never usually made to feel proud. I wanted to throw my arms around him and tell him I had always believed in him. Instead, I said, "Florida? Nice!"

"Yep." He gnawed at his meat. "Not stuck in the house twenty-four-seven like you thought."

He didn't say it in a bitter way. There was no I-told-you-so about it. He was simply stating a fact. I dropped my eyes to my plate of dismembered chicken wings.

"Hey, babe!" My neck snapped up to see Tristan bearing down upon us.

"That was a quick tutorial." Simon couldn't hide his disappointment at the intrusion and I tensed as Tristan pushed his way in beside me. He was normally a passive guy and this possessiveness bothered me. I knew what my roommate would say – be glad he's putting up a fight for you. But I didn't like it; I felt like a bone two dogs were fighting over.

My new boyfriend shrugged in response to Simon's remark and helped himself to the last scraps of my wings. "So what do you guys have planned for tonight?"

"I'm only here for the day," Simon answered but never took his eyes from me.

"No way, man," said Tristan. "You've come this far, you've got to stay for the party tonight."

I frowned. "Party?"

Tristan smirked patronisingly at me. "Gayle Duke's party! Everyone's been talking about it for weeks."

I creased my brow even further. Of course everyone had been talking about Gayle Duke's party. The first ten kegs were free and rumour had it entertainment was being provided by professional strippers. But since when had Tristan any interest?

As far as I had been aware, he never had any intention of going before Simon arrived. I was going, of course. I never missed a party. I would drink and flirt and dance, and in the end call Tristan to come bring me home. Which he would, gladly, after a night in front of football. I felt my body tense in anger. Tristan should have been happy that Simon was leaving but instead he wanted to keep him here so he could flaunt his ownership of me.

"I've nowhere to stay so I should probably be getting back," Simon said uncertainly.

"No problem, dude. You can stay in my room. I'll be crashing with Mattie so the bed will be free."

I cringed at the pointedness of his statement. Tristan might as well have pissed in a circle around me.

"Fine."

Simon's acceptance rendered me temporarily speechless and, before I could collect myself to object, the guys were standing. It was all sorted.

That was the night, Ben. The night I will always regret because it lost me Simon. Yet I will always cherish it. Because it gave me you.

FIFTEEN

Mattie

I should not have started drinking so early.

My roommate's minibar had tempted me before, though I did not raid it nightly as she did. My mistake was telling Angela about the Simon versus Tristan predicament. Her scandalous nature did not usually invite confidence but I was so uptight when I arrived back that I felt the need to vent, even to her.

She listened with a serious demeanour. Once I had finished, she threw her head back and laughed raucously.

"It's not funny, Angela," I snapped.

"Oh, come on, it'll be a story for the morning if nothing else!" She grinned wickedly and flung open the cupboard door to her mini-fridge with great fanfare. I stared at the baby bottles of vodka, whiskey and God knows what other spirits lined up in perfect height order. Angela's side of our dorm room was a mess but her minibar was ordered to perfection. It gave the impression of clarity and precision. It drew in my scattered soul.

Fretting about how Simon and Tristan were coping with each other in my absence, I had consumed more than I intended by the time they arrived at my dorm room to collect me. My roommate bounced off the bed as they entered.

"You must be Simon!" She skipped over and jerked her hand out in welcome. As he made to take it, she slapped his hand away playfully. "Oh come on, Si. No need to be formal."

She leaned in for a hug and then thrust her hips against him. He leapt back and I spat out the vodka I had been swirling in my mouth.

Angela merely laughed. "I'm just kidding around, Si! We're friends now." She pranced over to where I was sitting at the minibar and threw her arm dramatically around me, speaking with a confident drawl. "When you live with someone, you get pretty close. What's hers is mine, ain't that right, Tristan?"

She winked at him but Tristan wasn't fazed by her.

"Shut up, Angela," he scoffed in apparent amusement.

My new boyfriend didn't like my roommate. She had treated him with that same condescending seduction routine when they first met and for weeks he refused to come to my room to pick me up. Over time he learnt to ignore her and even slept over when she was there. It was never much of an issue – by the time she stumbled home, she usually collapsed straight away into a drink or drug-induced coma.

Angela was dancing happily to the radio as she waved us goodbye.

"She's fun, isn't she?" Tristan grinned as we left.

I threw him a filthy look.

He kept up the charade the whole way to the party. He punctured his wild stories from a recent guys' weekend away with boring facts from his World History class in an embarrassingly transparent attempt to appear both worldly and wise. Simon made a decent show of seeming interested.

Frustrated, I walked a few paces ahead of them, watching my breath turn to white puffs of air as I exhaled into my gloved hands for warmth. The snow had stopped falling but the thick blanket from earlier that day slowed our progress.

Gayle Duke didn't live on campus. Her rich father put her up in a house about half an hour from the school. She only threw three or four parties a year but they were legendary.

By the time we arrived, the party was rocking. When we opened the front door, a stench of smoky humidity burst out. The house was jammed with sweaty, boozing students. We pushed our way in, barging through swaying strangers in the hall until we made it to the kitchen. Tanked-up guys were pooling out the back door into the garden with glazed-eyed women hanging off them.

Tristan took my hand and pulled me past a bong-chugging competition in full swing on the kitchen counter. I reached out my other arm to drag Simon with us. He was staring through an open door at the strip-poker game in the next room. Girls were screeching in mock indignation as they enthusiastically removed their bras, the white residue of cocaine visible on their noses.

We found space in the garden and some relief from the heavy pumping of music. The three of us stood looking up at the heaving house.

Tristan ran a hand through his hair. "Some party, right?"

"Oh shut up, Tristan!" I could hear my words slurring but had consumed enough drink with Angela not to care. He was impressing no one with his frat-boy impersonation – not Simon, and certainly not me. "Everyone knows you hate it so just shut up!"

I couldn't judge what Simon thought of the party from his blank expression but, when I started to yell at Tristan, he left us straight away.

"I'm going to get us some drinks," he called back over his shoulder and I stared after him.

"What's your problem?" Tristan asked aggressively.

"What's *your* fucking problem?" The alcohol was warm in my veins and I started to shake off my heavy coat.

Tristan grabbed my wrist. "Leave it on, Mattie. It's freezing out here."

"Stop being a total dick."

"You tell him, sister!" A girl I recognised vaguely from lectures passed by me, delighted by our drama. She thrust a shot glass of something green at me.

I looked at Tristan's alarmed face and downed the drink. It licked my insides with a further flame of recklessness.

Maybe it was my steely expression as I knocked back the shot that bested him. More likely he'd been acting like an idiot all day and couldn't keep up the front any longer.

"I'm sorry." He stepped closer to me. "I'm sorry, all right? I don't like that guy."

"You don't know him." The words came out even as I tried to shut my mouth over them. "You're just jealous because he was my first."

Tristan's eyes opened wide and the girl who had given me the shot gasped. "No way! Burned, man!" She was grinning stupidly, watching us like a television show.

Realising that I had gone too far, I grabbed Tristan's arm to drag him away. "Let's get out of here, this party is lame."

But Tristan jerked his arm out of my grip and marched away. I called after him, more desperately than I would have done sober. He ignored me and kept walking.

Simon appeared at my side, fumbling awkwardly with three beers. "Where's Party Boy?"

I glared at him and he tried to hold his hands up in surrender. He laughed at his own inelegance as he slopped the beers onto his jacket and I couldn't help joining in. One of the things I missed about Simon was his ability to find the joke in any situation. And the way his smiling mouth seemed a fraction too wide for his long face.

I took one of the beers from him with a condescending head shake and started to guzzle greedily. Simon stared but didn't comment. He didn't say anything as we stood drinking and watching the party screech around us. When two jocks streaking through the garden with a wild-eyed delirium knocked into him, he grinned acceptingly, even as the beer flew from his hand to the ground.

I concentrated on speaking as distinctly as possible. The result was robotic. "Do you want another?"

He looked at me strangely. I sighed and without a word motioned for him to follow me back through the thronging house and out the front door. I was impressed that I made it with just two phantom hands groping me from the crowd. The front door slammed behind us, muffling the noise of the party.

We trudged along the path, kicking up snow. I ignored the tingling cold as some of it slipped into the tops of my boots. My roommate's boots that I had borrowed without asking.

I conversed with Simon in my head. I heard the questions he was longing to ask but was too polite to inflict on me. How did I enjoy those meaningless gatherings? Was experiencing that drunken madness so important to me that I could leave him behind? Could he not compete with that?

The truth was I did enjoy them. I liked being in with the in-crowd – the group attention could satisfy me for a while before I made it back to Tristan. I was happy being alone with him, with the affections of one man by my side. But I craved the parties too. I got a buzz from college life, from merely being there. Seeing new faces. Watching new bodies move. Catching eyes with total strangers and smiling for no reason. I could feel myself expanding.

I looked up at Simon. "You know how on Thanksgiving when you're so stuffed full of turkey you think you'll explode but you move on to the chocolate anyway? That's what this place does to my . . . my *soul*, Simon."

It was a stupid analogy and I was sure the impact was further undermined when I stumbled over my own feet trying to squint him into focus.

He caught my arm to steady me and didn't take it away when I was upright once again.

I managed to get us back to the dorms, although Simon's notoriously solid sense of direction may have been more helpful than my vague wanderings.

"Hey, Mattie, look!" His grip tightened on my arm as he swung me around towards the all-night diner opposite the college.

"You don't want to eat the hotdogs there." I shook my head vehemently. "Tristan got food poisoning." Immediately wishing I hadn't mentioned his name, I exhaled wearily and took Simon's hand to lead him across the road.

He shook off the frost from his jacket as we shuddered into the warmth. I plopped without grace into a booth while Simon ordered for us at the counter. I looked around. At one end of the diner, a table of college boys I didn't know were munching messily on burgers. Behind us, a couple leaned close together, whispering in a conspiratorial manner. A lone man in a red baseball cap leaned over the counter, muttering to the waitress while she filled Simon's order. It's amazing the details I can still remember, despite my intoxication at the time. Perhaps I sensed, without knowing how, what an important night it was going to turn out to be.

"Here you are, Mattie." Simon placed a large strawberry milkshake in front of me.

"Hey, Simon," I grinned, recalling another diner from long ago. "Do you remember the night before Joseph's prom?"

That infectious laugh rippled from his lips again. "I haven't thought about that in ages! Only my brother would crash a party the night *before* his prom. "

"When we caught him about to fall in the door of your house smelling like he'd bathed in a beer keg, we took him out for burgers and shakes to wake him up and – "

"The legless moron fell asleep at the table –" Simon snorted.

"So you ate his meal on top of your own –"

"And I ended up puking alongside him in the bushes outside my house!"

I let out a squeal of laughter and the boys at the end of the diner turned to look in amusement. I clapped a hand over my mouth. There's something about childhood friends that brings out the hysteria in otherwise ordinary memories.

More history came pouring out. Sneaking Joseph past his mother more than once after his late nights on the town. Telling Lena we were going to the cinema but instead sitting on the swings in the local park with Ruth's good whiskey concealed in paper bags. The night I fell asleep in a club in town and the girls from school reluctantly let Simon into the ladies' restrooms to help when they couldn't move me themselves.

"Yeah, you were a big help," I smirked sarcastically. "All you did was throw cold water in my face!"

"It worked, didn't it? Woke you up."

"You're such a dad," I grinned. "Always minding us!"

"And you're a mess!" He threw the insult back light-heartedly but his words fell heavy on me. "I always have to take care of you – even tonight when I'm not on duty."

My smile disintegrated and his face fell with mine. He started to stammer an apology. I shook my head. He had meant it as a joke but the truth was too real to be laughed away.

I whispered that he could have gone home tonight. He answered quietly that he hadn't intended to stay.

"I just wanted to see you, Mattie."

He blurred in front of me. A coming-of-age flutter re-awakened my feelings for him and I tasted the caramel quality of my question. "Why?"

The soft lighting of our Hollywood love scene was sharpened harshly with his answer. "I'm seeing someone."

Saliva filled my mouth. Who is she? Have you forgotten about me? Do you love her?

But I said nothing, knowing I had no right. Not after leaving him. Not after Tristan.

Simon hurried on, thumbing overspill from his glass. "Her name's Ingrid. She works in the business. She's a secretary."

"How clichéd!" It was out of my mouth before I could stop myself.

Simon grimaced. "There's no need to be that way. It's not like you haven't moved on, Mattie."

I tried to think of a smart answer but my brain spun uselessly. The wet noise of the couple kissing behind me was distracting. "I'm too drunk for this conversation."

"Well, maybe that's a good thing." Simon got louder in agitation and the man from the bar cocked his head at us.

I made a shushing sound. "What's that supposed to mean?" I hissed.

"Well, we have to talk sometime and you'll never open up to me sober."

I gaped at him and my lack of a retort seemed to spur him on.

"I came to visit you because I didn't feel right committing to Ingrid if there was still a chance for us. But you're as closed as ever. Always an excuse not to talk. You just want to do things your way."

The whole diner was staring at us. I could sense their collective gaze though I kept my stare locked on Simon. He had never spoken to me like that before. He was the kind one, the thoughtful one. Tears pricked my eyes.

"I'm sorry." His response to my upset was immediate. He leaned in and touched my fingers with his own, delicately, like the sensation might electrocute us. "Mattie, I'm sorry. Here's the truth – I want you. But if you're moving on with Tristan, I have to too."

I glared at him. He was going to make me choose, here and now? I opted for silence and his defences leapt across the boundary of trust into hurt: painful hurt.

"You still won't talk to me, Mattie? How can you expect to love anyone when you're so closed? Just like your mother."

He knew he had gone too far as soon as he said it. There is a line you should never cross, Ben. You may not know it until it's too late, but that line is when you take a person's greatest insecurity – like the fear that a mother's distance is a lack of love – and throw it back in their face to protect yourself from rejection.

Even as I gasped in horror, I felt the meaning of his words. He knew me; could he see what I could not? I went to him for holding as a girl and a teenager, when Lena closed her arms to me. Had I become her? Pushed Simon away as she had me? I shook my head, shutting my ears to his sincere apologies.

In my heart, I knew he hadn't meant to wound me. He loved me, I was sure of it. But self-righteous anger was all I had to shield me from his accusation and it raised me to my feet. The boys from the end booth were staring. I turned to avoid them only to see the couple behind me, his arm around her shoulder protectively, shielding her from us.

I looked down at Simon.

"Mattie," he held up a hand, offering it to me, "please."

That was the moment, Ben. The moment Simon asked me to choose him. And I could have done so. I could have changed everything, the whole course of our lives.

Instead, I let myself wallow in glorified victimhood. I

whipped my cell phone from my pocket and hit speed dial three. Lena was number one. Simon was number two from a long time ago.

"Tristan?"

"Yes?" he said curtly.

I begged him to come and get me, hating my soppy plea even as I made it.

On hearing it, Tristan's tone changed from clipped to concerned. "Are you okay?"

I watched Simon as I spoke. "Yes, yes, I'm fine. Just come."

Closing the phone, I took my seat again, knowing I only had minutes before Tristan arrived from the dorms. It was my last chance to make things right. But Simon's evaluation of my coldness stung me like burnt nerve-endings. Pride – that inexplicable swell that comes before a fall – equally empowered and belittled me. We sat in silence. Simon was clearly sorry and I felt warm with smugness as he squirmed.

After a few minutes Tristan, who was now more wasted than I was, threw open the door of the diner. It smacked against the wall. The man at the counter leapt, spilling his coffee, and cursed.

Simon stood. "Go. I'll make my own way to the station."

Tristan was beside me, thankfully not squaring up for a fight. He seemed already flushed with victory. "Let's go, hon."

I turned from Simon and marched out with Tristan. I did not look back.

As we walked across campus, I mulled over Simon's bruising comparison with my mother to block out the shame and regret already building within me. I was still inebriated but was steadier than earlier and certainly more in control than Tristan. He had obviously raided his own stash of spirits to drown his humiliation from the party. His arm, tight around my shoulder, was suffocating but I didn't shake it off. I felt cold, even as we bundled into the heat of the dorms.

I scraped the key into the lock. Angela was in, as usual passed out face down on her bed, fully clothed. The stench of booze and weed filled the room but for once I didn't care. Perhaps it would relax me. She hadn't gone to Gayle Duke's party – it would have been too pedestrian for her. I guessed she had spent the night with the hash-heads under their usual bridge.

I wanted Tristan to leave. I wanted to raid what was left of Angela's minibar and justify the night in a wash of self-pity.

He was upon me as soon as we stepped into the room. I let him kiss my neck but my body did not tingle in response as it usually did. I felt too sad to be stirred. Pushing him away, I tripped backwards and landed sitting on the bed. Standing in front of me, he cupped my face in his palms and reached down to kiss me. I tried to press him backwards but his frame was heavy with intent and, unable to propel him away, I leaned back.

"Tristan," I whispered, the cushioning duvet swallowing me like a marshmallow, "stop!"

He leaned over me and kissed my cheek gently. "Why?"

"Come on, Tristan," I said, louder now. "I'm not in the mood."

He sat up, clearly disappointed. "Where's your boyfriend gone?" he asked bitterly, not bothering to whisper for my roommate – we knew from experience Angela would sleep through more than conversations.

I looked at his bloodshot eyes and sat up to run a hand through his tangled hair. However sad I was about Simon, I didn't want to deal with another loss tonight. I pressed my forehead against Tristan's.

"My *boyfriend*," I emphasised the word, "is right here."

"Mattie!" He responded to my devotion loudly and urgently.

Suddenly, we were lying on the bed again but I still couldn't feel the thrill of delight I normally enjoyed when Tristan laid me down. Simon's face, filled with remorse at his stupid accusation, swam before me. My casting of myself as the wronged woman began to seem wrong.

I felt guilty about denying Tristan even as I pushed him away. But I needed to clear my head, or muddle it more with my roommate's liquor. Either way, I wanted to be alone.

"Seriously, Tristan," I mumbled as his mouth moved to mine hungrily, "not tonight."

He ignored me and I realised that my left arm had become trapped under his body. My other hand shoved at his chest but he leaned into the force, thinking I was trying to connect with him rather than push him away.

My resistance was useless and my body tensed with fear. Not of Tristan, but of what was unfolding. I didn't want this but it was happening anyway.

"Tristan!" I tried to scream to make him realise but in my powerlessness the words fainted into a wispy breath.

He misunderstood my whisper and answered passionately. "Oh Mattie!"

His sweaty fingers fumbled under my skirt and down into my tights, ripping them open. In a panic, I arched my body and again he mistook my reaction. One final stretch of his fingers released my voice in a cry of denial.

He jerked his head up, staring at me in confusion, his hand frozen in place. "Mattie, what . . .?"

"Get off her, you fucking creep!"

Gasping, I propped myself onto my elbows in time to see Tristan land on the floor with a thud.

He began to protest but Angela's bare foot caught his jaw.

"You bastard! What the fuck do you think you're doing?"

Another kick, this time to the groin, missed its target and connected with his stomach.

Winded, he scrambled back from Angela's attack and I leapt off the bed.

"Angela, no!" I grabbed her arm and she turned to me with a gaze of such motherly concern I almost burst into tears. "I'm fine, I'm fine! It's not what it looks like."

Tristan panted his way into a sitting position, staring up at my roommate in shock.

"Not what it looks like?" Her voice leapt an octave. "He was pinning you down while you were screaming 'no'!"

Tristan was on his feet before I could respond. "Wait a second, that's not what I . . ."

Angela wasn't listening. Picking up the nearest object to her – a battered, dog-eared library book – she whacked him repeatedly around the arms and head, forcing him back to the door. "*And stay out!*" she yelled, as she brought the book down square on his nose and slammed the door in his face. It would have been comical if it hadn't been so serious.

"No, Angela!" I cried again, pushing past her and throwing open the door.

Tristan stood before me, incredulity distorting his already bruising face. I took the front of his shirt in my fist and returned him to my room.

"It was a mistake, Angela," I said.

"Come off it –"

"I mean it," I cut her off vehemently.

She stared at me.

I moved towards her, Tristan cowering behind me. "Thank you. Thank you for trying to help me. But, seriously, Tristan wasn't trying to hurt me."

Angela looked from me to Tristan and back again. Her face hardened. "Fuck this!" With a dramatic flail against me, she stormed from the room.

I turned to Tristan. The two of us were sober as saints now and the weight of the day hung heavy in the air. Tristan made no move towards me as I stood before him, my chest heaving.

"Mattie?" he said weakly. "I didn't mean to . . . Jesus . . ." He took a step back, brushing his hands through his hair desperately. "Fucking hell, Mattie, I'd never hurt you."

"I know." His genuine horror at what had happened moved me. Strangely, I felt more protected than ever.

He backed away when I tried to kiss him. "Mattie, do you want to?"

I nodded in reply but he moved from me again, insisting on an answer. I spoke the words out loud. "I want to. I do."

It was true. As he took me in his arms and laid me gently on the bed, I experienced a rush of tender affection like I had never felt before. Not for Tristan. Not for Simon. I just felt it. A waterfall of the dearest, truest love imaginable cascaded over me.

I cannot explain it any other way, Ben, except that somehow, deep inside, I felt you arriving.

SIXTEEN

Lena

I am ready. On hearing Mattie come in the door after her walk and up the stairs of our apartment, I am fully prepared to tell her my story.

But when she turns at the top of the stairs and faces me, my stomach lurches.

Since coming to Italy, Mattie has improved. She is still sad, devastated. But she gets up in the morning. She talks to me, even if she doesn't say much. And, more importantly, she listens. She takes in something other than her loss. She went to the *seminario* yesterday without me and to dinner with Aaron's family, even though Simon was there. It is an astonishing improvement on the past few months. I should have known she could not sustain it forever, and certainly not for long after meeting Simon.

The girl at the top of the stairs is the Mattie of recent months. She is not merely crying, her face is contorted with lines, all frowning. She weeps loudly, her shoulders hunched and her hands trembling at her temples. She has been pushed too far and I want to wrap her up and swaddle her like I did when she was a baby.

I reach out my arms and, surprisingly, she walks straight to me and buries into me.

"Oh Lena," she whimpers, like a dog being kicked. "I've messed it up. I've ruined everything."

I push her back from me and hold her at arm's length. Usually she screams Ben's name over and over. This is different.

"What do you mean, sweetheart?"

She wipes her face with her hand and hiccups out more sobs. "I should never have let Simon go. He loved me and I just threw him aside – and for what? I don't know why I did it." Her words come fast and run together. "And I told myself I could do it without Tristan, that I could do it on my own, but I wasn't able . . . able to grow him. I couldn't do it, Lena, and now he's dead. Ben's dead and I can't breathe. Why can't I breathe?"

I recognise hysterics when I see them. Her anguish is burning her like poison. Her body heaves gulping sobs to expel the feeling, but it doesn't work.

Tears stinging my own eyes, I manoeuvre her onto the bed and speak to her slowly. She is convulsing now, panicking.

"Do as I say. You trust me, don't you, Mattie?" I smooth her hair gently. I wait until she nods through the shaking.

She obeys my instructions, taking slow deep breaths, concentrating on calming one limb at a time. After a few minutes, her breathing normalises and she regains some control. Embarrassed, she sits up and apologises. I shake my head and rub her back gently.

"I'm sorry," she sniffs again.

I tell her it's okay. It's perfectly natural. She has done amazingly over the past few days and I'm proud of her. That sets her off again.

"I just," she gulps again, "I just can't see past Ben, Lena. He's everywhere. There are holes inside me where he used to be." She presses parts of her body – her stomach, her heart, her head. "My womb feels empty. I can't find my heartbeat. My brain can't process anything without him." She presses on her breasts, her head bowed, talking now to herself. "They feel drained." She looks up at me. "I'm dying, Lena. I don't know who I am any more. I'm nothing without him."

"You are someone," I stress, "other than Ben's mother. You are my daughter." I pause. "Do you want to know about me? Who I am? We can share things, Mattie. We can be close." I am not used to talking to my daughter in this way. Beads of sweat break out on my forehead but she is looking at me with the open innocence of a baby so I continue. "I can help you through this and not because I'm your mother and think I know best."

Mattie gives me a watery smile. Suddenly, opening up to her is not as terrifying as I expected.

"I can help because of the story I have to tell you. The story of who I am." I grip her hand. "Try, Mattie. Listen to me and try to see past Ben. See past him to me."

PART TWO

SEVENTEEN

Lena

It began with an ending.

The skin on Papa's hand felt papery. I caressed it gently, fearful of rubbing it to nothing. He had been asleep in his hospital bed for almost two days. I had stopped noticing the wires and tubes and smell of disinfectant.

The nurses asked me repeatedly if there was someone I would like to call. At first I waved them away. I could take care of Papa myself. When it became clear their concern was for me, not Papa, my chest tightened and I pressed into his worn hand. Who would gather me up when he finally left me? Who would take care of me?

It was strange not having Damien to run to. I had made him my rock during our college years, to the exclusion of all other friends. But he had been clear that my Florence Nightingale lifestyle was not to his taste and I had not particularly missed him during my months of nursing Papa. I'd heard he found a new girlfriend from his graduate programme. I was surprised at how little I cared. Still, his absence left a void I had not filled.

Papa's old colleagues might have come if I'd asked. But the ones who knew him best were older men. Their coughed sympathies would have been awkwardly endured until they left me alone again. I thought of my high-school friends, Susanna and Liz. We had not kept in contact since leaving for college and I didn't know if they were living in the state, or even the States. I was too embarrassed to call. I settled for Mrs Carowitz, one of our neighbours who had lived next door since I was a kid. She said she would be there as soon as she could.

Papa awoke to find me crying. I felt his hand twitch under mine. "Lena." His voice was raspy, yet somehow retained the strength of a father.

I knew I should have trapped my pain inside me and been strong, whispered assurances and smiled serenely. A parent dying: the exact time to embrace role reversal. But I was scared. I didn't want him to leave me. I didn't know what I was going to do. I had no one. So I leaned forward, tipping the heavy hospital chair onto its front legs so I could bury my face in the sheets beside his body.

He did not make a sound as he lifted his arm to pat my head but the room seemed to vibrate with the effort radiating from him at the simple movement. All the authoritarian orders of my youth, the tensions from my late teenage years and his frustrated tirades of the last few months at being reduced to a patient – they were all gone. All that was left was a man minutes from death. I want to believe that in those final hours he had already started to tip over, that his advice was inspired by something larger than himself, larger than the mortal, living world.

"You're not alone," he whispered, swallowing a lump so dry I could feel it in my own throat.

I grabbed his arm, not caring if it hurt him. "Papa, don't leave me," I begged.

"Italy." He spoke lighter than a whisper now. Every word expelled another part of his soul from his body. I knew these were the last words he would ever speak. "Go to Italy, Lena. For me. You will not be alone."

He waited for me to nod before closing his eyes once more.

I watched his heartbeats jump on the monitor for what could have been hours or days. Mrs Carowitz came and went; I barely acknowledged her caresses and whispered consolations. Eventually, the monitor stopped flashing and Papa, his tired body ready to return to the rest of his families, slipped away. I screamed.

Looking back, I can remember only shadowy scenes from the hours and days after Papa died. Screaming as the nurses pulled me from him. Men I knew from my childhood shaking my hand. Kindly neighbours leading me from the house to the church to the graveyard. I didn't break down at the funeral. There was no point. He was already gone. Days passed in that dream-like vacuum. I don't remember details, just the heady heaviness of my body.

"Lena?" It was Mrs Carowitz, who had practically moved into the house with me in the days after the funeral. I hadn't objected. "There's a man at the door for you."

I turned and recognised him at once. The lawyer. The man with the will. I waved him in and Mrs Carowitz brought us a tray of refreshments. I thanked her and she scuttled away, pleased with my acknowledgement. I felt bad. It was the first time I had thanked her since the funeral, though she had taken care of everything, including me, since.

"He left all he had to you, Lena," the lawyer said brightly, as though it somehow helped. "Your father amassed a considerable fortune, although he did give a lot of it away during his lifetime to the refugee charity he worked with in the city."

I already knew this.

"Still, you can live comfortably on what he has left you. Can I ask if you have any plans for the immediate future?"

I watched him shift in his seat and rearrange his papers. This is the moment, looking back, that the blurry memories start to take form. I made my decision.

"Yes," I sat up straight. "I'm going to Italy."

I fell for Italy instantly. I flew into Rome at night and, exhausted, paid for a taxi to my hostel and slept for nearly a full day. Other travellers who shared my room came and went but left the room in darkness for me. When I woke up, they were all out. I was alone, despite Papa's promise. Feeling a toxic pull on my spirits, I opened the shutters to let in some light, and flow in it did. A gasp was ripped from my mouth at the magnificence of what lay before me.

Rome was a world apart from Chicago and DC. The buildings were so old I could almost hear stories of the ages being whispered from them. Buildings with off-white walls and orange-topped domes were not neatly laid out like the coordinated streets of America. They curved and wound their way around street vendors, squares and sculptures. The heat was different than home. More than hot, it smothered me and my chest constricted as I tried to take a breath. Paradoxically, it awoke me.

I felt Papa everywhere and for the first time I understood his obsession with buildings, rather than art. The homes, churches, shops, galleries of bustling Rome created the noise, the pull and push of the crowd, the clicking of tourist cameras. I fell in love with the place. But every so often I would turn, beaming, to make a remark to Papa.

The loneliness was like a swallowed rat chewing its way through my vital organs from the inside out. To have shared this journey with Papa would have been such a bond for us. Sometimes I thought of my mother and wondered if she was sitting up there, holding Papa's hand and watching me. I liked to think of them being in heaven together.

For the first few days, I wandered with a purpose. I visited museums, galleries and all the tourist sites. When I entered a building, the cooling burst of air-conditioning refreshed me; when I stepped outside again into the busy streets, I was warmed by the glow of the European sun. Awe and sadness washed over me in waves. The result was exhaustion but I found sleep eluded me in the night with images of Papa's last, painful days. So I started staying out later.

Drink was cheap and plentiful. The locals were friendly. They spoke English to me, pulling me from my lonely bar stool into their midnight sing-songs. I talked and talked to whoever I could but something kept me from succumbing to the greasy-haired locals whose hands moved quickly down my young body.

I had my hair braided by a fat Italian mama and my skin

tanned by the blazing sun. I read the few English language papers I could get my hands on. I drank so much I could not stomach food. It was a time before mobile phones, before the internet was conveniently accessible. I was necessarily, forcibly immersed in the moment.

A week into my trip, I was days away from moving on to another part of the country. It was around noon, when the heat overpowered me, that the *seminario* found me.

I passed a church of unusual black marble. I needed to escape the burn of the midday sun so I ducked into the shade by the steps to hear a tour guide lecture a group of bored-looking students.

"The paintings which adorn the walls inside this house of God caused some controversy in recent years. They are so exquisite, art-lovers flocked to see them. The priests were not disposed to think kindly of patrons treating their church as a museum. Their threats to take down the paintings caused near riots and ultimately the Vatican bishops, being so near, intervened to insist they remain up. After all, they were religious drawings. The publicity only made the church more famous. I hope you find them insightful."

By the blank stares and fingernail inspections, I did not believe that particular group of visitors cared about art, churches or their politics. But, as you can imagine, it was an intriguing speech to an art lover like me and I followed the group inside.

It had not appeared especially large from the outside, dwarfed by the many others around. However, inside it was more cathedral than church. High ceilings tilted my head past the statues towering every few rows. I took my time, strolling past the paintings, which were indeed magnificent. Bible stories were depicted with extreme gore, colour and detail. I shivered at some of the images. The Stations, each showing Jesus taking a further step on his road to destiny and doom, were accompanied by newer, richer paintings and copies of the masterpieces.

I was standing under a particularly dark picture when a sudden exhaustion enveloped me. The background of the painting was an abyss of blackness and the angel who swooped down on a fearful man was wrapped in a swirling sheet that seemed to bind me too.

Without thinking I reached out a hand for Papa. Weak from the sun's heat and further thoughts of him, a combination of tiredness and unhappiness swayed me on my feet.

The gentle hands of what felt like a mother steadied me. She said something in Italian, which I knew from the tone must have been, "Are you all right?"

I replied in English and let her lead me to a pew to wait for the dizziness to subside. When she finally fuzzed into focus, I realised she was a nun. Her round, plump face oozed concern. The light blue cloak covering her habit matched perfectly the colour of her wide eyes. She must have been only a few years older than me but her expression of concern massaged the need for a parent's support that I had been craving since Papa passed. Before I could stop myself, I was crying.

Not merely weeping, but wailing. I was too distraught to be embarrassed by the turning heads of tourists or hushed whispers around me. It was as if every sad thought that had ever invaded my mind burst out through my eye ducts. The nun held me close and whispered mixed Italian and English reassurances.

Eventually, my breath regularised and the tears clotted somewhere behind my pupils. Mortified, I could not bring myself to look up, so the nun dipped her face under mine, like I was a petulant kid hiding under a kitchen table.

"You must feel better now."

I nodded. When she asked, I told her my name was Magdalena – I don't know why I used my full name – and she replied warmly. I noticed that two other nuns were hovering nearby, clearly unnerved by my display of emotion. I gave them a feeble smile and the nun by my side helped me to my feet. I felt disorientated. I remember a blast of sticky air as she led me outside, then a rush of cool ventilation as we entered a café around the corner.

She introduced herself as Sister Agata and sat at a table with me while the other nuns took one by the window. I couldn't tell if they were annoyed at the attention their friend was giving me or merely unused to tending to snivelling laity. Either way, their darting looks made me squirm in my seat. I sat sipping the tea that Sister Agata had ordered for me, tasting only dust and feeling utterly spent. I just wanted to go to bed but I was strangely drawn to Sister Agata. Perhaps because of her kindness, I didn't want to leave her. She said nothing, asked no questions, she didn't probe or lecture.

We sat in companionable silence until one of the other nuns – a young woman with a sour mouth and impressively smooth skin – came over. She began to speak in Italian but Sister Agata nodded meaningfully towards me. "Let us not be rude, Marthe," she said curtly.

The nun's heavily lidded eyes narrowed further but she complied, speaking instead in English, though she made no effort to address me. Her words were pronounced in an accent that was noticeably different to Sister Agata's – it had a romantic, colourful texture that I immediately placed as French.

"Agata, we really must be getting back. Vespers is in an hour."

"Thank you, Marthe," Sister Agata nodded and the other woman slunk away.

"Magdalena," my new friend said softly, "we live in a seminary less than an hour out of the city. Would you be interested in coming to Vespers with us?"

"Oh, Sister Agata, thank you," my voice sounded hoarse, "but I'm not very religious."

"That's all right," she laughed. "Think of it as an Italian experience. It's in the hills and particularly scenic this time of year."

I looked up. She was being nice to me for no personal gain – unless she was trying to lure me to the mountains for some religious sacrificial ritual, but that seemed unlikely. Even Papa, who had terrified me into never accepting anything from a stranger, could not disapprove of Sister Agata.

When Papa died, it dawned on me how few friends I had. It had always been just the two of us. The girls from school had moved on and I hadn't sustained the few college friends I initially made, devoting my time instead to Damien. Something about Sister Agata – something other than the fact that she was a nun – captivated me.

"Okay," I answered quietly.

"Excellent!" she beamed, clapping her hands together. She led me over to the table where the other two nuns sat, one with her arms folded, the other watching our progress passively. "Sisters, this is Magdalena, my new friend. She is going to join us for Vespers in the *seminario*. Will Levi have room for her in his car?"

I stared at my feet, not daring to look into their cross faces. The pleasantness of the voice that spoke shamed me into meeting their eyes.

"You are very welcome, Magdalena," the smallest and youngest of the three said, pronouncing her heavily accented words carefully. "I am Sister Lucia."

I forced myself to speak. "You can call me Lena. I mean, everyone calls me Lena."

"Lena, then!" Sister Agata patted my shoulder.

The sour-faced nun began speaking in Italian again but swiftly changed to English at a pointed cough from Sister Agata. "We'll have to get the train though, Agata," she said, without looking at me. "Don't you remember Levi saying he would be leaving Rome early? He had to go back to lead Vesper's chant practice."

There was an urgent dash to the train station and I felt like changing my mind, especially when Sister Agata insisted on paying for my train ticket. But I was hurried along with no time for objections and within half an hour I was speeding away from the city of Rome into the countryside, to the place that would change my life.

I had thought the city was picturesque. The *seminario* was the type of landmark you would find on a postcard, if anyone could possibly capture its beauty.

Another nun collected us from the quaint hillside station less than an hour out of the city. The short drive from the station was mostly vertical. I felt my ears pop and my stomach slosh as we weaved around bends, narrowly avoiding the trees lining the very edge of the road. Even 'road' is too generous a description for the winding trail that led us finally out of the shade of the trees at the hill top.

As I got out of the car, the light of the afternoon sun dazzled me. I looked around at the collection of stone structures that made up the *seminario*. Beyond them lay a sea of mountains, each more grand and lush than the nearer one. The *seminario* buildings would have been a blight on the scenery if they had not been so charming. With only small, crisscrossed windows cut out of the walls, their yellow shade was bright like the sun.

"Welcome," Sister Agata opened her arms wide as she stepped from the car, "to *Seminario dei Discepoli di Pietro*."

We walked along a gravelly path to a large building, where the ground became a cobbled walkway. I stumbled but the sisters were evidently used to it and navigated the rocky ground with ease.

"Sister Agata, it's beautiful here."

I followed her through a rounded arch in the wall, into what I thought was the inside of the building. In fact it revealed an inner courtyard hidden within the walls. Only further in did steel iron doors allow entrance to the indoors. The ground in the courtyard was different again. Flat slabs had been chiselled out and filled back in with ornate designs that gave it a stately impression. Thick round pillars were strategically keeping the building upright. We cut through another arch on the other side of the courtyard, into the sun.

The younger nun Lucia turned, gesturing back longingly towards the cooling shade. I flicked my eyebrow up in agreement and she grinned in return. I remembered the slow and stilted way she greeted me in the coffee shop and surmised that she probably had very little English. Agata had done all the talking on our train journey. Still, I thought it polite to try to make conversation.

"I thought seminaries were for men, not women?"

It was the olive-skinned, sour-faced Marthe who answered.

"It is. The men here are training to be priests. It can take up to ten years. We work here to assist them and the priests who teach them. It is a worthy vocation."

I wanted to assure her that I had no doubt their jobs were worthy but at that moment Sister Agata, who had walked ahead in the sun, called back to hurry us on.

"This way, Lena!" She beckoned me to follow her. "We'd better go straight to Vespers, we're late already."

I responded with a "Coming, Sister Agata!"

"No need for 'Sister' – just call me Agata," she threw back with a grin.

It was at that moment I heard the chant. As if the visual wonders had not been enough, the soothing low hum of seminarians chanting somewhere nearby made me shiver. Filtering from the open vents, it quite literally halted me.

Realising I had stopped, the nuns accompanying me turned.

"What is wrong?" Lucia asked.

"That music." My exclamation came out in a sort of gasp. "It's so . . . haunting."

Agata and the sour-faced Marthe exchanged a smile.

"They are much better than they used to be." Agata came over to me and propelled me on with a gentle push. "Since Levi took over the classes, he has made a real difference. Don't you agree, Marthe?"

"Yes." The stiffness fell from Marthe's expression. "God has blessed him with a very real talent."

The heavy steel door opened with a creak to reveal a chapel. Entering from the back, the full view of the interior spread out before me. It was glowing with distorted light from massive colourful stained-glass windows on either side.

The space appeared dwarfed by the altar which somehow loomed over the rest of the chapel. The pews at the top half faced each other rather than the altar in a shape I had always associated with Protestantism.

A black velvet rope cordoned off the area at the back where we had entered, and this section was covered by a low roof held up by columns that partly blocked my view of the altar. I realised there must be a balcony above. In the back section, wooden chairs and benches were filled with nuns and people in lay clothes. The five of us shuffled into the last row, with Agata explaining in a whisper that the villagers often joined them for Mass and Vespers. However, they sat at the back with the nuns. The main part of the chapel was reserved for the priests and seminarians.

I had expected turning heads with condescending glowers of disgust at our tardiness when we entered. But no one had moved. All remained sitting or kneeling, listening to the choir. Although there was plenty to see, I closed my eyes, giving in to another sense.

The music was a living breathing entity. Notes fine as string sung in perfect unison – a high crescendo then, like rain, crashing to a still lake.

I had been forced to sit through many Vespers during my teenage years, as well as the obligatory High Mass once a month – a long, Latin service performed through music, mostly plain chant. Our weekly Ordinary Masses and sometimes our daily prayers were also punctuated with the flat monotone of Latin song. We hated it, of course. It went on and on and on and on. The songs belted out by our high school choir were not merely uninspiring, they were an active deterrent to us. The notes we sneaked to each other with the latest girly gossip could serve only as a brief distraction. Sister Mariah was lethal with her wooden ruler and any hand she caught passing on anything but a prayer book earned a sharp whack.

This was different. This whole place was different. Opening my eyes, I saw the small group of singers standing in the centre aisle just in front of the velvet rope, huddled around a music stand, transforming the one-noted mantra into a lullaby. They intoned in swells and dips, yet their bodies remained motionless. Only their mouths moved, creating music from inside.

The music stopped temporarily as a priest on the altar began speaking and everyone stood. I scrambled to my feet, looking around at my companions. Agata had her head bowed and her eyes closed. I was too fascinated by what I was seeing and hearing to retreat into prayer. Arching upwards to see past the heads in front of me, I watched the men in light purple cloaks file to the altar to receive a blessing. I waited, expecting us to follow, but no one from the back section moved. Apparently this was a special blessing for the seminarians alone. I was leaning even further to see around one of the many gilded columns when the congregation sat in one swift motion. Agata, back from her prayers, grinned and pulled on my sleeve to lower me onto the bench beside her.

"Have you never been inside a church before, Lena?" she murmured as we watched the seminarians shuffle forward.

"Actually," I replied, "I went to a Catholic school. We were forever at Mass."

She snorted a laugh and I could feel my eyes bulging at her reaction.

She touched my arm lightly. "Don't look so frightened. I'm guessing your experience of the Church wasn't exactly spiritual."

"It was nothing like this," I admitted, gazing around.

The inside of the chapel was not crumbling like the outside. Efforts had clearly been made to give it a regal quality. The gold-plated columns were not real gold, of course, but the effect of grandeur was accomplished. There were historical carvings on the wooden seats and the bumpy roof had been painted a clean white to signify the purity of the heavens. The artist in me was drawn to the paintings that hung close together on the wall. From the stable to the Passion, the life of Jesus was fully displayed.

The seminarians who had received their blessing now walked calmly back into the side pews, facing each other rather than the altar. I could only imagine the frenzy that would have ensued if our school chapel had been constructed that way, with the benches pushed back against the walls. We would have been staring directly into the eyes of our girlfriends and would have lasted barely seconds with our lips pursed to stay serious before spurting out wild teenage laughter. Susanna, Liz and I would never have survived. Sister Mariah's Ruler of Pain would have been broken from overuse within minutes.

Here, the seminarians read their prayer books or turned their heads sideways to face the altar. If they did look straight ahead, it was a solemn stare that seemed to see past the men opposite into something else. I shook my head, not understanding. This serenity was so far removed from the boredom with which I had always associated religion.

I felt a sudden rush of my papa's scent in my nostrils. Was this calmness what he felt when he prayed? No wonder it had helped him survive the war.

Before I could dwell too much on Papa, the seminarians stood and, to another repetitive chant, began filing out of the side door by the velvet rope. This time, they all sang. The words were crisp and light on their lips and on leaving the chapel they did not fade out. They continued pressing into the words as they left, each syllable an offering, even if a parting one.

It was that day, that very hour – when Agata and little Lucia insisted I accompany them to afternoon tea before I left for the city – that I first set eyes on Levi. The Hollywood analogy perhaps undermines the true intensity of feeling. In the *seminario*, where the glamour of modern life was stripped away and raw emotions venerated the creator of the earth, there had to be something more than mere spontaneous lust.

My first connection with Levi locked us in a truth that neither of us could deny. Papa used to tell me that friends make the best partners because they know each other on a level beyond the physical. It is difficult to explain how all that knowledge was transferred through a look. But it was. I knew Levi immediately.

The room where we had afternoon tea could only be described as splendid. While the outside of the *seminario* showed its age, the inside, though old-fashioned, was clean and ordered. Drawings of saints and photographs of modern-day pontiffs hung with an elegant stateliness. A long oval table was covered with pristine white linen and young men were busy setting out tea, cakes and sandwiches. I hovered close to Agata as the room began to fill with priests and seminarians. Most stared at me curiously when they came in.

A man about my age came over to us. "Agata, who is your friend?"

"Christoforo, this is Lena. We met in Rome and she came up for the service."

"Hello, Lena." Christoforo stuck out his hand awkwardly.

He was tall and extremely thin – his garments hung loosely off his shoulders. His beaming welcome was infectious and I shook his hand happily, and gratefully.

"Did you enjoy Vespers?" he asked.

I nearly laughed. No one had ever asked me that before. I never thought of religious services as something people enjoyed. Prayer as I knew it was an obligation. I was glad that I didn't have to lie. "I did," I nodded eagerly. "The music was very moving."

Christoforo smiled and popped a slice of cake into his mouth. "I wish I could sing," he mumbled, "but I would never inflict my terrible voice on the *seminario*!"

Buoyed by their friend's bravery, other seminarians shuffled over, some offering me refreshments politely, others approaching more boldly just to say hello. There were Americans amongst them, though most were from continental Europe – Italy, France and Germany. They happily chatted to me about my travels, giving me hints about where else to visit in Italy and sharing their own stories of journeying throughout the country. I don't know exactly what I expected from them but certainly not the jovial, easy conversation that would not have been out of place in a college dorm back home. The religious types I had grown up with had always been pious to the point of dour. I felt ashamed again that I had been unable to see another side to religion, a side that had meant so much to my papa.

Christoforo and another young man had turned from me to argue about whether I should cross over the border into France on my trip when a gap formed in the circle around me. Through the space, a man at the far side of the room glanced across. His eye caught mine and I heard myself gasp. He stood tall, with sallow skin and dark hair. A quintessential Italian. One bushy black eyebrow rose high when he saw me, his full lips parting in something like confusion.

While those around me talked animatedly I could only stare – and watch as he stared back. He looked shocked, like I was a long-lost friend he had forgotten existed. My whole body shook and my legs trembled. I was, at once, both at peace and completely exhilarated.

Our Hollywood moment was exceptional but could not last. The room was full of moving bodies and a group of priests vying for the food-laden table soon came between us. I strained to see around them, trying to find him again, desperate to see him for one more second. But even as I searched, I knew that would be insufficient. Nothing but eternity would have been long enough to look at Levi.

Christoforo and Agata drove me to the train station after our post-Vespers afternoon tea. As we said goodbye Agata invited me back to the *seminario* the next morning to sit in on the choir practice.

"If you liked the music today you would really enjoy it, Lena," Christoforo agreed.

"I would like to see you again," Agata added.

I wanted to tell her I was fine, that my breakdown in the church earlier that day seemed like a lifetime ago. That just being there and seeing their world had helped me somehow. But I could not think of anything except the man I saw across the room. Lucia had commented minutes after he disappeared into the crowd that the last train would be leaving soon and I was hustled out of the room with only a hurried farewell to those nearest me.

I agreed to return, if only because I knew curiosity would distract me forever unless I saw that man again.

I woke the next morning feeling excited. It took me a few minutes to remember why. I made my way to the train station in the centre of Rome and for once the city did not seem so spectacular to me. The crowds and history and art on every corner were made insignificant by the *seminario*.

I arrived at the hillside village station in a state of agitation and was thankful that Agata alone had come to collect me.

"How are you today, Lena?" she asked as she drove us upwards into the hills, so slowly I thought the engine might chug us to a halt.

I told her I was better for the time I spent with her yesterday. My clumsy thanks for her kindness was waved away. She said she was glad I had returned and she was keen that I have lunch with her and the other nuns after the music practice.

"One of our seminarians takes chant," she explained. "We have priests who teach, but they couldn't find anyone as naturally musical as Levi and he was glad to step in. They have practice for an hour today. Marthe will sit in with you. She has a terrifically musical ear and often joins the men for practice, though not for the services of course."

I nodded, though I didn't understand why she would not partake in the Masses. As we rounded up to the entrance I felt an unusual combination of relaxation and anticipation.

We stepped out of the car into the early-morning heat. Even in my light linen skirt and top, it was enough to cause me to sweat profusely. I had dressed carefully, sure to cover my shoulders and knees as a mark of respect.

The delights of the landscape were not diminished by familiarity. Beds of flowers danced in the warm breeze and birds chirped as we entered the grounds.

"Agata!"

I remembered as soon as I heard the French accent which one Marthe was. If only she had been the shy Lucia. She blurted out something in Italian, her tone aggressive.

Agata listened placidly and turned to me to translate. "Marthe is saying I am the slowest driver she has ever met."

Marthe looked at me as though just noticing me. She spoke in fluent English this time. "Are you coming to our practice?"

I faltered at her abruptness but she had already turned and was marching ahead. Agata gave me a gentle shove. "Go on, Lena."

I scuttled after Marthe, guilty that my presence was so obviously a bother yet annoyed at her rudeness. I followed her past the chapel, around the main building where we had afternoon tea yesterday and in through a side door.

Marthe turned to me.

"This is where the seminarians practise. It's important that they learn to fully sing the Mass before ordination."

I nodded, though again I wasn't entirely sure what I was agreeing to.

Marthe continued in perfect English as we started up the stairs. "They all know the Mass, of course. But to be able to lead it, and intone correctly and musically is another matter."

This building was less grand than the main one. The sweeping staircase was at first sight imposing but flecks of wood and dust loosened at a touch and up close the walls were a dull grey.

As we reached the second storey, I heard a rough-sounding hymn from a room at the end of the hallway.

Marthe opened the door and I gasped. It was him.

"Sorry I'm late, Levi." Marthe took my hand and pulled my frozen body inside. "This is Lena, everyone."

Through my shock, I noticed from his dropped jaw that he was equally taken aback at seeing me again. I felt somehow vindicated. Whether he felt what I did yesterday or not, I must have triggered something in him. Ten other men, all wearing black, turned to stare at us.

He came towards us. I wanted to say something but was suddenly conscious of my slight frame next to his broad build. He ignored me, motioning instead at Marthe to join him in the corner of the room. She went with him and I was left standing in the doorframe, looking at my feet as they shifted the weight of my body from one to the other, aware of the choir watching me curiously. Marthe and Levi conversed quietly in Italian, their words indistinct but their tone undeniable. Levi was angry and Marthe was annoyed that he was angry. After what seemed like forever, Marthe came back to me.

"Lena, we will sit here and listen." She directed me to two chairs at the side of the room.

Levi returned to his position at the front and began barking instructions at the men. The other seminarians glanced at us every now and again but mostly their attention varied only between their leader and the old, leather-bound chant books they held in their hands.

"Don't you sing with them?" I whispered.

Marthe answered at her normal volume but the men ignored us as they sang. "Sometimes. When they sing polyphonic hymns, I can take the higher parts. Or with this plain chant, I help the weaker ones with their sight-singing."

"I hope I'm not keeping you from it today."

Marthe's response was less severe. "No. Listening to the music is enough for me."

It took a while to relax but after some time I started to enjoy it. Levi stopped the men often to issue directions. I could not work out why. They sounded perfect to me, and in a way like my papa. Not his singing voice, but his comforting temperament when he tried to calm me if I got upset. The lower basses and baritones started with a deep sound that, if I closed my eyes, seemed to vibrate the floor beneath me. I knew the higher vocals would soon come in to harmonise and I wished they wouldn't, not wanting the resonating masculinity to be compromised. But when they did enter, they heightened the majesty and more than once made me draw in my breath sharply.

I watched Levi a lot. His hand movements were not those of a wild, impassioned conductor, yet his whole body arched into the smallest gesture to implore the men to go louder, quieter, quicker, more urgent. He brought the music beyond mere sound.

More than once he instructed the men sharply, bringing his hand down firmly on the beat.

"What is he saying, Marthe?" I asked, unable to contain myself.

She pursed her lips but answered me quietly. "They are too *legato* – too smooth – for this piece. He is trying to make them detach the notes. They must sing more detached." She added her last sentence loudly and crossly, as though hoping the men would hear her and take heed.

I watched his movements more keenly, trying to interpret. By the end of the practice, I was restless. Not from boredom; quite the opposite. The music had energised me and I wanted to join in.

When Levi dismissed the men, they gathered their belongings silently, casting their eyes at me as they left. Levi made to walk past us without saying anything but, inexplicably infused with confidence, I opened my mouth as he reached us.

"Thank you for letting me sit in."

He stopped and looked down at me. His face instantly unstiffened and his forehead smoothed. I wondered what age he was. Surely he could not be much older than me – I guessed late twenties.

"You are welcome."

He paused and I felt Marthe's hand on my arm, ready to lead me away. With nothing else to say, I bowed my head and went with her.

"Do you enjoy music?" Levi called after me as we reached the door.

I turned in Marthe's grip. "I do." I wished I could say something interesting, like I played an instrument or sang. All I had was a few childhood years of piano lessons and the basics of music theory from junior high.

Levi bent to rummage in a pile of old books.

"Here." He pressed a thin, worn paperback into my hands. "It has some of my favourite chants."

"The most *basic* chants," Marthe said pointedly.

"Sometimes the more simplistic, the more wholesome and truthful they are, Sister Marthe." Levi kept his tone light but I could sense a frustration in him.

"Thank you," I said to him, as Marthe urged me to hurry along.

I followed her downstairs and across the courtyard to the nuns' quarters, grasping Levi's chant book tightly in my hands.

Lunch was not a decadent affair like the previous day's afternoon tea. I sat with Agata, Marthe and little Lucia at a plain wooden table in a side room just for nuns. Other women dressed in their habits came in and sat at other tables but no one else joined us.

Aside from a crucifix at the top of the room and an image of the Virgin at the other end, the walls were bare. The windows were high on the wall and small and the room, despite the stifling heat outside, felt cold.

Agatha and Lucia talked animatedly, if quietly. Marthe said nothing the entire meal. I ate the bread and trimmings eagerly and answered any questions that were put to me, including some about Papa. The one time Marthe showed any interest was when I spoke about his death. She looked up then and I thought I saw compassion in her face, if only for a fleeting moment. She ate quickly and made an excuse to leave before the rest of us had finished, walking off without so much as a goodbye. I felt like I should thank her for sitting with me at practice but something stopped me calling after her. I was happy to see her go.

After lunch, the three of us went for a stroll outside with Agata gladly translating where Lucia found English difficult. Not for the first time since I arrived in Italy, I was embarrassed by my lack of Italian.

I was admiring the colourful yet understated gardens around the main buildings when we made our way through a rusted wooden gate, almost hidden by vines creeping along the stone wall.

Then I saw him. He was not coming our way but was walking from the dining hall back to the building where he had taken chant practice.

"Lucia," Agata said, spotting him as well, "Levi must be finished lunch. Will you ask him to drive our guest to the train station?"

I began to object at causing more inconvenience but Lucia had already scurried off and Agata was busy apologising for a prior engagement that prevented her taking me. She directed me into a tiny rose garden by the entrance. Well tended, it was tiny, no larger than the table at which we ate. It would not have admitted more than two other persons with us. There were two benches, whittled from wood. We remained standing.

"Lena, will you visit us again?" Agata asked with sincerity.

I was torn. My plan to venture out of Rome should have made me refuse but something was drawing me back. Perhaps it was the aura of serenity that brought Papa back to me, or Agata's comforting presence. Or him.

I stammered that I didn't want to be a burden, and there was something else I needed to make clear. "Agata, I don't know how to say this without being rude. I don't want to be a nun." I blushed, feeling ungrateful but knowing it had to be said. If she thought I was a candidate for the habit, I had to set her right.

"I'm glad you think I'm so optimistic," she said, with an amused grin. "I know you have not been called to religious life. We don't get many visitors here. If you're staying in Rome, ring me." She pulled a notebook and a pen out of a pocket I hadn't known existed in her habit.

I stared at the phone number she handed me. "You must be melting in that thing." I nodded at her habit.

"I feel like I'm living in my own tropical climate," she grinned, tilting her head in agreement. It was so easy to talk to her. She had none of the harshness or contriteness of the nuns who had educated me.

We were interrupted by a man greeting us from the edge of the rose garden.

It was Levi.

He did not acknowledge me but spoke with Agata in Italian. His expressions were transparently impatient and her voice rose in frustration. I loitered in embarrassment, knowing he did not want to drive me to the train station. He must have seen the feeling behind my look when we locked eyes across the dining hall. Aware of the insult, my cheeks burned with mortification.

The conversation ended with Levi storming off to get the car.

"I hope you call again before you leave," Agata said as she hugged me goodbye.

"Agata," I said, "if he doesn't want to take me to the station, I'm sure there's another way." I tried to keep my voice impassive.

"Actually, there isn't," she answered, linking my arm and leading me back out into the main courtyard where Levi was pulling up in the same white car I had been in before. "Unless you want to walk or cycle but you don't know the way. Don't worry about Levi – he's just being difficult."

She hugged me once more and opened the passenger door for me.

Levi kept his gaze fixed straight ahead as he took off.

I don't think I have ever felt so awkward as I did sitting in that car, racing down the winding roads. He drove like a maniac, not slowing for turns, and I closed my eyes, certain that if another vehicle rounded a corner we would crash straight into it. But we were entirely alone. We did not meet another car on the ten-minute journey from the *seminario* into the village.

Levi and I didn't speak for the first half of the journey. I thought I might pass out with the tension. Eventually, he broke the silence.

"Have you enjoyed your time with us?" His voice was not naturally deep, yet it seemed to hum low.

"Yes, thank you," I answered quickly, a gasp escaping me as the car felt like it almost tipped over on a sharp corner.

"Am I going too fast?"

"No, it's fine." I just got the words out before I sucked in another audible breath.

Levi's face broke into a smile as he slammed on the brakes and slowed almost to a crawl.

"I apologise. The other seminarians always scold me about my fast driving. I do need to be more careful."

I studied his side profile. The smile transformed his sallow face, smoothing the creases and raising his cheekbones. His English was incredible. Only the accent betrayed it was not his mother tongue. I wanted to ask him questions about who he was or where he was from. But I stopped myself. Levi was a trainee priest – I had to remember that.

We sat in silence for the rest of the journey. I watched the rolling fields of vines give way to rustic houses dotted along the road until we arrived in the quaint, noiseless village. The train station was empty. Levi instructed me to wait in the car. I watched curiously as he approached a window in the wall and conversed with the attendant.

He returned and abruptly opened the car door. "There is a train in one minute – hurry."

I scrambled out of the car and marched quickly after him to the platform. A warning hoot in the distance indicated the train was on its way.

"I bought you a ticket." He handed me a piece of paper and I stuttered a thank-you.

Our fingers brushed and he curled his around mine. I looked up at him. We stared hard at each other for what seemed like an age until suddenly the train was there and he was handing me up onto it. We said nothing but continued to gaze at each other even when the door closed between us. Like a Hollywood diva, I pressed up against the window until the train had taken me out of sight.

Only when he had disappeared into the distance and my breathing regularised did I fully grasp that from the moment he handed me the ticket until he helped me onto the train, he had not let go of my hand.

The day after Levi and I held hands on the platform, I did leave Rome as planned. I sat on a train to Naples, straining out the windows into the fields, wondering if we would drive through the village beneath *Seminario dei Discepoli di Pietro,* but we did not.

I slept on the train, having tossed and turned all night in confusion. I stood bleary-eyed as we pulled into the main station in Naples and a waft of stale food hit me when the doors opened. The bustle of the streets was more urgent than Rome and I felt as overwhelmed as when I first stepped off the plane in Italy. Papa seemed far removed from the rowdy shouts and, ominously, the quiet stares of moustached and leering men.

From the train station, I spotted a church with a sign for an art exhibition outside. Perfect, I thought, as I ducked in. It was empty and a choir were practising on the altar. Thinking of Vespers from my first day in the *seminario*, I sat into the back row and watched. Their tunes were punctuated with angry instructions from the choir master and their lacklustre bashing of the notes robbed the music of meaning. The choir's irreverence as they whispered and giggled with each other when the choir master's back was turned was completely removed from the solemnity of the *seminario*.

I thought of Papa. He would tease me for my virtuous indignation and remind me of the many times I shouted at him as a teenager that Mass was stupid, pointless, boring.

The first Sunday that I had refused to accompany him to Mass, I was thirteen. I had spent the night at Susanna's house with her and Liz. We had stayed up until nearly two in the morning whispering idle gossip about The Police, Bryan Adams and the cuties from the older classes in school. We had been excitable enough to think it would be clever to sneak some of her father's Scotch. When Papa came to collect me for Mass my head was thumping and I knew my eyes were sunken. He did not give out, suspecting only an innocent lack of sleep.

"I don't want to go, Papa," I moaned at the door, still in my pyjamas, as my friend's parents shuffled back into the kitchen, suspecting a scene. "Can you come back and get me after Mass?"

"I most certainly cannot. Get dressed this instant, young lady, or we'll be late."

"But Papa . . ."

"Lena," he breathed, dangerously, "we do not overstay our welcome in other people's homes."

Suddenly feeling unwanted in Susanna's house, I reluctantly threw on some clothes but did not brush my hair or teeth. I left sullenly, looking like, as Papa would later yell, "a tramp". His jaw remained tight throughout Mass. I knew the wrath was coming but he couldn't unleash it in the church so I smirked with a short-sighted vindictiveness.

When we arrived home an hour later, my head-thumping had intensified. As soon as he slammed the front door behind us, all sense of triumphant rebellion receded and I just wanted to crawl into bed.

I stood and listened as he shouted his anger at my behaviour. At his words of "disappointment" and "humiliated", I felt tears prick the back of my eyes and I apologised.

Too sensitive to my distress, Papa tried to understand. "You don't want to go to Mass any more?"

"No," I sniffed. "I get enough of Mass from Sister Mariah."

He smirked at that. "I moved away from religion for a while when I was your age too," he said, stroking his chin thoughtfully, all the anger from the previous few minutes dissipated by my tears. "All right, Lena, I won't make you come to Mass with me any more if you don't want to. But it would make me happy if you did come."

I glared at him but he just shrugged. What I saw as emotional blackmail was nothing more than honesty to Papa.

"I'd like you to keep coming with me so you don't forget it. You might need it someday."

As I sat in that church in Naples, cringing against the flat rendition of ancient chant from a secular choir, I thought of how Papa must have clung to religion as a lifeline during the war. I wished I had used the opportunity of that conversation, one of the few times he hinted about his past, to find out more about him. But the selfishness of teenagers knows no bounds and I was soon tucked up in bed, knowing he would have my dinner cooked by the time I woke up.

Papa was forced back to the Church because of the hatred directed at him by others. It was love that drew me back and I knew I had to embrace it, like Papa had.

I arrived back in Rome later that night and it was all I could do to wait until the next morning to phone Agata. Unable to sleep once again, I wrapped myself protectively in a light cardigan and ambled around the tourist centre of Rome. Though it was past midnight, the streets were busy. Courting couples kissed on the Spanish steps. A group of young women about my age threw pennies into the Trevi Fountain. I watched until one caught my eye and grinned. I smiled shyly back, homesick for my old school friends.

Lonely thoughts could not temper the excitement I felt about returning to the *seminario*. I chastised myself as I wandered the streets, knowing disappointment must follow another meeting with the seminarian they called Levi. He was giving himself over to a life of chastity. He would take no wife. He could devote himself to no woman, only God. Yet he had not let go of my hand on that station platform. He had not moved his eyes from mine for one second, even as the train carried me away. I knew I had to see him again.

"Lena!" The next morning, Agata sounded pleased to hear from me.

I coiled the telephone cord around my fingers, facing into the corner of the phone box as though someone might spy me committing this deception.

"Hi, Agata." It was still strange to address a nun so casually. "I'm staying in Rome for another while. I thought I might call up to see you this afternoon."

"Oh Lena, I am working with the children in the village today and having an early dinner with their families. If you like, you could come up for the evening. There won't be much excitement, I'm afraid. It's early to bed here. But we can have some supper and you could stay the night. We'll take you back to Rome in the morning."

I paused. "I don't want to put you out . . ."

"Don't be silly, it would be lovely to see you again!" Her assurance shone with sincerity and I grinned into the phone. The frantic activity of tourists outside the phone booth seemed all of a sudden less irritating and more like a carnival. "One of the priests is collecting me from the village this evening to bring me back to the *seminario*. I will walk to the train station and he can collect us there, if you can be there by seven?"

I told her I would be there.

My gait was buoyed with a skip for the rest of the day. The heat of summertime Rome mirrored my mood and I gladly sat in the sun instead of making my usual dash to the shade.

I arrived at the station in Rome early, images of Levi collecting us propelling me. I was in time to catch an earlier train to the hillside station and was waiting impatiently when Agata hurried up to me from the village. At the sight of her, all thoughts of Levi left my head. I never thought I'd strike up a relationship with a nun. She had a calming maturity but it was combined with a gleeful giddiness. Though almost thirty, as she had admitted over afternoon tea that first day, she had a young, endearing countenance.

Her hug was powerful and I thought that this was what having an older sister must be like. I leaned into her.

"And here is our lift," she cried over my shoulder. "Perfect timing."

I felt my delight at seeing my new friend fade in disappointment as a seminarian I had never seen before pulled up.

Unable to contain myself, I asked as offhandedly as I could, "Who owns the car you all use, Agata?"

"It's a seminary car," she answered. "Anyone who can drive is insured on it."

The young seminarian driving did not speak any English but he beamed engagingly at me. It astonished me that anyone would chose to live a life so sequestered that a grisly, travelling American who didn't speak their language was a source of entertainment. I tried to imagine my life as a nun. I'd be bored to distraction. It wasn't that I didn't believe in God. But surely there were better, more imaginative ways to spend the life He had given? For me, there was more truth and holiness to be found in art: a soul on paper.

Agata chatted enthusiastically for the short journey about the workshops she had spent the day running for the local children. As soon as we reached the *seminario*, she pulled me from the car. I barely had a chance to nod and smile my thanks to the driver, who returned the gestures fervently.

"Where are we going?" I asked as she steered me away in the opposite direction to the nuns' quarters and past the dining hall.

The sky was reddening, casting a glow over the hills and vineyards that spread from the height of the *seminario* down to the village. I would have stopped and admired the sight had Agata not been dragging me with such vigour.

"Agata? Seriously, where are we going?"

Putting her finger to her lips, she ducked around the side of the chapel into what looked like a dead-end alley. At the very end, a door opened into the side wall, revealing an empty classroom. Agata weaved between the desks and chairs, me in her wake, until we reached the teacher's bench. Behind it was another door leading to what I thought must have been a staff room. When I walked through it I stopped short. I was standing – almost teetering – at the top of a winding staircase that descended far deeper than I could see.

"Where are you taking me?" My question bounced off the stone wall, magnified.

Agata signalled me to follow her. The stairs was hard under my feet and electric lights, displayed in candle holders to look authentic, kept me steady. It wound to an end into a small circular room. It was empty except for a wooden table, which took up most of the space, and the cluster of people around it.

"Agata . . . and Lena! Welcome!" Christoforo opened his lanky arms to greet us with a mixture of delight and astonishment.

"Hello, Christoforo." Agata nudged me forward. "Lena, you know Christoforo – and Lucia of course."

The petite nun inclined her head shyly and I smiled back warmly as Agata introduced the other seminarians, a couple of whom I recognised from afternoon tea on the day of my first visit. I did my best not to display in my expression the plummeting sensation of disappointment at Levi's absence from the gathering.

As the small group beamed back at me Marthe stepped out from a side room. Agata hailed her smilingly and I tried to react as pleasantly as I had to the others. She merely tipped her head sideways, studying me.

Christoforo rescued me by directing my attention to the table. A selection of cheeses and bottles of unlabelled wine were spread out in a circular formation.

"That's very artistic," I blurted out before I could stop myself.

Agata turned to Lucia and babbled in Italian. The young girl bowed her head and blushed. I didn't need a translator to know the arrangement was hers and that Lucia did not usually receive compliments for her efforts.

"Gwenaël went home for his mother's birthday last week."

Christoforo indicated a slightly older seminarian at the end of the table, then added cheerfully, "He's from the south of France and his family trade cheeses."

"They are very tasty," Gwenaël confirmed in a slow, deliberate tone and we all laughed at his effort. He grinned too, pleased with himself.

"We have these little meetings whenever one of us comes back from visiting home," Agata explained.

Christoforo rubbed his hands together. "Let's eat! Marthe, would you like to say Grace?"

They bowed their heads and Marthe delivered a short prayer in monotone, almost belligerently. I kept one eye open to cast a glance around. Their eyes were all shut and it was clear each was conversing separately with God. It seemed like a contradiction. Here they were, sneaking around like teenagers to gorge on treats from home, yet they clearly had no desire to rebel against their own devotion.

Christoforo, Agata, Marthe and the others accepted purity as a worthy lifestyle. They loved God more than each other. But it didn't mean they couldn't take a night off – stealing down to the cellar for an evening feast. It was sweet, really.

I shook such condescending thoughts out of my head and tucked in, the wine warming me from the chilly air of the basement. Christoforo accosted me, apparently fascinated by America. I asked questions in return but it was only when he mentioned Levi that I was properly distracted from the feast.

"Levi and I are roommates here. He is a great man."

"Why isn't he here?" I tried to keep my question neutral, coughing on a piece of cheese.

"He's a bit funny about rules. He would be uneasy if he was down here. Looking over his shoulder and afraid of getting caught."

Agata joined in. "I say to him that he's a grown man, he can do what he likes. And it's not as though we're doing anything wrong, only meeting slightly later than our timetable schedules. But he's a worrier. Gwenaël," she held up a particularly mouldy block of cheese, "what on earth is this?"

The conversation moved on and after an hour, at only half

past nine, the feast was over. We all snuck back up together and I had a longing to go with Christoforo to meet Levi. Instead I waved goodbye when we reached the alleyway and followed Agata across the cobbled square.

The nuns' sleeping quarters were sparse but comfortable. Agata shared a room with Marthe, who I was told had decided to bunk with Lucia so I could take her bed. At first I objected, sure Agata had imposed this on her and even more sure that it could only fuel her unexplained coldness towards me. But Agata insisted Marthe had offered and was happy to take another room.

We talked for a while. I thought about how it might have been if Papa had not died and if Susanna, Liz and I had kept in contact after high school. The three of us could have travelled to Italy together. I would have written letters to Papa detailing the magical art I had discovered, while Susanna, Liz and I would have had whispered night-time conversations about the European men we encountered.

Instead, I was listening to a nun describe the personal effects around her bed. Pictures of an elderly man and woman were stuck to the walls and perched on her bedside table. She told me she was an only child and, though it meant no grandchildren, her religious parents were so proud when she chose to become a nun. And even prouder when she asked to work in the *seminario*, taking care of the men.

"Women have an important role to play. Like mothers, I believe nuns have a great capacity for caring. We are privileged to be helping these young men, who will one day lead the Church in spreading God's message."

Ignoring a snide thought that surely the men could fend for themselves, I focused instead on Agata's comparison between the convent and motherhood. I had never given it a great deal of thought, but supposed that one day I would have children. Would I do as good a job with them as Agata did taking care of the seminarians? I thought about my own mother, who died just after I was born. I never missed her because I had Papa. But sometimes I would watch other children being hugged and caressed by their mothers in a way that was different to a father's touch in its unembarrassed femininity. I knew that if I was ever to have a baby, I would smother her with love.

Later that night, I couldn't sleep. The mugginess of the air had intensified and it smelled too hot for breathing. I threw back the sheets and walked to the window. The view was not of the rolling fields but of a small, enclosed courtyard. Wiry garden tables and chairs were spread around the circular space and I imagined it was where the nuns relaxed during hot summer days, without the seminarians.

As quietly as I could, I pulled my cardigan over my makeshift pyjamas of shorts and a T-shirt and stepped into my white slip-on shoes. Agata rolled over but didn't wake up as I eased my way out the door.

The ground crunched under me. I ambled along the edge of the compound, searching for an exposed hillside where a gush of wind might cool me. The sound of my feet on the cracked paving, and on bits of leaves, vines and garden debris, made me conscious that I might wake someone up. I stumbled to the nearest bench and sat alone, thinking of Papa and what he would make of my being there.

I was so lost in thought I didn't hear the steps along the noisy path.

"Hello, Lena."

My head snapped up. Levi was standing, leaning against the wall opposite me. His pose reminded me strongly of a James Dean poster but the flowing cassock mocked the image and I couldn't help smiling. He responded in kind.

"What are you doing out at this late hour?" he asked.

I blushed, though I had no reason to. "It's too hot. I couldn't sleep."

Levi gestured to the landscape behind me. "I am glad you are seeing our *seminario* at night. It is even more striking in the darkness, in my opinion."

I looked around. The moon's glow illuminated the fields of vines and houses spread across the mountainsides. I drew in a breath at its beauty.

"I often come for solitary walks at night, away from the business of the day, to appreciate my good fortune in living here." Levi paused as I turned back to him. "I heard you were coming back to visit Agata. Are you thinking of a vocation?"

"Oh God, no!" I answered with a snigger.

I immediately realised my offensive mistake but Levi chuckled forgivingly.

"I understand. It's a common reaction. But you clearly were not too put off by our way of living." He studied me carefully. "You came back, at least." His eyes were boring into mine with the same intensity I had seen before. "Would you like to take a walk with me?"

We strolled in the dark, side by side, not touching. Happily playing the tour guide, he pointed out the cracked and painted buildings we passed, explaining their functions as school rooms, chapels, living quarters. He gave me some of the history of the *seminario* and I asked questions where I could think of them, dragging out the conversation as long as possible.

We rounded onto a small look-out. Hidden by the largest building in the grounds, the semi-circular nook was sheltered and seeped in darkness. Only the looped crescent of the moon provided light through the buildings. My eyes adjusted quickly and I willed myself to remain calm. It was in that moment, just before one of my favourite memories of him, that I felt the wind stop. The clammy heat of the night was even more stifling in the enclosed nook. I had a strange urge to rest my head against his arm.

"We often have early morning prayers here in the summer when it's warm enough," he was saying, staring out over the hills. Just when I thought it safe to look into his face, he bowed his head down and his eyes fixed on mine. He turned his body in to me and I mirrored the movement, wishing for a clear blast of air.

"Do you pray, Lena?"

I nodded. It was all I could do.

His voice was a whisper. "What do you pray for?"

I swallowed. My mind wouldn't work. His scent was warm.

"I don't know."

He closed his eyes. I copied him and in the utter darkness felt his desperation echo my own. "I don't know either," he said.

It is impossible to say who initiated it. All I know is that we were suddenly bound together in a desperate tightening of limbs. I felt my feet leave the ground as his arms wrapped around me, pulling me up towards him. I hung there as we kissed, feeling like I was dangling from the crescent-shaped moon.

Then the sky lit up with a crack and the heavens opened.

Levi ignored me the next day. I saw him across the pews at morning Mass. He caught my eye but looked away again. I hung behind with Agata after the service, talking in simple English to Lucia, waiting for him to come to me. He did not. I watched him stride ahead of us into the dining hall, deep in conversation with Christoforo. I asked Agata would she mind if I went back to bed for a few hours, as I had a headache.

"Of course not," she said and promised to wake me for lunch. The nuns were to spend the morning in prayer and she would say a special one for me.

Surprisingly, I did sleep and had to be shaken awake by a worried Agata at one o'clock. I told her it was just the humidity but she raised an eyebrow at my poor excuse – the storm the night before had cleared the air. The ground was damp and the sky cloudy but at least the air was breathable.

Lunch was a communal affair that day and, as we milled around after eating, plenty of seminarians and nuns who I had not spoken to before approached me, curious to know what I was doing there. Levi did not.

Agata introduced me to everyone with gusto until an older priest glided over. She bowed her head and stepped back as he shook my hand. He was a short man with hunched shoulders but he still managed to give off an air of grandeur and authority. His handshake was firm.

"My name is Father Pietro. I am the head of *Seminario dei Discepoli di Pietro*. I hear that you have been visiting and stayed with us last night?"

The accusatory inflection in his question distracted me from my search for Levi. I answered as evasively as I could, babbling about the beauty of the location and Agata's kindness. It was obviously the wrong answer.

"My dear, we welcome anyone who is looking to find the Lord into our midst. But this seminary is a place of serious study and contemplation. It is not a holiday camp or free hotel."

Agata made to interrupt on my behalf but I stopped her. I had spotted Levi glancing over, then hastily away again. A feeling of being wronged by him, coupled with this man's presumption which reminded me strongly of Sister Mariah, spurred me into defiance.

"No, Agata, it's all right. Father Pietro is right. I did not mean to overstay my welcome. My papa passed away only weeks ago and he was very religious. This place," I gestured around, "and everyone here reminds me of him and his devotion to the Church."

Father Pietro appeared slightly mollified. "In that case you are, of course, welcome."

"Father, I was thinking," Agata was suddenly her jolly self again, "the retreat next weekend – may she come, Father?"

"If she likes." His gaze persisted as if expecting a frown of doubt to betray me. "You will understand that there is not room here in the meantime?"

Levi was looking over again, this time with visibly widened eyes. He must have been wondering if I was betraying our kiss to his leader. Indignation rose in me and I sought not to make his life any easier.

"Of course, Father Pietro." I sweetened my voice. "I am going back to Rome today. One of your seminarians, Levi, drove me to the village station the last time I left here. Perhaps he would be kind enough to drive me again?"

"I'm sure that will not be a problem," said Father Pietro, evidently pleased with my intention of leaving.

Agata piped up. "Actually, Levi told me a few days ago that he has ordered new sheet music from the city and needs to collect it. Why doesn't Levi go to Rome today to pick up the music? That way he can drive Lena all the way back to her hostel."

I eyed Agata suspiciously but she gave no sign that she was aware of my desire to be alone with Levi. She couldn't know about the kiss. I hadn't told her and she hadn't stirred when I fell back into the bedroom the night before, soaking wet from the thunderstorm.

Father Pietro didn't look happy with the suggestion but Agata was already calling Levi over to us. With no viable excuse, he agreed to take me. I smirked spitefully until I caught Father Pietro observing me and tried to reform the expression into one of humble gratitude.

With a falsely relaxed gait, Levi left to get the car.

As we stood outside waiting for him, Agata explained about the retreat.

"It's for those considering a vocation. So if you'd rather not partake, I understand. But, Lena, you do seem content when you are here with us. You are welcome to come."

I stared at her, ignoring the hum of the car as Levi pulled up behind me. "Why are you so nice to me?"

"I like you," she answered bluntly and without hesitation. "We don't meet very many women from outside the *seminario* so I am not inclined to give you up so soon. Especially when you seem to be happy here."

"I did enjoy the cheese party." I elbowed her playfully and she giggled.

"Levi's here," she nodded behind me.

I hugged her tightly.

Agata waved at the car until Levi sped around the corner. Instinctively, I drew in a sharp breath and he apologised, slowing to a normal speed. After a few minutes of tense silence, it became obvious that he might not speak to me for the entire journey. It had felt mutual, but perhaps I had thrown myself at him last night. He must have been so angry with me. I had to repent.

"I'm sorry about last night." My voice wobbled. I made myself look at him. He maintained his silence, staring straight ahead, his face like marble. "I don't know what came over me." When he remained mute, I started to babble. "I didn't mean to insult you. I know you can't – I mean, I know you'll have to take a vow . . ." I took a deep breath and gave up. "I'm sorry."

Suddenly, so suddenly a little scream escaped my lips, Levi swerved into the side of the road. Revving the car between a gap in the row of trees so we were hidden from the road, he cut the engine abruptly. Gripping the dashboard ahead of me, I panted from the unexpected turn. For a wild moment, I thought of all my papa's warnings about taking lifts from strangers and stories about young women found murdered in mossy green woods.

Levi got out of the car and leaned against the side of it, his head down. Unsure, I opened the door and stepped out too.

"This is difficult for me," he said, and began to pace alongside the car. I stayed silent. "I don't know what it is I am feeling." He pressed his hand against his chest with force, worry lines etched deep into his face.

I wanted to help him, but what could I possibly do? The whole situation was ludicrous. I said the only thing I could – I apologised again and made to get back into the car.

"You're sorry?" Levi faced me across the car, his expression hard, and my trembling fingers slipped from door handle.

"Yes. I'm sorry."

His face broke into a sad smile. "I'm not."

That was the first night that my loneliness was not in the form of grief for Papa, homesickness for my childhood or pining for my girlfriends. As I tossed in the heat, I felt cold from the emptiness of my arms.

It was only when he told me what I should have known from the beginning – that it could never happen – that I felt the full strength of our instant connection.

We had carried on our journey in silence for a while. Eventually, Levi took his eyes off the road long enough to give me a meaningful stare.

"I made my decision a long time ago to enter religious life. I have never been tempted by a woman to seek another life for myself. But when I saw you, after Vespers . . ."

He trailed off. I knew what he meant because I had felt the same way. It was as if we had been lovers all our lives; as though

I had been looking across that room into the eyes not of a stranger, but a husband of many years.

"I'm not sorry it happened. But it can't happen again, Lena." This time he watched the road studiously as he spoke. "I am to be ordained a deacon in the next few months and a priest a year later. That is my vocation, my life. I am glad I met you," he glanced at me, "but we must forget."

I opened my mouth to object but had no rational argument – no argument at all beyond the sensation in my heart. We spoke hardly a word the rest of the journey back to Rome. When we arrived at my hostel he walked around to open the passenger door for me. I got out and looked up at him, waiting for him to change his mind.

"Goodbye, Lena." He patted my shoulder insipidly before returning to the car and driving off without so much as a backwards glance.

The next morning, having tossed restlessly through the night, I dragged myself out of bed. An English girl with dreadlocks told me I looked like death warmed up. When she asked me what was wrong, I answered that I was fine. Where would I have started if I was to tell her the truth? I felt bad that I wouldn't see Agata again but I couldn't go back to the *seminario*, not with Levi there.

The train station was my first stop, even before breakfast. I booked a one-way ticket to Tuscany for that night with a view to travelling north and maybe continuing into France as Christoforo had suggested on my first day in the *seminario*. Only vaguely aware of my movements, I spent the rest of the morning wandering around the now-familiar streets of Rome. I ate lunch outside in the shade by the Forum before realising I had not cancelled the rest of my stay in the hostel. I shrugged, to no one in particular. I would do it later. I kept going through the city, slowly, knowing it would be the last time I ever saw it.

When late afternoon beckoned evening, I walked back to the hostel, prepared for a last-minute pack and sprint to the train station. When I turned the corner onto the side street, my whole body surged forward. The white seminary car was parked outside the hostel steps and Levi was leaning against it.

I approached him cautiously. "Levi? What are you doing here?"

He stood up from the car and I noted he was not dressed in his cassock. Instead he was wearing black trousers and a black shirt with the top button open. He looked down at me with such anger I almost leaned away. Suddenly he was upon me, pulling me up towards him, his lips finding mine with a desperate urgency.

He pulled back just as quickly, leaving me open-mouthed and panting. "God help me," he whispered, before reaching for me again.

Levi was completely distracted. He paced the pathway outside my hostel. The road was a side street and mercifully mostly empty, although the few people who came and went from the hostel while we stood there cast worried looks at him.

"This is wrong," he kept saying. "This is wrong."

I tried to calm him but every move I made agitated him further. After fifteen minutes of his mutterings in Italian as well as English and crazed glances at me, my patience started to wane.

"For God's sake, Levi," I snapped, pausing as a young couple emerged from the hostel, staring openly at us as they passed.

I waited until they rounded the corner, the woman looking back over her shoulder for one more glimpse of a drama.

"Listen, if this is so wrong you can go. I thought you had left for good last night." I held my breath, scared he would agree.

Levi ignored my tone and continued his pacing. "Of course I left. What was I to do – stay here?"

I stayed silent.

When he spoke again, it was as if he was trying to convince himself as well as me. "I cannot let myself be taken over this way. My ordination is in months, not years. This is nothing more than a last-minute crisis."

"Like cold feet at a wedding?" I heard the sullenness in the words, but Levi did not.

"Exactly, that's all it is. Nerves."

"So there is a feeling?" I stepped out of the shade towards him.

He stopped abruptly and looked at me, out of breath. "Of course," he said, leaning back against the graffitied wall for support.

Vulnerability leaked from his very pores and I knew I had to be careful. "Levi," I said, matching his delicate timbre, "why don't we go for dinner? We can talk. Sort this out."

He nodded. I took his hand boldly and, although it jerked at the contact, he did not let go. His hand was coarser than I'd imagined and his grip, though not forceful, was firm. We walked without destination until he dropped my hand outside a quiet restaurant.

"Let's try here," he said, tightly.

I nodded and followed him inside. He spoke to the maître d' who sat us at a table near the back.

It was a relatively unassuming restaurant and the weak air conditioning bothered me. I buried my head in the inexpensive menu while Levi reached for the wine list. I watched him pore over the options, amazed at how natural it felt to be sitting opposite him, how much he was a part of me already. I believed in that moment that I would never be able to let him go.

He ordered a bottle of red.

"Do you know a lot about wines?" I took a stab at ordinary conversation after the waiter left.

He picked at the cheap tablecloth, looking around as a large group entered the restaurant. "Yes. We grow grapes at the *seminario* and make our own wine."

"Wow!" I said, impressed. I chastised myself immediately for my inarticulate response. "I mean, that's very interesting. Do you sell it?"

Levi coughed, looking around again as he answered. "Locally."

"But you're not millionaires from the proceeds?"

He stared at me like I was stupid. "It helps us with the upkeep of the *seminario*. That is all."

I blushed and immersed myself studiously in a tourist leaflet someone had left by my place mat as Levi resumed his observation of the comings and goings. We sat in silence until our food came, and ate with polite small talk. When the plates were cleared, we ordered coffee and Levi sat up straight, appearing to steel himself. He leaned forward on his elbows.

"It was wrong that I kissed you, Lena. I'm going to become a priest. I will be taking a vow of chastity. I will be devoting my life to God, not another person."

I wasn't willing to let him off the hook. "Then why did you kiss me?"

"I don't know, Lena. I honestly don't know what came over me."

"I understand." The colour rose hot in my cheeks and I looked past him to the bright mosaics on the opposite wall.

"I don't know the first thing about you. Tell me something."

I paused, wondering how to define myself in a sentence. "I studied art." It seemed as good a place to start as any.

"Are you Catholic?"

The bluntness of his question stunned and emboldened me. "Yes, but I don't define myself that way, like you do. My religion is like my hair colour. Just something I was born with." I didn't want to offend him but on that matter I had to be clear.

"My religion is everything to me." His tone was calm. "My parents are dead. The *seminario* is my home, and the order of *Discepoli di Pietro* is my family."

My eyes stung as the repercussions of our kiss played out in my mind. "I'm sorry, Levi. I won't take you away from your family."

"You're not taking me away." He sounded surprised. "Lena, I make my own choices. I know I shouldn't see you any more. I am being tested."

"Tested?"

"Yes," he responded casually and took another sip of his coffee – I had yet to touch mine. "My vocation is not an easy one. I am giving up the possibility of a wife and children. I will be a priest, a leader. It comes with responsibilities. I must prove that I am worthy."

My mouth dropped. "You see me as a test? What, as some sort of distraction God put in front of you to see if you could be lured to the dark side?"

He leaned back in his seat, studying me, clearly puzzled by my tone. I felt dizzy. My stomach swam and I lifted my hand to summon the waiter. In choppy Italian I asked for some water. He brought it straight away, perhaps noticing the red flush creeping up from my neck. I drank the glass in one gulp.

Levi stared at me. "Lena, are you feeling unwell?"

"It's the weather. I'm not used to the heat."

I blinked away the spots sparkling in front of my eyes. I lay my head in my hands for a few minutes and the near-faint dissipated. When I looked up, his face was white.

The corners of my mouth twitched. "You're not used to women, are you?"

"I didn't mean to offend you."

"Levi," I half-laughed, "I'm not a prop dropped onto the earth for the sole purpose of testing your commitment to the priesthood. I'm just a girl. A girl who likes you," I finished with a whisper. "I know it's wrong, and I'll leave Rome and never come back if that's what you need. But it's not what I want."

"What do you want?" He searched my eyes for an answer.

A gust of night wind blew in the door and reached us right down the back of the restaurant. I turned to see a group of elderly men enter. Behind them, darkness had fallen outside. A totality of blackness was all we had to venture into after this dinner.

Levi gripped the sides of the table with his hands.

"Levi?" I leaned in towards him.

"I know those men," he said.

I raised my hand again and the waiter was over to us in seconds, seemingly afraid I was still on the verge of collapse. "May we have the bill, please, and quickly?"

Levi reached a trembling hand into his pocket but I reached out to him. "I'll pay," I said with authority. "You get up and leave. I'll meet you outside."

He opened his mouth to object but I shook my head. "While

they are settling into their table and won't see you – go."

He obeyed and kept his head down passing the five men who were fussing with their coats, glasses and menus. They did not notice him and I breathed relief as he escaped.

The bill arrived and I paid, adding a generous tip, before following him outside. For an awful moment, I thought he had left. Then I saw a tall figure waiting at the end of the street.

I walked to him. It was not as warm as it had been earlier but there was still a comfortable heat.

He said nothing.

"Do you have to go back to the *seminario*?" I asked quietly.

"No," he answered without moving. "I told them I would stay with a friend in Rome tonight." He looked up. "I can call on that friend but I don't think we're finished here."

My chest lightened. "Do you want to go somewhere private, where we won't run into people you know?"

He nodded gratefully. I glanced around, as if a solution would present itself out of nowhere. My hostel was out of the question, with six strangers sharing bunk beds.

Levi spoke cautiously. "There is a hotel I know near here. We could get a room and just talk." His eyes were wide with worry that I would be insulted by his offer.

I nodded and, once again holding hands, we walked down the road. He kept a studious eye out for anyone else who might know him but the streets remained deserted.

The woman behind the reception desk barely looked at us. She asked for identification and I handed over mine. When Levi admitted that he didn't have any with him she merely shrugged, saying one was enough. I took the room key from the receptionist with a shaking hand. Could she tell he was a trainee priest? Was she aware that I was perspiring despite the cooling fans blowing in my face? She appeared oblivious or at least uninterested and passed me the key without comment.

I let out a strong sigh when Levi clicked the door closed behind us. He walked over to the furthest corner and sat on a hard, upright chair. I sat cross-legged on the bed, conscious of the old springs creaking under my weight.

"I think she thought I was a harlot," I said. "And I was convinced she knew you were a priest."

He smiled and picked at his shirt. "I'm not a priest yet and you are certainly no harlot. There is no need to be uneasy. This hotel is known for its discretion so we will not be found out." As though he had said nothing wrong, he stood and adjusted a tall fan in the corner so it blew at me.

I watched him and tried to steady myself as, simultaneously, my heart dropped and my body tensed. I shifted against the emotions. "What do you mean?"

Levi stopped fiddling with the heavy base and frowned at my frostiness.

I took a deep breath of the fan's cold air. "'Known for its discretion?' Is this some sort of . . . whorehouse?"

"What?" Levi's voice leapt an octave. "Of course not! What would make you think that?"

I didn't trust myself to speak.

"Lena, all I meant was that it's a hotel that doesn't ask questions. I'm not the first priest to have doubts, you know."

"So this is where all the seminarians come to have their final fling, is it?" I spat out the accusation and Levi baulked.

"No! Lena, that's not what I meant at all. Do you think I would treat you that way?"

He walked over and tried to take my hand. I flinched away.

"Lena," he said, "I know another man who had a relationship while he was in the *seminario*. He joined the year after me. He was my roommate before Christoforo." A grin full of memories lit up his face. "I was so excited when I arrived. I couldn't wait to be part of the order. But Alexandre – he wasn't cut out for our way of life. It wasn't his real vocation. Perhaps they sensed it in the interview and that was why he was given me as a roommate – someone who had a year's experience, who could guide him. I had no idea the priesthood was not his true calling. I don't believe he knew himself – until he met Thérèse." Levi sighed. "Alexandre fell in love with a chorister who sang in the church around the corner from here. She was shy, lonely for her home in France, and they developed a friendship that quickly blossomed into something more. He left the *seminario* after a few months. Once, in passing, he told me they came to this hotel in the beginning."

"So I was right . . ."

"I didn't want us to be caught," he interrupted. "I wanted some privacy for us. Do you really believe that I have so little respect for you?"

I dropped my face. "How do I know? I don't know anything about you. Maybe this is as crazy as it seems."

"Maybe," he repeated and I looked up to see him scratching his head absentmindedly. "We need time to figure it out and that is what this hotel room is for – privacy." He walked back to his corner and sat down. "Ask me anything."

So I did. We talked for hours. We touched on sensitive topics about which, over the next week as we took our first tentative steps at a courtship, we would elaborate. My papa. His older brother who died in a tragic accident when Levi was only ten. Art. Music. I was curious about the latter.

"We all learn chant. We have classes three times a week and I lead the rehearsals. Those who sing in the choir practise every day." He smiled. "It is said that when you sing, you pray twice."

I could see how the role of conductor worked for him. Conveying the mysterious truths he believed through the soft singing I had heard at Vespers.

He had considered taking a step back from the choir, he admitted – with his ordination fast approaching he wanted to dedicate more time to his studies. But he loved it so much, he could not bear to hand it over. At the mention of his approaching ordination, I looked away. Guilt washed over me again and something long forgotten floated up from the depths of my memory.

Once, for Hallowe'en, Susanna dressed up as a sexy devil. Red hot-pants, with a round fluffy tail, that the boys had pinched with wicked hoots. She had pretended to be offended but I knew she loved it. She whacked them with her plastic devil's fork, constantly adjusting her top as her newly sprouted chest bounced against the costume. I still remember Liz's reaction, dripping with awe at our friend's confidence – "Temptress!"

I felt like a temptress in that room, but not innocent and impish like Susanna. I was enticing a man away from a life of goodness and virtue. And for what?

"Lena," he whispered my name, as though he knew I was pulling back.

He stood up from the hard-backed chair and came towards me, surprisingly confident. I couldn't resist when he dipped his head to reach my lips. I gave in easily.

He pulled back, standing by the side of the bed as I remained sitting cross-legged on it, my hair being blown across my face by the fan. He brushed it away.

"Lena," he whispered, "*Discepoli di Pietro* prefers the seminarians to practise chastity. It prepares us for life as priests. But it is not a prerequisite. There have been men who have struggled with it and given in to temptation. They ultimately make their decision to stay and the priests support them, if they can prove they are truly ready for their vocation."

I said nothing, watching him.

"I am near the end of my training." He leaned over and trailed a finger across my cheek. I closed my eyes, expecting the dismissal. "If I was in my first year, and I succumbed to a woman's charms, they would not discard me as a lost cause. They would counsel me. But at this stage, if I am not fully committed, they will be reluctant to ordain me."

"I understand." I pushed his hand away. "We can't see each other any more."

"No," he said, his tone suddenly aggressive, "that won't do." He was not speaking to me then. He was not even looking at me. His eyes focused on something behind my head, something he was squinting to see but could not make out. "I can't make this choice now. I can't just abandon my ordination, everything I've worked for. I want it. I want to be a priest. I would be a good priest."

"I'm sorry," I whispered.

"But I can't give you up either. Not today. I can't choose,

Lena." His voice cracked with desperation and I reached out for him automatically.

"Then don't, Levi." I took his hand in mine. "Don't make the decision today. Give it time."

"I don't know what this is –" He pressed on his chest and for an awful second I thought he was going to cry. "I shouldn't be feeling this way. I've never felt like this." He looked at me. "It is as if I have known you forever."

"I don't get it either, Levi."

He raised my hand and kissed my knuckles, like a prince. "I know you were insulted when I said you were a test. I'm sorry. I don't know what to say, what to do. I'm afraid I'll hurt you if I let this continue."

I smiled sadly. "It's too late. Whether you let me go now or later, it's going to hurt."

"I am as much at home with you as I am in the *seminario*. That can't be a lie."

I leaned in and kissed him. He moaned and pulled away, looking searchingly into my eyes. "What's happening between us? What is this?" he whispered.

"It's a secret, Levi. Our secret."

His mouth found mine again and we dissolved into ecstasy.

The retreat was a yearly exhibition of life in the order for prospective priests. Although its sister convent was miles north of Rome, the retreat also welcomed women contemplating a vocation, because of the strong links between the convent and the nuns who ministered at the *seminario*. The retreat lasted for three days, during which time there were prayers, talks, prayers, discussions, prayers, question time and more prayers. By the end, I was convinced that they could have fit the entire retreat into one day if they had skipped the Masses. But that was not the ethos of the *seminario* and was certainly not the message they strove to deliver to their visitors.

Agata was silly with excitement about the retreat. Levi confided in me that although she was secure in her vocation, the world outside of the order stimulated her. He believed she should be working in the missions, or at least in a parish where community work was a nun's bread and butter. But, during a deep conversation with Levi a number of years ago, she had insisted that taking care of seminarians was her ultimate calling. The few workshops she ran in the local community were enough to satisfy her sometime wish for diversity.

Still, she could not contain her enthusiasm for the visitors and drew patient smiles from little Lucia, booming laughs from Christoforo and stern looks from Marthe.

Thankfully Marthe had moved to a separate building for the retreat. There was not enough room to accommodate the twenty would-be seminarians and five prospective female postulants. Some – those with personal connections to the current occupants – had been invited to stay in the grounds. A number of disused rooms had been converted for the occasion with some priests moving out of their quarters to bunk with the visiting men. The nuns also amended their sleeping arrangements and, of course, Agata insisted I take Marthe's bed again, rather than take a hotel in the local village with the rest of the visitors.

I did not object. Both Levi and I knew it was unlikely that we could sneak time alone during the retreat but there was at least a chance if I was staying in the *seminario*.

"You won't say anything to Agata, will you?" Levi asked the day before the retreat.

He had taken the car to Rome without informing anyone where he was going. He would come up with an evasive excuse on the way back, he had insisted when he first arrived, as he pushed me up against the wall in our usual hotel room. Our lovemaking had developed over the past three days, from tender to passionate embraces. I felt naked when he was gone and clothed only when he wrapped my body in his.

"Of course not." I was slightly peeved by his question. "You know I'd never tell anyone."

He was quick to pacify me. "I trust you completely, Lena. But Agata has that compassionate personality that invites confidences. I have felt able to unburden difficult memories to her in the past. She really listens. And she doesn't judge. Of course, none of us in the Church are supposed to judge but we're only human."

"You have me now." I stroked his cheek with my finger and he closed his eyes with a contented sigh.

"Thank God for you." He opened his lids halfway, as though emerging from a dream. "All I'm saying is that I would understand if you were tempted to tell Agata about us." His eyes were fully open now and he leaned up on an elbow. "But I am not yet fully committed to religious life and she is. She has the authority to report me to Father Pietro."

A tense silence pervaded the space as reality weighed heavy on our shoulders once more.

I had no intention of confiding in Agata, or anyone. Levi was mine, for now. Revealing him would ruin our relationship. If he was to leave the *seminario* for me, it had to be on his terms, or our kisses would be tainted with a bitter tang of regret.

Our first week had been like something out of a dream. Levi found it difficult to make excuses to leave the *seminario* every day, especially since he was so close to ordination. But he re-arranged his free time and got up earlier for his morning prayers. He made more excuses about visiting friends in the city. He gave the choir a break from daily practices under the pretext of their being too busy preparing for the retreat. So we made time like gods. Sometimes just an hour. If we were lucky, the whole day and, once, an entire night.

My intimacy with Levi was so different to the rushed, self-congratulatory game it had been with Damien. Though totally inexperienced, Levi wanted to know my body, to connect with me as a person through our physical bonding. He took his time, he let me lead him where he was ignorant and he spoke my name, loud and urgently, quiet and tender, over and over, until I felt our love was the purest to have existed throughout the whole of history.

We talked. I wanted to know what had drawn him to religious life. He told me of his childhood – a happy, playful early life. He described in vivid detail the small flat he had lived in with his mother and older brother. A poor home richly filled with love by his big mama whose faded pink apron was always splashed with dough and who offered toothy kisses with every cuddle.

"My father died when I was young but I never missed him," he told me on our last afternoon.

We were sitting on the floor in the hotel, leaning against the side of the bed, eating ice-creams I ran down to buy after the fan broke. I told him it reminded me of Sunday treats with my papa. He didn't need a papa, he told me, not with a mama like his.

"Mama could be happy without my father because she had me and Luke. I would spend hours playing out in the street with the other boys. Soccer balls made out of rolled-up plastic bags if nothing else could be found. We were heroes, warriors. Our games only ended when our mothers called us in for dinner. Piping hot pasta mostly, exactly what a growing boy needed. The smells of my childhood are clothes drying in the heat and fried tomatoes."

"You make it sound idyllic." I trailed my fingers along his arm.

His face hardened. It had been perfect, he agreed, for him at least. Until the day his brother Luke didn't come home. Levi had been one of the most popular boys on the street, because his big brother Luke had a motorcycle.

"It was ironic, you know? They thought he was the coolest thing but aside from the motorcycle he was everything the boys would have scoffed at. He had been an altar boy since he could walk. He was forever studying religious texts and made Mama and me pray all the time – in the mornings, before and after meals, at bedtime. I wasn't into that lifestyle back then. I just wanted to play. I was going to be a world-famous soccer star when I grew up. Luke, he was always going to be a priest."

When Luke crashed his motorcycle, Levi and his mother were eating alone at the table, wondering where he could be. In his absence, they had skipped the prayer before their meal.

Witnesses told the *Polizia* that Luke had lost control on a slippery road. He was dead before the motorcycle slid to a halt far from his broken body.

"My mother," Levi's voice became taut, "was never the same after that. She cried all the time, day and night. Nothing I could say or do would make her happy. I was sad too. I'd lost a brother. But she was so wrapped up in her own sadness, she couldn't see my pain. She couldn't see me at all."

"I'm sorry, Levi," I said, trying to imagine how a mother could become so absorbed in one loss that she could forget her own child.

"Everyone said it was a natural period of grief. That she would get over it. But that wasn't what happened. She got worse. She stopped eating and stopped making me food too. I began to cook for us and, one day, I made her say 'Grace before Meals' like Luke used to. That was the first time she looked at me rather than through me." Levi shook his head sadly. "I didn't notice it at the time but I can see it now. I started trying to be like him. Any semblance of Luke and my mother would smile at me. So I started studying the bible as he had, searching for him in the pages. The local priests welcomed me with open arms as Luke's brother. They made me feel like I had a family again. Then something miraculous started to happen. I began to really read the words of the bible and they affected me. I fell in love with the Lord and knew that it was my life's calling to serve Him."

Levi described how his mother wept with joy when he told her he would enter the priesthood as Luke had intended. He was fifteen. She died some months later.

"The priests of the parish looked after me and, on my eighteenth birthday, Father Pietro showed up at my door. Apparently Luke had contacted him before his death, enquiring about training in the *seminario*. Our local priest had described to Father Pietro how I wished to follow in my brother's footsteps and he spoke to me about it. I didn't realise it was an interview at the time. Shortly afterwards, I was offered a place. I know what you're thinking." Levi looked down at me. "You think that because I moulded myself into my brother that this life isn't really for me. But you're wrong. I believe in God with all my heart and soul, and I truly believe the best thing I can do with my life is to serve Him."

I held my breath but Levi said nothing more.

It was nearing the end of our day together and I didn't want him to leave contemplating a reason to choose the *seminario* over me. I stood and began to gather my belongings which I had strewn all over the room.

"I understand your commitment," I said. "My papa had it too. He was as devoted as any priest, but he wanted a family."

Levi watched me move around, talking happily like we were the most normal couple in the world.

"I have a question." Levi stood and began helping me to make the bed. "Your papa was Polish?"

I nodded.

"And this is your first trip to Europe?"

I whipped the sheets vigorously and nodded again.

"Are you planning on visiting his old home while you are on the continent?"

I stopped working, my arms drooping with a sudden tiredness. Levi watched me. The truth was Papa had not asked me to go to Poland where he had married his first wife and had his first two children, the half-brother and sister who died before I was born. Poland was a place of tormented memories. He wanted me to have a positive piece of his past, one where architecture, art and the Vatican lived. I tried to explain this to Levi but he still seemed confused.

"It's time to go now," I cut him off as he attempted to ask further questions.

We looked around the hotel room where we had spent many happy hours during the past week, making love and learning about each other.

We walked down the stairs hand in hand but he dropped mine when we reached the door outside.

"Agata is going to collect you from the train station tomorrow," he said. He paused. "It will be different in the *seminario*."

I nodded, trying to focus on the sensual way he pressed into the "*ar*" of the word, but all I could hear was the tension.

"We will all be busy with the retreat. I really should not have given the choir so much time off – they will need to be at their best for the visitors or Father Pietro will kill me."

"Levi," I said, "would you prefer I didn't go?"

"No," he answered immediately. "I want you there. I will try to see you when I can. Maybe it will help."

"Help?"

"I have to make a choice, Lena. Between you and my vocation. When I'm in the *seminario*, I pray and sing and am wholly committed. But this week, every second I have spent with you has made me see a new life I could have."

I couldn't stop myself. "It would be just as holy, Levi. You would be spending your love in a different way. It wouldn't mean you love God any less."

He looked down at me. "I love you, Lena."

It was the first time he had said that. I said it back straight away. We did not kiss, or even touch. We just stared at each other and felt the truth of those words seep into us.

Without checking for others, he grabbed me and pressed me against the wall. Not with violence, but desperately. His head bowed low so our eyes were level. "Lena, it is very important to me that you understand how difficult this is for me."

"I do," I breathed, "I do understand."

"I don't want you to think that, because I cannot make a decision, my love for you is somehow diminished."

"No, I don't think that . . ." I began, but he cut me off.

"I need more time." He loosened his grip on me and stood upright.

I stayed where I was, staring up at him.

"Take it," I said. "I'll wait for you, Levi."

"I won't keep you much longer," he said solemnly. "By the end of the retreat, I'll know."

I watched him walk away, towards the setting sun and around the corner. I stood staring at that corner for a long time after he left.

"Go away!" I groaned into my pillow.

Loss stirs only cherished memories so it had been a long time since a negative image of my papa had invaded my mind. But as Agata shook me awake at an ungodly hour, I remembered all those mornings as a child when he pulled me whining from my bed for school or Mass or other tedious obligations.

"Agata," I whimpered, squinting at my watch through the harsh bedroom light, "it's five in the morning!"

"I know, Lena. So hurry up or we'll be late. Father Pietro will be mad if anyone sets a bad example for the guests, even the nuns."

Only the flurry of panic in her urging could have roused me enough to sit up. I perched on the edge of my bed, hair askew and arms and legs floppy from rest. Out of nowhere, a cutting taunt jolted me like the cup of cold water Papa once playfully spilled on my face to force me out of bed.

"Still not up?" Marthe tutted at us as she strode into the room and across to a desk in the corner.

I stood in defiance.

Agata placed a calming hand on my arm as she passed by me on her way out to the bathroom. "We'll be on time, Marthe," she called back.

"I came to get my rosary beads. All the ladies from our room are ready to go." Marthe smirked as she turned from the desk drawer in which she had been rummaging, beads dangling from her fingers. Realising Agata was gone and that she was alone with me, her expression shifted from one of contempt to awkwardness and she walked quickly out of the room, her head down.

"What's her problem?" I asked Agata when she bustled back into the room.

"What?" Agata asked distractedly. "Oh, Marthe? Nothing, nothing. She just acts stern. Are you nearly ready?"

I wanted to say that it wasn't her sternness that irritated me, it was her haughty smugness, but Agata's focus was elsewhere.

Marthe was still running through my mind as we walked as speedily as serenity would allow to the first early-morning Mass of the retreat. Anger at Marthe's superior attitude made me surge forward faster than Agata. At least it woke me up.

What possible reason could they have for scheduling a Mass before dawn, I thought in frustration as Agata practically shoved me into the second-last row of the chapel.

My question was answered by Father Pietro, not once, but three times. Of course, I only understood the English version of his homily. Agata had explained that he would deliver it first in Italian, the official language of the *seminario*, before repeating it in French, and then in my language in deference to the visitors. I couldn't imagine Father Pietro deferring to anyone, although humility was one of the virtues he lauded in his speech. He explained that the seminarians were always up before the sun so that when the day finally broke, they would already have given thanks to God. Papa would have liked that, I smiled internally. Nothing calmed him more than getting a head start on the day. By the time I would trudge downstairs for breakfast, Papa usually had two hours of work done.

"You get up at this time every morning?" I whispered to Agata.

"No, just the seminarians," she hissed back. "Now, pray!"

I didn't disturb her again but suddenly noticed what should have been glaringly obvious from the beginning. All the nuns and female visitors were sitting in the roped-off section of the chapel, at the back. The priests and seminarians were crammed into the front section, where the pews faced each other, with the twenty male visitors scattered amongst them. A burning sense of injustice winded me and I wanted to run. A long forgotten fight with Papa played out in my mind. An argument born of teenage angst and entitlement when I had railed against the sexism of the Church.

"Don't be ridiculous, Lena," Papa had said. "God loves you just as much. The Church has men and women in different roles, that's all."

"Yeah, Papa, with the men in the roles with power. How convenient! It's all a power play. Keep the women down, put them in their place."

Papa had called me melodramatic and refused to argue about it after that. It wasn't the Church alone I attacked during those rants of misuse. Feminism was a popular way to rebel in the early eighties and there were plenty of ready-made examples for me: government, big businesses, sporting teams. Any organisation dominated by men I took as a personal insult. Papa had sympathy for many of my arguments, but failed to see the Church's structure as a problem.

I felt the full weight of my teenage arguments as I viewed the chapel. Determined not to ruin my chances with Levi by indulging in secular logic, I bowed my head like Agata and prayed to my papa for patience. After Mass, we returned to the nuns' quarters for breakfast. My stomach rumbled impatiently and I was too busy stuffing myself with bread and jam to notice that I had been separated from Agata.

A young girl in her late teens lowered herself onto the bench beside me. Her American accent instantly grabbed my attention and her thin frame and red, pimply face made me disposed to act motherly towards her, almost like Agata behaved with me. She launched straight into a passionate speech about how the Church had changed her life. I felt a squirm of embarrassment that the laity often experience when Jesus-freaks gush openly. The young girl wanted to know about my calling and I fobbed her off with a half-truth.

"I'm here because of Agata," I explained, thinking of the day she found me crying in Rome. "She saved me, I suppose."

The girl's eyes stretched wide with understanding. "It's a miracle when God sends that one person who can open our heart and mind to Him."

"Yeah," I nodded, feeling like a fraud.

Thankfully, at that moment, Marthe clapped her hands like Sister Mariah used to and ordered us out to the courtyard for prayer, with instructions that each visitor should walk with their assigned nun. I felt Agata's hand touch my shoulder and I followed her away from the young girl gratefully.

I felt sorry for Agata that she was stuck with me. The five other women were keen to learn and were diligent about prayer. When Marthe gave an hour-long lecture on the daily work of nuns in the *seminario*, they scribbled notes and asked questions. I listened out of politeness rather than personal curiosity.

Outside, the women interrogated their assigned nuns for information about religious life while I craned my neck around Agata's body to get a view of the seminarians as they passed, hoping for a glimpse of Levi.

I did see him that morning but he did not greet me. I had expected that – we had agreed in advance not to interact in front of the others unless absolutely necessary. Yet a mild annoyance tickled me. I couldn't figure out why, until the same thing happened later that day. As he passed our little group without acknowledging us, I realised why I was angry. It wasn't that he had ignored me; it was that he had overlooked Agata and the rest. And it wasn't just him. The cluster of robed men with him walked past us without so much as a nod of greeting. Agata bowed her head as she was ignored, like it was perfectly normal. Rage twisted in my gut at the manner in which he cast us as unworthy of notice.

Of course, not all of them acted that way when we crossed their paths. Father Pietro tilted his head politely in our direction and Christoforo's tall, skinny frame could be seen above them all, waving at us a few times during the day. But Levi – and he was not the only one – had by his inaction dismissed us.

I wanted to discuss my feminist qualms with Agata that evening while we were changing for a communal dinner in the dining hall. But my awareness of my deception, coupled with her anxiety around the success of the retreat, made me hold it in. As a result, I was positively hyperventilating with resentment by the time I met Levi that night.

There was a rotating list of chores for the seminarians. Every week, a new group cooked while a separate group tidied the dishes away. Some were responsible for laundry, others cleaning, gardening or light office work. They fitted in the 'housework' between their prayers, study and reflections. It was a self-sufficient system that was not changed because of the retreat.

That first night, Levi was on tidying-up duty and so finished up later than most of the other men. The nuns were all exhausted from their unusually early rise and retired early. I told

Agata I was not tired and wanted to take a walk. She was already snoring lightly when I left. I wandered with determined stealth while trying to act nonchalantly. Nothing suspicious about a late evening stroll, I repeated to myself as I slid behind bushes and weaved between buildings to avoid detection. After going the long way around by the edge of the vineyards, I arrived at our enclosed nook. The moon was full and sparkling white that evening. I remember because it mirrored so aptly my own blistering sense of being wronged.

I sat watching the sky where it met the mountains. In the distance, the tops of the trees were silhouetted against the dark sky in the shapes of travellers – like a cluster of villagers, some with bicycles, or knapsacks on their backs, on their way to heaven. A couple of lone birds flew across the sky's star-speckled vastness.

Eventually, he arrived.

It was not our first argument but it was one of our most intense. He constantly hushed me, which of course enraged me further.

"For God's sake, Lena!"

I knew he was frustrated when he took the name of God in vain.

"I'm not asking you to be quiet because you're a woman. Honestly! We both agreed we don't want to get caught."

The fact that he made complete sense did nothing to soothe me.

"Levi, I have a question for you. Do you agree that women should be priests?"

"No," he said, then raised his voice for the first time to overrule my triumphant "Aha!"

"Look, Lena," he was not bested by my logic, "it has nothing to do with equality. Jesus had male apostles and the Church is modelled on him."

"What about the woman whose name I was given?" I faced him straight on with my hands on my hips. The glow of the moon behind me illuminated his face with an eerie whiteness. "What about Mary Magdalene?"

"She was important to Jesus. Lots of women were. But the

apostles were men. Priests must always be men."

"Do you hear yourself?"

"This is my religion, Lena." He spoke louder now. "This is my life."

I looked at him, the strength of his belief shining in his eyes. More problems with the Church and his lifestyle bubbled up inside me but I held my tongue. I became aware in that moment that Levi was not right for me. Even if he had not been a seminarian, his views of the world and what I could only describe as a lack of normal social skills would have been enough to make us incompatible. But that realisation was utterly outweighed by another. None of it mattered. The pompous ceremonies he held so dear, the truisms he believed without question, his inability to see the world in any light other than that sent down by the Lord – it was all secondary to the connection of our hearts.

When I thought about it, I had known of our discordance from our first real conversation. Hadn't he seen me as nothing but a test of his commitment to the Church? I smiled slightly as I remembered how easily he'd insulted me, without meaning to of course, when he brought me to that hotel. But it hadn't mattered then and it was still irrelevant.

I looked up at him. He was standing firm, unwavering in his view, and yet I loved him. My love extended past our first physical attraction to everything about him. We might have disagreed, even on important issues, but somehow his unwavering convictions elevated him in my eyes. His sneaking around the *seminario* at night should have undermined his declared dedication to his vocation. I knew that wasn't the case. He was simply desperate, like me. For he loved me too, in spite of my qualms about his beliefs, in spite of my returning with the express goal of taking him away.

"I'm not saying women aren't important," he said more gently. "Of course they are." He took a step towards me and bravely reached out a hand to touch my arm. "Look at how important you are to me."

That was the first night we made love in the *seminario*. Taking my hand, he ran us along the side of the vineyard until, far from the buildings, we reached a crumbling structure. I was inclined to call it a shack; it had the appearance of an abandoned outhouse. Wrenching open the door, a cloud of dust puffed into our faces. Levi pulled me in, slamming the door behind us. Inside, it was empty. Just four stone walls, with a dirt floor, and a boarded-up window. No ventilation, no furniture. A small space that would have reached capacity with three or four more entrants.

"What is this place?" I looked around, searching for any sign of habitation – a shelf, a broom, even a prayer book. Aside from corner cobwebs it was empty.

"It was used as a resting room," Levi explained. "If the summer sun got too hot when tending the vines, this room provided some shelter. It hasn't been used in years, now that the new buildings are accessible on the other side. Don't worry," he sounded relaxed, "everyone sleeps too far away to spot us."

Complete privacy, who would have guessed? We discarded our clothes quickly and made love against the wall as quietly as possible. If he was uncomfortable being with me that way in the grounds of the *seminario*, he did not show it. With no bed to rest on and with the fear of being missed, we did not stay long.

Agata did not stir as I crept in our door. I crawled under the covers, exhausted and exhilarated at the same time. I couldn't believe we had got away with intimacy in the *seminario* and I grinned boldly into the pillow as I drifted off. Perhaps our success made us careless, and that is why we were eventually discovered.

Levi and I met in the hut the next night and, despite it being the last day of the retreat, the night after that too. We were both exhausted: Levi from his extra retreat duties and me from surviving on much less sleep than usual.

On that last night, I brought a blanket. It was too thin to cushion the stoniness of the ground beneath but it kept us clean. The stone structures of the wall had been built on a relatively level piece of earth but no flooring had been constructed. We sat huddled together on the blanket, our hold tighter than usual.

With the retreat having come to a close, I did not know what the future held for us. Our time together had been a romantic adventure plucked from a Hollywood film, or at least from the lives of two people more glamorous than a grieving traveller and apprentice priest. I sighed into Levi's chest and squeezed closer. He seemed to understand and kissed the top of my head. No doubt his own side of the dilemma was consuming him.

"Levi?"

He murmured in response.

"When I'm with you," I whispered, "I feel normal, and happy. I haven't felt like that since Papa died. He would have liked you."

Levi let out a snicker. "I can't imagine he would have approved of us."

I joined in, and we giggled like schoolchildren as we imagined the 'grown-ups" reactions to our affair.

"I hate the word 'affair'," I interjected. "It sounds morally wrong. But how can this be wrong?"

He kissed me, communicating a raw truth. Whatever we had, and however misguided it might be, we both knew it was a real and beautiful union.

"I could . . . teach." He stumbled over the words but he did not look away.

I gasped audibly. "Levi!"

"You could teach too," he rushed on. "Art. Here in Italy. We could work it out."

I stared hard into his eyes, searching for a twitch of hesitation. None came. Visions of a future – a real, unencumbered future – played out before my eyes. I grabbed him, impatient to make love once again on the ground of that tiny hut which in three short days had come to be a home. We fell back together, thudding heavily onto the flimsy blanket.

At that same second, the door flew open and a body filled the threshold.

For a heartbeat that lasted an eternity, nobody moved.

My breathing slowed in shock. I tried to gasp but my throat constricted and I threw my head against Levi's chest. I could feel his heart pounding with a different quickness than when he took me in his arms to make love.

Slowly, the intruder stepped forward, revealing a face riddled with indignation and something more than surprise – alarm.

With a scandalised blurt of disbelief, she turned and ran.

"Marthe!" I gasped.

Fast as a backdraft, my breath returned and I scrambled up to run after her. Levi's arm halted me.

"Levi! Come on, we have to go after her. She'll go straight to Father Pietro."

He shook his head and threw my clothes at me. I looked at them, then down at my uncovered chest. Moaning, I pulled my shirt over my head while Levi stuffed his feet hastily back into his shoes.

"Lena, you don't know Marthe –"

"I know she hates me!"

He grabbed my arm again as I made to sprint out the door. "Lena, please. I know how to handle her. I can make this right."

"Make it right?" I was aware my words were screeching like my vocal chords had sawed them but I didn't care. Why try to keep it a secret any more? If it had been anyone else, we might at least have been able to persuade them to wait until Levi confessed himself. Not her, I was certain.

"Lena, please." The panic in his voice matched my own and that alone made me listen. "Go back to your room. Don't say a word to anyone about this. I'll meet you straight after breakfast in the rose garden."

I tried to argue back, knowing that by then it would be too late. He refused to understand and insisted on walking me back to the nuns' sleeping quarters. I tried to impress upon him that he was wasting time.

"Don't let her get to Father Pietro before you do, Levi," I begged as he left me at the door of the building.

He merely nodded as he landed a light kiss on my mouth and ran away into the night.

Watching him leave, I felt keenly the importance of him

making the choice alone. We had just discussed seriously for the first time him leaving the priesthood and spending his life with me. But he had to do it his own way, in his own time, or it would all be ruined. Papa's death had made me see that. His mandatory lectures on Europe's architectural wonders had made me stubbornly shake my head against them. Only when I crossed the waters and saw for myself did I appreciate their beauty. If Levi was kicked out of the *seminario* in disgrace, forced to spend his life with me because choice had been taken from him, he would naturally blame me. Resentment would devour him and sour us. If Marthe made it to Father Pietro before Levi did, it was over.

Agata, the world's deepest sleeper, remained comatose even when my trembling body bumped off the bedside table as I quite literally fell into bed. I touched my lips with my fingers and a tear trickled from my eye. I knew that might have been the last kiss we would ever share.

"Lena, you look awful!"

The next morning, Agata wasted no time in worrying about me. I mumbled something about not sleeping well. When I saw myself in the bathroom mirror, Agata's description sounded generous. My eyes were bloated and puffy and the rest of my face was blotchy from crying. My hair was scrunched, tangled and sticking awkwardly out from my head like broken limbs.

I splashed cold water on my face but it didn't improve things much. I took longer than usual in the shower, scrubbing my head and body viciously as though I could massage away the self-reproach and fear. I looked marginally more normal when I returned to our room but the hollow indents cupping my eyes remained.

"Are you sure you're all right, Lena?"

Agata's voice was soothing like Papa's and I couldn't help it – just like that day in Rome, I broke down in tears. Her arms encircled me and I let myself give in to her comfort. I would not break my promise to Levi but I had to tell her something and, more than that, I needed to unburden. Papa and I had been unusually close, I suppose because each of us was all the other had. I didn't tell him everything of course, but he was always there, and I could confide in him about the big worries in my life. Agata's motherly concern brought home how lonely I had been before meeting Levi, and now that it was all about to end and with her surely hating me, the tears flowed fast and my voice shook.

"I guess I'm feeling lost, Agata," I sniffed. "I know I can't stay but I don't know where to go from here."

"Oh Lena," she stroked my hair gently, "everybody goes through something like that at least once in their lives. Even when you are settled, secure and your whole future is mapped out, it's normal to sometimes feel aimless. After all, so much is uncertain in this world."

I looked at her, wondering if this bubbly woman who was doing exactly what she wanted in life felt just as alone and frightened as I did sometimes. She spoke as if reading my mind.

"We all find ways of getting through, Lena. For me, it's faith. I believe God is guiding me on my way so when I find life hard, I know I'm not really alone. I hope you can believe that too. It will help, I promise."

I nodded and stood, unsure her theory would endure when she found out about me and Levi.

Agata mistook my shivers of dread for a cold and made me take my cardigan even though the summer sun was drying the already cracked rocks outside. The breakfast room was less busy that morning. Father Pietro had allowed the seminarians who helped with the retreat have a late start. No such luck for the nuns. Where before my stomach would have leapt at the inequality, it gave only a slight tremble. I could barely breathe as I looked around for Marthe. She was not there. There was no sign of Levi either.

"Good morning!" Christoforo was upon us suddenly and I jumped at his greeting. He laughed at my reaction. "Sorry, Lena, I didn't mean to scare you."

"You're up early, Christoforo," said Agata.

He shrugged and I tensed at his next words. "Levi couldn't

sleep. He was saying prayers quietly but I heard him in the distance and, once I am awake, I can never get back to sleep. I do not mind." He winked at me. "With everyone else still in bed, there is more breakfast for us, I think!"

I tried to fix my face into the shape of amusement but Christoforo was all business again.

"I was coming to find you, Lena, as soon as I'd eaten. Father Pietro would like you to visit him in his office after you have had breakfast."

Agata touched my arm on seeing my jaw drop. "There's no need to be nervous, Lena. I know he can seem strict. I'm sure he just wants to talk to you about your experience here."

"Exactly, Agata," Christoforo nodded, raising his eyebrows encouragingly at me. "You must be leaving us soon, now that the retreat is over. He probably wants to know how you have found life at the *seminario*. Make sure you say good things about us!"

I attempted a good-natured smile but don't know if I pulled it off. I had never found facial expressions such hard work before.

The rest of that breakfast is a blur in my memory. I concentrated on blinking back the tears that prickled constantly at my eyes and pushed my food around my plate absentmindedly. Christoforo and Agata chatted to each other and to the two poor seminarians who had been lumped with breakfast duty on a morning they should have spent in bed. I nodded along with the conversation and felt my eyes open wide when Christoforo finally stood, full, and offered to show me to Father Pietro's office.

"Bye, Agata." My farewell sounded flat. I was certain that the next time I saw her, she would know everything. So I drank in the warmth of her reply and turned to follow Christoforo, as though on a death march.

Proceeding up the winding staircase of the old building, I felt like I was on a tour of an ancient stately home. The furnishings were old but would have been considered splendid at one time. Christoforo relished being a guide, pointing out the age of the faded paintings and the history of the house before the order of *Discepoli di Pietro* took it over thirty years before – it had been a wealthy family's summer home. I was glad of the conversation. All I had to do was murmur with interest at his pauses, leaving my mind to wander into my trial a little earlier than my body.

Father Pietro's office was more like the backroom of a house converted into a study. Christoforo knocked on the door and ushered me inside before I could prepare myself. I turned for support but he had already left, closing the door firmly behind him.

With a deep breath I turned to face them. To my surprise, Marthe and Levi were not there. Father Pietro alone sat in front of me, writing furiously.

"Sit down, dear." He waved me to a chair without looking up.

I sank gladly into it.

"Please let me finish this last sentence . . ."

I coughed as politely as I could as dust, floating through the air, clouded my nostrils. Father Pietro dotted a full stop on a page with satisfaction, looking up contentedly as he set down his pen. I had never seen him so welcoming and it only heightened my sense of anxiety. Where was Levi? And Marthe? Would I be interrogated alone first before she burst in, pointing and accusing?

"I apologise for being rude – I wanted to finish my thought before I forgot it."

His slightly formal way of speaking reminded me that I was a stranger amongst them.

"You all have excellent English," I breathed.

He stood and walked around the table to me. "If one truly wishes to be a servant of the Church, one must be able to communicate with as many of his flock as possible. This is particularly the case in Italy, where people of all nationalities and languages come on pilgrimage."

I felt the weight of his authority as he towered over me.

"Besides, I always knew I would lead someday. I was drawn to the idea of running an order. So it was important that I could attract and speak to people from all over the world. I speak seven languages fluently."

"Seven!" I repeated, momentarily distracted and hugely impressed.

"Oh yes." Father Pietro beamed proudly. "Mostly European but I have begun to study some of the African languages also. After all, Africa is providing more faithful young than many European countries these days."

"That's because they are less educated." I heard the insult immediately and clapped a hand over my mouth, horrified.

He merely raised an eyebrow and settled himself into a chair by the window. The daylight streaming him behind gave the impression of a halo.

"Lena, Lena," he shook his head in amusement, like a father would to a naïve child, "contrary to popular belief, I am not averse to debate. Do you believe, like so many of the educated do, that religion is the opiate of the masses?"

I stared at him, my upbringing refusing to let me lie outright to a priest, yet I was terrified of further rudeness escaping me if I spoke the truth.

"It is interesting, is it not, that so many in the western world believe this, yet few of them would declare any allegiance to the very man who wrote those words: Marx himself?"

"Father Pietro –" I tried to cut off a discussion that could only end badly but he talked over me.

"Look around, Lena. I am an educated man, can you not see?"

I stared around his office, seeing it properly for the first time – the absence of Levi and Marthe were the only details I had noticed on entering. Books lined not just shelves on the walls but everywhere the light fell. Old and new editions were stacked on the floor and spread across the heavy wooden desk that sat immobile in the centre of the room. There was a simple crucifix hanging behind his desk but otherwise the walls were bare. Aside from the table and chairs, there was nothing visible except books. No wonder the room was so dusty.

"You see, Lena, education is not a premise of secularism. I

have read about all of the world religions, about theology and philosophy. There is one thing that trumps them all. Can you guess what it is, child?"

His eyes bored into me and I believed the moment of my expulsion was upon me.

But Father Pietro opened his arms and smiled. "Faith! Yes, dear Lena, faith is the greatest joy, the only truth. It sets us free."

I nodded weakly.

"So, let us talk frankly." He stood and I shrank into the seat. "I am not in the business of conversions. It is my job to help those who already believe, and who have been called to achieve a life of prayer and devotion. But I would never let the chance pass me by to help a troubled soul."

A flurry of anger coursed through me. He was not interested in me or my life. Just my soul. I don't know why that enraged me so much. Papa would have been delighted.

"You have been staying with Sister Agata, have you not?" he asked, settling back into the seat behind his desk.

I nodded again, feeling like a dumb child.

"Sister Marthe informed me this morning that she will be taking a week away from us to spend time with her brother. Now, usually we require notice from our nuns but, since this is a family issue, I allowed her to go. She deserves a break after all the hard work she put into the retreat." He leaned forward onto his arms. "So, Lena, there will be a spare bed in Sister Agata's room. If you would like, you are welcome to stay with us for another week."

I barely heard his offer. My mind was reeling. Marthe had left and it appeared she had not turned us in. It could not be true.

"Lena?"

I ignored him, my mind working in overdrive. I did not believe for a second that Marthe had suddenly been possessed with a need to see her brother. If she even had a brother. The timing of her leaving had to be connected to her discovery of us in the hut last night. Did that mean Levi had caught up with her? What on earth had he said to silence her? Perhaps she had her own secrets but it was unthinkable that Levi would blackmail her. Yet I knew it was equally impossible that Marthe was protecting me.

"Lena, dear, did you hear me? Are you feeling unwell?"

I shook myself. If our secret was not out, I had to keep it together. I thought of Levi waiting for me in the rose garden and was overtaken with a longing to see him.

"I'm fine, Father. That is very kind of you."

"Of course, if you would rather leave . . ."

"No!"

He looked surprised but satisfied at the eagerness of my response.

"Father, no, I would love more than anything to stay for another week."

"Excellent!" He rubbed his hands together. "I will be honest with you, Lena, I was not convinced your presence here was advisable. We are not a charity or refuge from the world. We are a school." He sounded strict again. "A place of worship for men devoting themselves to the Church." He surveyed me across his table, joining his hands together, in a prayer-like pose. "Sister Agata spoke to me about you again before the retreat. She believes we are helping you. I trust Sister Agata completely."

I felt my body shake at his words. I didn't want any of the shame Marthe was sure to expose to fall on Agata. "She is helping me," I said quickly. Father Pietro said nothing and I was fearful again of giving the wrong impression. "But, Father," I tried to make my declaration firm, "I do not want to become a nun."

"No, dear," he replied knowingly, "I do not expect you to depart in a week for a convent. But perhaps you will leave as a more fulfilled Catholic."

With awkward thanks, I stumbled from his office and raced down the stairs to the rose garden. The sceptical side of me wondered if he suspected and just wanted to keep an eye on me. Perhaps Marthe had spilled our secret and this was some cruel game to lure me into a false sense of security, only to reveal all at the right time. Deep down, I did not believe that. Despite his friendly manner and generous offer of board for a further week, I still saw him as an authority not to be defied. I felt certain that if he knew he would be too honest and angry for games.

Amongst all my jumbled thoughts, one shone through. I had to see Levi.

Levi was sitting in the rose garden, with his eyes closed and his face tilted up to the sky as though drinking in the sun, except he was in the shade.

I called his name and his head jerked around. He beckoned me over but, as I made to sit beside him, he shoved me gently to the seat opposite him.

"Here, take these." He handed me one of two small books he was holding, dog-eared at the edges.

At first I thought it was the bible. Atop it was a black, steel rod about the length of my hand; halfway along, it split in two, like a fork with two prongs each as long as the sleek handle.

"It's a tuning fork," Levi explained at my puzzled look as I picked it up, taken aback at how light and cold it felt in my hand.

He took it from me, smacked it lightly off the bench and held it to my ear. A high, piercing note sang from the fork. I took it back, holding it steady as the note sang on. The sound was oddly comforting.

"If anyone asks," he murmured, leaning forward in his seat, "I'm teaching you chant."

I opened the book to pages of music. I mirrored Levi's movement and leaned across the thin pathway separating our wooden benches. Our heads almost touched.

"Tell me," his voice was low and he peered into his own copy of the music as he spoke, "what did Father Pietro say?"

I gave him an abridged version, then demanded to know what had happened with Marthe. Before he could answer, we were interrupted.

"Lena!"

I jumped, but Levi remained calm. "Hello, Agata."

Agata ignored him. "Lena, Father Pietro has just told me that you're staying for another week?"

Her excitement quashed the desire I had felt only seconds ago to dismiss her. I answered with a genuine grin.

"That's wonderful!" She sat beside me on the bench.

Thankfully Levi stayed where he was. "I haven't been able to find Marthe though – have you seen her, Levi?"

"She has left already." He caught my eye but Agata was frowning into space and did not notice.

"Marthe left without saying goodbye? Is her brother sick? I got the impression from Father Pietro it was a social visit, although it is not like her to leave without checking with the rest of us. After all, we'll have to cover her work now."

"I saw her this morning, Agata, and there's nothing wrong. Her brother called and wanted to see her."

"And she went? Just like that? To visit her brother?" Her tone was as disbelieving as my thoughts had been on hearing the news. "They don't see each other very much, you see," she added for my benefit.

I shifted nervously at the suspicion in Agata's response.

Levi did not falter. "I think she had been hoping to see him for some time, actually. When she got the call she felt she could not refuse. She asked me to tell you that she is sorry for any trouble it causes you."

Agata accepted this with a shrug of her shoulders. I was distracted by the easy way in which Levi lied to his friend, especially as I remembered Agata and Christoforo's description of Levi as a man who worried about rules. Was I changing him for the worst?

"What do you have there, Lena?" Agata asked.

Levi answered before I had processed her question. "Oh, Lena was taken with the choir's singing during the retreat so Father Pietro thought it would be a good idea if she learned some chant, since she is staying for a while."

I glared at him. Father Pietro had said nothing of the sort and, if he wasn't careful, he was going to get us found out.

"Do you read music, Lena?" Agata asked.

I flicked open the book again and saw it contained the same type of music as the thin chant book Levi had given me when I sat in on his practice for the first time. I had played the piano as a girl but, while at first glance this music looked similar, it was strange. The stave on which the notes were written had four lines rather than the usual five, and instead of normal crochets and quavers, the notes were printed as squares and dots with squiggles and signs all around them.

"Yes, but not this kind," I answered.

"Chant looks different, doesn't it?" Levi said and began pointing out notational differences.

Agata stood. "I never studied music myself so I will not join you. Enjoy your lesson, Lena."

I could not tell if she was wary of the odd situation she had found us in. I didn't care. All I wanted was for her to go so I could get to the real truth about Marthe. Unfortunately Lucia then stumbled upon us with two other nuns who, delighted by the news of my extended stay, insisted on 'rescuing' me from class with Levi. With no excuse to linger, I managed a quick glance over my shoulder as the nuns linked my arms and led me away. I could not help but wonder whether, regardless of his decision, this week could end in anything other than tears.

The next few days were a nightmare.

Agata got it into her head that she needed to tend to me every waking hour, which meant I could not find time to be with Levi. When I bumped into him in the dining hall or about the grounds it was plain awkward as we tried to converse as part of a group, like we were mere acquaintances, not madly in love. Being so close without being able to touch him was torture.

The worst times were seeing him at Mass. His serenity when he bowed, knelt and sang was inspiring. He looked like he was born to be a priest. It was while observing him during the services that I came closest to leaving, with no goodbye or explanation – just walking out of his life and leaving him where he belonged. But sometimes, at the end of Mass, he would catch my eye and smile sadly and I knew our love could not be erased so quickly.

Now that the retreat was over, opportunities to meet during the night dissipated. The first evening, Christoforo arranged one of their suppers in the basement, with me as guest of honour. The next night Agata stayed up talking for hours like we were twelve-year-olds at a slumber party.

On the third day, I was determined to arrange a night-time meeting, if only to sit with him in silence. The urge to be held by him was overwhelming. Then Levi announced he was being sent for the night to a nearby school where a pupil had died in a car crash.

"*Why* do you have to go?" I tried not to whine but my annoyance still cut through.

We had managed to spend half an hour together in an unused classroom under the pretence of chant practice. Every few minutes one of us had to sing, in case passers-by questioned our meeting. It was funny at first. The humour soon dissolved.

"They want religious support on the ground. It's a Catholic school and they are in shock. It's a tragedy, Lena."

I dropped my gaze to my music book, abashed. "I know, Levi, of course. I just don't understand why it has to be you? You're not even a priest yet."

He turned away and looked out the window. "But I am nearly a deacon. Father Pietro thinks it will be good for me to be out in the community more. I was hoping to minister in a parish after my ordination."

I held my breath.

"Maybe it will do us good to be apart." He turned back to me and my heart dropped like a stone to my stomach. He grimaced at my bulging eyes. "It has been stressful, all this sneaking around. Perhaps some time away will help clear my head."

I twisted my hands together. The night Marthe found us in the shack, he had been about to announce his intention to choose me. What could have changed?

"What did Marthe say to you?" I asked again, furiously. When he shook his head, my temper flared. "If you want me to leave, all you have to do is say, Levi!" I spat out the words, then sang a bar of chant loudly and roughly.

He sighed. "I know none of this is fair or easy for you. I'm sorry, Lena."

As usual, his earnest desperation stirred my sympathy and I took his hand. "If only Catholic priests could have girlfriends, right?" I spoke light-heartedly but he pulled from my hand.

"No, you don't understand, Lena. I do not believe – Catholics do not believe – that priests can do their job if it is secondary to a family. I either want to serve God with everything I have, or commit myself to a woman wholeheartedly. I can't do both, at least not properly."

Fury roused me once more. "So, bottom line, you have to choose. When are you going to do that?"

"Look . . ."

"No, *you* look!" The empathy that had cradled me moments ago was drowned by a familiar feeling of misuse. "I'm willing to love you. To stay in Italy and be with you. Or move wherever you need to as long as we're together."

"That's different, Lena – you have nothing else."

I knew what he meant. I had lost my father and was looking for a life elsewhere. It was no sacrifice on my side to stay in Italy or move on. Whereas he was throwing away everything he had worked for, the core of his very identity. But I didn't care any more. I was sick of waiting.

"If you're leaving so am I," I said. "I don't want to stay here without you. This is your home, not mine. You can drive me into Rome before you go to the school."

Not allowing him time to answer I stormed from the classroom. I heard him call me back but thankfully Agata was crossing the courtyard and I beckoned her over.

"Hi, Lena, how is your chant coming along?"

"Fine, Agata." I paused to give Levi a chance to catch up. "Listen, I rang the hostel I was staying in and there was a message for me from a friend. She will be passing through Rome for one night only and wants to meet me. Levi was kind enough to offer to drop me into the city on his way to that school."

Levi pursed his lips but Agata simply stared at me.

"That's a pity, Lena." Her sincerity dropped a further weight of shame on my heavy shoulders.

"I'll be back tomorrow," I assured her. "I'll get the train back up first thing and I can make my own way here from the train station. The walk will do me good."

"Well," Agata frowned but accepted my excuse, "it is unfortunate that her visit coincides with your week here. But, since she is only in the city for one day, it cannot be helped."

I could tell that Agata was not impressed by my abandonment of the *seminario* for more interesting entertainment. I sensed it was the beginning of the end.

She hugged me as I sat into the car with Levi some hours later and made me promise to call if I had any problems getting back in the morning.

I glanced in the side mirror and saw her forehead crease as she waved us away. For a frantic second I wondered if she suspected us but I pushed the thought away. It did not matter what she imagined; it would all be over soon. One way or another, Levi was going to have to make a decision.

I was glad of our time alone in the car, if for no other reason than I needed to hear the truth about Marthe. When I had finally got him alone in the classroom earlier that day, he dodged my questions, posing his own and evading the subject. Now I was determined to get an answer.

I waited until we had reached the main road, not wanting to distract him on the winding road; his driving was reckless enough with full concentration. Every now and again he would remember that his speeding scared me and slow down. But he would soon drift back to his default of at least thirty miles over the limit. Neither of us spoke until we had left the village and I felt tears burning the back of my eyes. I didn't want there to be a cooling between us.

"I'm sorry I got angry earlier, Levi," I said. "I am trying to be supportive but it's difficult."

Levi's voice was hard in response. He put his hand to his eyes, blocking out the setting sun. "You didn't have to leave, Lena."

"I couldn't stand to be there another night without you. And it feels dishonest to Agata."

Levi swerved to pass out another car, ignoring my reactionary body clench. "This whole charade is dishonest, Lena."

I shivered. He sounded like he had made up his mind, made his choice, and I wasn't going to like it. Suddenly terrified of hearing the truth, I almost shouted my question about Marthe. Anything to distract him. It only seemed to anger him more.

"I already told you, Lena. We talked and she agreed not to say anything. She had to go visit her brother anyway . . ."

"Don't lie to me!" I barked. "You're lying to everyone else – don't lie to me!"

"I'm trying to protect us."

"What 'us'? You think this is an 'us'?" My voice shook.

Levi turned his head to look sideways at me and opened his mouth to argue back, perhaps even to end it for good. But his eyes widened in horror at something behind my head. I started to turn and heard the start of a scream before I was jerked sideways into Levi, his call to me lost in a violent smash. A squeal burst from my lips with a spurt of blood. Then there was nothing.

I can only remember snippets from the next few hours as I drifted in and out of consciousness. My first memory is of frantic screaming and beeping of horns. Yet throughout the madness I heard Levi calling to me. I turned towards the sound and saw him reach for me, a trickle of blood trailing down his cheek. Blackness dissolved the image and closed my eyes again.

Next the screams were closer and hands were pressing against my neck and my face. I could not decipher the Italian. The words were just sounds, running together faster than our car.

I murmured Levi's name, and he was there.

An ambulance ride, with the siren so shrill I tried to pass out again.

Doctors prodding me.

Nurses smiling serenely, almost blankly.

Each a fleeting flash of the world before sleep took me over.

Finally I awoke to proper consciousness with its sharp edges and piercing noises. I lay in a single bed. A drip pierced my arm. I turned my face away from it. A light curtain blocked my view of a group of men arguing loudly in Italian. I tried to remember what I was doing in hospital and why there was shouting there.

Panic burst the dam holding back my tears and I cried out for Levi.

The curtain whipped across and he was there. I breathed out, relieved, as he sat on the bed beside me and took my hand. I looked past his bandaged face to see who he had been arguing with: a man in a white coat, and Father Pietro.

The head priest stared down at our tender scene with thinning eyes and I tried to push Levi away but he held onto my hand more firmly.

"Father . . ." My throat felt scratchy.

"Don't try to talk, dear." Father Pietro shook his head unsmilingly. "You will be all right. I must go telephone Sister Agata. She will be very anxious to hear about you."

I watched as he pulled across the curtain, then I gaped at Levi.

"He knows about us!" I coughed.

Levi reached into a cup by the bed and took out a chip of ice. "Here," he whispered, "this will help."

I sucked it gratefully but was not to be distracted.

He held up a hand in defeat when I tried to speak again. "When we were brought in, the hospital rang the *seminario* – that is why Father Pietro is here. Don't worry, I have not told him anything and he will not suspect. He believes I am overcome with guilt. Which I am," he added, looking down at me. "Oh Lena, I'm so sorry." I started shaking my head but he rushed on. "I was going too fast. After that poor child was killed by a car only this morning . . . I should have known better. I should have learned." He slid another piece of ice into my mouth. "I was arguing with you. I should have been concentrating on the road."

"Levi," I began then stopped, not knowing how to go on. I wanted to beg him not to leave me. I didn't care that I had been in a crash. I had no desire to ask about my injuries. As long as he was there with me, I would be fine. But I was worried about him. "Your head." I reached up and lightly touched his white bandage with my finger.

"It's nothing." He waved away my concern. "A bump off the steering wheel. The other car crashed into the door on your side. It crushed into you. The glass shattered. It cut your face. The cuts will fade after a few weeks . . ." He leaned over me and I thought he was about to kiss me. He reached behind my left ear and touched my head gingerly. I flinched at a sharp sting. "The worst you have is a gash behind your ear. It is the only wound that will scar. You are so lucky, my love. *I* am so lucky."

As he made to move his hand away, I reached up to keep it there a bit longer. I felt a pull on the line entering my arm. "What is this?"

"Merely fluids," he said, sitting back. "You are not used to the heat here, so you were a little dehydrated. The doctor wants to keep you overnight because you were knocked unconscious by the crash. It's a precaution. You can come home with us tomorrow."

I was too tired to point out that the *seminario* was not my home. I felt a wave of nausea wash over me and shifted uncomfortably. Levi stroked my arm and questioned me but I convinced him I just needed to rest. I told him to go back to the *seminario*. At first he refused to leave me. I tried reasoning with him that Father Pietro would suspect but he didn't seem to care. Confused thoughts crossed each other as I drifted towards slumber. Before the crash we had been on the verge of splitting up. Now he was refusing to leave my side. Had his decision changed? Or was it merely guilt?

My turmoil ended there. The night's sleep was dreamless.

The next morning, Levi was gone and I was awoken by a nurse removing my drip. She was a middle-aged, plump woman with an unattractive pudding-bowl haircut. She took my temperature and prodded me some more before nodding to herself in apparent satisfaction. We conversed for a time. She recommended a follow-up test the next week and, though she insisted I would make a full recovery from my injuries, I was confused by what she was telling me, sure her broken English was the problem. When I cried, she held me and told me I would be all right. I thought that must have been what a mother's hold was like. Finally she left me to weep alone.

Sometime later, when my eyes had surely leaked all the extra fluids my drip had provided, the nurse reappeared to announce I had a visitor.

"It is not yet visiting hours," she said but without any real disapproval as she acknowledged the special treatment afforded to the clergy.

I pushed myself upright, hoping eagerly for Levi. Or perhaps Agata or Christoforo. For the first time I started to doubt my grand declarations that the *seminario* was Levi's home, not mine.

My visitor rounded into view and my whole body jerked in shock. She looked down at me and I was overcome with a mad urge to scream.

"How are you feeling? Your face is cut – are you in any pain?" Marthe's enquiries sounded kind as she eased herself into the chair beside me.

Instinctively, I shrank back from her.

"I was sorry to hear about your accident," she tried again. "Levi contacted me last night. He was very upset."

Searching her face for her usual dismissive expression, I found only grace. I was sure it was a trick. "What are you doing here?" The words came out more accusatory than I had intended but I didn't retract. Sitting in front of me was the very person who could destroy Levi so I was not inclined to be kind.

"After Levi left you last night, he came to meet me in Rome. I'm staying there with my brother," she explained.

I cocked an eyebrow, not believing for a second her excuse for fleeing the *seminario*.

"My brother and Levi are friends," she added, frowning at me. "Levi really hasn't told you? He is a good man."

Her cryptic words kindled curiosity but protecting Levi was my priority. "Marthe, what do you want?"

She paused. "I'm sorry for the way I treated you when you first arrived, Lena." For some reason, her use of my name tempered my stressed emotions. "It was not very Christian of me, but I was suspicious."

"Suspicious? Of me?" I rubbed my stinging arm where the drip had been ripped from my veins by the nurse with the pudding-bowl haircut and positive attitude.

"It is complicated. I will try to explain it to you." She removed her cloak to reveal her full nun's habit and settled back into her chair. When she spoke, she looked past me, as though speaking to a ghost shimmering in the air behind me. What I heard astonished me.

Marthe and her younger brother had a tragic childhood. Like Levi, they lost another sibling and, not long afterwards, their parents. They were moved from their family house in the city to stay with an aunt in the French countryside. Their aunt was a harsh woman who quelled any complaint with the promise that, if they gave her reason to send them away again, Marthe and her brother would surely be split up. There were no beatings and no abuse. Just resentment and an ever-pulsating node of envy at their youth.

Marthe and her brother huddled together at night for warmth while their aunt slept cosy under her many rugs and blankets. They threw each other scheming eyebrow-raises across the dinner table and developed a rudimentary sign language that she never decoded. The four years between them dissolved until they were more like twins, best friends, each the other's crutch.

All of their plans, from childhood plots of escape to their serious teenage discussions, were hatched together. They considered opening a café. Marthe was an excellent baker, having been forced to spend many years in the kitchen, but they would need start-up capital which their aunt would never provide. Her brother preferred the idea of teaching but further schooling was also out of the question without money for tuition. Unless, of course, he joined the priesthood.

This was not a new idea. Their aunt had often threatened Marthe with an enclosed convent, knowing her niece was terrified of it. Not of being a nun, but of being a cloistered or 'locked-up' nun. If she could live in an active convent with her brother nearby, it didn't seem like a bad idea. So they hatched their plan of a religious life together, the brother and sister. They choreographed it down to the last detail. Marthe, the older, would be forced to leave home before her brother. She would join a local French sisterhood which she knew had links to a seminary in Italy. That seminary was relatively new and recruiting nuns who were willing to assist. By the time Alexandre was ready to enter the seminary, Marthe would be ensconced there. After his ordination he would have to move but he could take her with him. They were willing to beg and bribe their way to a life together.

Their co-dependence was entrenched and everything initially went to plan. Thrilled to be rid of them, their aunt did not object and the local priest used his contacts to ensure their route to the *seminario*.

There was one major flaw in the plan, which was not discovered until years later.

After some months as a seminarian Alexandre figured out why his stomach sloshed constantly and his head pounded at night when sleep refused to come. He was not where he was supposed to be. He loved God, but was not meant to be a priest. His dream was of a brown-eyed woman who waved him off in the mornings with a clatter of dark-haired little girls who were the image of their Aunt Marthe. He dreamt that he would pass by his sister's house, on his way home from teaching, and collect her and his nephews to take them to his house for dinner. He longed for a family life he knew he'd once had but could not remember.

The fantasy could be pushed to the side, dismissed as an idle dream like so many of his childhood musings with Marthe, until a dark-haired, brown-eyed girl sang her way into his heart.

The worst part of the affair was not lying to Father Pietro or sneaking around his roommate Levi, or even his moral conscience that in betraying his ministry he was insulting the Lord. It was telling Marthe. At first, he did not think he could do it. But Thérèse had asked him to leave and he would have done anything for her.

Marthe's screams brought priests and nuns running from every corner of the *seminario*. The coffin-filled image of her dead parents was never so vivid to her as when Alexandre revealed he was leaving the priesthood before he had properly started.

Marthe's eyes filled with tears as she relayed the devastating exchange to me, a stranger, with brutal honesty. "'I'm not leaving *you*,' he said to me."

I watched with wide eyes while she dabbed a tissue to her face.

"But it felt like he was leaving me. He was my whole world."

I dared to ask the question. "Did you consider leaving too?"

She shook her head. "It was different for me, it always was. Alexandre was too young to remember more than a blurry outline of our parents. He grew up a lonely boy with a sister for a mother. He had dreams of another life. He had something to leave the priesthood for. Not me."

I said nothing; my head was noisy with Marthe's memories. When I looked at her, I saw a story much worse than mine. How awful it must have been to have lost her brother and for everyone to have known the reason why. No wonder Levi did not reveal her to me.

"I feel now that I have come to terms with his desertion. But we did not speak for years."

I gaped and she shrugged resignedly.

"I was too hurt. Too angry to see him. It took a long time before I was able to develop a new relationship with him. Now I see him more regularly. Alexandre and Thérèse had every reason to leave the country where their *amour* was a scandal, but they didn't. He left the *seminario* because she asked him but he has stayed in Italy for me, not for his dark-haired love." A sad sort of pride emanated from her for no more than a couple of seconds before she continued. "Somehow, his desertion has cemented my devotion to the *seminario*. I am useful there, more useful than any of the other nuns. I never knew that my brother was having doubts about his vocation. Now I watch the seminarians closely. I want to help them early if I can. No one else noticed but I could see Levi changing, and I knew you were the reason."

If possible, my jaw dropped still further. Marthe smiled. She was the only one who suspected, she assured me. No one else inferred anything from our behaviour. Her watchful eye had made her naturally distrustful of a youthful girl with all the opportunities of the world at her feet.

"Marthe," my voice cracked, "what did Levi say to you that night you found us?"

"He didn't say a word, Lena. He knew I would never 'turn him in' as the saying goes. If someone had done such a thing to Alexandre, I would never have forgiven them. I was the one who did the talking. You know what I told him, don't you?"

"To leave me?" I whispered, thinking of her pain when her brother was tempted away. But then I shook my head, sure that she would never wish her brother unhappy. "To leave the *seminario* and be with me?"

She sat back, staring at me with her old patronising glare. "You really weren't listening to my story, were you?"

Before I could decipher her meaning, the curtain scratched across and Agata was upon me. She started at the sight of Marthe sitting in the chair but did not let it distract her for long.

"Lena!"

I reached out a hand and began to reassure her but she spoke over me, claiming guilt and worry and confusion all at the same time. Marthe tried to calm her and the nurse with the pudding-bowl haircut stuck her head around the curtain, threatening to remove her if she didn't quieten down.

"I apologise," Agata breathed, shifting on the bed to find a groove, as though settling in for the day. "I didn't expect to see you here, Marthe. How did you hear about the accident?"

"Levi telephoned Alexandre," she answered softly.

I interrupted before Agata could delve deeper. "You're both so good to visit me, but really I'm fine. They're letting me go today."

"Well, you are coming back with us and no arguments," Agata said firmly. "Christoforo is driving down to collect us."

I glanced meaningfully at Marthe and she acceded to my silent request to ask what I dared not say. "What about Levi, Agata?"

"Oh, poor Levi. He feels awful. I saw him only briefly. He wanted to collect you, Lena, but Father Pietro would not allow it. After a knock to the head like that? He is probably in shock, the poor man. Lena, dear, you're shaking, are you quite all right?"

I tried to steady myself but my body was out of my control. Perhaps Father Pietro was not keeping Levi from me because of his injuries but because he had figured out the truth. Marthe intervened again. With a pure face she insisted gently to Agata that the *seminario* was too far a journey for me to make immediately upon leaving the hospital, and that I should spend the night with her and her brother in Rome.

At first, Agata dismissed the notion. After all, the *seminario* was less than an hour's drive away. Marthe was quietly insistent and when she played her ace – the fact that her sister-in-law was a nurse – Agata gave in.

Christoforo arrived shortly afterwards but was refused entry to see me. Visiting hours were coming to an end and there had been too many people in already. I felt suddenly humbled that I had managed to collect such a number of people who cared for me. Papa would have been pleased, I thought, as I wished more than anything for his fatherly touch.

After much ado, I was prepared, clothed and bundled out into the arms of a welcoming couple – Alexandre, a thin man with Marthe's sallow skin, and Thérèse, a surprisingly plain woman with brown eyes and long dark hair. Though not much older than me, they grabbed me from Marthe with parental care and manhandled me out of the hospital and into the back of their car.

Thérèse drove, her husband by her side.

She spoke to him in French and Alexandre twisted around to face me. "Thérèse wants to know if you are warm enough, Lena?"

I nodded back, slightly overwhelmed as Thérèse fired more questions at her husband in rapid French which he in turn directed at me. I saw Marthe smiling smugly. I got the impression that, with a childlike glee, she was enjoying someone else being at the receiving end of their overpowering affections.

The hospital was on the outskirts of the city and we travelled further out from there. The streets and sights were far from the tourist attractions I had been used to. After Thérèse exhausted all of her motherly questions, she settled for watching the road studiously. I observed her and Alexandre just as keenly from the back seat. Marthe had whispered to me as we descended in the elevator that I should not mention children, as people often do in an attempt at conversation. They had already lost two before birth and Thérèse had been told her chances of carrying a baby to term were slim.

I remembered Marthe's story about her younger brother craving a family to replace his own lost childhood. My eyes welled with tears. Unfortunately Alexandre noticed and, thinking I was unwell, began gesturing at his wife to drive faster.

"We live outside of the city." He turned again to engage with me, keeping up a running commentary of the areas we passed by. Thérèse drove us through a wealthy neighbourhood which gave way to a dreary sort of area where the graffiti were less colourful and more violent, and litter added to the general sense of neglect. Thankfully she continued through it and stopped on a street that was, if not affluent, at least clean and lively.

Marthe helped me out of the car and gestured upwards. Alexandre and Thérèse's home was a small apartment above a bakery. Smells of fresh bread comforted me like a warm bedspread and followed us up the stairs.

Alexandre breathed it in as he opened the door for us.

"Wait until the morning when it is delivered," he smiled, ushering me gently towards what was to be my bedroom. He was nudged out of the way by his wife as she took my arm to complete the final step of the task.

From the narrow doorway, Alexandre apologised for the cramped sleeping quarters. Fearful of being more of a nuisance, I tried to protest when they insisted on giving me the only spare room. Marthe called from the other room that I should not bother arguing – as the patient and wanderer alone in a strange land, I was to be given the space to recuperate. Marthe and her sister-in-law were to sleep in the main bedroom, while Alexandre would take the couch. Thérèse tucked me into bed and, surprisingly, I fell asleep within seconds. No thoughts of Levi kept me awake. No thoughts at all.

When I awoke it was dark and eerily quiet. My tongue ripped

like Velcro from the roof of my mouth and I reached out for the nightstand. No water. Sluggishly, I peeled myself from the bed and tip-toed into the main room of the apartment. Alexandre was sprawled on the couch on the carpeted half of the room, only a few steps from the kitchen.

As quietly as possible, I reached up and opened some presses until I found glasses piled atop each other. Taking one down, I filled it and let the cooling water replenish me. I thought of the nurse with the pudding-bowl haircut and how she told me everything would be all right. In that moment, alone and far from home, when all I wanted was for someone else to get the water for me and even tip my head back and pour it into my mouth, I didn't know how she could be right.

"Lena?"

I leapt, my hand flying to my mouth. I lowered it at seeing Alexandre ease himself sleepily into a sitting position. He waved away my apology for waking him and joined me for a glass of water in the kitchen.

"How are you?" he asked, gesturing to the two high stools at the kitchen countertop. I felt the lack of a kitchen table and the shabbiness of the furnishings.

I answered generically and he probed no more. We sat for a while in silence until my predicament started to overwhelm me. Such troubles always seem worse at night; somehow darkness adds a weight.

Alexandre spoke with concern into the silence. "Lena, are you sure you are well?"

He mistook my woolly eyes for sickness, though in truth my stomach was starting to churn. I could no longer bring myself to respond with the standard and untrue 'I'm fine'. I looked into his eyes, wide and earnest, and wondered if he was the one person who would understand. Before I could make up my mind, he pre-empted me.

"Marthe told me about you and Levi. I'm the only person she has told," he added, seeing my body tense. "I'm surprised he did not tell me. After all, I am the perfect person to confide in."

"Maybe he isn't planning on following your lead."

Alexandre looked at me sharply, then patted my hand. "Perhaps not. But he has not made a decision yet, which tells me he is at least considering the road I took. That shows how important you are to him."

I heard someone sigh deeply through the open bedroom door.

"Your wife does not speak English?"

Some of the lines in his face smoothed. "No. French is our mother tongue. We both also speak Italian. I learned English because I thought it would help me secure a place at the *seminario*."

"Are you sorry you left?" I asked it so fast he had barely finished his sentence.

He answered just as quickly. "No. I am not sorry."

I waited, as he did not seem finished.

"I have often wondered, especially when Thérèse and I went through hard times, whether life would have been easier – better, even – if I had stayed there."

Marthe had warned me to say nothing but in the dark whispers of the night I knew it was the right time. "Are you talking about your children?"

"Yes."

I watched in horror as a tear dripped onto his cheek. "I cannot regret them, though I never saw them, never held them. You will understand one day if you have children of your own."

I remembered what Levi said about his mother dissolving to nothing after losing a child and hoped I would never have to suffer what she or Thérèse had been through.

Alexandre wiped his eyes. "I do not believe in regrets. I made the only decision I could have at the time. I followed my heart."

Instinctively, I pressed a fist against my chest and Alexandre made the same motion.

"The heart, Lena, is where God stamps the blueprint of your life. Not your brain. Not your body either. When you tremble with passion – that is lust or love. It is not your heart. Your heart is where your purpose, your divine reason for existence dwells. I knew that if I stayed in the *seminario* I would be living a half-life. That was not what God wanted for me. I have no regrets.

And neither will Levi, once the decision is made."

I slid from my high stool, unable to stay sitting any longer. I had hardly paced more than five steps before I reached the end of the room. Alexandre watched me.

"Are you still friends with Levi?" I asked, building up to my real question.

Alexandre nodded, cautiously. "We did not speak for some time after I left but not because of the manner of my leaving. Levi was a rock of strength for Marthe. I knew she needed that and was grateful she had him as a friend. So I kept my distance. When my sister and I reconciled, Levi and I began to converse more regularly."

"Can you tell me about him?"

Alexandre laughed. "I think you already know him."

"But, Alexandre," I used his name familiarly, like he was my brother too, "every time I think he has made a decision, he does something that convinces me I'm wrong." I glanced quickly at the main bedroom, conscious I might wake the women. "Alexandre," I moved closer to my confidant, "I'm not a bad person. I don't make a habit of luring men from their life missions . . ."

Alexandre cut me off with another laugh. "I know, Lena." He covered my hand with his own in a gesture so paternal it made me ache.

"I want him to pick me," I said, "and I want him to do it soon."

Alexandre stared at me as though seeing me for the first time. He tightened his hold on my hand and led me to the main bedroom door. We watched his sister and wife sleeping soundly side by side.

"Take a look, Lena." He nodded in the direction of the women. "Tell me, do you think my sister had good reason to be jealous of Thérèse?"

"No," I answered at once. "She seems lovely."

"Look again," he whispered. "All my life – all of it I can remember at least – it was me and Marthe. She raised me, and I took care of her too. We were a team. Now, Lena, think carefully: what was it about Thérèse that made my sister jealous?

Rightly jealous, I should add."

I looked at the sleeping women – Marthe snoring lightly, Thérèse still as a rock.

"I guess," I shrugged my shoulders, "because you chose to be on a different team?"

"And there is your mistake, Lena," Alexandre whispered with an air of triumph. "That is why you cannot see a way out. You have it all wrong."

Marthe stirred and I pulled Alexandre back to the kitchen, afraid of being interrupted before getting to the nub of the knowledge he so clearly held.

"Alexandre, I don't mean to be difficult but you are going to have to spell this out for me. I don't know what you mean."

Unexpectedly, Alexandre stepped forward and took my face in his hands. "Lena," he said solidly, "the choice is not Levi's. The choice is yours."

I pushed him away and took a step back, my breath quickening. Like my hand fitting so easily into Levi's, the truth crystallised before me.

Marthe was right to be jealous because Thérèse held Alexandre's heart and mind, as Marthe once had. Alexandre would not have chosen to leave his sister, if Thérèse had not asked him. I had answered Marthe in the hospital with what I thought were Levi's only two options – pick me or pick the *seminario*. But there had been a third possibility, one I completely overlooked. Marthe had advised him to do nothing, because ultimately *I* would make the choice.

Levi could not make a decision because he was choosing between two great loves. I alone could decide.

At once, my heart swelled. It was all in my power. My future with Levi was secure – all I had to do was ask him to leave, just like Thérèse had asked Alexandre. At this thought, my heart constricted once more and plummeted to my stomach. Deep down, Alexandre had wanted a married life. He craved a wife and children. Thérèse knew that and had done the right thing, not selfishly to fulfil her own wishes, but for Alexandre, when she asked him to pick her.

It was not the same for us.

Levi loved me. Despite our circumstances and differences he loved me, I was sure of it. But that love was superfluous to his real life. He was fulfilling his true purpose in the priesthood – a purpose that was not random but one he had inherited from his brother. He had never needed me to live a full life like Alexandre had needed Thérèse. More importantly, I was not enough for him to do that. The *seminario* was, and always had been, Levi's family.

If I had to prioritise Levi or anybody else, I would choose Levi. I would do what was right for him before I did what was right for me or anybody else. And I knew what was right for him. A part of me had always known. I recognised the cruelty of the situation – I knew Levi better than any other person, well enough to know that his destiny was not with me.

Alexandre watched the tears flow down my face. "Oh Lena," he shook his head, "I'm sorry."

I pushed past him to their tiny bathroom. It was so cramped there was no room to close the door behind me as I threw up. Thérèse was at my side within seconds, holding back my hair. I heard a whispered conversation between Marthe and Alexandre before fainting to the floor.

I could see the change in me, as I walked around Rome over the next few days. When the tourists bumped into me, I did not apologise. In restaurants, I tipped but did not thank. My eyes pulsated all day long but no tears ran down my cheeks. I was hardening.

I needed to be practical now. Hollywood was over.

I thought a lot about Marthe during the week I stayed with her brother and his wife. The *seminario* saved me from allowing my grief at Papa's death consume me and I had attributed that to Levi and Agata. Yet Marthe was the one who noticed my attraction to Levi and ultimately it was her family's experience that showed me what I had to do.

I knew it was the last emotion she would have wanted to inspire but I couldn't help feeling desperately sorry for Marthe. Her brother's choice was a desertion, no matter how justified. I had conjured up a vivid image of a young teenage Marthe, pudgy with puppy fat she would shed in later years, cuddling her younger brother in the middle of the night, his little hand twisting around her pigtails for comfort. Marthe wouldn't see that she probably relied on him more than he did on her. Boys naturally grow away from their mothers. But he was her purpose, her reason for living.

"Are you surprised," Alexandre asked me almost a week later, "at how friendly my sister is with Thérèse?"

We were wandering through the streets to escape the apartment – it was stifling hot after Thérèse's cooking. Marthe had joined us unannounced and, after our meal, we took to the streets for an evening stroll. Bars and restaurants, street sellers and busking musicians gave it an almost festival-like atmosphere. Marthe and Thérèse were walking ahead of us, laughing easily about something.

"I think it would be hard for anyone not to like Thérèse, once they got to know her," I said. Though we could not converse, we did communicate and always with an active eagerness on her part to be helpful. Thérèse oozed kindness and her generosity towards me was clearly given without effort.

"True." Alexandre linked my arm to steer me around a group of inebriated men in our path. "But that is also true of Marthe."

I said nothing. I guessed that in the beginning Thérèse had received from Marthe the same up-turned nose as I did on first meeting her. But Marthe's willingness to confess her family history to me made me admit she probably had more in common with Thérèse than I gave her credit for initially. With Alexandre as their link, it didn't surprise me that, given time, they bonded.

After that first night, when Alexandre made me see what had to be done, Marthe had to return to the *seminario*. She offered to come back the next night and bring Levi with her.

I said no immediately. "Don't bring him here," I could hear the hysteria sharpen my words. "I don't want to see him."

I couldn't stop my eyes from watering and at first she looked confused, but her brother merely touched her arm and her eyes opened wide. She nodded, turned and did not visit again until nearly a week later.

Alexandre and Thérèse insisted I stay with them to recover from the accident. So I did, wandering the streets as a hardened soul during the day. They took good care of me – they brought me back to the hospital for the follow-up test the nurse with the pudding-bowl haircut had recommended, and comforted me silently when I cried, as I did many times over that week. I watched Alexandre and Thérèse during my stay with them. Their interaction was a series of gestures, each tending to the other. Conversations were punctuated with kisses or a light stroke of the arm – nothing showy, all real. Thérèse's devotion to her husband was clear and I was sure that she would not have asked him to abandon his vocation had she not been certain it was the right course for him. My empathy for Marthe increased when I realised that, by giving her brother such valuable affection growing up, she had unwittingly instilled in him that need to find it for himself in his adult life.

We had looped around on our journey back to the apartment when Alexandre leaned in close to me again. "Marthe and Thérèse are both caring women. As I have already told you, when I first left, Levi was there for Marthe. I'm glad now that he has her."

I closed my eyes, knowing it was time.

When we arrived back, Marthe made to leave and I grabbed her wrist. "There is a flight in two days. I checked with the travel agent a few days ago. I can get a seat."

All three of them stared at me – even Thérèse, who could tell from my tone I was making an important announcement.

"The plane leaves in the evening. Can you take me back to the *seminario* in the morning, so I can say goodbye?"

She tried to talk me out of it. Even Alexandre thought I should give myself more time to explain to Levi, to come to terms with my decision. But there was no point. I knew what was going to happen. I owed him a goodbye. Then I would leave.

So, on the most glorious, cloudless day, after nearly a week with Alexandre and Thérèse, Marthe arrived to take me back to the *seminario* one last time. I asked her to wait while I stepped into a phone box outside their apartment. I breathed in the homely smell from the bakery as I waited, receiver in hand. The call to Washington DC took a long time to connect. A week before, I might have taken that as a sign of something. Now, I knew it was merely the logistics of international calls.

"Yeah?"

The rough, impatient voice on the other end of the phone was somehow soothing to me. I was hard now too.

"Damien. It's Lena."

There was a pause.

"Lena. Jesus."

"Yeah. It's me. I wanted to ring . . ."

"Lena? Are you there? I can barely hear you . . ."

I pressed the phone closer to my mouth and spoke loudly. He sounded crackly too. I told him I was ringing from Italy. That I had been travelling since Papa died but was on my way home. Could I visit him? I missed him. The words did not sound fake or false when I said them. Neither did they contain truth or passion. They didn't sound like anything.

He seemed reluctant at first. He told me he was sorry about Papa. I tried not to remember his absence from the funeral.

"I need to move on with my life now, Damien," I said distinctly. "There's nothing left for me in Chicago. I want to move back to DC. I want to be with you again."

"Jesus Christ, Lena. This is sudden."

"Can I at least call you when I get back?"

After some stuttering he agreed and I hung up, out of breath. One more thing to do. I looked out of the phone box at Marthe sitting patiently in the car.

"Are you sure you know what you're doing, Lena?" Marthe asked quietly as I sat into the passenger seat beside her.

"I thought you'd be happy." The words tasted acidic in my mouth. "Another man won't be lost to a sinful life."

Marthe would not indulge my tasteless jibe. "There is nothing sinful about the love between a man and a woman. All I want is for Levi to be happy."

I regretted my comment but did not apologise. "He will be."

Marthe did not force conversation on me as we drove out of the city and up into the mountains. The weather was cooler than it had been and I hugged myself as we drove through the shade of the trees lining the roads.

Scampering animals played chicken with the car as we approached the entrance.

Marthe cut the engine and turned to me.

"I've arranged for Agata to be in her room and Father Pietro will be studying in his office for the next hour. Once you are done, come to the chapel. It will be empty and I'll bring Levi."

The chapel, I thought. The perfect place to end it.

Agata was extremely agitated when I arrived into what had been, for a time, *our* room. "Lena!" She crushed me against her and I couldn't help squeezing her back one last time. I let go before she did – I had to get this over quickly. She cupped my chin in her hand as she started babbling, scrutinising the car-crash cuts that had not yet healed.

"Where have you been? We haven't heard from you in days and Marthe gave me a cryptic message to wait in my room . . ."

"I'm sorry, Agata, I had things to sort out. I'm going back to America."

Agata's eyes opened wide. "When?"

"Today."

"Today!" She took a step back.

I moved towards her and took her hands in mine. "You have been so good to me. I will never forget what you have done for me here. Can you promise to write?"

Agata shifted uncomfortably. "Lena, something is going on. Will you not tell me what it is?"

I felt my eyes starting to water, something Agata's invitations of confidence often triggered.

"I can't, Agata. I'm sorry, please don't ask me." My voice broke and I threw myself against her.

She hushed me and held me close to her. "I'll miss you," she said but I could see the disappointment in her eyes when I pulled back.

"Please write?" I said.

She said nothing, clearly still reeling from my announcement.

"I'll write to you, Agata," I said, desperation leaking from my every pore.

Agata's natural sympathy took over and her tense expression relaxed. "Do. I'd like that. I'll write back," she assured me.

"Goodbye," I said, before fleeing from the room.

I all but ran to Father Pietro's office, keeping my head down and ignoring anyone I passed. The conversation with him was shorter and friendlier. I think he was glad I was leaving. He must have suspected I was never going to be anything more than a freeloader. I was grateful he had not learned about me and Levi, for our sakes but also for Father Pietro himself. It was clear the *seminario* meant everything to him and I would not have wished to burden him unnecessarily.

I walked in a daze back to the chapel. I was not going to get a chance to bid farewell to Christoforo, Lucia or any of the rest. It doesn't matter, I thought. I was only a fleeting part of their lives. Soon, I would be forgotten. In a few years, would they remember my name? I would be nothing but a vague memory – a passing visitor who had once stayed for a few days.

Levi was alone in the chapel when I entered from the back. He was kneeling at the altar, head bowed, deep in prayer. He must have heard me come in, dip under the rope I had never before been permitted to cross and make my way into the side pews. But he remained still for several more minutes and I did not disturb him. Quietly, so quietly I would have missed it if I hadn't been so totally attuned to him, he began to sing. Not a chant, but a hymn – an evocative, sad hymn that made my eyes water. It was as if he was singing to God, and God in turn was magnifying the song just for me: a parting gift.

Finally he stood and walked to sit beside me. He took my hand in his.

"Were you praying for anything in particular?" I asked. My voice sounded unfamiliar.

Levi sighed. "For the strength to endure this conversation, and to survive afterwards."

I held my breath. He turned to me.

"You have not been in contact with me. Marthe would not give me any information all week then asked that I meet you here. All she would tell me was that you were leaving with her straight away."

I felt a duty to Marthe. "She did not want this outcome." I shook my head. "Any more than I did."

"If I choose you and leave today, we could make it work." His voice was commanding and sure but I saw in his eyes the hesitation. I watched his chest constrict while he waited for me to answer and I knew I was making the right decision. For him, if not for anybody else.

I shook my head a fraction – it was enough to loosen the tears. "No. Your home is here. This is your life. But it is not mine."

I stood and walked into the centre of the aisle. I couldn't bear to be near him, knowing I was about to leave forever. I turned. For the first and only time, I saw a tear fall from his eyes.

"Do you not believe me worthy?"

"You are the most worthy man I have ever met, and no one I have met or will ever meet could be as worthy."

I moved back to him and leaned over the front bar of the pews. I reached out and pulled his neck forward so our foreheads touched. The bandage from the crash was gone. I was glad – I didn't want to remember him broken and bruised because of me. Unless hidden under his thick black hair there was a scar.

"Live a full life, Lena." He gripped the sides of my arms. "Please. It is important to me. I must know you will live a long and full life."

I wanted to shout at him that no, I would not. That my life was ending, my very being disappearing – that it would all be gone as soon as I walked out that door. I swallowed and allowed myself to cry as I answered.

"We both will. We will remember each other . . ."

". . . and pray for each other," he added.

"We will love each other forever and be glad we met," I finished.

I prayed in that moment. I prayed that my speech and formal goodbye would give him closure enough to live the life he was born to live – without me.

As I placed a parting kiss on his lips I covered his eyes gently with my hand. He understood and obeyed, keeping his eyes shut when I took my hand away. It was better this way. When he opened his eyes again, I would be gone. He would see only the chapel – his true love. I stared at his perfect face one last time, soaking up every detail for the years ahead.

"Lena?" he asked into the silence.

I turned and ran from the chapel, knowing I would never set foot in it again. I raced to the car where Marthe was waiting and climbed into the back. I knelt on the seat and pressed up against the back window as she drove away. I leaned my hands hard against the glass, reaching for him, watching the *seminario* disappear behind the trees.

Within hours, I would be back in America. Within days, I would be in Damien's bed. But Damien was not who I was meant to be with. I was meant to be here, with Levi. If only, if only, he was meant for me too.

As the tall trees lining the road swallowed my last view of the *seminario*, I vowed never to let him slip from me. To never allow myself forget or be distracted by others. He would live the life he was meant to, without me. But I would protect what we had in my memory and, in that small way, I would live my life with Levi.

PART THREE

EIGHTEEN

Mattie

I lie in my single bed, watching my mother in the bed next to me. She is sleeping deeply after finally telling me her story. I try to imagine her in this place, in another time, moving towards the seminary to have an affair with someone like Aaron.

She looks peaceful. I wonder if she is dreaming of him.

It is clear to me now where she was all those times I tried to get her attention. She was, in her mind at least, here in Italy with Levi. With this understanding comes little comfort. She ran to my dad for rescuing. He and I were substitutes for her, a poor woman's Levi. When we couldn't fill the gap – well, my dad left. But she could not get rid of me. I know she loves me but I am not enough. What I have learnt about my mother is that no one will ever be enough for her, except her seminarian.

I stand quietly out of bed and walk to the window. I face the closed shutters, then turn to look at my mother again. Is this really why she brought me here to Italy, in my fragile state? To solidify once and for all my suspicion that I was not enough for her?

She said she wanted me to learn about and from her. By knowing who she is, I don't feel any closer to her. There is no great sense of family I can take from her past and apply to my present. If anything, I need you more, Ben, because Lena is never going to let this seminarian go.

I knew my dad was no great love for Lena. But I never imagined such an epic tale as her forbidden affair with a priest in a faraway land. What on earth would her papa have said had he been alive? Did she even consider that? It sounds like she thought about nothing but Levi.

Tristan and I never had that passion. We met as part of a group on a college night out. As our friends paired off we were left together and kissed for something to do. That is not to say we did not grow close. We became used to each other and he excited me as a new college experience. I allowed myself to fall for him. But I never wanted him as my baby's daddy any more than Lena wanted my father.

However, I hadn't counted on Tristan feeling the same way. His reaction will haunt me forever.

"Tristan, we have to talk."

"Uh oh." He set my coffee on the table in front of me and sat into his seat opposite me. "That's never good. You're not breaking up with me, are you?" His voice was light and teasing.

I felt a gnawing at my insides and suddenly wished we had not come to a crowded campus coffee shop to have this conversation. I thought it would stop him making a scene, but maybe we would have been better having it out in my dorm room than risking him freaking out in front of everyone.

To stave off the revelation a moment longer, I took a sip of my drink. I shook my head to reassure him I was not about to dump him.

"Good! Don't do that to me, Mattie. Oh, they were out of decaf so I got you regular."

I halted mid-swallow and coughed loudly as I tried to spit out the rest. Coffee squirted out my nose and mouth. I pressed a tissue against my face. The two tanned and toned juniors at the next table tittered bitchily.

Tristan looked at me with a mixture of disgust and humiliation. "Jesus, Mattie, it's just coffee. There's no need to be such a drama queen about it."

I glared at him and blew my nose. "I can't have caffeine, Tristan."

He gave me a patronising smirk, assuming this was a dietary or health fad. I could not stay angry – I knew that with my next sentence I would change his life forever. I leaned across the table and took his hands.

"Tristan," I said purposefully.

"Mattie," he imitated me sarcastically and laughed, eyeing me quizzically.

My eyes narrowed. "I'm pregnant." As soon as I said the words, I felt my face relax and all frustration with Tristan ebb away. I was pregnant! I could feel you inside me, Ben, though it had been mere weeks and there was nothing physical except nausea to connect us.

Tristan stared at me blankly.

"I know it's a shock," I rubbed his hand enthusiastically, "but it's okay. It's going to be okay, because we're having a baby!" I laughed and buried my face in my hands. Only when I looked up again, expecting to see him smiling too, did I notice that his face had soured.

"Mattie," he laughed too, but it was very different to mine – short, rough and devoid of any joy, "I can't have a baby."

"Well, you are!"

He stood abruptly and walked out of the coffee shop. The two girls beside me arched their eyebrows and I threw them a dirty look as I kicked back my chair. I followed Tristan out and caught up with him a block away. I tried to take his hand but he shook me off.

"You're pregnant?"

"Yes," I said, "I am. If you need some time to get your head around it, that's fine. But I don't want you to worry. We can still finish college. We can find somewhere to live and schedule our classes so that we can take care of the baby . . ."

"Are you out of your fucking mind, Mattie?"

I took a step back. Tristan had never spoken to me like that before. I felt drops on my face, and strangely all over my body. I looked up and saw rain falling from the sky. I didn't need to cry. Heaven was doing it for me.

Tristan, usually one to throw his jacket over my head in a fit of chivalry, did not move. My hair became wet and matted to my head and I instinctively placed a hand on my stomach.

"I have to get in out of the rain. It's not good for the baby."

I had half-turned when Tristan's hand was on my arm, his face close to mine. "Not good for the baby? Are you serious? You're keeping it?"

I jerked away from him. He knew from my face that it was not for discussion.

"Are you sure it's mine?" he asked.

I slapped him hard across the face.

He held his palm against his cheek, his expression inscrutable. When he spoke, his tone was conciliatory. "Look, Mattie, I like you. A lot. But I have plans for my future and they don't include a baby. Not right now. I can't be a father."

"It's a bit late, Tristan," I spat. "You *are* a father."

"No, I'm not."

I took a step towards him, astounded. "I'm telling you he's your baby. I haven't slept with anyone else since we've been together. He's yours."

"No, it's not." He shook his head. "I'm not having anything to do with it. You either get rid of it or get rid of me."

I took a deep breath. The rain was falling in earnest now. People raced past us to get indoors, ignoring our fight.

"Tristan," I said, "you've had a shock. That's normal. Think on it for a few days. We can talk about it then."

"No," he repeated. He stepped forward, put his hands on my shoulders and kissed me. "Goodbye, Mattie."

I watched him walk away with an open mouth. Shaking my head, I turned and ran back to my dorm to dry. He would change his mind, I told Angela as she attempted to distract me with virgin cocktails over the next few days. She kept repeating that I was better off without him, like it was already over. I waited for his call, fully expectant of an apology. I wasn't sure how forthcoming I would be with forgiveness, but I was convinced we would sort it out one way or another. He never called.

Four days later, when I was walking across campus with

Angela, she spotted him. She had been unequivocally on my side since she found me sobbing in our bathroom after telling Tristan.

"Oi! Tristan, you asshole, get over here!"

"Angela!" I whispered crossly at her but it was too late. Everyone in the square had turned to look at us.

Tristan bowed his head and walked over.

"A pleasure as always, Angela," he muttered. He turned to me, his face unreadable. "Hello, Mattie."

"Hello."

There was a silence, broken, of course, by Angela. "Well, I'd love to stand around talking but I'd hate to be a third wheel. Or fourth wheel, should I say?" She slapped Tristan hard on the back and walked away, laughing loudly to herself.

"How are you?" he asked.

I shrugged. "A bit nauseated but I'll be fine. Do you want to talk?"

He had the grace to at least look embarrassed. "I don't think there's anything to talk about. If you want to have the baby, I can't stop you. But I won't be involved."

That was the first time I really believed him. His eyes were shining, not from tears but from determination.

"What am I supposed to tell the baby," I choked, "when he's older and he asks who his daddy is?"

Tristan's face was hard. "Tell him he doesn't have one." Without hesitation, he turned and walked out of my life. I haven't seen him since.

I laugh at the memory. A bitter laugh of a beaten-down woman – and it wakes Lena.

"Mattie? What time is it?"

I pull open the shutter but it makes no difference. The darkness is everywhere. "It's not morning yet. Go back to sleep."

She falls back against her pillow and is snoring lightly within seconds.

I lie down on my own bed, thinking of Tristan and wondering where he is now. I realise I am jealous of my mother. To have experienced a love so powerful that twenty years later even her own child isn't enough to fill the void! I know, as I think I always knew, Tristan was not my great love. If I ever had one it was Simon and I flung him aside for the lure of a different type of life. I think, after you died, Lena expected me to chase that life again.

But you changed me, Ben. A great love – the type Lena talks about – does not have to be romantic. You were my great love. At least Lena chose to leave hers; you were snatched cruelly from me. With such thoughts, I close my eyes and hope sleep will come, for it is the one place I can still hold you.

NINETEEN

Lena

I stopped my tale for Mattie at the point when I left Levi. That was, of course, the end of the love story. But it was not the end of my life. Somehow that kept going.

Returning to America after saying my farewell to Levi was nothing short of traumatic. The familiar streets of DC were cold and artless compared to the beauty of the *seminario*. Even the most famous sights – Capitol Hill, the Lincoln memorial, the Washington Monument – could not inspire a sense of belonging in me. Indeed, their grandeur seemed overstated and lacking the truth of the simple, honest life lived in the *seminario*. The only sustaining thought was that I had made the right decision for Levi.

I had been tempted to go straight from the airport to Damien's place. But I knew I must have looked nightmarishly tired and defeated. Besides, he might have been there with his new grad-programme girl. I had to do this right. So I checked into a hotel, dismissing the inexpensiveness of hostels. I needed space to rest.

I slept for almost eighteen hours without waking. When I rose, I felt fresher. I showered and went shopping for clean clothes. I picked out the good stuff and did not begrudge the money. I had to remind Damien that I was the type of girl he could bring home. I went to a hairdresser and bought new make-up. Then I rang him.

"It's me. I'm back."

"Lena! You're here in DC?"

I nodded into the phone. "Can we meet?" I paused. "I've got a hotel room."

"Listen, Lena . . ."

I could see him standing in his apartment, scratching his head as he tried to fathom my game.

" . . . I'm seeing another girl now."

"Okay. Let's just talk," I said quickly. "For old time's sake, Damien."

He was still hesitant but he agreed. I asked him to come to the bar in the hotel where I was staying. It was some distance from where he lived but I pleaded and he gave in. I think he felt bad about ditching me when Papa got sick. I sat for an hour in front of the mirror, applying and removing layers of make-up until I had achieved the desired impression – that of a woman who was classy and desirable. I focused intently on the movements of my hands across my cheeks, eyebrows and lips. I did not let my mind think about anything except the physical actions. The decision had been made. I was going to be with Damien and there was no point doubting and arguing in my mind.

Damien and I had good times during college. We could build a life together. Had Papa's health not declined, he and I would still be a couple. I would be bringing him home for Thanksgiving and Christmas. Maybe we would have moved away or bought a house in DC. Whatever would have happened, we would have been together. I needed to undo my papa's death, undo the loss of Levi by rewinding and continuing the life I would have had. The *seminario* I would visit only in my mind.

Damien was over-strutting – a sure sign of nerves – when he walked into the hotel bar. It was very quiet with only a few business men and older couples. I was perched on a bar stool in a short and low-cut dress, a cocktail in my hand. I waved and tried to keep my expression light. His head jutted forward and his eyes widened on seeing me. I knew I had successfully erased the last image he had of me – red-eyed and unkempt with nothing but Papa on my mind.

He pecked me on the cheek and sat up on a high bar stool beside me. He gestured at the barman for a drink and scratched at his stubble as he surveyed me.

I scrutinised him in return. He had put on weight since we last met and there was a grey tinge to the area around his eyes.

"Lena . . ." he started, looking me up and down with a juvenile grin. Then he stopped. He reached out and took my chin between his finger and thumb, tilting my face to inspect it in the light. "What happened to your face?"

The cuts from the glass fragments were fading and I had used as much make-up as I could to disguise what marks remained but I hadn't been able to hide them entirely. I shook out of his hand as passively as I could manage. That he could touch me with such familiarity jarred.

"I was in a car accident," I said without feeling.

His eyes widened. "Shit. Are you okay?"

"Yes." I smiled as broadly as I could, remembering the importance of achieving my goal with him. "They won't scar," I assured him. "I'll be back to normal soon."

He still seemed concerned so I put a hand on his leg.

"You look well, Damien," I lied and he snorted in derision.

"Fuck off, I look like shit." He nodded thanks at the barman and took a large slug from his longneck. "The guys I work for are sadistic. I swear, Lena, they're slave-drivers."

"They're treating you rough?" I tried to inject a note of sympathy.

"It's not easy. I don't know how long I'll last." He glanced at me self-pityingly before checking himself. "You look gorgeous though." He flashed me a dazzling grin.

I raised an eyebrow and he squirmed in his seat.

"I only noticed those cuts up close. I mean, baby, come on!" He leaned back to take in my figure and I tossed my hair, knowing I had him hooked. "Seriously, you're a knock-out. Where have you been?"

I raved about Italy – the food, the wine, the sun. It was not hard to be passionate about Rome, though I had to pretend I had not strayed from the city.

"Sounds gorgeous, hon. Listen, I'm sorry I didn't make your dad's funeral. I couldn't get away from work."

I looked down, guessing the truth. He hadn't been bothered to travel to another state when there was nothing for him at the end of it.

He leaned in closer. "Seriously, baby, I would have been there if I could. How are you doing?"

I held back the tears I know would have fallen had Levi or Agata or Marthe asked me that very question. "I'm fine, Damien. I need to move on now." I tried to bat my eyelids flirtatiously and he sat back, contemplating me.

Within an hour, we were up in my hotel room. It was a rushed affair I'm sure he considered passionate. I was doing what I had to do. Levi would no longer be the last man to have touched me, held me. This was my only way forward. Still, afterwards I could not stop myself crying.

"What's wrong, baby?" Damien sounded worried. "Was that not good for you?"

I stroked his cheek, and his ego. "It was great," I sniffed, offering him a wan smile. "I just missed you so much."

It was a lie. I hadn't missed Damien in any meaningful way. If I felt his absence at all, it was at first and merely from the change in my routine of which he had been a part for so long. That should have been a sign that he was not the man for me. But I didn't let myself see it. I was committed to my plan. I was focused, clinical almost. Continuing alone was not an option. Damien, for me, was the only way I could survive without Levi.

We met every day over the next couple of weeks. Sometimes, all he had time for was half an hour at lunch. A couple of evenings we managed dinner before he was hauled back to the office. At the end of the two weeks, he finally realised that I was, in essence, living in a hotel room.

"How long are you staying here?" he asked, his hand running lightly down my arm.

I leaned over him and kissed him. "That depends on you."

"You can't live in a hotel all your life."

I took a deep breath. Now was the moment to lay out my grand plan and see if he bit. My future depended on it and my stomach churned as I breathed out the words. "Papa left me plenty of money. If you don't want me, there's no reason for me to stay in DC. I'll go back to Chicago. But there's nothing for me there." I kissed him again. "I can sell Papa's house and we could start over here. Find a place to live. We could live together."

I knew it was tempting for him. His family had money but they were not in the habit of carrying each other. Once Damien left college, he was on his own. Papa's money would ease his life greatly. And I knew he loved me, in his own way. We were college sweethearts.

He did not answer straight away. Instead, he rolled me over and we spent one final lazy afternoon of non-commitment together. After that, everything raced ahead.

He agreed, and broke up with his grad-programme girlfriend. Papa's house sold quickly – I posted the final papers to the lawyer in Michigan rather than travel there. I was scared if I saw the house again I would never be able to stop crying, knowing I was giving away the last physical link to my past with Papa. I was doing it for a reason, I told myself as I signed the paper and licked the stamp and walked to the post-box and let it fall from my shaking fingers.

Damien and I drove around in his vintage car like excited kids looking at houses and apartments. Ultimately we settled on one. Damien wasn't bowled over by it but we had to pick somewhere. I knew his problem – he came from money and always saw himself in a mansion in the suburbs with a penthouse city apartment he could use for work. "We'll work up to that," I placated him. The three-storey house was huge from my perspective and at the very limit of what we could afford.

More news followed for Damien and he shared his on the same night and at the same time that I made my revelation, each unable to wait for the other.

"I lost my job."

"I'm pregnant."

I stared at him and he stared at my belly. I was scared he would run. That he would see it as two pieces of bad news. But he didn't. He wrapped his arms around me and told me we would make it work. He had a few business ventures going on the side, he winked.

I transferred Papa's money into a joint bank account so he had full access and I got a part-time job doing admin in an art gallery. It was a hard few months. Neither of us had struggled for money before, not in that way. Tension bubbled around us.

The day Mattie was born was probably the last joyous day we had together. He was there with me, hollering for me to push. I wanted to scream at him to shut up. Levi would have known what to say. His encouragement would have been a low and soothing chant, not a hysterical mantra like I was about to make a home run.

Then it all stopped. Damien's cheers faded to nothing but a mere buzz. Levi's face melted away in front of my eyes. She had arrived. I hadn't thought of her as a real person before. There she was, with arms and legs, and the tiniest fingers and toes I'd ever seen. With tufts of dark hair far back on her head and gummy eyes and a loud, determined wail.

"What'll we call her?" Damien asked when she was finally sleeping.

I paused, gazing down at my girl. "I like 'Mattie'," I said.

"Mattie." Damien paused. "My grandmother was called Matilda." He ran a finger gently across her cheek. "My little Tilda."

I laughed, a contented laugh. It was almost perfect. "Her name," I said gently but firmly, "is Mattie."

The stresses mounted after that. Mattie would cry for hours and my patience wore like a fraying rope. I kept it in because Damien snapped all the time and someone had to be the carer for our baby girl.

The side businesses came to nothing. Papa's money was whittled away. Damien drank. He gambled. He fought with other drunken gamblers. Once he came close to being arrested. I was anxious that we would not be able to keep the house. But I couldn't talk to him about it. He would yell at me that I hadn't a clue about the pressure he was under to provide for us. His shouts would make Mattie cry harder and sometimes he would scream at her too.

I survived two years. Until one night in late winter when the wind was howling around the house, scattering debris and the last of the autumnal leaves that had refused to be swept away. Damien hadn't arrived home and Mattie came padding downstairs sleepily, whinging for her blanket. I picked her up, sure she had dropped it upstairs, when his key went in the lock. I froze. When it took him more than a few attempts to open the door, I knew he had been drinking. He fell across the threshold.

"Wha's she doin' up?" he slurred.

"Why are you home so late?" I was in no mood to be bullied.

Terrified by the sudden aggression, Mattie struggled violently out of my grasp and ran up the stairs.

"Yeah, you run, li'l girl!" he roared. "Don't make me chase you!"

"Don't yell at her, Damien!" I shouted.

He turned his face on me and immediately I saw my mistake. He was not merely drunk, he was completely out of it. His eyes were so bloodshot I could barely see any white at all. He staggered, turned and picked up the umbrella resting by our coat stand. He snorted an excited laugh and came towards me.

"Damien!" I put up my hands. "What are you doing?"

I don't think he knew it was me standing in front of him. He swung and I was shocked by the force with which he slammed the umbrella down. I dodged the blow easily, his balance completely impaired, and he hit the table beside me. He took one more swing but this time I wasn't afraid. I could see what was about to happen. He smashed the umbrella down on the ground and toppled over with it, collapsing into a dead sleep on his front.

I stood panting, staring at his comatose body sprawled on our floor. The truth came crashing down harder than he had. I had thought I could start a life with Damien, be a family. But he was not the right man for me. Certainly not the right father to raise

Mattie. I was able to tell her truthfully in later years that he never beat me, never struck her. But that was because I didn't wait around for it to happen.

It is only twenty years later, now that Mattie has lost Ben and I can't get her to open up to me that I realise I have treated her as badly as Damien did. He escaped with drink; I hid in my memories. He shouted at her for peace; I ignored her to find it.

In the end, he left her. And, in a way, so did I.

TWENTY

Lena

Mattie looks tired when she wakes so I send her out for some air and to buy us bread rolls for breakfast. I sit at the table and run a file over my nails.

Unexpectedly, I feel calm. Maybe it is due to the first decent night's sleep I have had since we arrived. Or perhaps because the waiting is finally over. Anticipation is the worst form of torture. The ordination is today; I can no longer put it off. I am prepared. I will stay close to Mattie and if I have the strength will point out to her some of the most meaningful parts of the *seminario* – our semi-circular nook behind the buildings, the chapel, the main dining hall where I first caught Levi's eye through the crowd.

Mattie has looked at me differently since I told her the story last night, like she is seeing me for the first time as a real woman.

"Lena, I'm back," she calls as she jogs up the stairs and hands me a plastic bag of warm baguettes.

"Thanks, sweetheart. Let's eat now and then we can get ready."

"What time do we have to be there?" she asks, as she takes down plates from a high press over the sink.

"The ordination isn't until the afternoon but Ruth wants us there early. I think they are putting on some light snacks beforehand."

There is a pregnant silence as we sit and begin to eat.

"Are you nervous?" Mattie asks eventually.

I shake my head but the cup vibrates in my hand.

"Do you think he'll be there?"

Again I shake my head, this time with true conviction. Levi left the *seminario* eighteen years ago after his ordination. Marthe sent me letters for many years after I left Italy, as did Agata, although only with the former could I be truly open with my questions. She wrote that Levi did get his own parish, in the north of Italy, one with a promising choir where his musical talents could blossom. I liked to think of him sitting out in the sun of a Tuscan village, listening to his choir practise through the walls of his church.

Abruptly, all contact stopped from both Marthe and Agata. I wrote frantically but neither replied until, months later, a letter arrived. It was wet on the back where the envelope closes. It could have been from rain, wet hands of a postman or damp from the mailbox. But I knew instinctively it was a tear – a tear that had not dried even as it was carried across the sea to me.

I lean on the table to steady myself, then look up at Mattie. "No, he won't be there. No one I know will be there. Except . . ."

"Except?" Mattie sounds astounded.

"I gather from Ruth that the man who established the *seminario* still lives there, although he is more figurehead and scholar than management now. I met him during my time there. I doubt he will recognise me."

"Does he know?"

"Of course not! Nobody knows. Nobody ever knew, except our friend Marthe and her family. If I have to, I can face Father Pietro. Just like," I pause and wait for my daughter to catch my eye, "you can face Joseph's baby."

I watch Mattie's face scrunch up tight as she sits heavily onto a chair. I think of the men we have lost – Papa, Levi, Damien, Tristan, Simon – and know her grief for Ben is so much greater than any other because her one great love lived inside of her.

TWENTY-ONE

Mattie

The day has arrived – the day of Aaron's ordination when Lena won't be able to avoid travelling back to the seminary. I'm surprised she slept at all. Maybe unburdening to me acted as a natural relaxant.

I hardly slept all night. My mind feels like my stomach does after Thanksgiving dinner: too full for comfort, and the rest of my body is useless as a result. My mother's story fills my mind but not enough to distract me completely from you, Ben. Joseph's wife will be at the ordination today with their baby. I should be sitting beside her with you on my lap, trading war stories of motherhood like happy martyrs.

The cab collects us at noon and drives maniacally through the streets of Rome, heading for the mountains. I look meaningfully at Lena, waiting for her to chastise the driver, but she merely smiles knowingly. I grip the edge of the seat and close my eyes.

Lena becomes increasingly fidgety as we near the seminary. She points out ordinary sites with a catch in her voice. "That's the train station," she says like no one else could have recognised it from the platform and tracks. "The trees completely shade the road," she observes another time. I can only nod without understanding.

I glance over at her every few minutes. Her eyes remain fixed on the window and she is biting her carefully filed nails. An uneasiness settles over the car. As we climb, the calmness takes on an eerie quality. It is as if the trees not only hide us from the sun but cocoon us in our own little world. No birds call, no wind whistles through the greenery. In the silence, my mind slips back to my childhood. The more I think about Lena's story, the more my past makes sense.

When I was ten, Ruth dropped Simon and me off at my house after school to play.

"Tell your mom I'll be back in an hour to collect Simon," she called to me as she drove away.

We bustled in the door to find my mother sitting on the floor, her eyes red and flowing, her shoulders jumping violently.

I ran to her and only then noticed the letters strewn about her. Those secret letters she read with such concentration that I had learnt not to bother interrupting her. Once, the pan on the stove went on fire and I threw a wet towel over it as we had been taught to do in school. My mother had merely grunted her approval and returned to her letter. But this latest one, the one she clutched in her hand, must have contained something truly dire. Ignoring Simon, she pulled me to her chest and I was too afraid and distressed to let go.

Simon, thankfully, had the presence of mind to know this was not normal and he phoned his mother. It wasn't long before he was opening the door to Ruth. She pulled me away from my mother and ushered me and Simon into the sitting room off the kitchen. We pressed our ears up against the door and, after a few minutes, I squinted through the keyhole to see Ruth pouring tea and putting an arm around my mother.

"Lena, you'll be all right," Ruth said and my mother nodded.

I sat back. She hadn't nodded when *I* asked her not to cry. She had cried more.

Their words were muffled by the kettle reboiling and noise from outside filtering in the windows but we caught some of it. The letter had brought news, Lena said. A friend of hers, who she didn't name for Ruth, had died.

I walked away from the door and sat on the couch. Simon watched me thoughtfully.

"Who wrote your mom those letters?"

I said nothing, ignoring Simon's quizzical look.

"Her friend died," he said.

I shrugged.

Simon walked over to the shelf and lifted down a pre-made circular train track. He put it on the floor and traced the tracks with his fingers. "I'd be sad if my friend died."

I stood up and lifted down a bag of model trains. I tipped them onto the rug beside the couch and Simon began rummaging through them eagerly. We fitted a couple onto the tracks and began pushing them around. It was an old toy and we had to concentrate to keep them from slipping off.

"Simon, honey, we're leaving now, come on."

I watched him stand up at Ruth's call.

"Hope your mom is okay," he said.

I re-arranged the trains on the track. "Lena can look after herself."

He laughed. "Do you call your mom 'Lena' now?"

I didn't say anything.

Ruth opened the sitting room door. "Simon, I said, let's go. Mattie, dear," she bent down, "your mom is a bit upset because she got some sad news, so I'm going to come back and stay the night with you guys, okay?"

I wanted to scream that I could take care of my mother on my own but Ruth was already leaving.

"I'll be back as soon as I've picked up my night things. Simon can come back with me and you guys can have a sleepover."

Simon beamed but I didn't react. I just kept pushing those damned trains around and around the circular track.

Lena never told me who wrote her that letter, or who had died. But I know now that there is only one place that letter could have come from. That was the first time I called my mother 'Lena'. She let the seminary and her priest shape our lives more than she realised.

Watching a tear fall silently down my mother's cheek as she

looks out the window of the cab, I feel something beyond my usual resentment. I cradle a pang of personal empathy for a woman who, despite knowing deep down that she hasn't lost everything, still feels like she has.

TWENTY-TWO

Mattie

"Stop the car!"

I leap at the sudden demand. The cab driver twitches in his seat too. He babbles in Italian but Lena screams it again and bangs the headrest in front of her. I shout at her to calm down, mixed with yells at the cab driver to stop. Muttering angrily, he pulls the car into a ditch off the narrow roadway. Lena opens her door forcefully and rolls out.

She stumbles over to the nearest tree and leans against it, gasping in huge breaths and retching. I run around to her.

"Lena!" I don't ask her if she's all right – she obviously isn't.

"Oh Mattie," her words tremble on her tongue, "I don't know if I can do this."

I take my arm from her shoulder and step back. "You said none of them will be there."

"I know, I know. It's just . . . the memories."

I run a hand through my hair. "Lena," I say softly, "I get it. I don't want to go either. I don't want to see Joseph's baby. I mean, what if they ask me to hold him?"

Lena looks at me and I know she can see her own fear reflected back in my face.

"But Ruth paid for us to come here," I say. "This is Aaron's day, not ours. We have to do this, Lena, okay?"

She shakes her head like I just don't understand. She walks further in through the trees and I follow her. The view of vine-covered mountain after mountain leaning against the vast blue sky catches my breath. I remember the letter.

"When did Levi die?"

"What?" Her head snaps up. "Levi didn't die! Did he? What are you talking about?"

I lift my hands in a gesture of surrender. "You got a letter . . ."

"A letter? When?"

The cab driver calls over to us but we simultaneously wave him away.

"Years ago, when I was a kid. You got a letter and you couldn't stop crying. Your friend had died. I thought . . . was that not Levi?"

Lena dips her head into her hands and shudders out great, hacking sobs. I go to her and try to comfort her with touch and voice but she is inconsolable. Eventually she lifts her head.

"I can't believe you remember that."

I give an incredulous sniff. "Ruth had to stay the night with us because you wouldn't stop crying."

Lena stares at me. Out of nowhere, she plants a kiss on my cheek, her eyes drying. "I made life difficult for you, didn't I?"

My mouth drops open.

"It was my friend Marthe," Lena shudders, "who wrote me that letter. She didn't mention Levi in it. He didn't die."

"Well, someone did. Simon and I heard you telling Ruth."

Lena nods. "Yes, someone did. Someone gentle and kind. Someone who saved me when she could have left me crying in a black church in Rome."

My chest tightens. "Agata?"

Our driver begins to beep at us and Lena starts to move back through the trees towards the cab. I follow her eagerly.

"Did she ever find out? About you and Levi?"

"No. She never knew of my betrayal. It was cancer. It took her over very quickly and she was gone within months. Marthe was with her when she died."

Her voice weakens, as though Agata's cancer is eating away

at her as she speaks. "They prayed right to the very end but Agata wouldn't let Marthe pray for her. She made Marthe pray with her for everyone else they knew. Including me."

"Oh, Lena."

My mother's eyes are wet again. "She prayed for me in her last hours. If I get into heaven when I die it will be because of her."

I bow my head and think of Agata, the woman I have to love because she took care of my mother before I was around to do that.

"Mattie," Lena grabs my arm urgently, "I'm here. I'm here for you."

I frown, not knowing what she means, until I turn and see that a car has pulled in to the side of the road. It is not a cab. The driver, who has got out to converse with ours, is Simon. I know without having to check who is with him. A violent bout of nausea punches at me from inside my stomach.

"Mattie, what's going on?" Simon picks his way over the ditch to us. "Lena!" He starts on seeing my mother's tear-stained face. "What's wrong?"

"Oh Simon, dear . . ." My mother wipes her face with one hand while halting Simon with the other. She is in control now and I hang back, concentrating on my breathing. "I wasn't feeling well and I had to get out of the car for some air. But I'm much better now, thankfully. We were just about to continue up to the *semin* . . . the seminary. Go on ahead. We'll follow you."

Simon falters, looking past her to me. "I'd offer to take you the rest of the way," he says, "but there's not much room. I have Joseph and his wife, you see. And of course there's the baby seat."

I stare resolutely at the ground, refusing to meet his eye. I can sense Lena glance shiftily in my direction.

"That's fine, Simon, dear, we have the cab. Why don't you get going and we'll meet you up there?" She physically pushes him back towards his car but I can already see it happening. Joseph is getting out of the front seat and his wife, an attractive brunette, is standing, bending back into the car, scooping something out.

"Let's do the introductions now," Joseph calls, walking over with his little family in tow.

They stop at Simon's side and Lena steps back in line with me. The gap between our groups seems to stretch for an eternity.

"Hi, Lena, Mattie," Joseph says slowly. "I'd like you to meet my wife, Serena. This is our son, JJ."

"Nice to meet you, Serena," Lena says calmly.

I look at the baby boy. He is flapping his arms and legs enthusiastically at these new surroundings and faces. His cheeks are chubby and puffy from teething but he coos with delight so it must not be hurting him. I wait for the anguish to envelop me, for my legs to give away but they do not. This boy isn't you, Ben. No other baby will ever be you. The thought makes me want to cry but relief carries me through. I don't see you in this baby's face and that means I can breathe. For Ruth and Simon and Aaron, I will be able to get through the day.

I take a deliberate step forward. Lena takes in a sharp breath at my movement.

"Hello, Serena. He's a lovely baby."

Lena grips my arm and the brothers exchange relieved glances. Simon looks down at me with something like pride.

"Thank you, Mattie," Serena whispers.

To spare me further effort, Joseph turns to her. "We'd better get going."

"See you up there!" everyone seems to be calling to each other while I stand, rigid, and watch their car drive on ahead. Our driver taps his watch and I hold up my finger for him to wait one more minute.

"Are you all right, Mattie?" Lena whispers.

I nod, then turn to her. "You know, forget what happened with Levi. I think Agata would have been happy at the thought of you coming back here, to the place where you were such good friends."

Lena smiles at me through watering eyes and takes my hand. "We can do this," she says, her voice strong.

Together, we walk back to the car and proceed to the seminary.

TWENTY-THREE

Lena

There are priests waiting to greet us when we arrive. Father Pietro takes my hand without the smallest sign of recognition. Nothing comes out when I try to speak and Mattie quickly steps in.

"We're here for Aaron. We're friends of the family."

I try to nod but I can only stare. Father Pietro had seemed old when I met him a lifetime ago. Now he looks simply ancient. Short and wizened, his white hair has receded to a few feathery wisps. But he shakes my hand with the strength of a much younger man.

A seminarian offers to take us through to the dining hall where there is tea, coffee and light refreshments being served before the ordination begins. We walk through the main courtyard, past the entrance to the chapel and by the building where the teaching rooms are. None of it has changed. I would swear even the cracks in the walls have not been fixed or added to in over twenty years. The warmth of the day lasts only in the direct sunlight. Once we enter the sheltered, interior courtyard, a chill settles over us. Our guide directs us with his hand into the dining room with a shy smile.

Inside is throbbing with bodies. I take Mattie's hand and we push our way through the mothers, fathers, aunts, uncles,

237

priests, seminarians and nuns all milling around the one long oval table that takes up most of the room. People are spilling out onto the balcony to admire the view and into the neighbouring rooms for space.

I see Ruth in the corner with her family and wave to her.

Beaming madly, she strides over to us, looking a million dollars. She has pitched it just right. Her dress is a mixture of loud and tepid colours splashed together. It screams celebration yet is an understated cut that suits her ample figure and acknowledges her age. Her hair is blow-dried into vibrant curls and her tall heels cover her toes respectfully.

"Congratulations!" Mattie and I gush together.

Ruth thanks us profusely, her whole being swelling with pride. People bump into us as they try to pass and Ruth smiles widely at them all.

"Where's Aaron?" Mattie asks, surely noticing with relief, as I do, that Simon, Joseph and Serena are staying in the corner with two men I recognise as Aaron's school friends who had joined us for dinner in Rome.

Ruth scours the room and I use the excuse to look around too, half-expecting to see Marthe, Lucia, Christoforo . . . Agata . . . coming towards me with open arms.

"Aaron was here a few minutes ago. He went for a walk with Ed. I know he must be nervous but he is acting perfectly calmly. It's such a big day for him, for all of us. I hope he's not too overwhelmed. He is prepared though. And he looks wonderful. The cassock suits him so well. Some people were born for it, Lena, don't you know what I mean? Born for it!"

I manage to smile weakly as she keeps talking and waving at various people across the room.

"Lena," Mattie comes to my rescue, "Aaron probably had the right idea getting outside. Shall we go for a walk before Mass starts?"

Ruth jumps in before I can answer. "Yes, yes, do. The grounds are magnificent. Wander around. There are seminarians on duty for the day to make sure no one gets lost. Just make sure you're back on time! You'll want to get a good seat!"

I wonder if the chapel has been extended. There will be problems fitting everyone in otherwise. I link Mattie's arm and we stroll back out the front and around to the left of the building. The narrow river still runs along the side, lined with colourful shrubs and plants. We make our way down a garden path and come out near the fields.

"The seminarians work the vineyards as part of their daily routine. Or at least, they used to," I say.

Mattie seems interested. She asks me where Agata and the nuns lived so I walk her back around to the front. We pass Father Pietro making his way into the main building. He nods at us, pausing ever so slightly longer on me. I speed up, hurrying Mattie along. The nuns' quarters are barred off but we crane our necks to see the beginnings of their own private courtyard.

"So little has changed," I tell my daughter but the absence of Levi makes it a completely different place. The memories leap out at me from every stone I once trod, from every door I entered and flower I picked.

A seminarian, so young that even Mattie adopts a motherly expression, comes over to us. "Excuse me, the ordination will begin soon."

We follow his lead back to the chapel and I notice the lack of the sounds I was used to hearing in the *seminario*. There are no crickets, no chirpings. I like to think they have all stopped to pay their respects to Aaron and the six others being ordained.

"Will you be able to go into the chapel?" Mattie asks.

At first, I don't know what she means. Then I remember all of the important occasions when I shunned Mattie to avoid entering a church. I assure her I will be fine and she shrugs. I open my mouth to explain but the words won't come. This chapel has been the reason for my avoidance all those years. I am back at the start.

Ruth is suddenly at my side and we join the queue waiting to enter. "I'm so excited, I can't breathe. And deacon is only the first step! Can you imagine what I'll be like next year when he actually becomes a priest?"

We walk in and I cannot help it – I gasp. Not one part of the chapel has been altered. The centre-facing pews, the elaborate gold altar, the decorative pillars keeping it all upright – they are unchanged. Without direct sunlight, the stained glass does not shine like it did during my time. I am overtaken by an urge to describe to Mattie and Ruth how spectacular is it when it is lit up properly.

Ruth and Ed are herded with the rest of the families towards the black velvet rope that separates the centre-facing pews from the benches for the nuns and laity. For this special occasion, family members of the six men being ordained are permitted to sit in the front.

Mattie and I take a seat in the back section which is filling up quickly. Aaron's school friends sit behind us. I notice Joseph and Ruth are conversing at the rope, holding up the rest of the line. Mattie and I exchange a look as Ruth pushes past her son and makes her way over to us.

She leans in to us. "Serena and Joseph want to stay at the back in case little JJ causes a fuss." She says this with an air of impatience, as though Joseph should know that no grandson of hers would dare need feeding, changing or do anything other than sleep quietly during an ordination. "You and Lena can take their seats. Come on!" She grabs Mattie's arm, pulling her up.

I hesitate. I was never allowed past the rope during my time here. The one and only occasion I ventured further than the back seats was to say my goodbye to Levi. I start to stammer an objection – that we would be imposing – but it is clear Ruth is not willing to let the numbers supporting Aaron dwindle and before I can really panic about the situation, we have passed the rope and a seminarian with a check-list is leading us up the aisle. I hold my breath as the two of us follow Ruth, Ed and Simon into the pews. They sit in the front row while Mattie and I take two free seats directly behind them. Other families sit beside and opposite us while the remainder of the centre-facing pews are filled by seminarians.

An elderly man leans towards me. "Who are you here for?"

I barely get Aaron's name out before he starts telling me about his own son. Ruth, sitting in the front, turns around to shush us.

I am wondering whether the seminarians will intone the Mass when a clatter of organ pipes make us all jump. I look up at the balcony, complete with organ, which stretches to cover the entire back section of the chapel. It is full of a choir, at least twenty, all dressed in black. I squint to confirm that there are women amongst them but, as soon as they start singing, it is confirmed. Unable to contain myself, I lean forward.

"Ruth," I whisper, "do you know who is singing?"

She turns back to me. "It's a choir from the city, I believe."

The man beside me coughs pointedly and I sit back. I wonder what Levi would make of them. I remember him telling me that he preferred smaller choirs, with one or two per part. It is more intimate, he said. He certainly hadn't needed a large balcony to fit his group – they usually stood in the centre aisle just in front of the velvet rope. I try to enjoy the loud and complicated piece they are singing, sure it is meant to be cheerful as part of the celebration. I would give anything for Levi to work his talent on them.

The choir stops but the organ keeps going and the six seminarians being ordained walk in from the back of the chapel, Aaron leading the way. I can see Ruth trembling below me and I know it must be taking all her effort not to clap.

I hadn't anticipated, though perhaps I should have, what an integral part music would play in the ordination. The high Masses and Vespers I attended during my brief stay in the *seminario* had been almost fully sung. It should not surprise me that an ordination would be the same.

As I watch Aaron and his fellow seminarians move through the stages of the ceremony, I think of Levi and what it must have been like for him at his own ordination. For once, not to have been focused on his choir, but to hear them sing for him as he committed to a life with God. I wonder if he thought of me on that day.

The service is long – almost three hours – yet I only feel the time slow during the long homily given by a grey-haired priest who I guess is Father Pietro's successor. Aaron is one of two English-speaking seminarians being ordained, the others are

Italian and French. We therefore have to sit through two translations.

"Welcome, all, to the ordination of the men before you. They are your sons, or brothers, or friends – but, most of all, they are fellow human beings devoting their lives to the service of the Lord."

He continues in the same general vein for over twenty minutes. It is obviously meant to be inspiring, with references to prayer, charity and a life-long mission of spreading the gospel, yet it somehow falls flat. I think back to Father Pietro giving his homily in different languages during the retreat. I cannot recall the subject but I do remember listening with interest. Anger flows through me at the dullness being injected into Aaron's special day. I look down at Ruth. She is sitting unnaturally still, drinking in every word. Mattie shifts in her seat beside me, evidently bored. She is staring into space, a space which I notice is conveniently located at the back of Simon's head.

When the priest finally finishes speaking the choir restarts, this time with a quiet timbre. I relax and feel part of the *seminario* again. Closing my eyes, I say a special prayer for Agata who first made me feel at home here.

Though the ordination is in Latin, it is easy to tell when the important part comes around. The candidates are invited forward individually by the bishop and they prostrate themselves on the altar.

Out of the corner of my eye, I see Ruth grasp Ed's hand when Aaron's name is called. Ed covers her hand with his free one. At their intimate gesture, I am hit by a gust of something like loneliness, or regret. I turn away and focus on Aaron. He is surrounded on the altar not only by the bishop in his ornate and decorative robes but by a group of priests, all raising up their hands and praying along with the bishop.

I keep my head down when lining up for Communion, and am relieved that I end up kneeling before the bishop to receive rather than Father Pietro, who ministers halfway down the chapel to those behind the dividing velvet rope.

Finally, it ends. As though the Lord Himself is partaking, a stream of light shines through the stained glass at the last blessing, lighting up the altar and the rows in which we sit. I lift my hand to shield my eyes, feeling like I am sparkling as the distorted light falls on me.

"*Ite, missa est.*"

"*Deo gratias.*"

As we all respond to the dismissal, I am surprised to hear Mattie sing the response softly beside me. She has been silent for the whole Mass. I look at her with a raised eyebrow. It must have been an automatic reaction from what they taught her at St Nicholas's. I am so glad in that moment that I forced religion on her as a girl, even if I could never bring myself to accompany her to Mass. She is able to appreciate what is happening here, in the place I found true love, and today that means something to me.

The procession starts to a lively motet from the balcony choir, the organ clanging over the voices. Ruth is dabbing her eyes as we stand to watch the new deacons follow the bishop and priests outside.

We begin to process slowly after them and I feel time teasing me once again. There is only about an hour left here before we have to leave. The newly ordained will be dining with their families tonight so we will meet Aaron later in the city. We will have two more days of sightseeing and packing before we fly home. All too soon, it will be over – again.

Outside, the families and members of the *seminario* are all pushing towards the main dining hall where Aaron and the other new deacons are waiting. There is a wildness about the surge – everybody wants to be the first to offer congratulations. I put a hand on Mattie's arm and we hang back.

"Nearly there, Lena," she says quietly and I stare ahead, glad the crowd is moving quickly ahead, giving us space.

But Ruth and Ed urge us on impatiently.

"Lena, Mattie, let's go, I want to see Aaron." Ruth beckons us on before melting forward into the throng.

I make to follow her, my head somehow clearer with less people milling about. I notice that the *seminario* sounds are back – the little creatures, the babbling of the river. The wind winds around the buildings, catching hollows and curves, producing a musical resonance.

"Lena?"

I stop. Even as I shut my eyes with the assumption that the voice is in my head, I feel Mattie turn beside me and know she heard it too. My heart freezes and melts at the same time. I gasp audibly. With all my soul, I pray.

TWENTY-FOUR

Lena

The wind catches my hair as I spin like a Hollywood starlet. There is no crowd this time. Just him, walking towards me against the backdrop of the *seminario* chapel. Dressed in black, same as I remember, this time with a collar. The whole world sways and I think I will faint. But he does not slow and I do not have time.

He stops in front of me, blocking the cooling air from my face. He is older. His thinning hair is not as black as it once was but is not grey either. Lines have matured, rather than ruined, his face. With an open mouth he looks down at me, the richness of his eyes unchanged. I cannot move.

"You're here?" His question is not angry or even disbelieving. It is confused, like a man waking from the depths of a vivid dream who is unable to place his reality.

For a moment we stare at each other, as we once did a long time ago.

Then his face breaks into a smile and this time his jubilant words ring high into the air. "You're here!"

Without hesitation he bends down, wraps his still-strong arms around me and enfolds me in a hold so solid my feet leave the ground. I hang from him, immobilised by my own disbelief. When he makes no move to release me, I start to breathe again.

With a raw anguish, I am squeezing him back, tears falling unrepentantly from my eyes. He hushes me gently. At the sound of my name on his lips, I yearn all the more.

I have been held by other men, but none like Levi. His body encircles me with an invisible layer of protection. I whisper his name into his neck as he returns me to the ground. The instant my feet find land again, Mattie returns to my mind.

I turn to see her staring at me. I step towards her.

"Lena?" she says gently, touching my arm.

"Darling," I wipe my eyes, wanting to reassure her.

"Who is this?" Levi's voice is enthusiastic, interested. "Lena, you have a daughter?" He looks at me with something beyond love – like he is proud of me. I see his mistake. He thinks I have done what he asked and lived a full life. Gathered a family around me and forgotten our short time as soul mates.

A wave of nausea hits me as he moves around me to Mattie. I had brought her here to tell her about Levi; to show her where I experienced the greatest love of my life. But I never, ever expected that he would be here. Twenty years later! This wasn't supposed to happen. Mattie was not supposed to meet Levi. It is too late to prevent it. I try to step in front of my daughter as she glides forward to shake his hand but my feet are stuck to the ground.

"Yes, I'm Lena's daughter. You must be Father Levi," she says with a hint of uncertainty.

I feel lightheaded. The *seminario* spins, worse than in my dreams. I realise I am holding my breath but I don't dare take in air. How to stop it, how to stop it?

Do I want to stop it? Maybe somehow, deep down, this is what I wanted to happen. To save one I had to sacrifice the other. For all these years I have been protecting Levi when I should have been on Mattie's side.

He laughs at my daughter's guess. "Goodness! I have not been known by that name for many years."

Mattie glances at me and does a double take at my terrified face. She returns her stare to Levi, as though transfixed. "Oh, sorry. Lena told me that 'Levi' was your name."

"Certainly that was how she knew me. But, as I explained to her once, Levi was my *seminario* name. I used it when I was training here. Have you studied the bible? Do you know who Levi was?"

My daughter tilts her head to the side, trying to remember what she learned in St Nicholas's. The breeze whips up again. My tense body withstands the blow.

"The Levites were priests, weren't they?"

"Ah, in the Old Testament, yes. People are less familiar with the Levi of the New Testament, as he is more commonly known by another name." He smiles again, that warm, loving smile. "My parents gave me that other name when I was born and I use it now."

"Levi . . ." I try to gasp it out but my plea gets stuck in my throat.

He continues, unaware of the damage he is about to inflict. "You probably know the New Testament Levi as 'Matthew'. So while your mother knew me as Levi, you can call me Father Matteo."

He is still smiling. He has not noticed her face drop as the enormity of his words hits her. But it will not be long.

"And what is your name, dear?"

My daughter looks straight into his eyes. She must see there what I have been looking at in her for twenty years – a wide brow, long eyelashes, hazel rings around the pupils. Her words croak out like the cry of a wounded sparrow.

"I'm Mattie."

I watch it unfold, helpless. The jerk of his head in disbelief. The gaze of my daughter at my love – her father.

Blackness descends and as I fall I see the ground rise up to meet me, as Lucifer himself draws me down, down, down for my sin.

TWENTY-FIVE

Mattie

The man for whom I was named and who actually has the word 'Father' as part of his name, looks at me in a way I know I will never forget. Like I am an angel sent from the highest heaven.

We stare at each other in agony and awe, until a thud breaks our mutual shock. I stare down to see my mother lying on the ground. Father Matteo bends at once and shakes her, trying to wake her. She stirs at his touch.

"*What's going on?*"

I hear Ruth's shrill call and look up to see her bustling over with Aaron and Simon in tow. A few others who had loitered after the ordination scurry over to help but thankfully most of the crowd are inside the dining hall. I back away to let Ruth kneel beside Lena. She questions Father Matteo without looking at him, thinking he is just another priest who happened to witness her friend's fall. I am overcome with a bizarre desire to laugh. Simon's hand on the small of my back steadies me.

When Father Matteo appears incapable of answering Ruth's questions, she swivels around to me. "Mattie, what happened?"

Every face is suddenly staring at me but the only person I can focus on is the priest. He gazes back. Before Ruth can explode at everyone's lack of response, Lena stirs and struggles to sit upright. The attention of the growing crowd is redirected at my mother as Ruth crouches down to help her.

Only Father Matteo and I look elsewhere – at each other. In that moment, we communicate in a way I never have with another person: total understanding through silence. I am his and we had not known it. Lena never had any intention of telling either of us. There are a million things to say, and yet nothing. This is a meeting that should never have happened. I hear Lena rasp my name and my own knees falter.

"Simon," I turn and grip both his arms hard, "I have to get out of here. Can you take me back to the city? Now?"

"Mattie, what's the matter?"

"Now, Simon." I lean against his chest and breathe deeply once before lifting my head, still clinging to his arms. "I need to go. Will you take me or do I have to start walking?"

Without another word he puts his arm around me and steers me over to his car. "Joseph," he calls to his brother, who comes running with an uncharacteristically serious expression on his face. "I have to take Mattie back to Rome. I'll call you later, okay?"

"You all right, Sis?" Joseph peers down at me but I turn my head away.

I am sure the brothers are exchanging looks of puzzlement. I don't care.

Simon hands me into the passenger seat and jogs around to his own side. I stare through the car window at my mother making uncertain attempts at standing. As he speeds away I don't look back or answer his anxious questions. I say nothing for the journey while tears flow and, following several unsuccessful attempts, he stops asking and concentrates on the road.

When Simon stops the car outside our self-catering apartment, the afternoon sun is fading and the tears I let fall during the journey have stopped. He switches off the engine and clutches the steering wheel tight in his fists.

"Mattie," he makes an effort to sound commanding and I roll my tired head across the headrest to stare at him, "if you don't want to tell me what's going on between you and Lena, I won't force you. But I've left my brother's ordination for you. I have to at least know that you're okay."

I don't know what to tell him but he's right, I have to give him something. "She had a secret, you see. Lena had. One she never planned on telling me."

Simon nods me on eagerly.

I twist my head so I am facing the front window. "It came out today. She knows I'll never forgive her. That's why she collapsed."

"Mattie," Simon touches my shoulder, "I don't know what she did but she's your mother."

I look at him. "And you were my best friend. Things change."

He stares back and I try to find truth and answers in his eyes, the only place I've been able to find them before. I know that my heart will be forever yours, Ben, but in this moment I wonder if Simon could be my other great love. Is there such a thing?

Simon and I never had any serious drama like Lena did with her Levi. No sneaking around seminaries in foreign lands. For us, love was getting through the normal days. I held his hand at his grandmother's funeral. We sat oblivious to others in the school yard, talking our way through lunchtimes.

When we first crossed that line from best friends to lovers, we both felt it, the possibility that this was forever. I lock eyes with him now and know we are both remembering that awkward moment of initiation.

We had been in his house. His family was away. We were alone. We spent the evening eating pizza, watching films and ignoring the oppressive tension that clouded the mansion.

"Do you want to come upstairs?" he had asked, clearly terrified, and I felt my own courage rise because of it.

"Okay."

We walked hand in hand to his room. I stared at the bed in front of us. It looked strange and unfamiliar. Then Simon's hands were on my shoulders, turning me towards him, staring at me not in a lustful way, yet with real longing.

"Will it hurt? They say it hurts," I whispered.

I expected reassurance, cajoling even. But Simon raised his

shoulders and let them drop with weight. "I don't know, Mattie. I've never done it."

I gaped and asked, "Bonnie?"

He shook his head and I believed him. I named the others girls he'd dated since her but I knew each answer before he denied them in turn. We were equals in every way. Young, vulnerable and in love. It was the start of what could have been an amazing life together if I had not later ruined it all.

Perhaps Simon is my Levi – a love I let go for a reason I thought was valid at the time, but which I fear now I will always regret.

I lean across the car and kiss him. He freezes – I feel his body tense against mine. Just when I expect him to respond, he pulls away.

Sitting back in the car, he brushes a hand through his hair. "I'm sorry I kissed you the night we first met in Rome, the night we went for dinner. I only wanted to tell you how sorry I was about Ben and words weren't enough. I'm sorry."

As usual, my chest constricts at the mention of your name. "You're still with her, aren't you?" My heart is too full of you for any more sadness, yet my body stiffens with his answer.

Simon lowers his voice. "Mattie, I went to you. I asked you to come back to me. I was willing to do anything for you. But you chose your college boy so I opened myself up to Ingrid. I liked her then, and I have grown to love her. Very much. More than I ever thought I would. You were my first love . . ."

". . . but she's the one," I finish for him.

Without waiting for him to respond, I open the car door to get out. It takes huge physical effort, like I am recovering from an illness. I step out in front of a cyclist who has to swerve to miss me. He rings his bell and swears in Italian as I flatten myself against the car.

Suddenly, Simon is beside me.

"Mattie, let me help you."

I shake him off. "It's okay, Simon." I try to sound sincere, but every inflection is a labour. I want to lie down. "Really. I'm fine. Go back to the seminary. Apologise to Aaron for me – tell him I was feeling sick."

He tries to object to leaving me but I wave him away. What he said is true – he did leave an important family celebration at my request. I am not his responsibility and will detain him no longer. And my bruised heart wants him gone.

"What will I say to Lena?" he calls from the bottom steps of the apartment as I make my way up.

I turn. "There's nothing to say. Goodbye, Simon."

I walk straight to my suitcase upstairs and thrust my hand into the interior pocket. I pull out the single white stone Lena gave me from your grave. I collapse face down on the bed and think of you, Ben, caressing the pebble between my fingers. I am half a world from your resting place. You are so far away from me right now, I wonder if I will ever get back.

TWENTY-SIX

Mattie

It is a beautiful thing, coming home. No matter how much the traveller or the world might have changed during time spent away, there is a sense of resolution and rest that only home can invoke.

Some might think it sad, Ben, that home for me is a grave. You are truly all I have left. Lena thought she could repair the damage she inflicted on our relationship when I was a child by taking me to Italy. She declared her intention to undo the neglect and the distance by revealing herself openly to me. Even in that she could not be truly honest.

She never intended to lay bare the whole truth to me, just that part of it which suited her. Perhaps her plan was purely selfish – maybe Ruth's offer of a ticket to the seminary was too much to refuse but she needed help, a crutch to get through it, so she brought me. Or maybe I am being overly harsh in my attempt to deal with the truth about my past.

Because it is *my* past, though Lena would claim it as her own. Her priest Levi, or Father Matteo as he is now known, is my father. Had she any inkling that he would be at Aaron's ordination, she would not have brought me there. She would have kept me in the dark forever. Uncovered just what was necessary to establish a relationship with me but not enough to satisfy my need for a true family.

It is too late now. I will never speak to her again.

Your grave has not changed much during my week away. I worried that it might have begun to tarnish or dirty. The willow tree that protects a number of graves in the area kept yours clean from any major travelling debris. I only need to do some basic tending. I rake the stones, remove some fallen leaves and polish the tombstone. Within half an hour it is like I never left. If only that were the case.

Italy changed everything. The knowledge of my real father made me lose the man I had thought was my dad all over again, but in a different way. I don't blame Lena for leaving Damien. He was a drunk and a bully who was no good for her. I don't remember much, except all of our screams. His, as a weapon. Hers, in defence. Mine, in a closet, in fear.

I always wondered why he didn't fight for me. My few gentle memories of him whispering his own version of my name – Tilda – had convinced me that he did love me. I could never reconcile that with his complete lack of contact after Lena took me away. Now I know. He must have left because Lena admitted the truth, that I wasn't his.

Once I used Damien's name for me, to provoke Lena. I made Simon help me.

"Say it, you wimp!" I hissed before running from the bedroom with him.

It was the week after my mother got the letter about her friend dying and only a few days since I started calling her 'Lena' to her face. The first time I said it she did a double take and looked down at me in confusion, as though she had misheard me.

"What?" I had stood upright in defiance. "It's your name, isn't it?"

She had merely shrugged.

Simon followed me out of the room, fidgeting nervously. I knew he didn't like getting in trouble with adults but I was beyond caring. Since receiving that letter, Lena had been approaching catatonia and I needed to do something to get her back.

I prompted Simon. "Will we watch TV?" I said, loud and measured.

Lena, nursing a cup of tea at the kitchen table, did not look up.

"Okay," he answered. I nodded at him to continue. He took a deep breath and spoke loudly. "Okay, Tilda, let's do that."

At first Lena merely twitched in her seat. After a second her whole body shuddered and she stood, glaring down at the quaking ten-year-old Simon.

"What did you call her?"

I froze, panicked at the anger rippling from her. Simon's mouth was wide as his eyes and only his fear could have made me act.

"He called me Tilda," I said, with attempted conviction. "That's my name, isn't it?"

Her face contorted and eyes bulged to the point where I thought she might strike me. Then she sat back down and opened her arms to me. Unsure but unable to resist, I went to her. She held me to her chest and, though no sobs choked out, I could feel her chest rising and falling with the intensity of an exorcism.

"You must never call yourself that," she said, her voice unrecognisable. "You can call me Lena if you like," she bartered. She gave me a wobbly smile and looked over my head to Simon. "I don't care if she calls me Mrs Smelly-Mom!"

He laughed, as much out of relief as amusement.

"But your name is Mattie. Not Tilda, not anything else. You're my Mattie. Agreed?"

Of course I agreed. I thought it was her way of telling me that we didn't need my dad, that I was enough for her. Now I see she just wanted to use me to keep a connection with the real love of her life.

I arrange some fresh flowers around your headstone – bunches of baby-blue hydrangea because baby boys should have blue. I sing you a lullaby and kiss your headstone. Finally, after preparing myself, I turn to leave.

I stop. A man is standing at the end of your grave, staring down at me. A man with a high brow, a natural olive tan and hazel eyes, dressed in black.

TWENTY-SEVEN

Lena

I knock the bottle back and it clinks against my tooth. Cursing, I press a hand to my mouth. The beer was supposed to help with the pain, not cause more. Stupid bottle. Silly bottle. I giggle into my hand, then sigh as all humour vanishes once again.

It has been two weeks since we returned from Italy. Mattie left me at the airport and has not spoken to me since. I have phoned her, called to her house.

One day I let myself in with my key. She walked straight past me out the door. When I shouted after her asking where she was going she called back, "To a locksmith!"

I am not surprised at her reaction, just saddened by it. I have failed her again. I should have chosen her back then, instead of Levi. But I didn't have that instant connection she seemed to find as soon as she heard she was having Ben. It was only when I held her in my arms as a newborn that my love for her flowed. When I picked Levi, she had not yet stolen my heart – he was still everything to me. That is not excuse enough. For years afterwards I could have told her the truth.

When we visited the *seminario* I truly had no idea that he might be there. Marthe had written to me years before to tell me of his new parish in the north of Italy. I think maintaining the connection was too much for both me and Marthe after Agata died – every drop of ink was a tear for a lost friend. So we stopped our letters and I never found out he'd moved back.

By the time I managed to pick myself up off the ground after fainting in the *seminario*, Mattie was gone. When I called for her Joseph came running over to tell me that Simon had driven her back to Rome. I cried out and pushed past them all, including Levi. My daughter was my one thought. Even in that moment of panic I knew this was my punishment for choosing Levi over her. For her whole life I withdrew from her, craving Levi. Now he was finally standing before me and all I wanted was Mattie.

One of the other seminarians who had rushed over to help offered to take me inside to sit down. I gripped my head, not knowing what to do. Ruth took hold of my upper arm and pulled me away from the concerned group, her face screwed up in anger.

"Lena, you're making a scene at my son's ordination. What on earth is the matter?"

I shook her off. "I have to find Mattie."

"Simon is with her . . ."

"I said I need to find her, Ruth!" The words screeched from my mouth and Ruth hushed me frantically.

"All right, Lena, fine. I'll ask Joseph to call you a cab. It won't be long. Why don't you wait by the entrance?"

She did not offer to stay with me and I was glad of the solitude. As I walked through the courtyard to sit on the wall and wait for my ride, I heard an almost violently whispered conversation behind me and then footsteps coming my way. At first, I thought Ruth was coming back but it was Levi who sat down beside me.

"You're leaving?" he asked against my determined silence.

"Yes, I have to." My words ran together quickly, as though the faster I spoke the quicker I could get to Mattie. I stared down at my hands, unable to look into the face I had dreamed of ever since I left the *seminario*.

"Is she mine, Lena?" he asked simply.

"Yes," I gasped. "I never told her. I didn't tell anyone. I

should have, all those years ago. She's my daughter, I should have told her." I blushed with a hot wave of shame. "I should have told you. I'm sorry, Levi."

"Why didn't you?" His voice remained impassive.

I kept my head down. I longed to read the sentiment in his face but I was too afraid. The day he revealed the truth about his name came back clearly to me. It had been towards the end of our week in the hotel, just before the retreat, when we learned all about each other. Talking about his brother's death had upset him, so I tried to lighten the mood.

"Little Luke and Levi! It has a nice ring to it. I bet you were the cutest kids."

Then Levi explained. "Actually, Levi is not my baptismal name. I only took it when I began my vocation."

My head jerked back in astonishment. I knew so much about this man, yet I didn't know his real name? "Why?" I asked, the word rounding strongly in my mouth.

"My childhood was happy until Luke died. Life was so terrible without him. By the time I joined the *seminario*, I needed a new start. So I took the name Levi."

"Why did you pick that name?"

"It wasn't a random choice. Most people think it is a reference to the Levites, the Old Testament tribe who were priests. But there is a Levi in the New Testament. In biblical times people often had two names. Peter, the head of our Church, was known as Simon until Jesus met him. Thomas was sometimes called Judas. I couldn't detach myself completely from my family. So I took Levi, who was a follower of Jesus, though more commonly known by another name – the name I had been christened."

I tried, unsuccessfully, to stifle a laugh.

"What's so funny?"

"Well, it makes more sense to me now." I patted his hand at his confused look. "I always thought of Levi as, well, essentially a *Jewish* name. My papa was a World War Two refugee, so I grew up around a lot of Jewish families. I've known a few Levis but none who were Christian. It seemed odd that a young,

Italian, Catholic boy would have been named Levi. But I see now it is a chosen name. So what is Levi otherwise known as?"

Levi's voice softened. "He was one of the apostles. Like Luke, he is a highly valued follower of Jesus because he wrote a gospel. You will know him as Matthew. My real name, Lena, is Matteo."

Recalling that intimate disclosure as we sat on the *seminario* wall gave me the courage to look at him. His eyes were wide, searching. He asked his question again, and added a new one. "Why didn't you tell me, Lena? When did you find out?"

I shrank away. I knew what he was asking. Had I known when I left him in the chapel that I was taking his child with me?

"After our car accident, there were tests in the hospital. I found out then."

"Is she the reason you left?" he asked breathlessly.

I nodded, my heart beating fast. He reminded me of Mattie as a girl when she would look to me for answers, for love.

"I knew from the beginning," I confessed finally, "that this was the place for you. I left to protect you, so you could lead the life you were born to live."

"And your daughter?"

"I thought I could give her a father. My old college boyfriend, Damien. He left us when she was still a toddler. It's just been the two of us since then." I bowed my head again. "I knew she'd be okay. But you – I had to protect you."

Levi's hand was suddenly on my own. It was the touch I had longed to feel for so many years yet I was incapable of any emotion beyond fear for Mattie. We sat in silence until the cab arrived.

I jumped up and ran to the car. Levi held the door open after I got in. "Will you come back here again? Bring your daughter if she will come. You will not leave for America without seeing me again?" It was half-question, half-demand.

I nodded.

"She will forgive you, Lena," he said in earnest.

He was wrong.

Mattie was sitting at the kitchen table in our self-catering apartment when I returned from the *seminario*. I glanced past her to the bedroom and saw her clothes askew all over the room. I sat beside her and she glared at me. She leaned forward.

"Yes or no answers, Lena."

I nodded, just as I had to Levi on leaving the *seminario*.

"That man, that Father Matteo – he is the Levi you told me about?"

"Yes," I replied with an unintended whimper.

"And he is my father. Dad – Damien – is not my real dad?"

I wanted to apologise, to take her in my arms and tell her it didn't matter who her father was, in the same way it didn't matter who Ben's father was – one parent can be enough. Like Papa was. Instead I answered as she had asked. "Yes."

Mattie stared at me with a look of hatred. Yes, hatred, that blackest of all emotions. I could feel it seeping from her pores. It made me sick that my own child could feel so poisonous against me.

"When did you find out about me?"

I sighed. Her 'yes or no' questions had ended – she needed more. As usual, she needed a reassurance I could not give her.

"I knew before I left Italy. That's why I left," I answered honestly. It was all I could do for her now.

"You didn't think to tell him about me?"

"I wanted to," I said with feeling. "Of course I wanted to tell him. But it wouldn't have been fair. I couldn't trap him that way."

She gasped.

"Oh Mattie, I didn't mean it like that . . ."

"Don't bother. I get it. Why would you inflict me on him? Bad enough you ended up with me."

"Mattie! It wasn't –"

She cut me off. "I've booked myself onto a flight tomorrow afternoon back to DC," she said. "You can do what you like. You can even move in with my priest-father in that seminary for all I care. I really couldn't give a damn. But you are never to speak to me again." She stood and turned her back on me.

I did not obey her instruction but I might as well have done.

She did not answer me as I pleaded. She packed in silence. When she was finished, she curled under the covers pretending to be asleep. I left her only to run to the internet café around the corner. There was a space left on the flight. I booked it straight away.

The next morning, she made it downstairs before me and got a cab without me. I tried to locate her in the airport but she avoided me. On the flight, when I walked down the aisle to speak to her, she asked the air steward to make sure "that crazy woman" did not come near her.

It seemed excessive. But I understood. She was not merely angry that I had kept the true identity of her father a secret or that I had let her think Damien was her dad. It was the fact that *he* hadn't known. The choice to keep the secret had been solely mine and I made that choice based on something other than her needs. Exactly when she should not have had to cope with it, after the loss of her son, the truth came out and I abandoned her all over again.

I risk another toothache by tilting my head back, tipping the bottle upside down over my mouth and smacking the end with my open palm, hoping for one last trickle. I open my bedroom curtain and see that the darkness has evaporated. I have made it through another night. The reflection in the mirror is not a pretty sight. My hair is sticking up, unwashed for days. My eyes are sunken and my whole face looks like it is in a battle with gravity.

I stagger into the bathroom and stare down at the bath. If there are no more liquids I can put into my body, maybe I should put myself into liquid. I laugh at my wit and turn on the tap. I let the tub fill to the brim so when I step in, water sloshes over the sides. The water is warm but not too hot. I was always good at making baths. Mattie used to love them as a girl.

I lean my head back against the tub and sigh. The combination of drink, warm water and a steamy room lets me unwind for the first time in days. I stare at the taps in front of me, behind which I have tucked the simple chant book Levi gave me when I first sat in on his chant practice in the *seminario*. I have taken to flicking through in while sitting in the bath but I am too tired now to look through it. Steam and sunlight warms the room. I close my eyes and feel my body slacken as I sink into the water.

TWENTY-EIGHT

Mattie

We both stare at each other. The silent communication we shared in the seminary two weeks ago does not come. Instead we are just two strangers, standing by a little boy's grave.

He breaks the silence. "Hello, Mattie."

I swallow. This man is my father. My heart beats powerfully against my ribcage. "What are you doing here?" I only meant to sound curious but I think it came out rude. I try again. "I mean, how did you know where to find me?"

"Well . . ." The priest shifts uneasily. He looks like I feel. "I didn't actually come here for you. I mean, I did want to meet you, talk to you. But that is not why I am here in this graveyard." He takes a deep breath and starts again. "I came to America to see three people. First and most importantly, I wanted to meet you."

"Really?"

"Of course. Lena told me . . ." he pauses, swallowing hard, ". . . she told me you are my daughter."

I nod.

When the priest starts speaking again, his voice is stronger. "I wanted to talk to Lena too. Aaron told me where I could find her. He also told me –" again he stops short, apparently gathering the courage to continue, "where I could find the third person I came to see."

"Who is that?" For a frightful moment I think he means my dad, or the man I thought was my dad, Damien.

"I believe," he steps forward, "that as well as a daughter, I have a grandson."

Instinctively, I move in front of your grave. He does not stir and, recollecting the reality of the situation, I stand aside. I have no need to protect you from this man.

"You *had* a grandson." I gesture towards your grave. "Ben. He died while he was still inside of me."

"What did he die from?" the priest asks.

I stare at him. It is a question no one ever asked, except for me. I hounded the doctors. I rang the man who performed the autopsy at his house demanding answers. Everyone else accepted without the indignation it demanded that 'these things happen'.

"The doctors say there is no reason." I force the words out but they twist my tongue into a knot too tight for unravelling. He says nothing and I feel I must continue. "They say it is usual – *common* – for a baby to just die. Even Ben, who was so alive, so active inside me for so long. There was nothing I could have done."

The priest tilts his head to the side and frowns. I stare back, appalled by his apparent scepticism.

"That's what they said!" I raise my voice, daring him to challenge me as I repeat my defence like a plea. "They said I couldn't have done anything."

"I believe you, Mattie," he says with a small smile. "But I'm not convinced you believe yourself."

For a second – for barely a micro-second – I want to shout at him. He has no right, no right at all coming here and speaking to me in this way. But I absorb the truth of his words. How can a man who I have met once, and for only minutes at that, know this is the weight that has been crushing me? It was my job to keep you alive for a measly nine months. And I couldn't do it. I failed. Just like I failed to make Lena happy.

"Everyone . . . says . . ." I stumble over the words, "it's not my fault. But how do they know?"

It is not tears alone that fall. My whole body shivers violently and I drop heavily to my knees. The skin bursts and the bone bruises under my jeans as I put out my hands too late. I turn and crawl onto the stones I have raked so carefully.

"Ben!" I cry, my voice as gravelly as the earth. "Oh son, I'm so sorry! I'm sorry, Ben!"

Father Matteo was right. Of course I don't believe myself when I parrot back the doctors' useless excuses. How could a baby so full of movement and life stop without a cause?

"It isn't right." I look up at the priest who is standing over me with a face full of something more than compassion – understanding.

"I know," he says.

I move closer to your headstone. "It isn't right. I should have been able to keep him alive. I had one more week until I was due. Why couldn't I keep him alive for one more week?"

I hear the priest move and wait for a comforting hand but he does not touch me. Instead he sits cross-legged on the earth beside me. Irrelevantly, I think about his black trousers getting dirty.

"I've seen you before," he says, as I shift into a sitting position on your grave.

"Where?" I sniff.

The priest's laugh is gentle and without superiority. "Not you, Mattie. I have seen a mother grieve for the loss of her son until it wore her away. Everything that she had been before – fun, bright, a mother to another boy – that all disappeared. Grief is like a parasite. It will feed on you until there is nothing left. Mattie?"

"Yes, Father Matteo?"

He smiles. "Call me Levi. Mattie, when my brother died I watched my mother fragment and each piece of her crumble to dust until that dust was crushed so finely the air gathered it back up and cast her to the heavens. I cannot bear to watch my daughter go through that too."

"But, Levi," I test out his name, "I can't stop myself. He's in my thoughts day and night. I feel him on my skin and moving inside me. When I sleep, I dream about him."

For the first time, Levi reaches out to me. At the last second, he jerks his hand away and strokes your grave instead. "And well you should think of him. Of course he should occupy your mind. You will never be rid of him, nor should you be. But you need not die also."

I open my mouth but he holds up his hand like a teacher. "It is no shame and no failure to live your life. I did. When your mother left me, I devoted my life to God with passion and lived it to the fullest. It does not mean I love her any less."

"*She* didn't." I rush it out, scared an old loyalty will stop me betraying her. "She didn't live her life. You were always in her thoughts and she couldn't love anyone the way she loved you. Not even me." I stop, my mouth dry. It is hard to speak it aloud.

Levi stares at me. "Do you think that was right? Shouldn't she have lived her life? Shouldn't you?"

"That's different," I speak with conviction. "Lena had something to live for – me. And your mother, I'm sorry, but she had you to take care of. I don't have another child. I don't have anyone."

Levi smiles. "Of course you do. You have Lena."

I think of her then as Levi would have seen her when they first met – a young girl, searching, just like us all. He stands and offers me a hand. I take it, letting him pull me to my feet.

"Will you show me where she lives?" he asks, dusting himself off and turning to lead us away without waiting for an answer. He gestures to me to walk with him. "If you don't mind, I will come back again and speak to my grandson."

I give my permission without hesitating. I like the idea of you having other visitors. I look over my shoulder and, as I always do, blow a kiss back to you as we walk out.

"Which way are we going?" he asks.

"Levi –" I break off, feeling awkward but there is no point in stalling. "I'll show you the house but I won't come in. I haven't spoken to my mother since I found out about you."

He stops walking. "You have not spoken to her?" He asks like it is the oddest thing he has ever heard, instead of the most reasonable.

I answer defensively, scuffing the ground with my shoe. "You should understand. Aren't you angry with her? She lied to both of us for years."

"Yes, I was angry," he nods, then immediately shakes his head. "But I know why she did it. She did it for me."

I pause. "Would it have been so awful? Being my dad?"

"Of course not! It would have been an honour. But your mother knew my destiny was life as a priest and she chose to spare me the knowledge of what I was giving up."

"So she chose you, over me. I get why you're not angry. But you must see why I am?"

"Of course. You feel betrayed, and all the more acutely because you and Lena have a special relationship. When you were growing up it was just the two of you." Levi shakes his head like he can read my thoughts. "Lena shouldn't have made you feel second to me. But I watched her after you rushed from the *seminario* – she adores you. And she needs you just as much as you need Ben. The difference is she can have you, if you let her." He sighs. "Who are we to cut from our lives any love we have been fortunate enough to receive? Look at what you can miss out on when you do," he adds, looking down at me tenderly.

We stop when we reach the graveyard gate.

"You must forgive your mother."

A burning resentment twists my stomach. "Just like that, after everything? You don't know what it was like."

"Mattie," he says earnestly, "I know what I'm talking about . . ."

"You don't even know me!"

He opens his mouth to retort but stops. "You're right." He shakes his head, "I don't know you. But I want to. Very, very much."

My anger ebbs away into sadness.

"I have forgiven Lena. You must too." He is doing more than asking, he is imploring me. "It is the only way either of you will find peace. I forgave my mother for succumbing to her grief at my expense. You must do the same." As I open my mouth to answer back, he holds up a hand. "And she's not the only one, as you should know. I don't need to tell you the other person you have to forgive, do I?" He leans in to me. "The doctors are right," he whispers. "But if you can't believe them, you need to forgive yourself. It's not your fault that Ben died."

No one has ever said that to me before. The doctors said it was a natural death. The nurses said I was bound to be upset. Lena told me not to be sad. But no one ever baldly said those words: *it's not your fault*. I expect tears to fall. They do not. I feel light, like the wind.

Levi straightens. "Now take me to your mother, and we can all talk."

TWENTY-NINE

Mattie

I start feeling woozy when I step out of the cab in front of Lena's house.

At first, I think it's the heat or the fact that I haven't been here since before we left for Italy. I stand in the street, looking up at the door in the huge frame, rusting and in need of paint. The plants in their pots on either side of the door are grey and wilting from lack of food and water. As I lift one foot to climb the steps I realise too late that the other cannot hold me and I stumble.

Levi is beside me, steadying me. "Mattie, are you all right?"

A blissfully cool hand presses against my forehead.

"You are very hot. Let's get you inside for a glass of water."

At his words, I gasp. A memory washes over me with such force that I am transplanted back to it. I no longer feel the ground beneath my feet or Levi's hand on my arm. I am sitting in a chair in Lena's house, having just arrived for dinner after a busy day, and she is pouring me a glass of water.

"You look exhausted, Mattie," she scolds, holding the glass under the flowing tap. "The apartment is as ready as it's ever going to be. You should sit and relax for the next week. You're not going to have much time to rest after the baby comes."

"I know, I know, Lena." I smile at my mother, excitement tingling me at the mention of your arrival.

"*Seriously though, Mattie, what were you thinking dragging yourself into town to buy new bedding at this late stage, and on your own?*"

"*I wanted to take advantage of the quiet.*"

Lena frowns. "What do you mean?"

"*He's so busy inside me all of the time. Always squirming and kicking. I haven't been able to do anything physical for months without him attacking me! Don't get me wrong, I love it. But he's finally quietened down, so I grabbed the opportunity.*"

Lena drops the glass. It shatters by her bare feet. I let out a small scream and jump up. Water splashes over the floor as fragments scatter.

Lena does not react. She stands rigid, her neck red and veiny as though holding an emotion hostage in there, leaving no room for air. Her eyes bulge.

I say her name over and over but she doesn't respond. "Lena? Lena?"

"She's not answering. Don't you have a key, Mattie?"

With another gasp, I am back in the present, with Levi still gripping my arm. I glance behind me. We have walked up the five steps to Lena's front door. I don't remember making the journey. Only then do I realise I am calling out her name, like I did that day she dropped the glass.

"Come on, Mattie, you need to sit down for a few minutes. Find your key and I can let us in." Levi's instructions are issued calmly but a touch higher in pitch than usual.

I sense the urgency. I grope around in my bag until the keys scrape against my hand. Levi takes them from me and opens the door. He leads me inside. I know straight away something is wrong. Nothing is overtly out of place but I feel it.

Levi calls out my mother's name. There is no answer. I push him from me and totter further into the house like a drunken infant. He follows me silently as I stagger up the stairs. Her bedroom door is open. My old bedroom door is open. Only the door to the bathroom is closed. I reach out my hand for Levi to take, not knowing why.

The hand that smacks into mine in reassurance is not Levi's, but Lena's. When I open my eyes, I have once more been hurtled back to that day.

Lena's hand is firm in mine, the pressure contradicting her words. "It's probably nothing, Mattie. This is just a precaution."

I ease myself out of the wheelchair, big fat bump first, and shimmy onto the bed. A young, overly eager nurse dances into the room. Lena makes to pull her to the side.

I shout out. "Don't try to keep anything from me. This is my baby. What's the matter?"

"You did the right thing coming in, hon," the nurse says to me. Her movements are bright as she moves to my side. "I'm sure everything is fine but, if you are worried, it is always best to come to us."

I cock my head to stare at Lena, who had dumped me in a chair the moment we arrived at the hospital before conversing with the staff out of earshot.

After she had dropped the glass, she demanded that we take a trip to the hospital. She refused to give a reason other than: "If the baby has been that quiet, we need to check he's all right inside there." It seemed stupid to me. If anything was really wrong, I'd know it, I'd feel it. But she insisted and it was easier to give in. We were silent the whole journey here and, despite my certainty that Ben was just taking a little rest, I felt a panic creeping through me.

The nurse works busily around me. "Mattie, can you lift up your shirt for me?" she says. "We'll do an ultrasound."

Lena watches the nurse squeeze the gel onto my stomach and lift the transducer. I smile. I love this part of the check-ups – hearing the rhythmic thump-thump of another heart in my body. Without warning, Lena reaches over and grabs the nurse's hand, halting her just before she makes contact with my belly.

"Why are you stopping?" I ask, my breathing quickening.

Lena looks at me with watering eyes and a trembling lip and I feel a surge of anger that she is scaring me like this when everything is fine.

"He's just sleeping, Lena!" I spit as much disdain as I can into the words. "He's been going non-stop for weeks – he's taking a little rest."

"When was the last time you felt him move, hon?" the nurse asks gently.

I think. I was out shopping for bedding all day. Yesterday, I cleaned the apartment, delighted I could reach under beds and stretch high into shelves without him denting me.

My voice comes out small. "Two days ago?"

Lena and the nurse exchange a fleeting glance across the bed and that is the moment I know. But it can't be right. I would have known if he was gone. Surely I am not such a poor mother that I didn't realise for two whole days that my baby was . . . no, it can't be. I feel my body begin to spasm. I reach out to the nurse's hovering hand and slam it down, forcing her to press the transducer onto my stomach. We all wait. And wait. I press it harder into me. So hard it bruises. No sound emerges. The nurse speaks loudly to me, trying to pull from me but my grip is iron.

I call your name. I call it when the doctor comes in to confirm. I call it that night as Lena feeds me the medication to soften my cervix for the induction. I call it the next day when they spread my legs to pop my waters. I cry then. You need those waters. You swim in them and breathe like a fish in my goldfish-bowl stomach. They pierce me with an epidural to numb the pain but it only affects the physical. I scream your name again.

Lena calls it too. She sits behind me in the bed where your father should have been, holding me solid while I push you out. When you finally slide out of me into the nurse's waiting hands, I stop calling your name long enough to gasp in air, but it does not fill the hole you left.

We all know you are gone but still we stare at you, hoping for a wail. The silence spreads and fills the room, crushing me inwards. I want to strike you, pinch you, burn you – I would do anything to hear the mere faintest of cries. You loll in the nurse's arms as she dries you tenderly, wraps you in a blue blanket and passes you to me. It is wrong. I know you – you are a kicker, a sportsman. You should be wriggling to escape your swaddle. But you just lie there, unmoving, with your little white face flecked red from my blood.

Behind me, Lena whispers, "He's beautiful." Those words,

and my sobs as I bend over you, are the only sounds to be heard.

A voice breaks the silence except this time it is Levi, not Lena, who interrupts, and it is he who is holding my hand.

"Mattie, maybe your mother isn't here? She might have gone out. Come downstairs and sit for a while, please? You are not well."

I shake my head, refusing to move back from the bathroom door. Carrying death inside me has left a trace – a sixth sense. I push open the door.

I hear Levi's cry even before my legs can buckle. Ben, you lay unmoving in my waters for two days before Lena made me recognise what your stillness meant. I look at the bath and see my mother sleeping in water, just like you.

THIRTY

Mattie

She's dead.

I take a long gasping breath but it's not enough to sustain me. My vision blurs like I am under that water too and my body desolidifies with her. I slide gently into the fall and cover my ears as I curl into the foetal position against the wall.

I have never heard a man scream like this – like a hysterical woman. He cries great blubbering tears and shrieks for help. I don't answer – he's not talking to me. He's raising his hands, his eyes, his whole body towards the sky and though I don't understand the racing Italian gushing from his lips, I know who he is calling on.

My mother is beside him on the floor now. He is kissing her. Her chest rises and falls. My heart leaps – she's alive! But then I realise it's only with each kiss, each puff of air from his own lungs into her that her body responds. Still, that split second of hope galvanises me enough to be of use. I crawl to her side and look searchingly at Levi. Despite his red eyes and blotched cheeks, he is in control. He reaches across my mother's lifeless form and seizes my wrists. He places them firm on my mother's bare chest. He interlocks my limp fingers, grabs my waist and pulls my body upright, so my arms are long and locked.

"Press down, thirty times," he instructs, his accent thicker than it was before. "Hard, hard as you can."

I start, trembling.

He shouts at me. "Harder! Don't worry about hurting her. She's dead. She's dead, Mattie! But we can bring her back. Harder!"

I look from him to my mother's body. Her breasts are drooping towards the floor on each side, as though she is splitting apart.

"No!" I shout. "No, you're not doing this to me! You're not leaving me like this!"

I press down as forcefully as I can, fearful of breaking a rib but not giving in to that fear.

It goes on for a long time. My energy wanes but I don't stop. Levi calls for help on his mobile phone in between giving her puffs of air, while I pump her heart. We keep going, working solidly. He takes over the compressions to give my arms a break. I puff air into her mouth, blowing life back into her, the life she gave me.

Levi and I do not speak again until we hear the crash of the firemen breaking down the front door. Our eyes lock in that moment and I recognise the fear in his, knowing my own face must express the same. We never would have stopped, for anything. We would have kept trying to bring my mother back until the end of time. But now others are here. Others, with their expertise and objectivity and willingness to say it is too late, she is gone.

My breathing accelerates as they pound up the stairs. They shout at us to come into the hall so they can fit into the small bathroom. I stand but Levi doesn't want to leave her.

I lean over and press my hand into his shoulder. "Levi, she needs them. Come on."

He responds to the sound of my voice, though I am unsure if he is processing the words. He lets me bend further and take his hand in mine. I pull him up and lead him into the hallway. Three bulky medics shove past us and kneel around Lena, prodding her and restarting mouth-to-mouth. Colourful pads are stuck to her chest, one of the men yells "*Clear!*" and Lena's body jerks upwards. I whip around and bury my head against Levi's shoulder, my eyes squeezed shut against the sight and sickening sounds.

He wraps me to him and a strange image appears before me, a redundant premonition of how the moment of goodbye might have been. Lena dying of old age in her warm bed and you, my strong, grown son consoling me in the way Levi is now. Instead I am standing with wet feet in a cold and sad hallway, with the Italian priest who unwittingly fathered me clutching me as much for his own comfort as for mine.

I keep my face closed into his chest for the longest time. More beeps, thrashing and urgent conversations between the medics confirm to me that time is passing. Time in which Lena is not responding.

Eventually, I hear an authoritative instruction, almost resigned, from the bathroom. "Last time . . . *clear*!"

I hold my breath against Levi's chest. I hold it while the silence stretches. My head spins and my body vibrates from lack of oxygen but I refuse to breathe. I will not leave her here. I will not let time move me on without the person I need, as it did once before.

I pray. I know Levi is praying too. I press my hand against his heart, beside my face, and think of you with all my might. Suddenly, all of Lena's guardian angels – her papa, Agata, you my darling Ben – join forces to save her one more time. A weak intake of breath leaks from the bathroom. The medics are shouting words I can't make out but which are dripping with relief. I turn to see her exposed, barely-living body twitch as sunlight streams in the window onto her.

In the second before my legs give way, Levi collapses and we crumple together to the floor. A medic darts to our side as we lie in a heap but Levi does not let me go. He whispers that everything will be okay while he sways us back and forth, like an old rocking chair.

THIRTY-ONE

Lena

I wake up and immediately know I don't want to be awake. I close my eyes shut again. I can't remember where I am but I know I don't want to remember. If I do, it will bring pain. But I can't stop my mind flashing the past towards me any more than I can stop my mouth from breathing in air. Both hurt.

There are noises around, all artificial – ticking, clicking and whirring. No one else is here with me. For some reason, that calms me, though I cannot place why. I open my eyes a fraction. When nothing happens, I open them more fully.

I am in a hospital. I can tell straight away from the sparseness of the room and the monitors beside me. What are they monitoring? A wire is sticking out of my arm. I look around and see curtains pulled across a window. They are flimsy – nothing compares to the dark shutters of Italy – and cold evening light bullies its way in through them. I roll to face the other direction and see a door with a round, portal-shaped window in the centre. I lift my head from the pillow. Through that window I see my daughter and Ruth. They are conversing seriously and Mattie appears to be weeping. I try to call out her name and my chest explodes.

I breathe in instinctively and pain shoots again across my torso. Holding my breath inflicts another extreme sensation. I squirm and bang on the bed with my fist. I need to cough but am afraid. Then Mattie is there, calling out to me, and someone else. A woman appears with a stethoscope swinging around her neck. She leans over me and takes my hand.

"Lena, I want you to take slow, short breaths through your mouth – can you do that?"

I shake my head frantically and her demand is issued again, firmer this time.

"Lena, come on now, slow, short breaths. Let's go. In . . . that's it . . . out . . ."

I press my eyes shut, grip Mattie's hand and follow the doctor's instructions. After some time, the pain in my chest fades away into mere discomfort. The doctor is talking to me but I ignore her, looking only at Mattie.

My daughter speaks tenderly. "Listen to the doctor, Lena."

I cast my eyes back to the doctor who smiles at me. "Welcome back, Lena. You are very fortunate. If your daughter had found you any later, we might not have been so lucky."

I try to remember. What happened? Where was I found? I want to ask her these questions but I am afraid my chest will constrict again. I look questioningly at Mattie.

"You were drowning," Mattie chokes. She runs from the room in tears before I can say a word.

I make to sit up, a precursor to running after her, but the effort weakens me and I collapse back on the pillow. I grab the doctor's arm. She seems young.

"What happened?" I wheeze and don't recognise my own voice.

The doctor looks at me sadly. "It appears that you fell asleep in the bath, Lena. You were lucky the water was so warm or you would likely have succumbed to ischemia or hypoxia."

I stare at her vacantly, her words meaning nothing.

"You had a build-up of liquid in your lungs, Lena. That is why your chest hurts. That, and the efforts to restart your heart. Don't worry, it is temporary. We gave you some warmed fluids intravenously to be safe but you should make a full recovery."

"Matt . . ." I begin but the doctor stops me.

"Don't speak unless you need to, Lena. Your daughter is upset – that is natural. She'll come around. They always do. Your friend Ruth is here too. She's beside herself with worry – she won't stop questioning us. Would you like to see her?"

I look around. Ruth's head is bobbing anxiously behind the portal-shaped window in the door. It is clear Mattie has gone. I nod resignedly and close my eyes. When I open them again, Ruth is sitting in a chair beside my bed.

"Hi, Lena," she says quietly.

The last conversation I had with her comes flooding back to me.

She returned from Italy a few days after me and Mattie. I had been so consumed with getting Mattie to talk to me, I had forgotten all about Ruth and the scene I made at the ordination. Until she arrived at my door, her face dark.

At first she said nothing. I stood back to let her in but she shook her head. When she spoke, her words held no anger, just sadness. "How could you, Lena?"

"Ruth, I'm sorry. Come in . . ."

Then the resentment hit. "I don't want to fucking come in!"

I gaped. Ruth never cursed.

"You *ruined* Aaron's ordination. You made him and us a laughing stock. Is it true what they are saying? That Father Matteo is Mattie's dad?"

I drew in a large gulp of air. Levi must have told everyone. Or else Mattie told Simon who told Aaron who told everyone. Whatever way it came out, Levi had been exposed. Everything I gave up to protect him, everything I made Mattie give up – the chance to know her real father – was in vain. I stared at Ruth, unable to bring myself to positively confirm it. I didn't need to. She knew from my twisted face.

"But how is that even possible?" She gestured wildly and I thought she was going to fall off the front step. "You knew the seminary? All this time I've spoken of it, sent my son there and you never mentioned? You lied to me!"

"I never *lied*, Ruth," I said, emphasising the word, but she cast my defence aside.

"Oh, a technicality, Lena. You lied by omission. You let me talk about that place and invite you to my son's ordination. You must have known what would happen when you got there!"

"I didn't, honestly!" I reached out but she backed away, her face full of disgust. "I thought he left years ago, Ruth. He did leave but he came back. If I'd known I wouldn't have gone – I'd never have done anything to spoil Aaron's ordination."

"Don't pretend you care about Aaron. You didn't think about him at all. Or me. Or Mattie, God love the poor child. What is *wrong* with you?"

My breathing quickened and shame twisted my gut in agony. "I don't know, Ruth. I don't know what's wrong with me."

She stared at me coldly. "Well, something's not right, Lena. You don't treat people like that, especially family and so-called friends. I don't want to see you again." She turned her back and walked down the steps.

"Ruth, wait!" I ran outside after her, not caring that I was in my bare feet. "Don't leave, please. I can explain."

"I think you've explained enough," she called back, continuing to walk apace.

"Please, Ruth!" I screamed it, and she turned along with several passers-by. I knew I must have looked utterly pathetic. No shoes or socks, my hair a mess, no make-up. I wrapped my cardigan tighter around my pyjamas as tears streamed down my face. "Ruth, please. Mattie won't talk to me. I don't know what to do."

She took a step back to me. None of the pedestrians moved but it felt like they were closing in around us.

"Back to you again, isn't it, Lena? Did you ever think about me and *my* family? What kind of a start is this for Aaron? To be caught up in your torrid affair. You didn't stop to think how he will be affected, did you?"

I had no response. I hadn't meant to hurt any of them but the damage was done.

"Goodbye, Lena."

She stalked away. I called after her again, desperately, but she continued walking out of my life.

Now she sits before me and I recall the intensity of her anger. I have a strange urge to call for help, like I had once before when lying in a hospital bed and a woman I thought was not my friend came to see me.

Before I can say anything, Ruth bursts into tears.

"I'm so sorry, Lena," she sobs.

I try to make eye contact with her. I know what people will think. It is important to make her understand.

"Accident," I rasp.

She looks up and I hope she believes me.

"I shouldn't have left you like that," she says. "All alone when even Mattie had cut you from her life. You were in need. It was so unchristian of me."

I shake my head again, longing to converse.

"Don't speak," she says firmly. "It's not good for you." She sounds more normal as her bossiness takes over.

"Sorry . . ." I say meaningfully and reach out a hand to her. She pauses – images of Aaron's humiliation clearly tormenting her.

Then, with real tenderness, she intertwines her fingers with mine and smiles. I open my mouth but she lets go of my hand and slaps it gently. "I said don't speak!" Her voice softens. "We have years left to talk, Lena. Rest your throat for now."

"Listen to her, Lena." The doctor reappears in the room. "She needs to rest now, if you don't mind," she says to my friend.

Ruth stands but I cling onto her arm. "About Aaron. I'm sorry."

Her lip trembles. She leans down and kisses my forehead, like a mother. "You'll be fine. I'll come back tomorrow. Mattie will be in to see you later too. It's going to be okay, Lena."

I watch her leave and the doctor turns to me.

"It makes a difference to have friends like her, doesn't it?" she says.

I nod wildly, then stop because it hurts. The doctor tells me to get some rest as it will help my chest heal more quickly. I obey, closing my eyes to let sleep take me over.

When I awake, the curtains are drawn and early morning sunlight is streaming in the window. A lone ray falls on an empty chair in the corner. I turn to see Mattie sitting in another chair beside my bed, reading a book.

At my movement, she closes it slowly and leans forward.

"How are you feeling, Lena?"

I pause, unsure of the answer. I am still tired, but there is only a tightening rather than the pain of yesterday, like someone is pressing down on a fresh bruise.

"Better," I say, trying to keep the rawness out of my voice. "But, Mattie . . ."

"Don't speak unless you have to," she urges. "Your chest is still tender."

It is vital that I tell her this. "It was an accident. Drank too much. Fell asleep. Accident."

At first she just stares at me. Then she stands and walks over to the window into the path of the solitary ray.

"I left you all alone," she says, her voice tight. "I wouldn't blame you . . ."

"No, Mattie!" I say it loud. My throats stings like it's on fire but I don't stop. "I just fell asleep. I'd never leave you like that, never!"

When she doesn't turn around, I push myself upright in the bed.

"Mattie," I say, softer this time, though it hurts just as much, "I know I wasn't the mother you wanted. I've done so many things wrong. But I lost the only parent I knew. I would never do that to you, not on purpose."

Mattie turns in the light and I keep talking, trying to reel her back to me.

"I did my best." She is visibly shivering. "I put Levi first – I didn't tell him about you. But everything after that – going back to Damien, then raising you alone – I did all that for you."

"Would you have asked him to leave his vocation, if it wasn't for me?"

I think about that for a minute, then shake my head. "The *seminario* was where he was meant to be. I guess having you simply made the decision easier to make. If Levi was going to leave, it had to be of his own free will," I whisper hoarsely. "In his own time, and when he was ready. If I had forced him to leave to take care of me and a baby, how could he have forgiven me?"

I close my eyes, exhausted from talking and memories.

When the nurse with the pudding-bowl haircut told me I was pregnant, I had wanted to confide in Levi. He would have gathered me up and run away with me. He would have been devoted to me and the baby, I was sure of it. But he wouldn't have been happy. Alexandre made me see that I had to save him from that. I had to be a mother, a leader, a protector – and not just for my baby.

I made sure Damien and I slept together as soon as possible after I returned, to make it plausible. It was sneaky and dishonest and utterly unfair to Damien, but I did it for Mattie, to give her a family.

I had never planned on telling Damien the truth. But he left me no choice. When he woke up the morning after the umbrella incident, he was face down on our lawn outside. I had dragged him out by the foot, taking no heed of the bumps he sustained in the process. I packed his things and tossed them out beside him. I dropped Mattie to a neighbour who started to ask questions but when she looked past me to Damien's comatose body, she patted my arm in understanding and took Mattie inside.

Damien was jerked awake by local teenage boys pelting him with fruit and stones. "The missus kick you out, mister?" they cawed.

I watched from the window as Damien staggered inside. I had locked the door but it did not take him long, fuelled by a hung-over rage, to beat it down. I held up the telephone in my hand.

"I press one button and the police will be here," I warned. "Stay away from me."

He opened his arms wide. "What do you think I'm going to do, Lena?"

"You tried to smash my face in last night." I jerked my head towards the battered umbrella lying by the stairs.

Damien's face fell. He apologised. He blamed the drink, said it would never happen again. But I knew who he was and that he would never change. I guess I had known that from the moment he told me I was selfish to choose my dying papa over him.

When he eventually accepted my mind would not be changed, he played what he thought was his ace. "You're not taking Mattie from me." His voice held something akin to glee.

I was prepared. "You think you stand a chance? A drunken, out-of-work gambler who tries to beat up his wife? Just leave, Damien. Mattie's staying with me."

With a vicious laugh, he threw his head back mockingly. "You're an ignorant bitch is what you are," he spat. "Where's your black eye? Where's your police report? Mattie has never wanted for anything in her life. I'm getting joint at the very least and you better keep those pretty eyes open because the second you close them the girl and I are gone, into the sunset."

His eyes were sparkling with power and I knew I would never sleep easy while he thought he had a claim over Mattie. So I told him. At first he didn't believe me. But I was brutal. I spared no detail about how I had seduced him, used him, lied to him.

"Ever wonder where she gets her black hair, her smooth complexion? It's not from you."

"My little Tilda," he whispered.

I almost felt sorry for him. But to make him leave, I had to hurt him. I ran up the stairs two at a time and pulled out the compartment under the bed where I kept all the important documents.

When I raced back downstairs he was standing in the same spot with a puckered brow. I thrust her birth certificate into his hand. "See? You might have poured the water on her head but I filled out the form. Her real name is Mattie, not Matilda. I didn't give her your grandmother's name because she's not yours. She was never yours." I swallowed, wondering what kind of person I had become. "She's named after her real father."

I was going to hell. Every member of the *seminario* could pray for me for the rest of their days and it would not be enough to undo the cruelty I inflicted on Damien. But it worked. He stared at me with a clenched jaw and I shut my eyes tight, prepared for the blow. It never came. I opened my eyes in time to see his back as he walked out of the door and out of our lives.

I suck in the stale hospital air, my throat sizzling from the long speech. I don't stop. "I was so sure I was doing the right thing at the time. Leaving Levi, I did it for him. Reuniting with Damien, that was for you. I'd do anything for you, Mattie."

She looked at me intently. "Do you wish you'd done things differently?"

I shake my head, from uncertainty rather than signifying the negative. "Sometimes, yes. Look at the outcome of my choices. You had a terrifying first two years with Damien, then no father at all. Look how you found out about Levi! It's been weeks since you've spoken to me. Of course I wonder whether I made a terrible mistake. But had I forced Levi to leave the *seminario* to take care of us, who's to say how that would have worked out? Would he have grown to resent us and left us to return to the priesthood? Maybe. Or maybe I'd be wishing I had let him go from the start. I'll never know. We make these life decisions, Mattie, but who's to say what's right?"

My throat throbs. Mattie pours me another glass of water from the plastic jug. She wants me to keep talking. That has to be a good sign.

"He's here." Mattie tips her head to one side, regarding me carefully. "Your priest – Levi, Father Matteo, whatever – he's here in DC."

I splutter out the water I'd sipped, moaning as the dullness hardens on my chest. Mattie strokes my arm as I unclench.

"He was there when I found you." Her voice splashes like the water in the glass. "He was great. I totally freaked out but he pulled you from the bath and gave you mouth-to-mouth. He made me do the compressions on your chest. Do you know what it's like to have to resuscitate your own mother?"

A tear slips from my eye. Just when I think I can't make any worse mistakes, I manage to destroy my daughter's sense of security all over again. And Levi. All I tried to do was protect him but, not only did I ruin his life, he had to save mine.

"I'm sorry if I hurt your chest," she whispers, her lip

quivering. "Levi said to do it hard. I thought I might break your ribs but I didn't care if it brought you back." She hesitates before handing me the book she was reading. "I found it beside the bath."

I stroke the damp cover. "Levi gave it to me in the *seminario*," I whisper, turning the pages of the simple chant book, now sodden and heavy. "It's the only bit of him I have left . . . except for you."

"He is in disgrace," Mattie says, sounding suddenly tired.

She tells me that on their way to my house, he filled her in on what happened after we left the *seminario*. Straight away he was confronted by Father Pietro who had watched from afar as I fainted and Levi tended to me. It was then that a vague sense of familiarity had taken the shape of a traveller he had housed during a hot summer long ago. Unable to lie to the man who had taken him in on the reputation of his brother, Levi confessed everything on the spot, in front of the other seminarians, including Aaron and his family.

"There will be ramifications," Mattie continues softly. "We don't know exactly what they will be yet. They are trying to deal with it tactfully and not create a Church scandal. Everyone who knows about it has been sworn to secrecy so there is no real fear of it leaking. No one wants dishonour brought on the *seminario*."

Even in my alarm for Levi, I am warmed by her use of the Italian. "What will happen to Levi?" I ask.

"They want him gone from the *seminario* for a time while they decide on his future. He has friends who would have taken him in but he came here. He wanted to see you. And me," she adds. "And Ben," she whispers finally. "Oh Lena!" She breaks down and buries her head in the sheets beside my body.

I stroke her hair.

"I'm so sorry I left you all alone," she whispers.

"No, my darling, that wasn't your fault . . ."

"What if you'd died?" she sniffs. "I'd never have forgiven myself, Lena."

"I'm not going anywhere," I promise her. "We'll get through this together, you and me."

"And Levi?" She looks up, her face stained with tears.

"That's up to you," I say. "The most important thing is that the two of us are together." I mean it and, more importantly, I can see in Mattie's face that she believes me.

I look at my beautiful daughter – Levi's daughter – and I see what I should have always known. The way to honour the love Levi and I shared during that glorious summer twenty years ago is sitting right in front of me.

THIRTY-TWO

Lena

Levi has been to visit me so often in my dreams that I wonder whether his appearance by my bedside is nothing more than a mirage.

It is coming to the end of visiting hours and Mattie has gone home. My chest and throat are still searing from my long conversation with her earlier in the day. The doctor prescribed some medication to help me sleep but it isn't working. I have a room all to myself – arranged by Ruth – and the silence contrasts starkly with my busy mind. Rest evades me.

The nurse must see me tossing in the dark through the portal-shaped window because she opens the door.

"Lena?" she says in a carrying whisper. "I didn't think you were expecting any more visitors this evening but this gentleman is quite insistent."

It is only his silhouette I can see past the nurse but I know it is him. I wave at her to let him in. I turn on the side lamp by my bed, squinting against the dim light it casts into the room.

Levi looks grave as he pulls up a chair by my bed. I try to sit up but he motions for me to stay where I am.

I blush, remembering what I've been told about how he found me.

"I won't stay long," he says, his pitch flat and unfathomable.

"I should have waited a few more days until you are better able for company but I had to give in to selfishness on this occasion. I needed to see with my own eyes that you are well."

I know I should say something but can't find where to begin. When he just continues to stare at me, the words fall from my mouth without thought. "I'm sorry."

He shakes his head. "Why did you come back to the *seminario*, Lena?"

I try to explain about Aaron's ordination and Ruth's generosity and my weakness in not being able to refuse. "I've dreamt about going back since the day I left, and here was a real chance to return."

Levi stands abruptly. "You were so surprised to see me – did you not suspect I might still be there?"

"Oh Levi," I sit up, anxious he should know the truth, "I didn't, I truly didn't. Marthe had written years ago to tell me you had moved to the north of Italy. I assumed you were still there." I cough harshly, not caring that the long sentences will hinder my recovery. "Levi," I hold out an arm to gesture him back to me, "I left you and the *seminario* for a reason. Why would I undo the value of those years by interrupting your life now?"

To my relief, he sits again but a frown remains on his forehead. "Did Marthe not tell you I was invited back to the *seminario* last year?"

I shake my head. "We haven't been in contact with each other in years. Not since Agata . . ."

His hand flies to his throat. "You heard?"

"Marthe wrote to me," I nod in reply. "I still miss Agata, you know, even after all this time. She was there for me when I needed her most. I'm so glad she never found out how we betrayed her trust, but I feel guilty. I never got to ask for her forgiveness."

"She knew." His voice is a whisper.

Mine is not. "*What?*"

Levi stands again and this time I throw off my sheet and get to my feet.

"Lena, lie down or the nurse will have my head!"

But I push against his hands as he tries to propel me back into bed. "What do you mean, she knew? Did you tell her?"

He shakes his head, sinking into the chair, leaving me standing. Then he lifts his eyes and begins to tell me the story of the last time he met her. At his words, I sink back onto the bed.

When the doctors had told Agata she only had months to live, she decided to leave the *seminario* for good, not wanting to be a burden on the men she was supposed to be helping. Marthe told her brother and sister-in-law about the diagnosis and the ever-generous Thérèse insisted Agata stay with them for her last months. As a nurse, she took care of Agata's medical needs while Marthe stayed with her friend, talking and praying.

A few weeks before she died, Marthe suggested that Levi should visit – Agata had mentioned some old friends she would like to see again, and Levi was one.

"I only saw her for a few minutes. At that stage, she was too weak to sustain a prolonged conversation."

To my horror, his voice catches.

"Oh Lena, it was awful. She was so pale and thin. Her eyes were just the same – full of warmth and compassion – but they were held captive in this sunken, waxy face . . ." He takes a large breath, and I can tell he has been holding his last image of Agata inside for too long.

I lean forward to stroke his arms. It suddenly doesn't matter what Agata knew about us. She died fighting an evil greater than her body and enormous spirit. I just wish I could have been there to support her, like she had been for me.

Levi's descriptions are vivid and I see Agata's fading face before me.

"Thank you for coming," Agata had said to Levi. "I have prayed for you, my friend. But there is someone else I want to pray for, and I think you can help me."

"Anyone, Agata," he replied, in perfect ignorance.

"Our travelling friend Lena. You remember her, don't you?"

Shocked, Levi said nothing but she kept going, her voice trembling with effort.

"Of course you remember her. She was with us for a short

time and left so abruptly. I thought if I was going to pray for her, you should be here. She meant more to you than anybody, didn't she, Levi?"

When he still said nothing, unable to fathom how she could know the truth, Agata reached out and took his hand.

"It's all right, Levi. I mean, Matteo," she said with a faint smile. "You gave in to temptation but you repented. I know you are a committed priest. I liked Lena. She was my friend. I don't have very long left to pray for her. I think my prayer for her will be strengthened if it is made with you, don't you agree?"

My body trembles at the thought of Agata using her last ounce of strength to help me. "But how did she know?"

Levi shakes his head. "Marthe swears she never said a word, and I believe her. Same with Alexandre and his wife. I can only surmise that she guessed, Lena, all those years ago. We did not discuss it any further. I prayed with her, for you and for me. Even though she told me not to waste my efforts on her, I included her silently in my prayers. She asked me to sing to her so I did until she fell asleep, and I left without waking her. She died three weeks later."

I lie back on the bed, feeling a strange sense of peace that Agata knew about us and didn't hate me for it. Not that she would have been capable of hate, but to have her pray for me in that way implies forgiveness. I love her more than ever in this moment.

"Agata was one of the reasons I accepted the position back in the *seminario*. I think my going there and praying for her in that place would have meant a lot to her."

"Did you pray for her at Aaron's ordination?" I ask suddenly.

He nods. "At every Mass, when we bow our heads for the dead, I ask God to take special care of her."

"Me too," I rush out. "At the ordination, I prayed for her too. Do you think she felt it, our combined prayers for her in the *seminario*?"

Levi smiles. "I do believe that. She was in the chapel with us that day, I am sure. Maybe it was she who put me across your path. If I had left the chapel a few seconds later, you would have been gone from the courtyard. I would never have known you came back."

"Levi, believe me," I urge, "I didn't know you were there. The choir alone convinced me someone else was in charge of the music. Not that there was anything wrong with them," I add hastily, "but they are not your type. Or have you changed so much?"

He looks at me, interested. "What did you think of them?"

I open my mouth then stop, not wanting to insult him but having nothing positive to say. To my surprise, Levi bursts out laughing.

"It was nothing to do with me! The choir's conductor is an aunt of one of the new deacons. So for that one occasion, I let them take over. I was relegated to page-turner for the organist."

"Thank God!" I laugh. "They were nothing compared to your group, Levi. I hope the conductor doesn't have any other nephews on the brink of ordination!"

"But, Lena," he asks, sobering, "did you really want to revisit the *seminario* without me? And knowing what you did about Agata?"

I bow my head. My raw throat, from which I had been completely distracted during our conversation, suddenly feels like sandpaper again. "I wasn't completely honest with you, Levi. I'm sorry. You deserve nothing but the truth from me now. Mattie was the real reason I returned. She's depressed. I did everything I could think of to lift her out of it, but nothing worked. So I turned to the only thing that helped me when I was aching in that way – the *seminario*. She wouldn't need to know you were her father but the beauty, the simplistic lifestyle, the welcoming people – I thought if I could show her all that, and open up to her finally about my own story, or most of it at least, she would be inspired to improve."

"Mattie is a beautiful girl. So tragic to hear about her son."

"Ben," I say. It is important that he knows the name.

"Yes, of course. Ben. Lena," he tilts forward, "I have spoken with her. She still needs help."

At this, I push myself upright again, ignoring his

protestations. "Levi," I make myself talk louder – I know I'll pay later for forcing it but I don't care, "I've tried everything. Even the *seminario*. I don't know what else to do."

"You're her mother . . ."

"And I failed her, all right? I know it."

I see my mistakes clearly – missing her sacraments, often distracted by my sorry past. How many times did I shut her out? I think about how I wouldn't let her comfort me when I read about Agata's death. How could she possibly have trusted me to help her when I taught her to deal with grief by crying alone?

"You'll find a way to help her. It's not too late." Levi reaches out a hand to comfort me for the first time since arriving at my bedside. "You are both young. You have the rest of your lives to be close."

I smile. Here we are, two parents discussing how best to help our baby.

Levi leans in close to me. "Lena," he says, with some urgency, "I understand why you kept Mattie a secret from me. I even believe I must thank you for it, because you did it to secure for me the future I always wanted. But that future has come and gone, and now I want to know her. I want to help her. I have come to ask for your blessing."

I don't have to think about it. I nod earnestly. "Of course, Levi," I say with as much emphasis as my dry throat will allow. "She's yours, after all."

"And so are you," he whispers. "I will never regret the time we spent together and not just because of Mattie."

I close my eyes to soak in those treasured words.

"You know," he leans forward, "when I was in the *seminario*, I learned about good and evil, heaven and hell, God and Lucifer. The black and the white of life – it was what we were taught to preach. But the more I live, the more I see the greyness in between. Perhaps when we think our choices are limited to two extremes there might actually be an alternative hidden in the middle."

I shake my head, the medication fuzzing my brain. "What are you saying, Levi?"

"Back then, we thought we had to choose between running away together and never seeing each other again. Have we grown up now? Can we possibly be in each other's lives another way?"

"You mean as friends?"

He pauses. "Yes, friends. But only because I can't think of another word to describe it. You will always mean more to me than even my closest friends."

"Levi," I put my hands on his, moving nearer to him, "it will never be the same as that summer in the *seminario*."

"No," he agrees. "Never."

I can barely breathe. "What exactly are you proposing?"

Our foreheads touch as they did when we said goodbye all those years ago. Our mouths are almost touching. I can't tell, because my eyes are closed but I am sure his are too.

"One last kiss." His words are so faint I might have imagined them.

Desperate as I am for that, I shake my head. "I don't think I can survive another goodbye."

He pushes his head forward so our noses touch. The line he is about to cross is worse than anything we did twenty years ago because now he is ordained. Yet when he speaks, he sounds more certain than he ever did during our summer together.

"It won't be like last time. We'll still be in each other's lives, if not the way we once hoped."

"One final kiss," I breathe into his lips and they press onto mine.

A tender touch, into which we put everything we ever felt for each other, every missed moment over the past twenty years and all the love in our hearts.

When we pull away, I ache with sadness at the knowledge that we will never be that intimate again. But it is coupled with joy for a reunion of another kind, and excitement that our lives do not have to be lived wholly apart.

There is something I have to say. "I'm sorry, Levi."

However well-intentioned my actions, I need his forgiveness.

Before I can elaborate, I am granted my need. He offers it to me generously and without qualification, except for an odd request. "I forgive you for anything you are sorry for. If you can forgive me."

"Forgive you? For what?" I feel my eyebrows shoot up into my forehead.

"For letting you make the choice. I should have had the courage to decide and not left the weight on your shoulders for twenty years."

The door swings open behind him and the nurse whispers into the room. "Father, it's time to go."

"I'll just say goodbye," he calls over his shoulder, turning back to me with a shy smile playing on his lips. "For now."

"For now," I agree, and reach out to shake his hand.

He grabs me and presses me to his chest. I stay there, knowing he will not let me go even as the nurse reminds him again to leave. I don't remember pulling away, or lying back in the bed, or falling asleep. I must have slipped naturally into slumber as I sat, being held by Levi, no longer needing to distinguish between the worlds of reality and dreams.

THIRTY-THREE

Mattie

I clean your headstone with a rag, dusting off the leaves from a late fall. I don't mind the shedding. It lets me be useful while I'm here. I like that I can still do something for you.

It is early and the sky is that milky white of dawn. I guessed that the graveyard would be empty at this hour. I want some alone time with you, Ben, before I leave. I will be back. I will always come back.

I hear the crunch of leaves under a boot and turn, angry to be interrupted until I see the loping form of the man walking towards me.

"Simon!" I stand and he gives me a jerky wave as he stamps across the broken branches and around the graves to reach me.

"Hi, Mattie," he says. "I didn't think you would be here this early."

"I'm always here," I say.

A silence descends. He asks me how I am. I answer that I am fine. Another silence. He asks about Lena. I tell him she is doing better. He nods.

"Is it true, Mattie?" he blurts out. From anyone else's mouth it would have been a grab for gossip, but not Simon.

I sigh. "Yes, it's true."

"That priest from Aaron's seminary. He's . . . your dad?"

I nod and give Simon a smile as weak as the sun trying to colour the early morning sky. "Surprisingly, it's not as sordid as it sounds."

Simon snorts, then immediately apologises. I give him a playful shove and throw my eyes up to heaven. How could I be angry with him?

I hear a strange sound and look down at his hand. "What have you got there?"

He lifts his arm and a clash of chimes tinkle. He eyes what he is holding almost sceptically. "It's called 'Mr Jingle', apparently." He shrugs with a wicked grin. "It's weird the stuff Joseph thinks is cool these days."

He catches my eye and we both burst into laughter. An image of the hard-as-nails Joseph fawning over cuddly toys is too ridiculous not to be funny, even though it makes me a little sad to think how time has moved on.

"Anyway," Simon finishes off a final chuckle, "he told me this is the ultimate toy for babies." He lifts it up so I can see, scrutinising it like an explosive device as it dangles from his fingertips. "It has everything – bright colours and noises, and Mr Jingle's face is a no-beat brand in the baby market. Apparently!" he stresses and I try to stifle another giggle. Suddenly, he is serious again. "People bring flowers, you know. What do babies want with flowers? I thought I'd leave this on Ben's grave. My mom says you're leaving for a while, and I didn't want him to be lonely."

I look up into Simon's face. There I see my first love, my childhood sweetheart, my best friend who is still willing to be there for me after everything.

"Thank you," I say.

I take a tentative step forward and he opens his arms at my gesture. I press against him and we stand together for a long time, me wishing things had worked out differently. But if Lena's life has taught me anything, it's that wishing will not make it so.

"I hope the squirrels don't take Mr Jingle," Simon says, keeping me tight against him.

We watch a couple of red-tails scamper playfully amongst the leaves. They move erratically, stopping at the slightest noise, frightened, before crawling furiously up the tree out of sight, their bushy tails shaking wildly behind them.

"Maybe you can come and check that Mr Jingle hasn't been taken while I'm gone? To make sure he's okay?"

"Of course," Simon says with feeling, giving me another squeeze. "Don't worry, Mattie," he is whispering now, "he'll be okay."

We step back from each other and Simon coughs awkwardly. "When are you going?"

I take a deep breath. "In a couple of weeks, once Lena's a bit stronger. She needs someone to take care of her for a while. I fly to Paris, and then who knows? I have a train ticket that I can use all over Europe." I hear the energy I exude when discussing my plans. It has been a long time since I have been excited about anything. But I am about the future.

"Well, you always wanted to go travelling." Simon's voice holds no trace of animosity.

Though I knew it already, his undiluted happiness for me confirms with an awful finality that he has moved on.

He knows I know it too, and pauses only for a second before admitting the truth to me. "I'm going away for a couple of days too – this weekend."

I nod. "Where?"

"Hawaii."

"I see."

The squirrels are gone now. A caretaker turns on a grass-cutter at the further end of the graveyard.

"Did you buy a ring?"

"I'm using my grandmother's."

I pause, remembering when I held his hand at her funeral. "Will she say yes?"

Simon looks down at me with a softened smile he used to reserve for me, but which is now hers. "Yes, she will."

A rush of jealousy darkens my mind. Not envy of Simon's future wife, but of Simon himself. He talked to me in the hours before I conceived you, Ben. When he told me about Ingrid I failed to see the real warning – that he wasn't like my family. Lena could never move on from Levi. I have been unable to live a life without you. Simon is not like that, he never was. He might always regret me, but he has an open heart that is big and brave enough to find love again. I envy him for that reason. I want to be like that. Maybe I can be. I'll start now.

I will go to Europe. Lena is planning to fly over for a vacation when I get to Italy. We might even meet up with Levi. Lena received a letter from her old friend Marthe who is now based in France. She says I am welcome to stop in if I make it as far as south-west France. Her brother and sister-in-law have a large home near her and because the children they foster come and go, there is usually a spare bed. Lena seems delighted at the prospect of me visiting her old friend, and is contemplating joining me. I haven't decided if I will call on them yet but it is good to know there are people I can turn to if I need help over there.

When I return, Simon will be engaged and you will still be in the ground. But I will be ready. For what exactly, I don't know. Just living, I suppose.

I will never forget you, Ben. You will forever own my heart. When I come back here I will do what Simon did and leave you presents you would have wanted.

I return from my thoughts to the present. Simon is looking at me.

"Do you want a ride home?"

I shake my head. "I'll take the bus. It will be quicker in the early morning traffic."

"Are you sure?" He sounds concerned.

I smile and am rewarded with his wide beamer in return. "I'm sure, Simon. But you can walk me out if you'd like."

He turns and gestures with a gentlemanly sweep of his arm to the path leading from your grave to the outside world of the living.

The sun is not yet fully up but it is risen enough to illuminate the graveyard in a soft, calming light. I stop for a moment to take it in. I must remember to visit at this time again – as dawn melts into morning, when the semi-bright sun glows gently and full of promises for the day.

"Bye-bye, Ben, darling. I'll be back as soon as I can," I call over my shoulder, as I blow a kiss back towards my son's grave.

EPILOGUE

Lena

It is a glamorous affair.

The five-star hotel welcomes us from the church with doormen to take our coats and gloved waiters offering trays of champagne. Chandeliers hang from the high ceilings and the guests mill like royalty, calling out flattering approvals of attire, hair and general beauty. Of course, every compliment is qualified by a reference to the bride and how she outshines us all.

Gasps had rippled through the church as she walked down the aisle, clinging nervously to her father's arm. All eyes, some being dabbed with tissues, were on the bride but I turned away, drawn instead to the priest. Aaron stood on the altar, bouncing on the balls of his feet, throwing the groom excited looks as he stared steadfastly ahead. Joseph, the best man, whispered furiously in the groom's ear, apparently giving a blow-by-blow account of the bride's journey to the altar.

"Welcome all!" said Aaron in a carrying voice as he stretched out his arms to the congregation. JJ's new baby brother cooed back and everyone laughed. "Yes, and a particular hello to our littlest page-boy! This is a long-anticipated day and I know our parents are very proud."

Simon turned around from the altar to beam at Ruth and Ed. Aaron continued. "After all, it is only once that this will happen . . . that a priest performs his first ever wedding!"

The bride and groom laughed along with their guests. Simon's smile was the widest I had ever seen it.

After his initial bright welcome, Aaron became earnest and it was clear he took his duty seriously. The atmosphere changed from light-hearted frivolity to solemnity and it was perfect.

Now darkness has fallen over the winter's evening early and I am glad of the warmth of the hotel for the reception. I wander through the crowd, most of whom I do not know as they are Ruth and Ed's friends, acquaintances and business associates. I imagine the happy couple might have preferred a smaller wedding but Simon wouldn't want to disappoint his parents. My hand is wedged comfortably through Alvin's arm.

"Quite the . . . *opulent* occasion, isn't it?" Alvin scratches the back of his head and, at the movement, the front of his shirt becomes untucked from his pants, exposing his stomach.

I laugh and pull it back down. I know he is wondering why he agreed to be my 'plus-one' for this wedding.

"It's what they wanted," I shrug.

He holds up the mini vol-au-vent he plucked from the tray of a passing waiter and peers at it suspiciously. "No hot dogs, then?" he grins, giving me a teasing nudge.

I met Alvin when the doctors suggested I join a walking group to help build my body back to health after the bath incident. A widower, and ten years older than me, we were still the youngest in the group of mainly old age pensioners so we stuck together. Alvin was cheerful company and we took to meeting outside of the group for coffee or the theatre. He even likes going to art galleries. It has been very difficult explaining to Ruth and Mattie that we are merely friends.

"What's the problem?" Ruth had been extremely disappointed when I insisted he was nothing more. "He's charming, isn't he? Handsome? Intelligent? What else are you looking for?"

As I tried unsuccessfully to explain to her, I am not looking for anything, or anyone in that way. The last thing I want is a boyfriend but I do need more friends in my life.

"If you're holding out for Father Matteo to leave the

priesthood, you'll be waiting a long time," Ruth said bluntly one day, out of exasperation.

I didn't need her to tell me that. I know there is no chance of Levi deserting his vocation or of us becoming a couple. More to the point, I don't want it. Our love – our Hollywood love – belongs to another place and time. A place where rivers flow alongside yellow buildings and male voices sing into the warm mountain air. A time before I had a daughter who is all the family I need.

I am not averse to meeting a man with whom I could spend the rest of my life if he comes along. After all, I am still a young woman, relatively speaking. If he doesn't, I will not be sad for want of a partner. It could never be like the love I shared with Levi.

Alvin is a good friend – a man who misses his dead wife and just wants company while he tries to get on with his life. He happily agreed to accompany me to the wedding and I am glad of his friendship.

The bride glides over to us with open arms. "Lena, I'm so glad you made it!"

"Thanks, Ingrid." I hug her back, careful not to crinkle her dress.

As I introduce Alvin, Simon joins us and I take his hands in mine. I want him to know that I am truly happy for him, that though he and Mattie have gone their separate ways I still think of him like I did when he was my daughter's best friend – the son I never had. I can't find the words to express that so I settle for hugging him very tight and hoping he understands.

Soon, the bell is rung for dinner. Alvin and I don't know the people at our table and spend most of the meal laughing with each other. I expect Ruth to have arranged long and inspiring speeches but there are only three – all short and to the point. Alvin booms out laughter with the rest of the dining hall at Joseph's cheeky best man speech. Then Ingrid's father, shaking with nerves, says a few lines of welcome to his new son-in-law before tearing up over his daughter.

Simon's speech is heartfelt and I am not the only woman

sniffing by the end. He places a hand on Ingrid's shoulder and looks down on her as though he has never seen anyone so lovely. His affection for her is clearly no less intense than it was for Mattie.

After dinner, there is dancing and my heart aches a little for my daughter as I watch Simon pull his new bride onto the dance floor. Whatever Mattie says, I know she regrets Simon.

She sends me a text message later in the evening. **"Hope wedding went well – tell Simon I said congrats. On a midnight tour of Krakow. Magnificent! Love you. M."**

I smile and show it to Alvin. He was fiercely impressed when I told him about Mattie's trip. "Such fearlessness to be working her way across a different continent alone," he had said with admiration and I relished the praise on her behalf.

Mattie is almost at the age I was when I first met Levi. I have lived so long in that time, I remember every youthful doubt, joy and fear. I send her a message back, a short one, telling her I love her and miss her. This is her second trip to Europe but I will not be joining her. She is not meeting Levi or Marthe as she did with me on her last trip. This time, she is doing her own thing. She was determined to take in Poland, where Papa lived. And she made it. I close my eyes and hope he is sitting up in heaven, bouncing Ben on his knee and pointing down at Mattie.

Alvin, sensing my reverie, leaves me to my thoughts and strikes up a conversation with the woman beside him. After a while, I feel a pressure on my arm and I open my eyes. Ruth is by my side.

"Lena," she whispers, somewhat awkwardly, "Father Matteo is here. I hope you don't mind," she adds quickly. "Aaron invited him to the afters when he said he was thinking of visiting DC . . ."

A calmness filters through me. "Of course I don't mind!"

I tell Alvin I will be back soon and he happily waves me away. I last saw Levi a few months ago. He visits often now. He comes to see Mattie but always makes time for me.

I find him outside. What looks like ornate windows are actually floor-to-ceiling doors which have been opened out onto a terrace. Large patio heaters temper the winter cold and groups of guests are already milling about outside – some are gathered in the centre, others are sitting at the many tables, smoking and talking.

Levi is standing at the outermost edge of the terrace, staring into the distance. A faraway mountain stretches wide like a boulder. The moon hangs delicately above and a few stars are dotted across the vast sky. It makes me feel peaceful.

"Hello, Father Matteo."

"Good evening, Magdalena."

We grin conspiratorially as I stand into place beside him.

"You look beautiful," he says quietly.

I return the compliment and we stand in companionable silence, looking out at the horizon-swallowing mountain.

"Is there any news?" I ask, after a while.

He shakes his head. It is a year and a half since he was exposed to the few who gathered around when I fainted at Aaron's ordination. Initially, it was hushed up and he left the *seminario* quietly, returning to his parish. Then, a few weeks ago, the news broke. We do not know who revealed it or why – it could have been an innocent whisper overheard or malicious gossip. Either way, higher authorities are currently deciding his fate.

"They might not do anything," I had suggested when he first told me over the phone.

At first he had agreed. "If they do not want word to spread further, inaction is best," he admitted. But he seemed resigned to the reality that he will have to leave his parish. "I was so happy there," he confessed to me, "and even happier when the *seminario* invited me back to teach music. I spent eight wonderful years there learning my vocation and it was where I met you. They will never let me return now."

I shake my head, baffled at the unfairness and waste of it all.

But he seems more accepting. "I have a child. One I conceived, possibly quite literally, in the *seminario*. There have been too many scandals in recent years. They have to be seen to do something."

The likelihood is the equivalent of a demotion, in

circumstance if not in rank. He will be shipped off to a parish under the radar in the countryside with few responsibilities.

"It wouldn't be so bad," he says, staring up at the stars. "A good priest can make a difference in the smallest community."

"You are a good priest," I say.

He smiles down at me. "Don't be sad for me, Lena. You gave me twenty years of borrowed time and I believe I have made a positive contribution to my parish. But we should never have believed that we could live on the same earth for the rest of our days and be forever apart. It wasn't part of the plan. And you gave me Mattie. Twenty years later, but I have her now."

He says it without regret or malice but it prompts me to say again what I have been repeating since I watched them meet in the *seminario*.

"I thought I was doing the right thing for you but I'm still sorry. I'm sorry for keeping from you the truth that you had a daughter."

The bands stops playing abruptly and he puts a hand on my shoulder. Our silence carries far into the night. I know he has forgiven me already. But I had to say it. I always will.

"It's a nice view here," he says.

"Not as stunning as the *seminario*."

"Nothing is. Shall we pray?"

I whisper, "You do it. Sing for me."

So he does. He closes his eyes but I keep my gaze on the stars. We are far enough from the groups of guests that his quiet voice is heard by me alone. He intones a simple *Magnificat*, a prayer from the gospel after which his brother was named – a prayer said by Our Lady, the mother. When he finishes I thank him and, with perfect timing, the band starts up again, this time a slow waltz.

"Dance with me," he says.

I go to him willingly. After all this time, I know there will be no passionate reunion, no choice to be made like there was so many years ago. But there is love and there is Mattie. That is enough.

As usual, he seems attuned to my thoughts of our daughter.

"She's so precious," he whispers, leaning his head against mine.

My whole being straightens. I am as proud as if he had complimented me personally. "She is," I say simply.

"You raised her to be a wonderful person."

We continue turning.

Then I blurt it out, as though the tiny circle we are cutting on the terrace is a confessional. It's something I've told him before, but I will spend the rest of my life trying to prove that I never forgot him, that I carried him forward with me, through Mattie. "You know I fell short as a mother in many ways. But I raised her Catholic, Levi. I sent her to a religious school and made sure she went to Mass every week. She's got all her sacraments. She loves music – she plays the piano. She stopped for a while during college but has starting playing again when she visits me."

Against my head I can feel his cheek rise in a smile. "And you named her Mattie."

"There wasn't much I could do with 'Levi'."

He laughs – a comforting, musical sound.

"You let her call you 'Levi'," I say, my statement a question of sorts. "Even though everyone calls you Father Matteo now."

"People associate the name 'Levi' with the Levites, and assume it means 'priest'. But the true meaning of 'Levi' is 'attached'. Mattie and I are linked through blood and her very existence has tethered me to you all these years. The three of us are joined together – we are a family. I want to be 'Levi' to you both."

He looks down at me and the moon casts a glow of no real colour onto his face. "Since my ordination, I have been known as Matteo. All the while Mattie was living on the other side of the world and we shared a name. A truly appropriate name." He pulls me closer, still turning me on the spot. The mountain comes into view over his shoulder. "'Matteo'" he whispers, "means 'given'."

I dig my fingers hard into his shoulders. "You gave me everything."

"That meaning is often phrased another way," he continues,

"which I think is particularly true in Mattie's case. Our names mean 'Gift of God'."

I feel the truth in the meaning and know I am unworthily blessed with whom I have been gifted.

We continue to move around the terrace, ignoring the other guests who, inspired by our moon-lit movements, start to pair off and move in circles beside us. In my mind, we are perfectly alone in both another time and place.

In many years, when we are finally done living our full lives, I hope Papa, Agata and Ben will have the strength between them to raise me up. When they do, I will arrive back to a moment like this with Levi and, like a harmonic cadence finally resolved, we will dance under the starry night sky of the *seminario*.

THE END

Acknowledgements

I want to begin by thanking all the team at Poolbeg Press and Ward River Press for believing in this book, especially my dedicated publisher Paula Campbell, my talented editor Gaye Shortland, and of course, the wonderful Ailbhe Hennigan, all of whom put so much time and effort into my dreams.

Thank you to Eileen Dennan, David Doran, Seán Farrell, Niall McCann, Robert Murtagh, Brian Ward, Liam Flood, Therese Nolan and Allyson Dowling – a.k.a. The Second Monday Writing Group. You have been with this book from the very first words to the finished story and I cannot thank you enough for your advice, encouragement and thoughtful critique. My gratitude to the Irish Writers Centre for facilitating our meetings.

Particular thanks to Martha Davis for helping me with the American aspects of this story and to Emer Muldowney for sharing your midwifery knowledge and experiences. Any inaccuracies in this book are entirely of my own making.

A special thank you to Dr Ite O'Donovan and the Lassus Scholars choir for immersing me in sacred music and opening my eyes to the beauty and musicality of Italy.

Since my first novel, *The Secret Son*, was published I have been fortunate to meet many of the talented authors Ireland has to offer. Thank you all for sharing your writing experiences with me.

Thank you to my friends who have been so supportive of my writing. I cannot overstate how much your interest and backing means to me. Particular thanks to Kevin Comiskey for so generously taking the time to set up my official website.

Finally I want to thank my family – my brother Richard and all generations of aunts, uncles and cousins – for your active support, and especially my parents Michael and Denise for always being there for me and for your constant belief in me and my writing.

This book is dedicated to my grandmothers – Mary Burke, who as a piano teacher and church organist kindled in me an early interest in music – and Kathleen Ryan, on whose piano I learned to play.

Interview with the Author

Where did you get the idea for Levi's Gift?

I sing with a choir called the Lassus Scholars. A couple of years ago, we sang in a seminary in Italy very like the one described in *Levi's Gift*. I thought it was an absolutely beautiful place. The timing was perfect because I had just finished a novel, and was waiting for inspiration to hit for another. The seminary stirred my imagination and the characters and storyline flowed easily.

Is *Levi's Gift* a love story?

I decided that if I was going to set a novel in such a beautiful place, the story would have to be epic. For me, the most powerful emotion I can write about is love. I wanted to incorporate different types of love – from familial to romantic to friendships – and I wanted the love in this book to be transcendent. So, all of the relationships in *Levi's Gift* push the boundaries of love. Mattie craves her mother's approval at a very basic level. The grief suffered by both Lena and Mattie on losing their loved ones (Papa and Ben) is extreme. Simon and Mattie's love is one that can never be erased fully because it is rooted in childhood. And, of course, Lena and Levi's connection is a rare and complex being. I tried to mirror the intensity of the love shared by the characters by focusing on the other transcendental aspects of the book – religion and music. So yes, *Levi's Gift* is most definitely a love story, but of a particular kind.

Your first book *The Secret Son* also dealt with revelations from the past and family relationships. How significant are these themes to you?

Apparently they are very significant! I didn't purposefully set out to incorporate these themes but, as the storyline developed, it was clear they were coming to the fore again. I come from a small, loving and close-knit family. I view family relationships as the most important ones we have, so they are usually an important part of my writing.

As for moving on from the past, I wish I could say I have dramatic secrets from my past that inspire this theme but I'm not that interesting I'm afraid! I am fascinated by history and even more so by people who think history doesn't matter. It repeats itself over and over, and I do not believe we can run from it forever. On a psychological level, I have always been interested in how an unresolved past can result in difficulties moving forward. It is an intriguing part of the human experience and a subject I am drawn back to again and again when I write.

Do you have favourite characters?

The narrators Lena and Mattie both mean so much to me – I wouldn't have been able to sustain a whole book through their viewpoints if I didn't feel very close to them. However, I think the character that appeals to me most is Simon. The most interesting character to write was definitely Marthe and, although she is only a minor character, I had the most fun writing Angela, Mattie's brazen roommate!

Levi's Gift **is narrated by two different characters and is told in the present tense with many flashbacks to the past. Also, Mattie's narration addresses her lost baby for the length of the novel. Did you have any difficulties writing *Levi's Gift*?**

It took a lot of work to structure *Levi's Gift*. I wrote it very haphazardly in the beginning – I would write scenes as they came to me even though I didn't know where they would appear in the novel, if at all. That is how I ended up with scenes from both Lena and Mattie's point of view. Initially, I had planned on interspersing Lena's history with the ongoing storyline but it soon became clear to me that it deserved an entire section in the book if I was to do it justice. Working all the scenes together and achieving a flow took a long time but it was worth the effort to get it right.

Having Mattie talk directly to Ben was a considered choice. It helped emphasise her extreme emotional distress and inability to move on after his death, and I also wanted to see how this type of narration would hold up for the length of a novel.

I'm lucky to be in a monthly writing group. Their feedback on the characters, the storyline and the readability of *Levi's Gift* was invaluable.

You have said that the names of the characters were deliberately chosen. Can you tell us about that?

Levi's name is a key part of the book, and I wanted to augment that by giving every character a significant designation. No name is given in this book by accident. For me, layering the characters in this way enriches the story. To give a few examples, Agata means 'virtuous or good', Ruth means 'friendship' and, in the Old Testament, Aaron is the name of the first high priest. If there are any other characters whose names you are interested in deciphering, there are plenty of helpful baby names websites out there!

Discussion Topics for Book Clubs

1. What is Levi's 'gift' to which the title refers?

2. How important is religion to the two main characters, Lena and Mattie?

3. In the last analysis, did Lena make the right choice for Levi? For herself? For Mattie?

4. Lena made the decision to leave Levi. Nevertheless, he could have followed her. Did he make the right choice by staying in the *seminario*?

5. Did Lena do the right thing when she married Damien? When she rejected him?

6. Is Lena a good mother?

7. Do you agree with Levi that celibacy is necessary for priests?

8. Do you agree that women should be excluded from the priesthood?

9. Some of Levi's beliefs are abhorrent to Lena. How is she able to accept the differences between them?

10. Should Mattie have broken up with Simon?

11. Will Simon be happy?

12. How well does the book depict Mattie's grief at the loss of her baby?

13. Do you think Lena and Mattie have grown closer by the end of the book? Have they moved on as individuals?

14. The inability to move forward without facing the past is a recurring theme for many of the characters in this book. Do you think they should be able to shake off the past?

15. Whose story touched you most?

16. In what ways is music important to the story?

17. In what ways is the Italian setting important to the story? Could the same story be successfully set in, for example, an Irish seminary?

18. In what ways are Lena and Mattie similar and in what ways are they different?

19. How important is the figure of 'Papa' in the book?

20. What is the symbolic difference between Papa's love of architecture and Lena's love of art?

21. Were the truths revealed throughout the book expected?

22. Which character would you want as a friend?

23. What, if anything, about this story will stay with you?

24. In your opinion, does *Levi's Gift* have a happy ending?

 WARD RIVER PRESS

Novels that demand to be talked about,
not just read!

NOW AVAILABLE

The Friday Tree by Sophia Hillan

Ruby's Tuesday by Gillian Binchy

Sing Me to Sleep by Helen Moorhouse

The Last Goodbye by Caroline Finnerty

Into the Night Sky by Caroline Finnerty

The House Where It Happened
by Martina Devlin

Kingdom of Scars by Eoin Macken

A Shadow in the Yard by Liz McManus

The Curtain Falls by Carole Gurnett